Th

That Cure

Arthur Herbert

2021 White Bird Publications

Copyright © 2021 by Arthur Herbert

Published in the United States
by White Bird Publication, LLC, Texas

ISBN 978-1-63363-512-8
eBook ISBN 978-1-63363-513-5
Library of Congress Control Number 2021932838

Cover design by Books Covered Ltd
https://www.bookscovered.co.uk/

PRINTED IN THE UNITED STATES OF AMERICA

Dedication:

For Amy. I thank God daily for your willingness to marry below your station.

Acknowledgements:

Special thanks to David and Amy Haynie, under whose roof this story was born.

I'd also like to thank my developmental editor Dana Isaacson for his invaluable advice which took the early drafts of the story to another level.

Thank you to Evelyn Byrne-Kusch for taking a chance on the project and giving it the opportunity to go from something in my head to something in your hands.

Thank you to Rafael Diaz-Flores, MD, MPH for giving the book a thoughtful and thorough sensitivity read.

I'd like to thank Joel Shulkin, MD and Nick Russell for being so giving of their only non-renewable resource, their time.

Finally, thanks to my beautiful wife Amy. You're patient, sexy, brilliant, patient, driven, independent, encouraging, patient, elegant, understanding, and most of all, patient.

The Cuts That Cure

**White Bird
Publications**

"If you only come face-to-face with your own mistakes once or twice in your life, it's bound to be extra painful. I face mine every day—that way they ain't usually much worse than a dry shave."

—Larry McMurtry, Lonesome Dove

CHAPTER ONE

3:16 a.m.—Saturday, December 22ⁿᵈ

Suturing the incision that ran from the bottom of Mr. Holub's breastbone to his pubic hair, Alex Brantley paused, needle poised over the patient's abdomen, for a jaw-clicking yawn. Stretching his neck until it audibly popped, he let his lids sag briefly and for a moment enjoyed this slight release of tension.

He opened his eyes. At this hour, there was none of the operating room's daytime energy— no hospital gossip, no background music, no chit-chat. The metronomic beep of the anesthesia monitor paced the bleariness, lulling everyone into a sleepy wakefulness. The anesthesiologist, Dr. Majumdar, a woman so tiny if Alex had to guess she didn't weigh ninety pounds with rocks in her pockets, leaned back in her castered chair on the other side of the turquoise surgical drapes. She scrolled through the electronic patient chart with one hand and fiddled with the engagement ring she wore on a necklace with the other. She ran the ring back and forth, left to right, over and over, making it buzz as the smooth metal of the band slid across the braided chain. In the corner, Charles, the bald circulator nurse, rested his chin on his palm, head cocked at an angle while he searched the internet for an anniversary present for his wife.

The operation had been routine. The intestinal blockage that had brought Mr. Holub to the emergency room earlier that night was caused by scar tissue, not a cancer as Alex had worried. Since there were no other surgeries posted on the OR board, the surgical team seemed eager to catch some sleep before the 7 a.m. shift change.

Alex's scrub tech, a rail-thin Jamaican woman named Cedella, moved the blood-stained instruments to the far edge of her surgical stand before crossing her forearms and leaning onto the metal tray to give her weary legs a break. She held the suture scissors ready and watched as Alex deftly tied a stack of knots, one atop the other, before pulling both threads up under tension and mumbling, "Cut." Cedella obeyed, bending forward to neatly cut the threads a few millimeters above the knots before resuming her position while Alex reloaded his needle driver. Thirty-five years old, Alex had now been performing the act of suturing for the last ten years, more or less, and muscle memory had taken over, his mind free to wander as he sewed.

While the others hoped this would be their last surgical case of the night, Alex hoped it would be the last case for the rest of his life.

Back out front by the OR desk, Alex took his white coat off the wall peg and tossed his blue paper surgical cap in a trash can by the door, hat-head matting down his medium-length brown hair. Catching his reflection in a chrome paper towel dispenser, he noticed his weight loss made his already-lean features sharper, a depleted look not helped by a three-day growth of beard and dark circles under his eyes.

It took two slaps of the saucer-sized steel plate set in the wall next to the exit's heavy double doors to make them open inwards with a whooshing electric hum. Alex remembered playfully tricking the young daughter of one of his colleagues at this very door. He'd stood with his hip leaning against the plate, then while she watched he waved his hands elaborately in an *abracadabra* at the doors. Holding the fingers-splayed pose, he'd discretely pressed the plate with his hip, causing her to squeal with delight, clapping and pointing when the doors opened as if by magic.

Hospital policy forbade wearing surgical paraphernalia in the waiting room, but those rules were never enforced after hours as the clipboards—the staff's nickname for the officious administrators responsible for enforcement—were home in bed. The rank-and-file joked that given the clipboards' lavish salaries, one would think they could afford cars with headlights, yet they were never seen in the hospital after dark.

Now close to finishing his last shift at Saint Vincent's, Alex walked into the waiting room with his surgical mask dangling on his chest and wearing his blue shoe covers. He exuded no spirit of rebellion in his rule-breaking, though, only fatigue. Bone-aching, mind-numbing, soul-crushing fatigue.

He stood in the doorway backlite and allowed his eyes to adjust to the waiting room's darkness. In the gloom, empty chairs and poinsettias sat surrounded by barber-poled tinsel looping along the walls. Standing on tiptoes, he saw a sliver of light peeking beneath a closed door in the furthest reaches of the shadows. Apparently, someone from the OR desk had put his patient's family in the counseling room before his arrival, saving him the trouble. *It figures.* After seven weeks of his preaching about it, they finally got proactive three hours before he was to leave.

Alex stopped at the door and gathered himself. Since Frieda walked out on him three years ago, crying, saying she was through with asking, in fact begging him to get help, moments such as this had become laden with risk for him. If he was honest with himself, she'd been right. His disillusionment with his chosen career had manifested in a dozen different ways, all unhealthy. He'd been depleted not just physically but emotionally for as long as he could remember, with energy left only to put one foot in front of the other. This compassion fatigue led directly to the professional and personal problems he now experienced, He needed to be careful here. Gathering himself, he took a moment for two deep cleansing breaths.

Fake it 'til you make it. He rapped softly on the closed door and, without waiting for an answer, entered.

The room was simple. Purposely built small and cramped to discourage crowds during difficult conversations, it went for spartan over intimate, an unobjectionable neutral tan, with a vase of fake gladiolas in the corner. A framed mat of the Brownsville, Texas skyline gave the impression of being in more than a backwater, but less than a metropolis.

On a small love seat, a gangly young towheaded girl slept deeply, mouth open, her socked feet tucked up under her, and her head resting on the shoulder of a teenaged boy. Her bulky maroon sweater swaddled her, only fingertips visible at the end of her long sleeves. She'd bitten her nails to the quick, the stubby remnants painted a chipped sparkly pink, like ragged lady beetles. The dull-eyed boy next to her stared off into the middle distance as he sat picking at his acne, his longish greasy hair dangling over one eye. With them sat a woman in her late thirties who wore matter-of-fact clothes with no makeup, her blonde hair showing a few lines of grey and pulled into a ponytail. Worry shone through her eyes, and Alex recognized the look of exhaustion he saw every day in the mirror. She clenched a crumpled wad of tissues in her hand. When she saw Alex enter, she sat up quickly and immediately began searching his facial expression and body language for clues as to whether her life was about to change forever.

Alex sat in the room's last empty chair and got right to the point. "Evening, everybody. Mr. Holub did just fine. The blockage looks like it was caused by internal scar tissue from the appendectomy he had when he was in college. I cut all the scar tissue loose from where it kinked the intestines, and then I looked all around and didn't see any signs of cancer. I did have to remove a short piece of his intestines to fix the blockage. It was only about six inches long. A small enough piece that he'll never miss it, and then I just sewed the two ends back together. Overall, the operation went real smooth. He lost about a coke can's worth of blood, but he shouldn't need any transfusions. He's still got a ways to go, but if everything I did tonight heals up okay, he should make a full recovery from this episode."

The woman sagged with relief. "When can I see him?"

Her eyes darted down. Following her gaze, Alex grimaced when he saw dark spatters of her husband's blood staining his shoe covers and scrub pants. Quickly, he said, "Give us just a few minutes. We're getting him tucked into the recovery room right now. He'll have a tube in his nose, but we removed the breathing tube just a few minutes ago. He'll be shaking off the last of the anesthetic for a few hours yet, so don't expect him to be particularly chatty."

"Thank you so much, Doctor. What'd you say your name was?"

"Alex. Alex Brantley." Shifting his weight, he pulled the left edge of his rumpled white coat taut so she could see his embroidered name above the breast pocket. *Almost out of here*.

"One last thing," he said as he rose. "I'm actually just the surgeon covering emergencies tonight, and this is my last day working here at Saint Vincent's. I go off at seven this morning and at that point one of the hospital's other surgeons, Dr. Montez, will be taking over as Mr. Holub's main doctor. Dr. Montez and I'll talk about Mr. Holub when she gets here, so she'll be completely up to speed when I leave. You'll get to meet her tomorrow in Mr. Holub's room when she makes her rounds."

She nodded and sniffed, looking down at her hands as she worried the Kleenex before using it to wipe her nose. "Thank you again."

He nodded and his face broke into a smile borne of relief. A different life was just a little over three hours away. If he could avoid creating any new problems for himself until then, if the universe would cooperate and give him a quiet three-hour nap, then in the morning he could get a handle on things and figure out where to go from here. He'd already made the big decisions. Now he just needed to get to the day and put them in motion. It was so close he could taste it.

The shrill sound of his pager cut through the quiet of the family room, its noxious tone set at top volume so it would wake him from the dead. Alex sagged and blindly silenced it on his hip.

Before looking at the pager's display, he told himself to relax. It was probably just the recovery room paging to ask for a clarification on the orders he'd written for Mr. Holub. Keep it together. *You're almost out. Do not, repeat, do not show your ass in here.*

Taking a deep breath through his nose, he unclipped the pager from its holster and looked at the text screen. The paramedic dispatcher's clipped shorthand read, *Level 1 trauma activation- 8 mo male, burns to bilateral legs and buttocks, here now.* An eight-month-old boy with burns to the lower half of his body. Alex sighed and smiled his goodbye to the Holubs as he left the room. He took the stairwell down to the ER feeling like he moved underwater.

Entering the trauma room, Alex found the baby red-faced and inconsolable. Tears rolled down his chubby cheeks as he lay on the stretcher surrounded by the trauma team performing their assessments. Two long mechanical arms extended from the wall with angulated joints and elbows, resembling a praying mantis. These supported twin overhead lamps the size of a manhole cover, their convergence casting the boy in white spotlights. The trauma team went about their business in muted tones, the less to scare the already-terrified child as he tried to pull at the elbow splint protecting his tenuous IV line. One nurse knelt by the boy's head, cooing as she stroked his downy hair with a purple-gloved hand, whispering to him in a maternal *sotto voce* that it was going to be all right.

Alex drifted over to a nurse-scribe typing at a monitor in the room's corner and sighed, "What's the story?"

Without looking up from his keyboard, the nurse said, "Parents said dad was giving him a bath tonight in the sink and he didn't check the water temperature before putting the baby in. When the kid started crying, dad says he pulled him out and thought the skin was just a little red. When the kid wouldn't stop crying afterwards, he says that's when he figured something was wrong and brought him in."

"What time did this happen?"

"Dad says about one o'clock."

"Giving him a bath after midnight?"

"That's his story and he's sticking to it."

"Anybody else around the house to see all this?"

"Mom says she was there too at the time of the bath, grandma was in the house but asleep."

"Where're mom and dad right now?"

"Social worker just walked them over to the family room over by the triage desk."

Alex watched the baby's feet bicycle-pedal in the air, keeping time with his wails. "What's his name?"

For the first time, the nurse stopped typing and looked up at the child. "Buford McEwan. Mom says they call him Bubba."

"Okay. Let's start by doing Bubba a favor and lettin' him have point one per kilo of morphine."

"Mmm-kay."

As Alex walked to the bedside, the wall of trauma

nurses parted, making room. Murmuring, "Shhhh, shh, shh, shh," he delicately examined the child as one of the nurses began to administer the pain medicine, injecting it slowly through one of the rubber ports in the baby's IV tubing. Gradually, the baby's howls tapered off to sniffles, his lower lip sucking in with each hitching breath, snot running down his nose. The child gave Alex a plaintive look.

Starting at a line so sharply circumscribed it could have been drawn with a pen, the burned skin had sloughed from the baby's waist to his toes, leaving wounds tinted a deep cherry red, like dull crimson pants.

"Doesn't look like a bath. More like being dipped," Alex said. Gently pressing on the boy's abdomen to look for any signs of tenderness suggestive of internal injuries, Alex spotted a fresh, purple bruise on the left side of the child's chest. The bruise had a sharply demarcated, upside-down "V" at its apex before becoming more diffuse and ragged at its opposite end. *Shaped like the tip of a boot.*

The scribe nurse announced to the room, "Babygram's up." The babygram—a head-to-toe, single-shot x-ray done on injured children—appeared on a monitor in the corner, bony arms and legs akimbo, like a miniature skeleton doing a frenetic dance. Leaving the bedside, Alex inspected the picture with Talmudic concentration. He drew his face within inches of the screen, moving the mouse to adjust the light/dark contrast, bringing it up and down to better examine the subtleties of the image. With a long-practiced gaze, thorough and persistent, Alex scrutinized the outline of every bone in the child's body.

Then he saw them, subtle but unmistakable. The x-ray showed a broken rib on the right side of the chest, it's sclerotic lines of scarred bone showing it to be an old fracture that had already healed, as well as two broken ribs on the left, their edges sharp and clean and new.

"Child's been beaten," he said, so low no one else in the room could hear. Alex felt something inside him, long bent and straining, finally snap, like a broken bone of his own.

An hour later, having cleaned and dressed the baby's burn wounds and transferred the child's care to the intensive care unit team, Alex shambled out to the emergency room's triage desk. A dozen worried-looking people milled about nearby in the ER lobby, their anxious chatter drowning out the TV's banter between two hosts on a Brownsville morning show.

Alex spied the social worker on call, a plump middle-aged woman named Lupita, holding a steno pad with scribbled notes as she talked to a security guard by the triage desk. Dressed smartly in navy slacks and a frilly cream-colored blouse, she and the guard were the only people in the room who didn't look like they'd just rolled out of bed and thrown on whatever clothes were at-hand. She acknowledged Alex's approach with a nod, holding up her index finger to him while finishing her conversation with the guard.

"—still sorting things out, but if you wouldn't mind just staying close down here for now. Everybody here in the lobby's with the family of that baby. They've been steady showing up for the last hour or so and a couple of these folks smell like they've been drinking. You never know who might decide to do something stupid. Mom and Dad are from Encino so since it's so close to daylight I'm not going to worry about trying to find them a hotel voucher for now."

Thumbs hitched in his belt, the security guard scanned the crowd. "Sounds good, Lupe. Need anything else from me?"

"One thing: Dad parked illegally in the ambulance bay. He says he was freaking out, just pulled in to the first spot he could find. If you would, please, tell the department not to tow it. I'll ask him to move it a little later in the morning once things have settled down. He said it's a brown Cutlass. Thanks, Antonio."

The guard winked, then ambled to the plate glass windows looking out on the parking lot, acting casual while securing a spot where he could eavesdrop on the crowd to pick up trouble early.

Leaning on the triage desk while he waited, Alex saw himself in the waiting room's CCTV monitor behind the counter. The carelessness with which he'd pulled on his white coat left the collar flipped, like a half-ass Elvis impersonation. His expression was vacant and lifeless, his gaze blank and unfocused. He looked like he was filming a hostage video.

Turning to Alex, Lupita's all-business demeanor broke when she observed Alex up-close. She asked with genuine concern in her voice, "Dr. Brantley, are you alright? You look terrible."

Ignoring the question, he asked one of his own. "Where're Mom and Dad?"

Lupita pursed her lips and gave him a skeptical look before answering, "All these people out here are extended family and friends. Once the crowd started getting this large, I moved Mom and Dad into the crisis room over by the vending machines."

Alex stifled a yawn. "What do they know?"

"Just that y'all are assessing the baby."

"Okay, let's get this over with," he said as he shuffled towards the crisis room.

"Don't you want to change first?" she called after him. He was still spattered in Mr. Holub's blood.

"Nope." He kept walking.

The odor of unwashed bodies hung thick in the air when Alex and Lupita entered the ER's crisis room, strong and musty, tempting Alex to leave the door open. A squat, older woman with gray hair and thick glasses sat in one chair, fingering rosary beads in her gnarled hands. Across from her, an obese teenager with braces on her overbite rocked back and forth, whispering a lullaby to a baby asleep in her arms. A woman with a half-dozen facial piercings and a neck tattoo sat on a short bench and swayed as she sobbed. Her gym shorts rode up as her legs bounced, heels tapping on the sole of her flip-flops. Next to her, a short, skinny man with a scraggly mullet sat brooding. His sleeveless concert shirt revealed wiry arms that looked coiled and cocked. As Alex looked him over, he noticed cowboy boots with a sharp "V"-toe sticking out past the frayed hems of the bristly man's jeans.

Without preamble, Alex pointed to the couple and asked, "Mom and Dad?"

"Yeah," the short man said as the woman nodded and wiped her studded nose, then her eyes.

"Bubba's been put in I.C.U., and we've called Child Protective Services. Somebody's gonna be going to jail over this."

The father's eyebrows knitted as though he hadn't heard Alex right and he leaned forward slightly. "Jail?"

"Yeah, jail. It's where people go when they beat their kids. Don't know yet if the charges'll be for assault or murder. If you have any questions about how the process works, Lupita here will be happy to answer them for you." Alex turned on his heel and reached for the knob as Lupita shot him a furious look.

The matter-of-fact manner of the announcement made it hang in the air for a few seconds. The silence was broken with the mother's wail of "Oh fuck, oh fuck, OH FUCK, *OH FUCK, OH FUCK!*" Her words morphed into a primal scream, fists balled and jammed into her squeezed-shut eyes. No one in the stunned room moved to comfort her.

The crowd in the lobby heard the muffled shrieks and surrounded Alex as he exited, barraging him with questions and requests for news or updates. He ignored them, pushing through the group firmly as he made his way back to the main ER. On his way, he took off his white coat and stuffed it in a trashcan, leaving half the garment sticking out the receptacle's swinging lid.

A doctor waved him over as he cut through the Emergency Room. "Oh, good, Dr. Brantley, I was just about to page you. I've got a consult for you, fifty-four-year-old man with abdominal pain for the last six hours. I'm sending him to C.T. scan now, but—" He broke off with a quizzical expression when Alex walked past without acknowledging him. The doctor followed, speaking to Alex's mute profile as he tried to keep up. "Excuse me, Dr. Brantley? Are you still on call? It's only five thirty." Alex shuffled through the sliding glass doors that led to the ambulance bay and continued outside to the doctors' parking area. The consulting doctor shouted after him as Alex ambled away, "Don't y'all change over at seven?"

Between the sports cars and foreign imports sat a ten-year-old copper-colored LeSabre with a dent in the rear quarter panel, a souvenir from the night Frieda had left, vision blurred by tears as she backed up her car. Cranking the engine, Alex followed the one-way lane in the direction of the lot's exit. As he passed a short row of ambulances parked adjacent to the ER's entrance, he impulsively hit the brakes hard enough that the tires chirped, and the car swayed a moment before coming to a standstill. He idled, thinking, then pulled over to the curb. He left the engine running as he popped the LeSabre's trunk.

Amid the clutter, he found the tire iron under the spare. Alex walked past the ambulances and toward the cockroach-brown Cutlass at the end of the row of emergency vehicle parking. Rearing back, he swung the tire iron at the car's back window with all of his might. It exploded in a starburst, like a plexiglass supernova. Two more violent swings took care of the taillights, leaving the asphalt covered in ruby-colored plastic shards. He worked his way around the car, taking care of the passenger windows and windshield in turn. The only sounds were birds chirping in the predawn punctuated by intermittent detonations of glass. Alex's feet crunched on glass chips as he circled the Cutlass, dragging the tip of the tire iron along the low-gloss finish.

Like an art critic, he stepped back and appraised his work. For a final touch, he finished smashing out the driver's window with three more blows, then reached across the driver's seat to pluck out a honey bun that sat in the center console, still in its wrapper. Ripping it open with his teeth, he spat the small piece of plastic back onto the driver's seat, and then took a bite of the pastry on the way back to his car. He tossed the tire iron back into the LeSabre's trunk and slammed it before looking straight into the CCTV camera perched over this portion of the lot and giving it the finger. Then he settled behind the wheel and drove off into the purple dawn.

CHAPTER TWO

9:10 a.m.—Monday, February 4ᵗʰ

"Okay class, now that we've covered introduction, body, and conclusion, we're going to put it all together. Y'all's assignment will be to do a five-minute presentation that I want you to title, 'Who I am.' I want y'all to have some fun with this. Really try to let us know what makes you tick. Take it anywhere you want so long as at the end of the five minutes we have a better idea of what you're really like."

Sitting in the back row, Henry Wallis inwardly groaned. He detested few things in life, but Mrs. Lee's sophomore Communication Arts class at Lorenzo de Zavala High School in Three Rivers, Texas made that short list.

While Mrs. Lee preached the virtues of opening a speech with humor, Henry began crafting the fairy tale this assignment would force him to deliver. Because if he knew anything, he knew this: he was different from other kids in a way Mrs. Lee wasn't ready to hear about.

It wasn't anything about the way he looked—medium height with glasses, athletic appearing with dimples, and a cleft chin. When he'd turned fifteen about a year ago, he'd gotten his braces off and started wearing contacts, and as he'd gotten over his baby-giraffe clumsiness when he grew into his body, girls had started to think of him as cute. If he walked by in the mall among a dozen other teenagers, with his letterman's jacket and vacant expression, he didn't have the sense anything made him stand out.

Nor could he blame it on the fact that his father had been killed on deployment in Afghanistan. Henry'd been a toddler at the time and had no memory of the man, only a picture of him in his Army dress uniform that his mother kept in a trunk since re-marrying when he was nine years old.

His mother, Rebecca, doted on him in a way that Henry considered excessive but not pathological. She believed in traditional gender roles and sought out men who felt the same way. From a young age Henry recognized that she believed in keeping up appearances at all costs. "What will people think?" was her rejoinder for many of her husband's more outlandish suggestions. It drove her selections of decorations, social engagements, fashion choices and friends, but Henry didn't see this as the cause of his problem.

He couldn't blame it on his stepfather either. Patrick Sullivan—Sully to his friends—was a kind man, not terribly bright, but honest and thoughtful. Good with his hands and competent at life, he seemed to enjoy teaching Henry the manly arts. Sully treated his mother well, and she'd taken his name, while having Henry keep his own. To the community—and to Sully's mistaken belief as well—they seemed to be a small-town version of the Cleavers.

On his fourth birthday, he'd fallen off a horse at a petting zoo and cracked his skull badly enough that he needed emergency surgery for bleeding on the brain, an operation that had left him with a curved scar, like a ram's horn, on the right side of his scalp that was still visible. He often caught himself fingering its bumpy edges absent-mindedly when he concentrated on something, especially now that he clipped his hair short. Back then the doctors had told his mother there would be no long-term aftereffects, but he still wondered occasionally whether that injury had scrambled something in his brain, like Humpty-Dumpty.

While the origins of what set him apart, made him different, remained an enigma to Henry, from a young age he'd understood the need to hide it from the world. In retrospect, he thought he'd been able to hide that side of himself from his parents and teachers for a remarkably long time, a fact he considered to be a testament to his careful and meticulous nature. The world didn't discover the real Henry until he was ten years old.

The events behind this revelation began innocuously enough. Henry's chronically underemployed uncle found work clearing brush on the deer lease of a friend's friend and asked to borrow Sully's chainsaw. His promise to take care of it only lasted until the first refueling when, in his haste and inexperience, Henry's uncle tried to top it off with gas with the engine still hot. The vaporized gasoline fire-balled and set the chainsaw aflame, leaving it a misshapen pile of melted plastic and scorched metal, and his chagrined uncle with second-degree burns on both hands. Knowing his brother-in-law would never replace it, Sully hadn't bothered asking. As Sully headed to the hardware store late on a Saturday afternoon, he asked Henry if he wanted to tag along. Henry enjoyed Sully's company and bounded out to the truck.

The hardware store was located in a strip mall, and they passed a pet store on their way. Henry's eyes grew wide and he begged Sully to go inside, pulling at his arm. Sully relented, but insisted they would only look. Inside the store, Henry wandered the aisles, oohing and aahing at the gerbils playing in their cedar chips and tapping the glass of the snakes' aquaria.

Henry stopped in his tracks, though, when he saw a

hutch containing six small rabbits. Palms splayed and nose pressed against the wire cage, his face lit up, but even at ten years old he could recognize in Sully's face the man's regret at the decision to enter the store. Henry complied with no argument when Sully gently reminded his stepson, they needed to be getting to the hardware store if they were going to make it home in time for supper.

Later that night in his room, Henry had emptied the jar in which he kept all the money he got for his allowance. The next weekend he returned to the pet store, this time alone, his pockets bulging and jingling. The store owner watched with amusement as Henry pulled handful after handful of loose change and a few crumpled bills from the many pockets of his cargo shorts and dumped it all on the glass countertop next to the old-fashioned brass cash register with pop up numbers, then counted out the purchase price. Smiling as he handed over the wire cage with the rabbit inside, he told the delighted, wide-eyed Henry, "Best part of m' job is making young boys like you so happy."

It had been difficult riding his bicycle home with the small cage balanced on the handlebars, but Henry managed.

For years afterwards, when Rebecca thought back on the day her life changed, usually alone on the porch swing after Sully had gone to bed and she'd had a little too much wine, she couldn't help but think how different her life might have been if she'd just ordered a pizza for supper that night. It's funny, the little choices on which things hinged. If she'd ordered a pizza, she wouldn't have been peeling potatoes for dinner on that early evening, and if she hadn't been peeling potatoes, she wouldn't have had the opportunity to glance up at the window over the sink. But she did, and she had, so that was now just so much spilled milk.

Squinting, she saw through the window a thin wisp of white smoke rising out of a stand of oak trees about the size of a football field behind their house. She suspected teenagers went back there to smoke marijuana, and now she feared one of them may have carelessly tossed a cigarette and started a small fire. Drying her hands on a dishrag, she went to investigate.

Entering a clearing, she saw a rabbit in a wire cage, suspended by a coat hanger looped over a low-lying tree branch. The cage sat just a few inches above a small fire that was the source of the smoke. The animal was hurling itself in an agonal frenzy against the wire walls, trying in vain to escape as it slowly burned to death.

Oblivious to her presence due to his intense concentration, with his jaw clenched and his eyes wide, her ten-year-old son masturbated furiously while listening to the animal's death squeals.

She'd shrieked and rushed forward, burning her hands as she swatted at the cage causing the branch to sway wildly as she tried to knock it from its spot above the flames while her startled son zipped up. Once the enclosure was on the ground, she had no means to euthanize the tortured animal. Knowing that she couldn't take it to a veterinarian due to the questions such a visit would generate, she felt she had no choice but to let it slowly succumb to its injuries over the course of three hours. She'd beaten Henry for the incident, but that was the only part of the episode that had brought him to tears.

Furtively, she'd taken Henry to see a child psychiatrist after the rabbit episode. She made the appointment all the way up in Austin because as she saw it, the seventy-five-mile drive was worth it to mitigate the chances of bumping into someone she knew while walking her only child into the office of a doctor for crazy people.

The psychiatrist kept up a mask of professionalism while Rebecca described the reason for Henry's visit, but she saw when it slipped for a moment and the revulsion of the human being underneath the white coat showed through, like a stumble in high heels. Paying cash for the visit to avoid filing an insurance claim, Rebecca never took Henry back.

She needed solutions, she thought. No—she frowned. She needed normalcy, not solutions.

She'd never told Sully about the incident fearful he'd leave her had he found out. After all, what man wants to be told his new stepson is torturing small animals?

She always looked at Henry differently after that. When months later Sully announced he'd gotten a job offer an hour away in the small town of Three Rivers as a prison officer at the Federal Correctional Institution—or as most of the town's few thousand residents referred to it, The Clink—she was the one who suggested they move there to save him a commute. She told the family she'd like a change of scenery, but the truth was she never wanted to see that small stand of trees out the kitchen sink's window ever again.

CHAPTER THREE

6:05 a.m.—Saturday, December 22nd

Twenty minutes after leaving the ER parking lot, for the last time Alex walked through the door of the apartment he temporarily called home. Prior to beginning this assignment seven weeks earlier, the recruiter had promised him upscale accommodations, but that wasn't an adjective Alex would have chosen to describe his lodgings.

During the last two years, Alex had covered practices for a surgeon taking three months of maternity leave, a national guard reservist who'd been deployed to Afghanistan for six months, a doctor who'd broken his arm in a car wreck and couldn't operate for twelve weeks, and an elderly country surgeon who'd decided to go part-time. Seven weeks ago, Alex went to Brownsville to substitute for Dr. Montez as she recovered from donating a kidney to her sister.

Prior to starting his surgical training, there'd been a plan, and it most certainly hadn't been working as a professional temp. In the halcyon days of finishing medical school, he and Frieda had talked of moving to a small town in west Texas, some place like Pecos where she had people, or maybe Fort Stockton with its easy access to the Big Bend's desert wilderness. He would join a smallish group, they thought, carving out a practice doing general surgery while she worked as a physical therapist. Laying in the dark in each other's arms, they dreamed about buying land, something with lots of limestone and maybe a creek, and having kids. After finishing four years of medical school and in the run up to beginning his five-year surgical residency, they had it all figured out.

He'd expected surgical training to be a beat-down, and he hadn't been wrong. The stress, the backbreaking hours, and the accountability wore on even the strongest of personalities. In his first few years, he'd assumed his struggles were no different from any other surgeon. Sure, he'd noticed that his weight had dropped when he began punching new holes in his belts. He'd also thought it odd that despite his chronic exhaustion, he had trouble going to sleep when he lay down, his brain running full tilt, ruminating on issues back at the hospital. But he'd assumed all of his peers dealt with these problems too. While half of the surgery residents in his program were female, the culture of the training was far from nurturing. "No one ever died from a lack of sleep," was a common saying among the program's leadership.

As the years of his residency crawled by, Frieda picked up on the fact that something was wrong with him even before Alex himself. She'd gamely coped as best she could, telling him she understood when he turned his back to her advances in the dark, and making excuses for Alex's withering enjoyment of social interaction. She watched helplessly as his fastidious nature morphed slowly, almost imperceptibly. He began living with stubble, his clothes rumpled, and his lab coat sported week-old coffee spills. When she finally raised her concerns, he'd dismissed them, at first gingerly, but over time more stridently, assuring her that this was just the price to be paid, that everyone went through this, that he just had to put his head down and power through for himself and for them.

When she asked him to see a psychiatrist, he rebuffed the idea out of wounded pride. When she begged him to quit the job, saying they could figure out the next step together, he'd refused, saying he was in too far. When she gave him an ultimatum, the job or her, he'd foolishly snubbed her. When the end came, the remark that still stung the worst was when she called the hospital his jealous mistress. Her last words as she walked out the door in tearful anger were that in all the years the residency had spent teaching him to care for his patients, they'd never once given him a lesson in how to care for himself or her.

Since leaving, she'd moved on. He'd heard she married an Episcopal priest in Corpus Christi a few months ago, with a promise of a better life.

After she left, Alex's downward spiral accelerated. His interactions with colleagues became less professional. His paperwork missed deadlines and his appearance continued to decline. While these red flags were picked up by his program it was testimony to the department's priorities that he was allowed to graduate because, at the end of it he still managed to take care of his patients, both in the OR and out. One of the remarks that he saw on his final evaluation came from the oldest member of the faculty, "While I don't know what's going on down in the core of this man-child, the one thing I do know is the son of a bitch can operate. Progression to graduation approved."

He'd found that private practices were more concerned about these red flags, though, as professionalism problems made him radioactive to community surgeons who had to court referrals and lived and died by their online ratings from past patients. The frustrations of his failed job search were compounded by the fact that graduation had brought with it the obligation to start paying off student debt, which between college and medical school now totaled well over three hundred thousand dollars. In desperation, he'd turned to the only place where almost anyone could get a job, short-term temporary assignments with no commitments.

Through these temporary assignments, he'd become something of an expert on the décor of corporate housing. The Brownsville apartment was standard issue for these gigs. Eleven hundred square feet of worn dark brown carpeting, faux-wood paneling on which hung reproductions of generic autumn scenery, mismatched green couch and yellow love seat, and ten-year old appliances in the kitchen. He'd never bothered to put sheets on the bed since he watched TV on the couch until he fell asleep, so he'd chosen instead to just use the mattress as an open-air hamper.

With the exception of a sticky brown film on the bottom shelf of the refrigerator, the place had been passably clean when Alex moved in. The maid service was scheduled for Wednesday mornings, but Alex had been put on call at St. Vincent's every Tuesday night during his time in Brownsville and was therefore trying to sleep every time they arrived. They refused to reschedule, and he sent them away each week without cleaning the place. Food splatters in the microwave accumulated, and dirty dishes stacked up in the sink. Once all the stocked cutlery and dishware had been used, Alex bought paper plates and plastic utensils to avoid washing dishes. The mattress, stacked high with dirty laundry and stained scrubs, made the condo smell like a locker room.

On this, his last morning, he kicked off his tennis shoes in the front entryway and dipped his left shoulder so the strap of his overnight bag slid off and landed with a dull thump. Alex searched between the cushions for the remote, then collapsed on the couch and scrolled to SportsCenter only to find a screen message that ESPN was no longer available on his satellite package. Apparently, the temp company had decided to try to save a few dollars with some cord-cutting.

He continued to stare at the TV for a few moments before turning it off. His reflection in the powered-down screen matched his mood, black and dull. He sat in that position without moving, deep in thought, for a long time, the room totally silent. Eventually the sun peeked over the rooftop across the street, the harsh light slanting through the blinds and throwing shadows like prison bars across his face, making him squint as he rubbed his whiskers.

With Frieda's leaving, he'd lost the only thing that really mattered. Despite his wounded pride, he'd managed to keep it together long enough to graduate from his residency, but he saw she was right. He found the highs weren't as high as the lows were low, and now in retrospect he could see it had been that way for far too long. The night of his graduation, after the ceremony had ended and his colleagues ran off into the night to celebrate, Alex stayed behind, sitting by himself at his round table in the Marriott's ballroom, the vest of his three-piece suit unbuttoned, his tie loosened and crooked, drinking warm champagne and reading his surgical certificate. There, amid the wait staff bussing tables and housekeepers vacuuming the paisley carpet, he had a moment of clarity. In that moment he saw that really there was no decision to make. There was no way he could do this for the rest of his career.

That left him with a problem, though. Or rather, three hundred thousand of them. Then and there, staring at the bubbles rising to the top of his flute, he'd decided that every spare nickel would go toward debt reduction, and once his loans were paid, a new life. A life of what, he couldn't say, at least not then, but something different. And that night at the Marriott, that had been enough.

But it had been harder than he'd thought. The numbers barely seemed to move when he looked at his invoices every month while he ate Ramen and changed his own oil to save money. Slowly, he'd come to realize that he was still looking at years of this to retire his debt, years of dreading each tomorrow. And as the reality of that sunk in, he began to contemplate more drastic measures to make his problems go away.

Coming back to the moment, he thought, I need a cigarette.

Management only allowed smoking behind the complex in an area adjacent to a massive culvert. Grabbing a half-empty soft pack of Marlboro Lights from the plexiglass coffee table, Alex weighed whether he had the energy to put on shoes, make the walk out to the drainage ditch, and stand there in the December morning chill. Deciding he didn't, he shook out a cigarette and put it to his lips before padding into the kitchen where he surveyed the mound of dirty dishes filling the sink and counter space. He found a large skillet at the bottom of the stack and tried to extract it from the crusted mountain of pots and cutlery with a careful pull, like a game of Jenga. The pile shifted then came tumbling down with a clatter onto the linoleum as he jumped back to protect his toes.

The frying pan was bigger than a dinner plate and heavy. With a few waggles of his wrist, he tested its heft then, satisfied, swung it at the smoke detector set in the kitchen ceiling. He connected solidly and the white circle's plastic housing disintegrated, leaving red and black wires pig tailing from the mount. Alex sauntered into the bedroom and disposed of the smoke detector there in a similar fashion. After destroying the device in the living room, he nonchalantly tossed the frying pan onto the love seat before collapsing onto the couch and lighting up. He took a long drag, savoring it before exhaling through his nostrils in twin dragon-like plumes.

He finished that cigarette and lit another as he shuffled into the bedroom and opened the French doors on the closet. Kneeling and groping in the dark recesses, he retrieved two olive green Army surplus duffle bags and from his knees began stuffing them with clothes, heedless as to whether they were clean or dirty.

Alex dragged the duffel bags outside and muscled them into the rear seat of his car. Squinting as the smoke drifted into his eyes, he pulled out onto the highway, leaving the front door of the apartment standing ajar.

His first stop was Party Central.

The party favor store was located on the first floor of a dingy-looking building just outside downtown. An electronic bing-bong announced him, causing a skeletally thin older man to glance up from his seat on a stool behind the register where he read the *Brownsville Herald*. His ears stuck straight out, accentuated by his thinning hair, and his short-sleeved pearl snap shirt seemed to hang on him. He only regarded Alex for a moment before returning to the sports section.

Alex scanned the store. He seemed to be the only customer in the place. A tinny version of "Bette Davis Eyes" played overhead, accompanied by the sound of footsteps clomping around on the second floor where he heard muffled voices, like a blanket over a speaker.

He wandered down the aisle directly in front of the entrance, skirting a display with row upon row of bubble-blowing jars. Alex pulled a random one off the shelf and fished out the plastic dipper. Dunking it back into the soapy solution, he blew a long string of bubbles into the store's still air before returning the jar to the shelf.

Moments later Alex found what he was after on the aisle with balloons and streamers. Several large helium tanks, stood as high as his chin and secured to DIY racks with chains. Waggling one cannister, he decided he needed something more manageable. Further down were tanks about the size of the small plaid thermos he remembered his father taking to work every day when he was young. Alex selected one of the small ones and found a brass regulator on the shelf above it. He screwed the regulator on to make sure it fit, and briefly spun the handle to make sure he heard the hiss of gas. Pleased, he closed the valve again and brought both items to the register.

The next errand, at a retailer for home improvement supplies, went quickly. Alex easily found the large oven bags in the outdoor patio and grill section, and while he'd had to ask for help in finding the rolls of silicone tubing the whole affair had not taken more than twelve minutes.

Sitting in the retailer's parking lot, he looked up and down the street before him. In his line of sight were two closed-down storefronts with soaped-over plate glass windows, a liquor store, and a pawn shop. Beyond the pawn shop he could just see a sign whose bottom was obstructed from view but whose top clearly read "Motel..." He started the car and headed in that direction.

CHAPTER FOUR

11:10 a.m.—Saturday, December 22nd

Viewed fully, the sign read "Motel El Cielo" in bold red cursive. Beneath it, a large black arrow outlined with light bulbs pointing into the parking lot, and magnetic letters tempted prospects with Kitchenettes-Free cable TV-Free Wi-Fi-Low weekly rates-Jacuzzi.

The motel occupied three sides of the parking lot's square, interrupted by a breezeway in the middle, all of the rooms opening onto the lot. Alex pulled into a spot along the stucco wall next to the office's acrylic door. Inside, a runty-looking flowerless plant stood next to a rack of brochures for visitor activities, and a half-full pot of percolator coffee sat on the counter top. Behind the desk, a varnished wooden plaque held small hooks with room keys on plastic fobs. No one was at the front when he walked in, but he could hear Judge Judy's voice coming from a door behind the desk. Not seeing a bell, he asked loudly, "Hello? Anybody home?"

A diminutive woman came out of the back room and lay down the crochet hook and yarn she'd been working. Bespectacled and braless, her sleeveless sundress showed withered, lined arms. "What can I do for you, sugar?" she asked, her edentulous mouth flattening out the "sh" sound.

"Need a room."

"No problem there, we got plenty. How many nights?"

"Just the one."

"Anybody with you?"

"Nope."

"Need a kitchenette?"

"Nope."

"Smoking?"

"Please."

"Oughtta give that up, you'll live longer."

Alex smiled at that.

She turned her back to him and studied the board with the hanging keys. After brief consideration, she pulled the key for room sixteen off its hook and handed it over. "Sweet sixteen, here you go."

"How much?"

"Well, let's see here. We got a single king, smoking, no kitchenette. That'll run you fifty-five, after the governm'nt gets his, come to sixty-one and some change."

"I'll take it."

The woman handed Alex a slip of paper. "Name and address here, license plate, make, and model here, then sign here." While Alex filled out the form, she looked him up and down in his stained scrubs. "You some kinda doctor or somethin'?"

"Or something, yeah," he said without looking up. He handed the slip back, paid her in cash, took the room key, and left.

Entering room sixteen, the pungent smell of industrial-strength disinfectant grabbed his nose and wouldn't let go, like the chemical smell of a portable john. Dark faux-wood paneling contrasted with the alternating blue and tan diamond pattern of the polyester bedspread, and a thick TV was mounted in a bracket up in the corner.

It was cold in the room, and Alex knelt by the AC unit under the front window, selecting the warmest setting. It kicked on after a brief pause, and he savored the heated air blowing against his face and hands as he held them in front of the slats.

He closed the thick blackout shades and stripped, kicking his boxers and scrub bottoms away with his big toe. Turning the water on as hot as he could stand it, he stood in the shower stall leaning forward, hands splayed on the lime-green tiles and elbows locked.

He stayed like that until the water turned cold, then reached for the folded towel on the back of the toilet tank. The showerhead continued to dribble as he caught a glimpse of himself in the mirror. The water beaded as it ran down his face and chest, red-rimmed eyes above his scruff, hair akimbo. The yellow-tinged bulb above the sink made him appear jaundiced. He bared his teeth in the mirror and stuck out his tongue. Finally, he just ran his fingers through his hair rather than comb it, wrapped the towel around his waist, and went back into the bedroom. He lay down without bothering to get under the bedspread and was asleep instantly.

Alex didn't know how long he slept, but when he awoke there was no light filtering around the edges of the blackout shades.

It felt near.

When he closed his eyes, he could feel his heart beating in his chest, banging away with ferocity. His body knew what was coming, and tens of thousands of years of self-preserving evolutionary biology was kicking in.

Opening his eyes, he swung his legs over the side of the bed and stood, re-knotting the towel around his waist when it slipped. He pulled the heavy blinds open and studied the scene, popping his knuckles one-by-one in nervous anticipation.

He watched a man and woman talking while they smoked on the sidewalk next to the office, oblivious to his standing in the dark room's window, bare-chested in a towel and watching them. Their body language suggested they were or soon would be intimate, as she laughed at something the man said and let a hand linger on his forearm for a few seconds. Standing this close to the window, Alex's face was reflected back to him in the glass pane, and he refocused to study his own features in the black mirror.

The hair on his forearms stood on end and his breathing quickened. *Okay, enough of this. Time to do what you came here to do.*

Closing the shades, he went outside to the LeSabre still wearing only his towel. He only bothered to retrieve the helium bottle, oven bag, and tubing before kicking the car's door closed behind him with the sole of his bare foot.

Deliberately, he smoothed out the bedspread, so it once again looked pristine, then he lay all three articles down, side by side, adjusting them so they were in a perfect row. With the space lit only by the low light of the bedside lamp, the room took on a more ominous feel.

Alex pulled the chair to the edge of the bed and sat ramrod straight as he picked up the bottle and put the nozzle to his nose, then turned the handle to allow just the smallest amount of helium to escape. He knew from his premed days that helium was supposed to be odorless, and indeed, he didn't smell a thing. That curiosity satisfied, he set the bottle down so the regulator nozzle and knob hung over the edge of the bed, then picked up the spool of silicone tubing and reeled off an arm's length before pausing. The plastic spool didn't come with any sharp edges to cut the tubing in two.

In frustration, he scanned the room where his eyes

landed on the ceiling light's glass globe. Climbing on the mattress and standing tiptoe, he could just reach the globe's screws and unthread them. The globe bounced off the mattress and cracked when it hit the floor. Now working with purpose, he shook a pillowcase free and placed the globe inside, twisting the end twice to secure it before bringing it down on the carpet with one swift overhanded motion. The globe broke apart noisily. He rooted around in the bottom of the pillowcase and selected a shard that looked suitable. On the third swipe, the shard cut through the silicone and left Alex with a three-foot length of tubing.

His heart pounded, but his hands didn't shake as he cast aside the pillowcase. He picked up the oven bag and shook it open, trying not to give himself a chance to think. Pulling the bag over his head, the smell of neoprene was so strong he could taste it.

The translucent bag gave the room an ethereal, ghostly quality. He cinched the bag's drawstring around his neck so that it was snug but not uncomfortable. Picking up the tubing, he pushed one end onto the regulator's nozzle far enough that it was secure and tunneled the other end under the drawstring. When he looked down, he could see the open end of the tubing sitting above his jawline, next to the right-hand corner of his mouth.

He heard a roaring in his ears. With slow determination, he reached out and first touched, then grabbed the knob on the regulator. The metal was so cold it burned.

Come on, come on, do it! Fuck sake, do it! Don't be such a chickenshit! Do it!

He willed himself to twist the knob, but it was as though his arm belonged to someone else and he could no more force it to obey him than he could characters on a TV screen. The simple act of rotating his wrist seemed to be beyond his body's ability to execute.

Alex began panting from the exertion, holding his breath every few seconds as he bore down, eyes squeezed shut with effort. He became aware of a keening sound, a high-pitched, primal noise, guttural, like he was straining to lift a too-heavy weight. It got louder as his exertion increased, his forearm veins bulged, and the regulator shook. Spittle began to fleck the inside of the bag, and the condensation from his wheezing breath fogged the plastic, both combining to obstruct his vision. With one final gasp, his higher brain shrieked at him *Goddamn you, do it*!

Slowly, the regulator turned a quarter inch, then another. Inside the bag, he heard a low, soft hiss as the helium began to trickle. Sagging with relief, Alex began to pull long deep breaths in through his nose to accelerate the process. He tried to let go of the regulator's knob, but found tetany had set in, forcing him to use his other hand to pry his contracted fingers off until his right claw lay useless in his lap. As Alex continued to inhale deeply through his nose, his mind emptied, leaving him calm, knowing that the end of his pain was only a few minutes away.

His toes and fingertips began tingling, but he still felt lucid. Once the sensation marched to his wrists and ankles, like ants crawling, he began to feel light-headed. With it came a sense of disembodiment, like he was an observer to this event. He stopped inhaling deeply and sagged back in the chair, no longer feeling the need to push this experience along, content to just let it happen, like a skiff following a current.

He began to hallucinate, seeing bright strobing flashes of red, white, and blue, shining in sharp lines, outlines around a black square in his field of vision, like some bizarre patriotic movie screen. He studied the display with detached interest, considering its origins as the edges of his vision turned grey. A part of his brain realized the square was the blackout shades in the room, and he congratulated himself on solving that part of the puzzle. He was working on the mystery of the red, white, and blue lines of light at the edges when he heard what sounded like three rapid-fire rumbles of noise, like cannon shots. This was followed by, "*ssssiiirrrrr, hhoooopennnhhuuuup, brrrrronvllllepooolleeessseee.*" His disembodied self considered this startling and strange, but intriguing, like a riddle as the sounds echoed through the fog and rattled around his dying brain.

His vision had narrowed considerably now, like looking through a telescope backwards. He could barely see the door fly open and two policemen enter, guns drawn. His dot of vision was shrinking steadily now, the gray about to take over his vision completely. He heard "Jeeesssuuuuuussss," and saw one cop kneeling in front of his face. He lost all sight, but was still processing noise, hearing a shouted, slurred word that sounded like, "Mmmmbulllannnsss." His last thought before he blacked out was, *Christ, was that weird or what?*

He was cold.

The chill surrounded him in the inky darkness, and he was disoriented but not in distress. For a moment he wondered if he was underwater. To test this, he tried a swimming motion, a breaststroke, but found he couldn't move. Then he became conscious of a light far above him, and he found himself drifting upward toward it, unbidden. As he floated upward away from the dark depths, the surface became brighter until he broke through.

Confused, he found himself flat on his back, stretched out on nylon carpet staring at blisters of paint peeling from the ceiling. A pretty, pony-tailed woman hovered above him, placing an oxygen mask over his nose and mouth before shining a penlight in his eyes. He couldn't remember anything, and when he tried to sit up, the woman gently put a gloved hand on his chest and told him to lie back down. Raising his head, he saw a cachectic older woman with Mr. Magoo glasses who looked familiar, speaking animatedly to a cop who scribbled notes as he listened. Behind them, an ambulance idled with its rear doors open, chuffing blue exhaust in the direction of the open door. While Alex watched, a man wearing the same shirt as the pretty woman pulled a stretcher out of the back of the rig. Collapsible struts unfolded like spider legs from the underside of the gurney and snapped into locked positions as the stretcher cleared the ambulance's doorframe.

Cutting through the cobwebs, the events of the night slowly came back as the paramedics loaded him onto the stretcher. Tears welled up, and Alex didn't bother to wipe them, letting them tumble down his cheeks as he lay inert. His chest heaved, and the sobs racked him in stronger and stronger waves, like a child's tantrum. He rubbed his eyes with his palms hard enough that he saw blinking lights. He asked the second of the two cops who stood nearby, leaning against the motel room wall and watching, "What happened?"

The cop was a burly man, lumberjack-big. He pushed away from the wall and answered in a tone as gruff as his appearance. "A bulletin went out for you and your ride this morning after an incident of criminal vandalism at St. Vincent's hospital. My partner and I passed by when we noticed your LeSabre out in the parking lot and ran the plates. The manager keyed the door for us. Lucky for you too, paramedic's say another few minutes, and we would've been calling for the coroner instead of the EMTs."

The cop sidled out to the sidewalk to catch the end of the manager's statement to his partner. Alex overheard her saying to the pair of officers, "All's I know is my light cover's broken like a rich man's promise. Mebbe that Mexican might notta screwed it in tight enough last time he changed the bulbs out, but that'd be surprisin', normally he does good work. I don't know why this fella'd go breakin' it hisself, but either way I don't 'spect I'll ever see that money again. Any chance we could just look in his wallet quick-like and I could get my money back to buy a new one? I figger a twenty oughtta cover it. I got the rheumatism an' that medicine ain't cheap. Ever' little bit helps."

The cop smiled patiently. "Sorry, ma'am. I can't help you there. Look on the bright side, it's only a little bit of money."

She grumbled, "When you got nothin', a little is a lot."

"You take care ma'am," the lumberjack said as the two cops walked back to their squad car.

As the paramedics loaded Alex into the back of the rig, he heard her say, "This ain't right. No sir, this ain't right at all."

CHAPTER FIVE

12:45 a.m.—Sunday, December 23rd

Walking down the hallway of the hospital that morning, the day started like so many others for Alex over the years, with the familiar smells of coffee and fresh paint. Passing down a brightly lit corridor past a busy unit clerk's station, he watched harried nurses draw up meds and chart their patient notes. There were differences on this particular morning, though. The scrubs they'd issued Alex here at Rio Hondo Hospital were light green instead of the sky blue preferred by St. Vincent's, for one. He walked these halls with an escort and wearing slippers, for another.

After leaving the El Cielo, the paramedics had taken him for a quick evaluation in the ER where one of the doctors made sure Alex showed no acute signs of illness after his helium-induced blackout. Now cleared, the psychiatric unit here at Rio Hondo and an involuntary hold on the lock down unit awaited him where the psychiatrists would decide if he constituted an ongoing threat to himself.

At the psych unit's locked door, his escort, a scrawny man with red-dirt hair and a pleasant, unthreatening demeanor pressed a button on the intercom. This was followed by a buzzing sound, and a dead bolt on the door audibly shot open. The man opened the door with his buttock, and gestured toward the ward with one hand while placing the other in the small of Alex's back, a move Alex knew was meant to both welcome him as well as allow the man to feel if Alex's muscles tensed in a last-second effort to escape.

Alex had no intention of making things difficult. Scanning the lobby as he entered, he saw three other patients, two men and a woman.

At the nurses' station, the charge nurse said with a professional smile and a slight head tilt, "Good evening, Dr. Brantley. My name is Ms. Hopkins. Housekeeping is just finishing up cleaning your room now. Would you mind having a seat in our common area for just a few minutes?"

Silently, Alex wandered over to a round white table and pulled up a chair. Across from him sat a light-skinned woman of about twenty with hair cropped tight against her skull and feverish eyes. She drew on herself with a black dry erase marker. She reached inside her scrub top and fixed her bra strap, then held the marker tip up to her nose and sniffed it deeply while casting a cautious glance at the nurses' station.

The chair to Alex's right scraped. A beer-bellied man in his forties with a bad comb-over dropped into it and clasped his hands in front of him, fingers interlaced as he considered Alex. Alex returned the stare, not saying a word.

After a quiet minute, the man said to Alex, "You can't blame yourself."

Alex looked down at the white Formica, hoping the man would go away.

The man continued, "I mean, if a man steps to you,

intent on doing you bodily harm, you're gonna protect, protect and serve, am I right? Forget that for even just a minute and you are up *arroyo de caca,* Jack. You do what you gotta do." He tapped his index finger against the table in emphasis of each word.

Alex turned his back to the man, not wanting to engage.

The man was undeterred, continuing, "I don't know what Anthony was thinking. I said to Marie, when Anthony started up, I said, 'You know somebody's gonna get clipped for this'. A fuckin' blind man could see it. But you know, you could never tell that kid nothin'. I was hoping his mother was just gonna have him cremated, something cheap. I don't know if you know, but she's on a fixed income, poor woman. She called me a few weeks ago to help when her fuckin' oven went tits up. I told her she's gotta do the Meals on Wheels, but she don't want to. Says she don't take charity. And now she's gotta deal with this, too." He shook his head in distaste, then said, "Swear to God, if I live to be a hundred, I'll never understand why that asshole would blow things up like he did. I mean, why? What was he looking to get? Makes me think back to what I heard Father Bob say one time."

Now, he reached out and grabbed Alex by the upper arm, squeezing so hard it hurt. Alex turned back, locked eyes with the man and said, "Take your fucking hand off of me."

The man kept his grip so tight his knuckles blanched and stared into Alex's eyes as though imparting some solemn truth.

"Father Bob said, 'Some men just wanna watch the world burn'." Then he released his grip on Alex and crossed his arms before tilting the chair back on two legs, the lesson concluded.

Alex rose and crossed the room to a half-moon of chairs that faced the television where a hawk-nosed old man wearing Bermuda shorts with nylon socks and garters sat watching the home shopping network through heavy-framed glasses.

Alex said, "Sir, are you watching this?"

The man didn't acknowledge the question, so Alex said, "Would you mind if I put it on SportsCenter?"

When the old man still didn't answer, Alex picked up the remote from the chair next to him and changed the channel. The old man never moved.

CHAPTER SIX

6:50 p.m.—Friday, March 8th

Rebecca only brought two plates of dessert to the table. With Henry's training like a madman, she no longer bothered asking if he wanted sweets.

As she handed Sully his plate of peach cobbler, she asked, "Henry, what are you doing tomorrow? I'm helping the Auxiliary get ready for the auction, and I could use a hand setting up tables."

Henry checked his phone. "Schedule coach gave me should keep me busy 'til noon. He wants us to really get after it on Saturdays." He'd discovered a talent for endurance running and had made varsity in cross country his sophomore year.

Hefting a spoonful, Sully smiled as he said, "'Sides, for the first week after I got my driver's license, all I wanted to do was be behind the wheel. Didn't matter what it was. I

41

remember my daddy sayin' I'd drive to go get the mail."

Rebecca said, "Oh, shoot that reminds me. You'll need one of the cars to go train. I guess that means I need to start thinking about that when I'm making plans. Sully, what does your morning look like?"

"I got the eleven to seven tonight. Any chance I could grab a nap in the morning before we head over there?"

"Sure."

Henry said, "May I be excused? I got a lot of homework."

Rebecca nodded, not wanting to speak with her mouth full, gesturing for him to clear his dirty place setting.

Moments later, he closed his bedroom door and locked it. He could hear them prattling about the upcoming weekend and with his homework excuse he knew they wouldn't interrupt him. He got a bottle of water from his mini-fridge and powered up his laptop.

The incident years ago with the rabbit had confirmed Henry's instinct that his urges—actually, call it what it was, his nature—needed to be concealed from the world, but he did so out of necessity, not shame.

The change in geography to Three Rivers had done nothing to slow his escalating aberrant behavior. In his adolescence he'd discovered sadomasochistic pornography, then as his digital savvy grew, he found the dark web. In its murkiest back rooms, he found snuff films from Eastern Europe, videos of cartel executions, and jihadi beheadings. With his parents' technical abilities limited to checking email—he'd actually had to help both of them create their Facebook pages—Henry knew there was no chance they could check up on his internet activities. Behind his locked door, he roamed freely through the web's darkest alleys.

But tonight would be different. He'd gotten his driver's license the day before. This new independence opened up all kinds of interesting possibilities.

He'd seen a headline recently in the Express-News about a park on the outskirts of San Antonio that had experienced an influx of homeless people. Most of the story consisted of complaints from park-goers and pleas from social workers for more resources, but it had piqued his interest. He'd mentally filed the story away. Now, he found the link and directions.

The next morning, he turned off his Android while sitting in the driveway, completely powering it down. Having rendered it temporarily untraceable, he set off toward San Antonio at first light.

His destination was Juan Seguin City Park, a heavily wooded recreational area on the southwest side of the city. When he arrived an hour later, he saw two other cars in the parking lot.

A map of the park's many trails in hand, Henry traced out a five-kilometer loop, the distance of his races. He set off running it lightly, not even breathing hard. He crossed the path of one other runner, a slim woman with a dog leash in one hand and pepper spray in the other. In the few moments of eye-contact as they passed each other, he gave her a nonchalant smile he'd practiced in the mirror, casual enough to be nondescript and not worth remembering.

As he wound his way through the park, he also passed several men and women who clearly made the park home. Just off the trails in semi-permanent encampments, their spots were marked by shopping carts filled with scavenged belongings, dirty white PVC buckets and torn suitcases stuffed with scrounged cold weather gear, scattered among smoldering campfires.

The homeless who bivouacked there sat watch over their meager possessions and monitored Henry with a flat affect as he trotted by. A few in the throes of active psychosis gave him a wide grin and exaggerated waves, waves he returned with a muted one-handed gesture. Twice Henry had to skip over-spent hypodermic needles laying in the trail.

When he returned to his car a few hours later, both of

the other vehicles had left. As he cooled down, he scanned the trees and the light posts around the lot. No cameras that he could see. As he started the drive back to Three Rivers, his mouth felt dry and his senses heightened.

CHAPTER SEVEN

7:50 a.m.—Monday, August 12th

Alex had no trouble finding parking at Lorenzo de Zavala High School in Three Rivers. The lot's few cars belonged to those sentenced to summer school, and with the start of the regular school year only two weeks away, both the teachers and students were limping to the finish line. Despite the numerous spots close to the school's entrance, he parked on the lot's far side next to the field house to get a start on his ten thousand steps.

In the eight months since his night at the El Cielo, he'd become fanatical about exercise. The counselors and psychiatrists at Rio Hondo had preached its benefits to him, and he had to admit they weren't wrong. At the end of his thirty-day inpatient stay, he'd emerged six pounds lighter with the most energy he'd had since he was a teenager.

With his briefcase in hand and with butterflies in his

stomach, he made his way past a motley collection of dented trucks and compact cars, a far cry from the sports cars and expensive imports Alex's colleagues drove in what he now thought of as his former life as a surgeon.

A state trooper wearing a grey Stetson and wrap-around Oakleys stood with thumbs hooked in his utility belt and his back to three sets of plexiglass double doors that led into the school.

"Morning, sir. Can I help you?" the trooper asked.

"Morning, Officer—" Alex glanced at his nametag, "—Hardy. I'm Alex Brantley. I've got an interview today with Principal Cunningham for a job as the new science teacher."

As he shook Alex's hand, Deputy Hardy looked him up and down. With his tweed jacket with elbow patches, too-thin tie, grey Dockers with a woven belt, and beat-up Larry Mahans, Alex knew he looked the part.

Principal Cunningham stood up at her desk and smiled widely as she extended a hand and said, "Dr. Brantley, thank you for coming."

He moved his Styrofoam cup of coffee to the same hand holding the briefcase and with his free hand pumped hers twice. She was short and well-dressed, with a smart red suit that set off her styled gray hair. She gave an impression of having class and an air that left no doubt as to who was in charge.

"Please have a seat," she said and closed the door herself before returning to her own.

"Thanks. It's great to be here. And please, call me Alex."

Principal Cunningham put on a pair of reading glasses and opened a manila folder on her desk. He couldn't read the label on the front, but on the first page he recognized upside down the passport-style picture he'd taken when he started with the Texas Education Agency. While she read, he sat in silence and examined her office. Undergraduate diploma from the University of Texas in Austin. Masters Degree in Education from Trinity. On her desk, two framed pictures sat at angles. In the first, she and a silver-haired man posed with rifles and broad grins over an elk carcass in the snow while in the other a younger version of the couple sat astride a Harley. In a curio cabinet with a small brass key behind her, small portraits of two teenage girls who resembled her around the eyes sat on the glass shelves. A paddle-bladed ceiling fan turned above them, helping stir the stale August air.

She flipped a page, then another. Then, satisfied, she closed the folder before taking off the glasses and tossing them on top. "Quite an eight or nine months you've had."

Alex paused, not sure what to say to that. "It's been challenging."

"That's one way to describe it. Another way is to say it's been the Bellagio fountains of shit shows." She put the glasses back on and, reopening the folder, read aloud.

"Doctor. Bouncing practice to practice. Suspension of your medical license by the state board around Christmas 'cause of a criminal charge of vandalism brought by the parents of a patient somewhere through that time, later withdrawn when the parents were in turn criminally charged for child abuse and the prosecutor did you a solid. Inpatient psychiatric treatment for thirty days. By the way, was that voluntary or involuntary?"

"It began with an involuntary hold for ninety-six hours, but I agreed to make it voluntary and stayed for a month. It helped me get my head screwed back on straight."

She kept reading. "Pursued a teacher's certificate after your discharge from the psychiatric facility. Successful completion of the Educator Preparation Program. Good evaluations by your proctors. Passed your certification exam and application to the state was just approved." She closed the folder and took off the reading glasses again, then leaned back in her leather chair.

"Son, let's make a deal. I'll be straight with you, and

you be straight with me. How's that sound?"

"I'd like that."

She brought the chair forward and propped her elbows on the desk blotter. "Mm-kay, I'll start. I agreed to interview you 'cause trying to find somebody to teach science for thirty-one thousand a year who knows more about biology than what they learned in junior high watching late night Cinemax is like looking for a goddamn unicorn. You've got red flags all over the place in here." She tapped the manila folder with a finger chewed up by arthritis. "But at least they aren't of the variety that disqualify you outright, like playing 'I'll show you mine if you show me yours' with a kid or sellin' pictures of your female students' feet on the internet. Now, I believe in giving people second chances, and that's what I'm thinkin' 'bout doing here. I can't argue if somebody called me selfish because, yes, we do need help. Hell, Friday when I walked by the natural sciences classroom, the sub we've got in there right now sounded like he was about five minutes from tellin' the kids that fossils were planted where they are by the Jews during World War One. But you've got to understand, you'd be on a short leash here. If I saw any signs of the behavior that landed you sitting here in front of me, we'd be having a conversation even more difficult than this one. Am I clear?"

"Crystal," Alex said.

"Okay, with that said, this is the part where I'd like for you to be straight with me. I'm thinkin' 'bout taking a chance like this—and make no mistake that's what I'd be doing here, taking a chance—because I think you bring a good bit of possible long-term upside for us here at the school. Your credentials speak to the fact that you're a smart guy, you come from west Texas, so you know the culture, and we have a hell of a nice little town here. It's the kind of place that would be easy to call home for a certain kind of person. Now, I know that what we're talking about is as far from the life that you had as can be. But son, no bullshit, how long do you picture yourself wanting to do this for?"

Alex smiled. "Principal Cunningham—"

"Call me Jen."

"Jen, I can't say what the future will look like, but I can say how it won't. There's no chance, zero, that I'm going to be doing the groundwork that needs doing to try to get my medical license back. The months since I quit...well, let's just say it took time and distance, but I can see now how miserable I was. That misery drove me to some pretty dark places. Once we get to know each other better I may share with you how dark, but for now I can say with certainty I'm never going back to that life. I'm okay with the idea that I've touched my last patient. I'd like to think of making some place home, and I'm open to Three Rivers being that place."

"Fair enough. But if we do this, what I need from you is to not go putting me in any difficult positions." She stood, signifying they were done.

"Deal," he said as he stood, and once again they shook.

CHAPTER EIGHT

11:15 a.m.—Wednesday, August 14th

With his feet propped on the corner of the folding table in a Brownsville laundromat, Alex watched the spin cycle and read *The Last Picture Show.* Hearing his phone ring, he glanced at the contact. It was Principal Cunningham.

"Morning, Jen. You doing alright today?"

"Better than some, not as good as others. You?"

The washer emitted a loud *clack* and the spinning cylinder came to a halt. "Living life to the fullest here in beautiful Brownsville," he said as he transferred damp clothes to the dryer.

"I'm happy to say we'll be offering you a one-year contract here in short order. It calls for teaching six classes a day, two each of freshman biology, sophomore chemistry, and junior physics. Our total student body is about two hundred, most years, plus or minus. So at fifty kids per year, we're going to have to stretch you for now from our normal class size of fifteen or so kids to about twenty five students per class while I keep trying to recruit you some help. That way we meet their basic science requirement for graduation. In the state of Texas, if a kid wants to graduate with Distinction, they'll need a fourth-year science credit, but that can be a mentored project of some kind. When that's needed, I'll assign that to someone other than you, 'cause you're gonna have your hands full.

"As long as I'm piling the work on, one last thing. I'll be needing you to help coach the varsity cross-country team in the fall and the J.V. baseball team in the spring.

"It sounds like a lot of work, and it is, but I suspect it's less than what you were used to doing in your former life. I really hope you'll consider taking the gig."

"Thank you, ma'am, I can give you my answer now. I really liked the school, and the job sounds great. I'll be signing whatever you send me."

"Outstanding. Then work on gettin' your ass out here. School's close to starting, and we're gonna throw you in the deep end out the gate. Glad to have you on board."

Barreling north from Brownsville the following day, Alex felt excitement at the idea of his next landing spot. The small town was located in the heart of the south Texas oil patch, and the surrounding desert was littered with pumpjacks, tirelessly bobbing away, sucking the crude that was the town's lifeblood from the hardscrabble ground. The local refinery was one of the largest in the region, and, along with the Clink, one of two major employers in the area.

As he made his way north, the low-rolling hills slid by, dotted with stands of creosote brush and cedar scrub, stock tanks marked by windmills, clusters of cattle wallowing in mud holes or bunching under mesquite trees to take advantage of the shade. Wavy lines of heat came off the cracked blacktop of Highway 281, creating wet mirages in the distance.

Just before getting to town, the highway crested a rise. The shoulder widened at the highest point of the bluff, so he slowed and pulled off the asphalt onto the gravel apron. Killing the engine, he got out and leaned against the fender, arms crossed, the metal hot on the seat of his pants. On the other side of the battered guardrail, a few hundred hardscrabble feet of sandstone and chert made a craggy staircase downward where it joined the desert pan and extended like a lumpy quilt to the horizon. A single cloud marred the bright blue sky, casting a small island of shadow on the escarpment. The dark silhouette drifted from his left to right, marching shade across the desert floor for several minutes, further and further into the distance until it disappeared. Once it passed, it left the desert in a great stillness, the only sound the subtle whisper of wind over the rocks around him.

Some people saw these miles and miles of limestone, scrub, and emptiness as a post-apocalyptic hellscape, but Alex had come to have an appreciation for it. He'd felt the crunch of the caldera under his boots on whitetail hunts with his father. While day-laboring as a teenager for Mr. Seigler, a neighboring rancher, he'd cooled off from the hot summer sun with a dip in a stock tank and spent cold January afternoons re-stringing barbed wire between beau d'arc fence posts, his collar flipped against a biting west wind. He'd seen the land's beauty up close. A hard land and unforgiving to be sure, but beautiful nonetheless. This prompted him to think of Principal Cunningham's words. Maybe this was going to be a place he could call home.

In the center of Three Rivers, Alex found a charming town square. Quaint shops and restaurants formed a ring, all facing a two-story building of cut stone, the county seat. In front, a statue of Jose Antonio Navarro, the influential Tejano who championed Texas' independence, kept watch from his view in the saddle. Making a loop, he found one of the storefronts was Dinah's Diner, the spot of his next reckoning in trying to move on with his life.

Gabriella Vazquez was already in a booth when Alex entered. The young lawyer's face was framed with short black hair that she wore straight, and behind her practical glasses were almond eyes that were sympathetic yet discerning.

Her menu was closed, and she was reading her phone. Alex slid in opposite her and pulled his own laminated menu out of the wire loop holder.

Without looking up Gabriella said, "Good morning. Give me just one second to finish up."

Inspecting the offerings, he attempted a smile and said, "Don't take too long. Remember I'm paying you by the hour."

Gabriella closed her phone but laid it on the table at an angle to monitor the screen. Looking across the table at him, she said with the faintest trace of an accent, "So, good news it sounds like?"

Alex closed the menu and said, "Yeah, I'm gainfully employed, the principal called with the good news. My first day will be the twenty-sixth."

"Is it still Principal Cunningham?"

"Yep."

"She was the principal when I attended school there. I liked her very much."

Alex stifled the urge to make a joke asking if that had only been two years ago. It used to annoy him when patients made cracks about how young he looked, and he didn't want to take a chance on getting on the wrong side of his lawyer.

A matronly waitress with fire-engine-red press-on nails that looked more like talons took their orders—meatloaf special for him and a house salad for her—and sauntered back toward the kitchen.

Turning to business, Alex asked, "So what have you got for me?"

Gabriella reached into a leather satchel and pulled out a yellow legal pad full of scribbled notes. Periodically checking them as she spoke, she answered, "Well, after reviewing your situation, I think it will be most advisable if we have you file for bankruptcy under chapter 7. We will have to liquidate your assets but judging by the list you gave me that will not be problematic. Now to go with chapter 7, we are going to have to show that your income is below the state median. That won't be a problem as in Texas right now, that's about fifty-nine thousand dollars. Have you found out yet what your salary at the high school will be?"

"About thirty-one thousand."

"As I said, not a problem then. Unfortunately, that is not the hard part. Student debt is not automatically considered to be a part of the debt that triggered the bankruptcy proceeding. I know that sounds strange, but that is a fact. We will have to go through the motions of asking your lenders to bundle your debt into the bankruptcy filing out of the goodness of their hearts, and they will of course say no because that is their corporate policy. Once they say no, we will have to file what is known as an adversary proceeding. This is paperwork that asks a judge to determine whether the student loan debt should be dischargeable based on your new circumstances."

"How often does that work?" Alex asked.

"About forty percent of the time."

"Odds don't sound that great."

"There is one other thing that makes this case much more difficult."

"Boy, the good news just keeps coming."

"I am sorry, but I do not see the point in sugar-coating things."

Alex said, "No, no, you're right. I'd rather know. What's the other piece of bad news?"

"The judge is going to easily see that a public high school teacher's salary would never be able to service the debt and interest that you have and will continue to accrue.

That is the good part, but there is a high likelihood that the judge's solution to the problem will be to have you return to practicing medicine."

"Wait, what?" Alex said, anger creeping into his tone.

"Think about this, Dr. Brantley. There are mechanisms in place which allow a pathway for physicians who have had their licenses suspended to return to practicing medicine, some of which you have already accomplished. You have articulated awareness of the psychiatric issue that was a root cause of your difficulties. You have also sought treatment for those issues in a way that is verifiable."

Alex sat in silence, looking out through the plate glass window at the courthouse as she continued.

"Physicians who pursue re-licensure have to undergo ongoing psychiatric treatment, perform some continuing medical education, and they can then be granted a provisional medical license which allows them to begin to see patients once again. Those patient encounters must be supervised by another physician picked by the board."

"Supervised?"

"Yes, this supervising physician will accompany the applicant through every clinic visit and consultation received from the emergency room. If the applicant is a surgeon, through operations as well. This supervisor will be watching for two things. First that the psychiatric problems that contributed to your license revocation are not showing signs of resurfacing. And secondly that the applicant for reinstatement is safe and competent in the performance of patient care. The applicant is required to reimburse that supervising physician for their time."

"How long would that go on for?"

"It depends, but usually for about a year. Once the supervisor is confident that the applicant is safe to practice independently, the applicant is granted a full medical license once again and can go back to the normal practice of medicine, although with the understanding that the applicant continues with psychotherapy and more frequent than normal assessments by the Board for continued fitness to practice."

Alex's mood darkened.

"So you see, Dr. Brantley, since this route exists, and you have already completed a part of it, the judge is likely to issue a court order declining to bundle your debt in with the bankruptcy, and to give you an unofficial recommendation that you return to your medical career. That would eventually give you greater earning power and the eventual means to repay the debt."

Alex twisted his napkin "But what if I hate practicing medicine?"

Gabriella paused before answering, "Frankly, the court is likely to say there is no constitutional right guaranteeing that you like your job."

Alex held the car door for Gabriella as she climbed behind the wheel, then closed it, and leaned in the open driver's window. "I'm having a hard time telling myself this is all going to work out," he said.

"Dr. Brantley, I am sympathetic to your situation. I really am. But I just think it's important that you realize this strategy of having your student debt dismissed by the courts is unlikely to be successful. I am happy to file all of the petitions, and we can see what happens. But as they say, 'Hope is not a plan'. As your attorney, I strongly recommend you have a backup plan ready for the likely situation in which we are not able to get your debt relieved by the bankruptcy courts."

Bemused, he looked across the plaza at the courthouse. "And I've always heard it's not a good idea to ignore any advice that starts off with 'As your attorney I would recommend...'" She smiled at that, and he said, "Let me think about it. In the meantime, please keep me updated on the filings. Thanks for all your help with this."

"It is nothing. And I hope you enjoy your time with us

in Three Rivers. I grew up here and have no desire to leave. It is a wonderful town."

He stood up straight and slapped the roof of the car, then stepped clear so she could back out. Once in the street, she gave him one last smile and a wave before driving away.

CHAPTER NINE

9:45 p.m.—Friday, August 16th

Beneath a thin-horned moon, Henry sat in the backseat of his stepfather's Buick sedan with his elbow propped on the door handle while he pulled at his lower lip, deep in thought, naked from the waist down. His flaccid penis lay against his thigh and his bare ass stuck to the vinyl upholstery, peeling off when he shifted his weight. With a circular motion, he wiped the fogged interior glass. Through the smear, the night-black waters of the Frio River rolled by in the inky darkness just beyond the bulrushes in the bar ditch.

Tracy Garcia's sweaty bangs stuck to her forehead. The lace panties she'd worn lay inside out, wadded up on the floorboard atop her puddled denim skirt. She pulled her feet up under her naked bottom and began to absent-mindedly trace her finger around the seatbelt buckle where it jutted out from the bench seat. The hard plastic square had been sticking her in the hip during their stilted love making, and Henry had seen her grimacing in discomfort with each of his thrusts but hadn't said anything.

"Henry, what's the matter?" she asked.

He didn't answer, just continued to stare out the window. The smudged condensate where he'd wiped his window was beading up, and he cocked his head, as though considering the view from a new angle.

"Am I doing something wrong?" she asked, reaching out and placing her hand on his sticky thigh. He still didn't look at her, but it was clear from her tone she knew he was no longer in the backseat with her.

This was the part he hated the most, her neediness. It was exhausting. This had been going on for about three months, and the effort it took to keep pretending wore him down like a rock in a stream.

It's not that he disliked her. He felt nothing towards her, never had. But he was at an age in a small town where it was expected you show an interest in girls, so that's what he'd done. For a while, he'd noticed couples his age holding hands in the hallways. Then Sully had begun making wry comments with a half-smile about how he was sure Henry would wind up being a lady killer. After considering it, he'd made the conscious decision one day that he needed to have a girlfriend.

A few days later, he'd run into Tracy at Three Rivers' only movie theater. She'd been faceless to him through their first few years at De Zavala. His only memory of her was that she'd always attended the cross country meets, usually bringing him a drink after he finished while making a point to congratulate him no matter how he'd done. She looked at him in a way that she didn't look at the other boys on the track team, a fact his teammates had also noticed. They teased him, but also spoke approvingly of her. At the time he took note of all this with utter indifference, as disinterested as if he'd been told a low-pressure system moved over the Great Lakes region the night before.

Seeing her that night in the theater lobby waiting to buy popcorn, he considered her for a moment, then walked up and tapped her on the shoulder. She turned around and smiled in surprise, her braces gone since their last encounter.

She'd giggled throughout their brief exchange. He'd talked while she tried awkwardly to flirt, and at the end of the conversation she told him that she was, like, having an end of school get together the following weekend and, like, some friends were coming over and would he want to come and it would, like, be totally cool if he couldn't or was too busy or whatever. He accepted. She walked away backwards as she blushed and said goodbye, then turned and ran to her friends who had been waiting and watching. The gaggle collapsed into itself, pulling Tracy in to interrogate her, then squealing as they headed en masse to their theater.

After their third date, word trickled back to him that she referred to him as her boyfriend, so he assumed he was obligated to do the same for her.

On the nights he took Tracy out, he usually made an excuse to borrow Sully's car because the bench seats were more conducive to their make out sessions. Truthfully, Henry could take them or leave them, but these trysts allowed him to have something to say when his peers gathered to recount their tales of teenage conquest.

The two of them had come to each other inexperienced virgins, but she showed enthusiasm, desperately wanting to please him. For the better part of the summer, things would end with her giving him a tug as the guys on the cross-country team called it.

Three weeks ago, however, she'd told him she loved him. He didn't know what to say, nor how to interpret the expectant look she gave him at the end of her tumble of words.

After several seconds of awkward silence, she said, "Do you have something you want to say to me now?"

Finally, some judgment gene kicked in and he parroted back in a monotone that he loved her too. Any thoughts he'd had that this lie would make the uncomfortable conversation end were dispelled when a look of relief crossed her face, and she followed by saying she'd decided they should go all the way.

They made plans to go through with it on their next date. She issued him a list of instructions and requirements: make sure he brought a blanket and a condom, downloaded a Taylor Swift album, and find a way to buy her a four pack of wine coolers. She said she wanted it to be romantic, perfect, the way it was when her girlfriends who were experienced talked about it.

And so, they'd fumbled their way through it in a pasture on her uncle's horse farm. That first time he'd not even taken his blue jeans all the way off, leaving them wadded around his ankles, tube socks still pulled up and glowing white in the dark. He lay on top of her, clumsily wriggling and thrusting in the moonlight, her thighs wrapped around his hips, her ankles locked in the small of his back while they slapped mosquitoes. Her breath had the sick-sweet smell of wine coolers, and her skin the odor of cheap soap.

After several minutes, Henry found he was having a difficult time maintaining his erection. Not sure what else to do, he stiffened and groaned, then rolled off and quickly removed the condom before discarding it into the dark so there would be no evidence of his mendacity.

He needn't have worried, though, as she wasn't looking for anything that would spoil the illusion of the moment.

She pulled him back on top of her, hugging him forcefully. "Just stay like this a little while longer," she said to him at the time. "I want to remember this moment forever."

He lay suspended awkwardly, looking down into her closed eyes beneath him for what felt to him like a long time.

On the drive back to town after that first time, she had a radiance that was less post-coital and more triumphant for an obstacle overcome. She leaned over and took his right arm, leaning her head on his shoulder and smiling in the silence, her face intermittently lit by oncoming headlights on the two-lane road. Henry suspected she was already composing the speech she was going to give to her girlfriends about how magical the experience had been, with fireworks exploding and the earth shaking beneath their physical demonstration of this, the perfect love.

After the first time, they'd abandoned the great outdoors. Tracy's requirement of efforts at romance from Henry had also disappeared. The itinerary for their subsequent attempts consisted of picking her up at her house, going to see a movie, then heading to the turnaround where Highway 72 crossed the Frio. There was a poorly maintained service road that peeled off from the turnaround's U-shaped asphalt and paralleled the river for a quarter mile. It was popular among teenagers looking for a place to park.

Tonight had been their fourth time trying to have sex. It had not gone well. Henry found he was having greater difficulty achieving and maintaining erections when they were together in this way.

In response to his silence, she repeated her question, this time more earnestly, "Am I doing something wrong? Henry, look at me."

He turned and looked at her. "No, it's nothing about you. I've just got a lot on my mind."

"Are you sure? Because I can try other things. If you wanted me to, I could try—"

"No," he said. Right now, it was all he could do to keep from just leaving her here by the river and driving back into town himself. He'd never wanted to be somewhere less than he did right at that moment.

"Then what is it? Do you think I'm ugly?"

For a second, he saw what she would look like on her back, arms and ankles bound, a bandana wadded in her mouth, looking up at him in bug-eyed, breath-clutching panic as he slowly put his hands on her throat and began to squeeze. He knew how to make her expression change from sadness into something much better. It was too easy to picture.

Tracy stared at him in bewilderment. But as he let his imagination run down this dark path, his expression changed, from indifference to intrigue. Then a trace of a smile appeared at one corner of his mouth, and he felt himself stiffening. Her face betrayed her as her bewilderment visibly turned into relief, not knowing what had just changed but looking grateful that it had.

Wiping the tears from her cheeks, she moved toward him in the dark.

CHAPTER TEN

10:20 a.m.—Saturday, August 17ᵗʰ

"…and I'd appreciate if, from time to time, you'd be willing to help with my computer when it acts up. My grandson normally fixes it when it gives me trouble, but I hate to bother him."

Dorothy Wright had been the librarian at Lorenzo de Zavala for thirty-two years. She still looked the part down to the reading glasses that bounced on a long chain around her neck. Pleasant and pear-shaped, she'd been thrilled to learn the applicant for the apartment over her garage was the new science teacher at the high school.

The studio apartment met Alex's simple needs. A splintered bureau and caramel-colored settee accompanied a Murphy bed that stuck out six inches short of its alcove, only clunking home with a *thunk* when Alex put a shoulder to it. The walls had built-in bookshelves that he had no idea how to fill.

"Happy to try, but I wouldn't get your hopes too high about what I can do," Alex said as they paused on the shaky metal landing so she could lock the heavy iron gate over the apartment's door. The burglar bars on the windows made him feel simultaneously comforted and nervous. "I.T. isn't my strong suit."

"Well, I guarantee you can do better than I could. Damn thing is the devil's machine sometimes but Lord it does make my life easier." She dabbed her neck with a red bandana. The sunlight blinded him, causing him to sun-sneeze as he followed her down the rickety steps bolted into the side of the garage. The glare cast her face in speckled shadows as it shone through her wide-brimmed straw hat. "You planning on moving in right away?"

"If that's okay with you. I holed up at a motel last night, and I'm ready to get settled."

"Sounds good. I'll call you later this afternoon with a final decision after I check with Principal Cunningham to make sure you are who you say you are, but assuming you check out I could let you move in as soon as tomorrow."

"That'd be fine, thanks." They shook hands, and she took a drink of water straight from the hose on the side of her house before waving goodbye one last time and ambling inside.

His spirits were good as he drove back to the motel, but he felt twinges of loneliness tugging at him. He was considering going for a run once he'd returned to the motel when he noticed a squat prefab building with the sign "Three Rivers Animal Shelter." The sign gave him pause and he made a U-turn.

Inside the shelter, he asked the technician to let him see whichever dog was next due to be put down, and the woman led him past a line of crates and cages to a small pen containing an English bulldog. Mostly white, the dog had a brown patch over one eye. Amid the din of the other dogs' barks and yips, the tech raised her voice to read off the cage's tag: he was about four years old and weighed forty-eight pounds. She added dispassionately that if no one adopted him he was scheduled to be euthanized the following day.

Through the chain link, Alex looked down at the dog as he lay on a brown towel, his head on his paws, eyes cast upward, tracking their movements.

"He seems to be friendly. We haven't had any problems with aggressiveness toward any of the staff," she said.

Alex squatted on his haunches and poked two fingers through the mesh door. The dog heaved himself to his feet and leaned forward to sniff Alex's fingers.

"What do you think friend-o?" he asked the dog. In answer, the dog began licking Alex's fingers. Mrs. Taylor had mentioned that a pet would be okay with an additional deposit, so thirty minutes later, the dog sat in the LeSabre's passenger seat, head swiveling slowly as he watched the world go by on the drive with his new master.

After smuggling the dog into his motel room, the two of them enjoyed a nice evening getting acquainted. He named the dog Brutus, and when it came time for bed, the dog jumped up to share the mattress.

Sleep wouldn't come, though, and he spent the night watching a square of moonlight crawl across the carpet and up the wall as he replayed his conversation with Gabby. Tightness built in his chest, and in the sensory deprivation of the motel room's darkness anxiety kept spilling into his thoughts, slopping over the edges like walking with a too-full bucket. Finally, he gave up and rolled out of bed, pulled on a pair of gray athletic shorts, and laced up his running shoes. Brutus's ear twitched as he slept, and Alex thought he'd be okay by himself while he broke a brief sweat.

His feet crunched rhythmically on the gravel of the highway's shoulder. Clouds of bugs swarmed the halogen lamps on his path. In the line of streetlights, his bobbing shadow telescoped, a silhouette within a silhouette.

Hitting his stride, Alex took a route toward the dancing orange of the refinery's flare stacks, their burn-off standing in stark relief against the grey-blue darkness. He felt his angst leave his body, washed away by sweat. Checking his watch, he picked up his pace. Just past the processing plant, the first predawn light showed a sky that threatened rain, and he turned back toward the motel. By the time he swiped his key card he had a stitch in his side and the right frame of mind to face the day.

CHAPTER ELEVEN

6:25 a.m.—Monday, August 26th

Setting his briefcase on the particleboard desk in the room that would be both his homeroom and main classroom, Alex used his reflection in the window to throw a knot in his tie. One of the summer-school teachers had decorated the space with scientifically themed wall hangings and left them up, presumably with the idea that if you can't be good, be helpful.

One wall held a large periodic table, while another had a hand-fashioned sign that read "SCIENCE in the NEWS!" Below it, a half dozen scientifically-themed stories were taped to the concrete wall. Black and white portraits ringed the room. Alex recognized Einstein and Marie Curie, and assumed the pair of men sitting next to a model of a double helix were Watson and Crick. There were several others whom he didn't recognize, and he made a mental note to

Google them before the meet-and-greet he intended to hold with his new students' parents, just in case anyone asked.

With well over an hour before first bell, he walked in the direction of the teachers' lounge to get a cup of coffee. On his return, he passed a wall of windows set in the main hallway and heard a loud tapping. Looking around, he saw a portly elderly man in an ochre tweed jacket standing outside, beckoning with a hand that held a pipe. The man had a thin moustache and a generous smile.

Retracing his steps, Alex made his way outside and toward the distinguished-looking gentleman. "Morning, sir. Can I help you?"

"I wanted to introduce myself. I'm Dylan Burrows. I teach English, have done so here for almost thirty years. And I'm guessing that you must be Mr. Brantley, the new science teacher I've heard so much about." Burrows tamped the bowl of tobacco down with his thumb and drew on the pipe to get it going. He waved the match out and extended his hand to Alex. His grip was soft, and the handshake was delicate, like he was squeezing an egg. "I'm in the classroom next to yours. May I say how thrilled we are to have you joining us."

"Why, thank you, that means a lot. I'm really looking forward to getting to know all y'all." Alex pointed at the pipe and smiled. "I thought there was no smoking on school property."

"Alas, you're right. The fascists have stripped us of this particular avenue of enjoyment. This is just my own little blow for freedom."

"Thirty years buys you some dispensation I guess?"

"Rank does have its privileges, dear boy. It's my sincere hope that if there's anything I can do to help with your transition, you'll ask. In my years, I've seen many young people come through here, and sometimes there is a sense of disappointment with what they perceive as a lack of glamour in small town life, like they've been trapped in a *Hee Haw* rerun. Don't be fooled, though. This town and this job offer things that feed the soul."

Alex laughed. "You don't need to worry about me there. I come from small town Texas. These are my people."

"Wonderful. That puts you ahead in the game already. And Principal Cunningham is the most wonderful supervisor. In our decades together, she and I have seen it all, and lived to speak of it. We've laughed and cried, she and I, and I owe her for protecting me on the little island I've carved out for myself here. She owes me for having introduced her to gin gimlets."

"Sounds like y'all have a real history together, you two."

Barrow leaned in conspiratorially. "I don't speak often of this, but years ago when she ran unsuccessfully for county judge, I was her campaign manager. Me. A campaign manager for a Republican. Isn't that priceless?"

"She didn't win, I take it?"

"Regrettably, no. The good citizens of Live Oak County were not ready for a strong female candidate who had a confirmed bachelor as her campaign manager. Alas, we were ahead of our time." He sighed and drew on his pipe again.

"Well, Mr. Barrow, I'll let you enjoy your pipe in peace before the day gets cranked up. It was nice meeting you. Take this as the compliment that I mean it to be. I can say without a doubt you're the most interesting person I've met so far in Three Rivers."

"Why thank you. And please call me Dylan. I'll be sure to have you over for cocktails one evening. If you are lucky, I will treat you to one of my recitations from Ezra Pound's *Cantos*."

"Looking forward to it," Alex said as he headed inside.

Back in his classroom, he took a seat behind the plain desk at the front of the room and worked on the week's lesson plans. Over the next hour, a trickle of noise in the hallway built to a swell as students drifted by, talking, laughing, yelling, the clamor echoing off the tiles. Gradually, a few students peeled off to enter Alex's classroom, paying little attention to the man sitting quietly at the front as they continued their conversations in the self-centered and self-conscious way of sixteen-year-olds.

Alex inspected the group and their noisy interactions, gathering his first impressions. His homeroom consisted of eleven sophomores, six girls and five boys. As first bell inched closer, he counted ten.

The ringing of the bell cut through the noise like a fire alarm. It continued for a five-Mississippi count in which the conversations became muted. When the shrill blast died off, Alex stood and came around the desk with the roll. The sound of footsteps pounding toward the room grabbed his attention and a long-limbed kid in a camo t-shirt and baggy cargo pants hurtled through the doorway before stopping abruptly, his eyes pleading.

Alex said, "Okay, on my first day I was going to give somebody one freebie. That was it. Take a seat."

Shoulders slumped, the kid took a seat and dropped his backpack at his feet.

"Morning, everyone. My name's Mr. Brantley, and I'm your new homeroom teacher. I'm also the new science teacher around here so since y'all are sophomores you'll be seeing me in chemistry. This is just homeroom, so I don't see a need for a lot of speeches, but just do me one favor. Be on time." He paused and looked at the sheepish kid. "Being late means I've got to send you to the office, which also means that I have to do some extra paperwork, and if there's one thing in life that I hate it's doing extra paperwork. We clear on that?"

Alex took the murmuring as agreement and continued. "Alright, let's call roll real quick before announcements start and I'll start working on learning everybody's names."

His first day was an enjoyable blur. He covered the states of matter in his physics classes, watching as the kids' eyes lit up when he started discussing plasma. He'd bought a softball-sized snow globe at a thrift store and he held it up as a metaphor for the sea of electrons that swim about freely in a plasma state, not associated with any particular atom. "Now imagine that these snowflakes are the electrons. Those carry electricity, right? Says so right there in their name. Well, now it's easy to see why plasma states conduct electricity so well. It's nothing for an electrical charge to jump from one tiny electron to another." He handed the snow globe off to be passed around while he turned the lecture back to the dry erase board.

In biology, they covered the beginnings of cell structures. Mitochondria, the nucleus, the cell wall and its role as gatekeeper, letting needed nutrients in and excreting toxins.

The chemistry class was more boisterous, but nothing he couldn't handle. As he introduced himself, one smart ass raised his hand and asked if he cooked crystal meth on the side like the chemistry teacher in *Breaking Bad*, eliciting a titter from the class. Alex considered this, then told the student no, he was no Walter White. Then with a grin Alex said, "But you know what? You kind of remind me of Jacob in *Glee*." The unflattering comparison brought an, "Oooh, snap" and some "Damns" from the class, followed by a collective laugh. Alex gave the kid a look that said, *You want to keep going?* Then launched into an introduction to the periodic table.

Managing the classroom came relatively easily to Alex, and the pace, while hectic at times, was slower than when he was practicing medicine. He'd found in his training for the teacher's certificate that he had a theatrical side he could tap into when needed. It served him well, and so far in these limited interactions the kids had seemed to respond.

After his last class ended, he was drafting an email when Dylan tapped on his door. "I see you survived your first day," he said.

"Yeah. Classes went well, no disciplinary issues of any substance. A couple of smartasses trying to challenge my authority, but just age-appropriate stuff."

"Wonderful. I hope you continue to enjoy this world's rich tapestry. See you tomorrow."

CHAPTER TWELVE

5:50 p.m.—Tuesday, August 27th

At first, Alex wasn't sure he was in the right place.

He'd spoken briefly with the varsity track and field coach, Jim Volkner, the previous evening by phone and they'd made plans to meet the next day fifteen minutes before the rest of the cross-country team was due to arrive for their after-school session. On the phone, the man's light, breezy voice and convivial manner suggested youth with a slender appearance.

So when Alex arrived at the trailhead of a worn path that roughly paralleled the Frio River, he assumed Volkner to be late since the only person in sight was a plump older man with a lip full of tobacco and wearing Elvis-sized sunglasses. Atop his crew cut sat a navy-blue hat that read, "Vietnam Veteran- All gave some- 58,479 gave all," and he spat a dart of tobacco juice into the brown dust. The man looked like a tow truck driver.

It caught Alex off guard when the man put out his hand and that same cordial voice he recognized from the phone said, "Alex? Jim Volkner, nice to meet you."

Recovering, Alex said, "Pleasure, coach. Looking forward to working with you and the boys."

"Well, let's both be honest," Volkner said, rubbing his ample belly with a smile. "You're gonna be working with 'em a lot more'n I will. If I tried to run with these boys, most of the exercise they'd get would be from doing CPR on me."

Alex laughed. "Funny you say that, I only got into running earlier this year myself. Most of my work sounds like it'll likely be yelling encouragement from behind while they leave me in the dust. So, what's your story?"

Volkner wrestled a cooler out of the bed of his pickup and started filling it with sports drink bottles. "Grew up in Houston, went to a big high school, place had a real developed track and field program back in the day where I found out I was pretty fair at the shot put and the discus. Graduated in '70 and got sent to 'Nam, when I finished up my tour, I went to U.T. on the G.I. Bill. I made it on the track and field team there, as a walk on, and was All-Southwest Conference. Even made the Olympic team in '80, but that fuckin' peanut farmer cost me my shot with his goddam boycott." He spat another brown stream with a wince. "Anyway, make a short story long, I moved here in '83 with the missus to be closer to her family, and been here since, happy as a clam." He tossed two bags of ice in the air and let them smack in the dirt before ripping the plastic and pouring the broken ice on top of the drinks.

As they spoke, an SUV pulled up and four teenagers in running gear piled out, cutting up and boisterous, all full of life.

Volkner waved them over and said, "Alright fellas, settle down and take a knee." They obeyed instantly. "This here's Coach Brantley. He's the new science teacher and gonna be helping coach y'all from here on out this season."

Alex gave a simple wave.

Volkner resumed, "Alex, left to right we got Patrick Harkins, Enrique Villanueva, Henry Wallis, and Jimmy Nguyen."

To the boys, he said, "I want y'all doing tempo runs today. Thirty seconds slower than your 5K pace, alright? Gonna do a set of three 3K runs with a four-minute interval between each one. Questions? Okay, fifteen-minutes to stretch then y'all are off."

Pulling Alex aside, he asked, "What would you say to tryin' to run with 'em this evening? I didn't want to put you on the spot in front of 'em, but if you got it in you I think it'd be a good idea."

"Yeah, I'll give it a shot."

"Sounds good. Harkins is the slowest. Swear to God, if I put that boy in charge of two turtles, one would get away."

"And who's the fastest?"

"Wallis, hands down. Boy runs like he stole somethin'. You keep up with him, I'll be impressed."

Volkner hadn't exaggerated. The Wallis kid ran like a gazelle. Alex hung in with him for the first two kilometers, but while his needle was running in the red, Wallis looked like he barely broke a sweat, his loping strides looking effortless. Alex had watched the kids while they stretched, and noticed that Wallis seemed quiet, reserved. He hadn't joined in with the other teens while they cut up during their exercises and seemed grimly serious. Now keeping up with the kid for the first kilometer, Alex tried some good-natured trash talk to engage the kid.

Huffing, Alex asked, "You embarrassed an old man's matching your pace?"

Listening to Alex's false bravado, he cracked a smile.

"Nothing to say?" Alex panted as they approached the metallic yellow 1K marker mounted on a small post off the trail.

Conversationally, the Wallis kid said without breathing hard, "Keep up your shit-talking. I think it's getting ready to stop here in a minute in the second K."

As they passed the marker, Wallis found another gear. It took all of Alex's effort to keep up the pace, all thoughts of conversation gone. Alex was no longer thinking about trying to pace himself, he now just wanted to see how long he could keep up with Wallis. He tried to ignore the burning in his legs and chest, sucking in great whoops of air. Periodically, Wallis looked over at him and gave a half smile that Alex pretended was grudging respect. The other three runners were somewhere behind them, but Alex had no idea where. He couldn't spare the energy to look back.

They were still elbow to elbow as the 2K marker crawled into view. Alex felt like he was sprinting now, the marker seeming like a finish line more than a milestone.

Seeing Alex's red faced-effort, Wallis smiled and said, "When you fall back, you guys decide who wants to go for second."

Wallis lengthened his stride, and got a serious look, pulling away from Alex rapidly. Alex's pace slowed to a trot, and he was soon passed by Nguyen, then Villanueva, then even Harkins. By the time Alex passed the finish line next to Volkner's truck, Wallis was well into his cool down,

Volkner said to him with a chuckle as he clapped him on the back, "I been waiting on you so long I need a shave."

CHAPTER THIRTEEN

6:15 a.m.—Friday, August 30th

"Starting the day with a touch of elegance is so important to one's well-being, wouldn't you agree?" Burrows asked.

The coffee in the china demitasse he set before Alex smelled rich, with a hint of vanilla. Finding over the course of the first week that they both arrived early, the two men had begun the last few mornings sharing a cup of coffee in Burrow's classroom. Burrows preferred to play host, showing off his tasteful and well-appointed classroom.

A great rosewood desk was the centerpiece of the room, and plants dotted the room's corners, bringing a touch of color. Three ceiling-to-floor oak bookshelves filled with hardbound classics and yellowed portraits of the masters in sturdy frames gave the room the feeling of a small library. A glass two-tiered serving cart held the coffee maker and china, and they tracked the time by a figurine clock on a shelf beside the chalkboard. As he sipped his coffee, Alex felt like he should be extending his pinkie.

Burrows asked, "What are you reading these days? And please don't say Stephen King or my impression of you will fall in a manner that would be irreparable."

Alex chuckled. "Actually, with trying to get my feet under me this last week, I haven't had the energy to pick up a book for pleasure. Anything you'd recommend? Something light?"

Burrows thought for a moment before saying, "I have just the thing."

Going to the middle bookcase, it only took him a moment to locate the book and he pulled it down. "Have you read *A Confederacy of Dunces* before?"

"Uh-uh. Good book?"

"Magnificent. One of only two novels Toole wrote before he committed suicide, this one won the Pulitzer. It's a charming picture of life in New Orleans in the sixties. I'm afraid it hasn't aged terribly well by the day's standards. There are elements of it that would cause an outbreak of Saint Vitus' dance among some of today's more censorious elements. You should read it now before the forces of progress require us to throw it on a metaphorical bonfire, or possibly a literal one, sad to say." He handed it to Alex.

Taking his seat once again, Burrows sighed. "I was sickly as a child, and books were my source of escape. I've reflected on a near-daily basis at how lucky I've been, making a living surrounded by them. It's like being paid to socialize with friends who never disappoint you."

Later, back in his room sorting through emails while the kids filed in, he looked up and a quick head count showed eleven warm bodies. He called the role anyway to help associate faces with names. With a group that small it took less than a minute, and he was about to let them resume their conversations at a lower volume while they awaited announcements when a girl in the second row wearing thick glasses and braces raised her hand.

Alex glanced at his seating chart. "Yes, um…Sheila?"

"Mr. Brantley, are you some kind of a doctor or something?"

He froze, then relaxed. He had to get over this reaction when people brought up his past.

"Why do you ask?"

"'Cuz, last night when my mom asked me who my homeroom teacher was, I told her your name and she googled you. There was something from the board of medical under your name. It said you were a doctor. The picture looked a lot like you." She sat looking at him, waiting patiently.

"Thank you for asking, Sheila. Yes, I used to be a doctor, but I'm not anymore."

"How come?"

"I didn't like it very much. I like doing this a lot more."

A massive boy with shaggy hair and bib overalls raised his hand.

"Yes, Robert?"

"What kind of doctor were you?"

"I was a surgeon."

"You mean like cutting people open and stuff?"

"Yep."

Expressions of amazement and admiration went through the class as the students now sat rapt, softly murmuring to each other, like he had just levitated, and they were trying to figure out how he had done it.

Another girl, now not even bothering to raise her hand: "What was the grossest thing you ever seen?"

Alex was amused for a moment, but answered, "Nope. Sorry guys, we're not going to play this game, okay? And do me a favor, remind your parents that I'm going to host a little open-house here in the classroom tonight so that I can get to meet them and they can meet me. I want to let them know what we're going to be covering in the curriculum for the year, and answer any questions they have. I sent an email to all y'all's folks on Wednesday, but help them remember, okay?"

Disappointed, they again murmured in the way that Alex was coming to see was their universal way of expressing agreement.

Moments later the P.A, broadcast began, but Alex could see from the way they were whispering to each other while sneaking glances in his direction that he was the main subject of discussion and not the announcement that spirit ribbons could be bought inside the field house before, but not after, school.

Later, with the day over and the hallways quiet, he sat at his desk grading homework. His thoughts circled back to what Sheila had said that morning about her parents googling him.

Reaching into his satchel, he retrieved his laptop, opened a search engine and typed in "Alex Brantley MD."

There it was—third link from the top. The Texas Medical Board bulletin describing his license suspension and a PDF of the proceedings. Alex had never actually read it, and he opened it out of morbid curiosity.

It was all there, the complaints, the mandated counseling sessions for anger management, the court-ordered psychotherapy, and the *coup-de-grâce*, his actions in the hospital parking lot with the tire iron and the car. The final paragraph in which the board made a unanimous decision for license suspension was almost anticlimactic. It was sobering.

He closed his laptop and sat, deep in thought. It was safe to assume this was now common knowledge. After all, it was salacious and publicly available in a small town where it seemed like everyone knew each other. Word of mouth traveled fast in places like this, and any parent who didn't already know about his past when they arrived for that evening's meet-and-greet probably would by the time they left. Alex wouldn't bring it up, but he would face it head-on if and when someone brought it up. Anyway, he thought, it wasn't like he had a choice.

As it turned out, Alex needn't have worried about being openly challenged during the parent-teacher meetings. In that sense, the sessions had gone better than he'd anticipated. In each, the parents sat politely in the students' seats while Alex leaned back against his desk, hands clasped in front of him as he spoke to each group. He introduced himself as Mr. Brantley, and simply sketched out his goals for what he wanted to cover in their children's classes for the academic year. He also notified them of his policy that students would keep their phones on a small table next to the door when they came into his classroom. He'd expected push back, but each group of parents accepted this with equanimity.

At the end of his patter, he always said, "And now I'd be happy to take any questions." Each time, he mentally braced himself when a few hands went in the air, but despite his fears, no one asked, "So when in the hell did the school system decide to start hiring reprobates?" Instead, they focused on mundane topics like absence policies or homework quantities.

Alex realized it was also likely that some of the quieter parents were there for the same reason people slow down to look at a wreck on the highway: how often do you get to see a real-life disgraced doctor up close and personal? He got this sense from the way they seemed to study him, like they were behind the velvet rope at a carnival freak show. *That's just the price of doing business now.*

As the final group of the night filed out, shaking his hand and nodding their goodbyes, Alex noticed that one man seemed to hang back. Medium height and fortyish, he sported a small paunch and deep tan that contrasted with his white dress shirt. While he wore boots and jeans, Alex spotted a Rolex on the wrist of the hand he extended.

"I just wanted to say we really appreciate your taking the time tonight, Mr. Brantley. I'm Stu Perry, my daughter's

Janine. She's in your ninth-grade biology class."

"Nice to meet you, Mr. Perry."

"Please, call me Stu."

"Thanks, Stu." Alex did not return the offer for familiarity just yet, instead continuing, "I hate to say but with the year just starting and me being new to town, I haven't really had a chance to get to know Janine very well yet. Does she have any interest in the sciences?"

"Yeah, she says she wants to be a veterinarian."

Here we go. He'd seen this before. Young kids who think being a vet is putting bowtie bandages on the paws of hurt puppies, when the reality is you spend most of your days putting animals down for insultingly low wages. He figured he'd hold off on that part of the speech.

"That's great, any scientific interest is music to my ears. I'm happy to help cultivate that."

"Thanks. Listen, I know you said you're new to town. I'm having a barbecue on Labor Day, whole mess of folks'll be over. It'd be great it if you could come out for a bit. Give people a chance to start to get to know you a little better. Good food, cold beer, and the river runs through my backyard."

Alex said, "Thanks for the invite. Let me think about it. I'm still getting settled in around here and I've got a million details to take care of. I was going to try to get a lot of it done over the holiday weekend."

"No worries. If you've got plans, I understand. Meantime, if you decide to drop by." He scribbled his cell on the back of a business card and handed it to Alex. "Think about it. If you come, bring some swim trunks." They shook again. "Take care, and thanks again for your work with my baby girl."

After Stu left, Alex looked at the card. It read, "Stewart M. Perry, The Perry Law Firm LLC, Real Estate Attorney," with a San Antonio address. He tucked it into his wallet and went about straightening his classroom.

CHAPTER FOURTEEN

7:20 p.m.—Sunday, September 1ˢᵗ

On days when Sully did an eleven to seven, the family would wait to eat until he got home. Rebecca liked to tell her friends at the church this ritual, sitting down at least once a day to share a meal, was an important part of being a family. They ate on TV trays in the living room so Sully could watch "Wheel of Fortune." She recorded it special for him.

"How was cross-country today, Henry?" Rebecca asked as she pulled the tray towards her in the rocking chair and cut up her meatloaf.

Without looking away from the screen, he said, "Pretty good. I shaved four seconds off my best five-K today." Scooping mashed potatoes, he said to Sully, "She should ask for an 'R'."

"I heard from Marsha Hopkins today that coach Volkner had to go to the hospital in San Antonio yesterday, something about his gall bladder? Was he at practice today?"

"No, Mr. Brantley ran things."

Spearing honey carrots, she asked, "Isn't he the new science teacher?"

"Yeah, but they hired him to also be the cross-country assistant coach. He's been working out with us."

Brow wrinkled, Sully asked, "Think that fourth word's 'R-I-V-E-R'?"

Trying not to sound concerned, she asked, "What do you mean, working out with y'all?"

"He's in a lot better shape than coach V. He runs with us...ask for 'B'."

"Are there any other adults running with y'all, or is it just him?" she asked. She ate more slowly now, thinking about implications.

Shoveling more potatoes, he said, "Noh, jush him. He pretty fash. Whennepaysheshhimshef, he c'n keep up wiv ush. He even shtuck wiv me for 2K on hishfirshpractish."

"Don't talk with your mouth full, dear," she gently reprimanded.

Squinting at the puzzle, Sully said, "She should buy a vowel."

Rebecca's face had unconsciously slipped into a grimace. The rumor mill around Alex was churning full force and had gone past the facts available on the State Medical Board website. They'd taken a particularly ugly turn of late.

"I'll tell you what I heard," Frances McKinley said to her in a hushed tone that morning while the two of them set up the church's bake sale. She stage-whispered to Rebecca, "There are other complaints out there that those medical board yahoos decided not to publish. Supposedly," —she looked around to make sure she wasn't overheard— "they caught him having sex with a patient in a hospital room. And that patient was a man. Then I heard he threatened to accuse the board of being prejudiced against gays if they tried to press charges against him, so they let it drop to make the whole thing go away."

"But how can they just let someone get away with that?" Rebecca asked in shock as she set out cupcakes.

Spiraling napkins, Frances admonished her, "Don't be naive, Rebecca. You know how things work. Everybody's terrified of being accused that they're anti-gay so those people can just run around now, doing whatever they like."

"Well, that doesn't make it right."

They tsk-tsk'ed for a few more minutes, lamenting the state of the world before going on to more mundane topics, but Rebecca's mind had drifted back to that conversation through the day. Now she found herself playing with her mashed potatoes, worrying in silence, appetite gone.

"Hope y'all been makin' him feel welcome," Sully said still without taking his eyes off the screen as he dug into his carrots. A movie title, the clue said, but he was stumped by,

"B R _ D _ E _ _ E R T H E R _ _ E R K _ A _ .

CHAPTER FIFTEEN

7:47 a.m.—Monday, September 2nd

Brutus's snores rattled the shingles, like someone dropped a handful of gravel in a blender.

Alex kicked off the sheets and padded into the bathroom to urinate then, yawning and scratching himself, shuffled into the kitchenette. The coffeemaker burped then emitted a hiss of air like a truck's brakes as it finished brewing.

The sounds woke Brutus, and he lumbered through the sunlit apartment. Blinking the sleep out of his eyes, he looked up at Alex expectantly. Alex considered him, then turned to face him square on and silently held up a small piece of granola, waiting a beat before showing his other palm extended out, as though Alex pushed against an invisible brick wall.

Now excited, the dog followed Alex's command and

sat, eyes locked, attention undivided. Still without saying a word, Alex then pushed his palm to the floor. Brutus eagerly laid down, sphinx-like, the nub of his tail twitching rapidly. Alex made him hold it for a few moments, then broke the command sequence and extended the granola. Brutus jumped up and devoured it, then began sniffing the linoleum to capture any stray crumbles that had escaped the gears of his jowls.

Alex roughly scratched between his ears, pleasantly surprised at how quickly the dog had picked up those two basic commands.

It dawned on him that it was Labor Day. As he considered his options, he found himself thinking about Stu's offer of barbecue.

He picked up his pants off the floor and dug out his wallet to find Stu's card. He texted:

Alex: *Alex Brantley here. Offer still good?*

Three shimmering grey dots appeared, then:

Stu: *Absolutely! Starts at 2. Going 'til food 'n beer gone*

Alex: *OK 2 bring my dog?*

Stu: *Sure! He can meet mine*

Alex: *Cool c u then*

Later that afternoon, Alex turned off a blacktop county road at a pipe-rail arch adorned with "Rocking-S Ranch" in soldered cast-iron letters bookended by the ranch's branding symbol: a capital S sitting at an angle on a curved rocker. Alex's teeth vibrated as he drove over a cattle guard at the ranch's entrance before heading down a graded gravel road.

He passed through stands of mixed cedar and willow, the land greener here than in town from proximity to the river. A quarter mile in, the road skirted a white barn where someone worked under a tractor's cowling in the machine shop, only visible from the waist down. Beside the barn sat two holding pens for cattle, the pie-shaped enclosures funneling down to loading and working chutes where the dirty work of branding, castrating, and palpating was done. Judging by the fresh manure about, the empty pens hadn't been that way long.

A hundred yards past the cattle pens sat two massive, century-old oak trees whose canopies flanked a plush single-story ranch house. A wrap-around flagstone porch surrounded the building with more than twenty cars and trucks parked in rough rows on the front lawn. After killing the engine, he put Brutus on a leash and ambled around back.

A light breeze carried the smell of grilling meat, and Brutus tugged hard at the leash, willing them forward. A screened-in back porch overlooked an expansive and manicured yard that sloped like a fairway down to the edge of a river he knew to be the Nueces. Beyond the civilized borders of the mowed lawn, thigh-high wild grass and pockets of cedar surrounded Stu's homestead.

Halfway down the yard, a face-cord of mesquite firewood sat stacked within easy reach of a seasoned two-barrel barbecue pit, which poured delicious white smoke from its stove-pipe vent. Six weathered plank picnic tables clustered like boxcars on the lawn while down by the river, children took turns on a rope swing. Their Tarzan-howls reached the house as they jumped off a retaining wall and arced over the water before letting go to plunge into the green depths. About thirty adults looked on from the yard and milled about, chatting and drinking.

Amid the crowd, Stu played host, dressed comfortably in jeans and a light-blue t-shirt, the chest and back stained dark with a deep V of sweat while he tended the pit's fire. When he saw Alex approach, he took off his worn cowboy hat and wiped his brow with his forearm before pointing him out to the attractive middle-aged woman with whom he chatted. She was done up in small-town Texas high fashion: heavy makeup, big hair, and a sundress with cowboy boots.

He replaced his hat and shook Alex's hand. "Mr. Brantley! Glad you could make it."

"Appreciate you having me."

"This is Allanah Davidson. Allanah, this is Mr. Brantley, new science teacher at the high school."

Allanah smiled and said, "Nice to put a face to the name, Mr. Brantley."

"Pleased to meet you ma'am." Brutus sniffed madly at everyone's boots and legs, straining against the leash. He gave a half-hearted jump at Stu's legs in excitement before going back to the olfactory delights in the grass around them. "This is Brutus. Don't worry, only thing he's liable to do is lick you to death."

Stu said, "Mine'll be finding you shortly. I've got three pointers, two English, one German short hair. They're running around here someplace. Same thing, they'll be coming up to love on you and check Brutus out but none of 'em have a mean bone in their worthless bodies."

Allanah leaned into Alex and said, "It's a good thing those three can flush quail 'cause they ain't worth a shit as guard dogs. Alex you got any kids?"

"No ma'am. Just me and Brutus against the world. You?"

"One. He's over in Iraq right now, bein' all that he can be."

Pulling a red bandana from his back pocket, Stu lifted the handles on the two-barrel doors and smoke billowed out, stinging Alex's eyes. Stu mopped the briskets and chicken halves generously, the slop causing a mouthwatering sizzle from the coals.

Closing the doors, he said, "Alex, beer and soft drinks down by the river. Food should be ready shortly, and plenty of company. I'll join you down there momentarily."

Getting the feeling he'd walked up on a private conversation, Alex took the hint and smiled his thanks then nodded, saying "Sounds good. It was a pleasure to meet you, ma'am."

He grabbed a beer from one of the coolers under a large pecan tree by the shoreline and used a church key tied to the handle to pop the top, pulling a long swallow in the shade. The only familiar face in the crowd was Deputy Hardy, in swim trunks and flip flops, with a fish-belly white paunch and thinning hair, the man lacked his usual air of authority.

Brutus was a great conversation starter, though, as strangers continually squatted and asked to play with him. Most of the conversations didn't get past pleasantries and the weather, but it felt good to be interacting with locals. Alex had been at it for twenty minutes when Stu came over.

"How long you been in Three Rivers now?" Stu asked as Alex finished a beer.

"Couple weeks."

"Getting to know the town at all?"

"Little bit. I'm working out with the cross-country team, helping coach them."

"Good. More you see of this town, the more I think it'll grow on you. My wife and I grew up here, childhood sweethearts, the whole nine. In fact, this pecan tree we're standing under"—he pointed at the leafy cover with a finger from the hand holding his beer—"was the first place we ever kissed." He got a wistful look. "Anyway, after she died three years ago, I thought about moving to San Antonio. My business is based out of there, and I thought the change of scenery might do me good, help clear my head. At the end of the day, though, I decided I just love this town too much."

"Speaking of business, I saw on your card that you're a real estate lawyer?"

"Among other things."

"How big's your group?"

"Just me. I always found I work best by myself. Votes by the board are always unanimous that way."

"So, you live out here?" Alex said, looking around again.

"Some of the time. It's still an active cattle ranch but that's more of a hobby. I've also got a place in San Antonio that I stay at some—"

A high-pitched shriek cut Stu off mid-answer. Co-mingled pain and fear tore through the air like the rending of a garment. The sound of frantic dogs barking and baying followed immediately as all conversation stopped and heads swiveled, looking around in shock to locate the source of the noise. Brutus moved between Alex's legs, the leash winding around his master's thigh as the dog looked in the direction of the tall grass.

Without hesitation, Stu sprinted to the fire pit and grabbed a long shovel used to spread coals before charging into the grass to their left in the direction of the howling. Now Alex could see two dogs in that vicinity, visible only from the shoulders up. They bounced as they circled something hidden by the tall weeds and scrub, continuing to bark madly, furious at something they'd found. He watched as Stu slowed upon approaching them, scanning the area, the shovel poised in front of him like a spear. He froze, then with lightning quickness thrust the shovel forward and leaned on it with all his weight. He wiggled the handle back and forth, driving the blade deeper into the ground. Raising the shovel overhead, Stu struck a second savage blow, then a third, his teeth clenched and bared in primal fury. Then, he knelt in the grass, almost invisible. After a moment, he stood and beckoned Alex to come over, then cupped his hand to his mouth and shouted, "Leave your dog there."

Handing the leash to someone nearby, Alex waded into the high grass. He found Stu kneeling beside a brown and white English pointer. Its head rested on his thigh, whimpering as he stroked its flank. Blood trickled from the dog's cheek and shoulder, and its face had already begun to swell. The hound began to shiver despite the heat. The other two dogs sniffed and circled, occasionally licking the stricken dog. The larger of the two protectively muttered a low growl as she saw Alex approach.

"Hush, now," Stu scolded the dog.

It fell silent but watched Alex suspiciously.

The shovel with its bloody scoop matted the grass where Stu cast it aside in haste. Next to it, the body of a four-foot-long rattlesnake lay in a scooped hollow under a cedar log. During the fight it had twisted itself into a Gordian knot and despite being decapitated, continued to sluggishly undulate in a death spasm.

Alex knelt next to Stu and inspected the wounded animal. "Looks like he got it twice. Face and leg there?"

"Yeah," Stu said as he continued to stroke the dog. "I've always heard that business of cutting an 'X' on the wound and sucking out the venom is Hollywood, John-Wayne bullshit, is that right?"

Alex nodded. "Best thing we can do is get the dog to a vet for antivenom. Plus, some good pain control. Snake bites hurt like hell."

"Sounds good. Can you drive?"

As evening approached, the two men sat in the emergency vet's waiting room. Brutus had gotten over the excitement and lay curled up under Alex's hard plastic chair, fast asleep. The vet had administered a dose of the antivenom shortly after their arrival and so far, the Pointer, whose name was Daisy, was still alive. Stu had called his ranch foreman who'd reassured Stu he could keep the party going.

"That Mexican's forgotten more 'bout grilling than I'll ever know," Stu said as he hung up. "Things back at the house'll be fine."

"Glad to hear."

"I appreciate you coming down here like you did. Helluva way to spend your Labor Day."

Alex smiled his welcome.

"I do love that dog," Stu said thoughtfully. "She and I've been through a lot together. Lot of hunts, lot of life for that matter."

Alex nodded, and they were silent for a while.

Eventually, the vet came out and said the dog looked like she was likely to be alright but needed to stay for a few days. They'd contact him if anything changed, but he could head home for now.

Relieved, Stu shook the vet's hand and thanked her. As they drove back to Stu's house, he told Alex, "I'm really glad you came out today. A bunch of us are hoping this town works out for you."

"Thanks, you've been really gracious. The food, the beer, the introductions. I don't know what to say."

"Tell you what. You dove hunt? Season starts in this part of the state on the fourteenth. I'm going out first weekend with a couple of folks. I'd be glad to lend you a shotgun if you'd join us."

"That sounds great, but you've got to know in advance I'm not much of a shot."

"Hell, that's alright. Mostly we just use it as an excuse to drink beer and get outside anyway. I'll send the details along once they're set. Now step on it, I'm starving."

CHAPTER SIXTEEN

3:30 p.m.—Thursday, September 12ᵗʰ

Rebecca arranged her coupons. She'd forgotten to check their expiration dates before she left the house, and even though her high-stacked shopping cart would take a few minutes to ring up she hurried now to get them sorted before she made it to the checkout girl.

The phone interrupted her calculations of the value of upsizing her paper towel purchase to utilize a half-off discount. Cradling the phone in the crook of her shoulder, she answered, "Hello?"

"Hi, Mrs. Sullivan? This is Alex Brantley, I'm Henry's physics teacher up at the school."

Rebecca recoiled in surprise. In her anxious ruminations, she'd built Mr. Brantley up into some kind of bogeyman in her mind, something larger than life. Getting a call from him out of the blue, well, it shook her. Unsettled, she fought to control her voice as she answered, "Yes, Mr. Brantley, I know who you are. What can I do for you?"

"I wanted to speak to you about Henry."

"Yes?" Her voice shook now, all thoughts of coupons forgotten.

"Did he tell you that he failed his physics test yesterday?"

Perversely, this bad news actually made her relax a little. "No, but he'd mentioned that he was having difficulty with the material a couple times. Says it doesn't come natural to him. I can relate. Math was never a strong suit for me or his daddy either."

"Yeah, he came close to passing, but this isn't horseshoes."

"Me and his stepfather will stay on him to make sure he studies. He's a smart boy, I think he should get the hang of it."

"I'm sure he will. But just to make sure, I'd be happy to tutor him after school a couple of days a week. Probably an hour or two per session. Once we see that he's turning it around, we can back off that pace if we need to."

"How much we lookin' at?" she asked warily.

"Oh, I wouldn't charge y'all. Making sure he gets the hang of it is part of my job as I see it. His part is to do the work. I've seen how disciplined he is when it comes to running, so his effort shouldn't be an issue."

"Well, I appreciate that offer. Course, I'll need to talk to my husband about it tonight."

"Great. This is my cell. I hope I'm not out of line, but I already touched base with Henry and he's eager to start. Once you and your husband make a decision, let me know."

That night while getting ready for bed, she paused in the middle of putting lotion on her legs to update Sully.

"I got to say, it goes against my better judgment to let that man be alone with Henry even more than he already is," she said as she went back to rubbing moisturizer into her tan legs. "When they're training, at least I know there's other people around. But now, you go putting them behind closed doors a couple times a week, just the two of them? I mean, Henry's a good-looking boy and the stories that're going around about the man—?"

Sully stood at the sink in his white jockey shorts and paused from brushing his teeth. "The school district would've done a background check, and wouldn't have hired him if it had turned up anything along the lines of what you and your girlfriends are worried about. Swear to God, when y'all get together you're worse than a sewing circle what with all the gossip. I mean, the man's talking about giving up his time for free tutoring. Ask me, I think we need more teachers like that."

She knew a losing battle when she saw one. "But do me one favor, then?" she asked.

"What's that?" He spat toothpaste into the sink.

"Will you call him back and tell him? Talking to that man makes me feel, I don't know…icky."

"Sure, no problem."

She texted him the number, but when she was done, she sat tapping her phone against her chin while low-grade anxiety gnawed at her stomach. She didn't like this at all. No sir, not one bit.

CHAPTER SEVENTEEN

1:35 p.m.—Saturday, October 19ᵗʰ

The birthday boy, Sully manned the grill in an apron that read "Veg-e-TAR-i-an- *noun*. Old Indian word for bad hunter," cracking jokes and drinking beer. Being Texas on a Saturday afternoon, much of the crowd clustered around the backyard speakers listening to the Longhorns play Kansas in a ritual every bit as devout as church while Rebecca flitted about in a calico dress, dipping in and out of conversations, refreshing drinks and beaming.

Turning forty hadn't seemed to affect Sully much, and with the exception of a card table piled with incontinence undergarments, fake swollen prostate prescriptions, AARP applications, and other gag gifts it looked like any other backyard cookout.

Henry circled through the crowd a few times, answering questions and being seen. Once he'd been long enough that he didn't think his absence would draw attention—not drawing attention, good or bad, had become something of a commandment for him—he excused himself back to his room.

As he played *Call of Duty*, his thoughts kept drifting to the park, ruminating on it. He'd been back a handful of times since that first trip in March, and now it felt like an itch he couldn't scratch. It consumed his thoughts, leaving no room for banal conversations.

That night, he had trouble getting to sleep from anticipation, and when his alarm went off at 5:00 a.m. on Sunday morning, he bounded out of bed. He left his mother and stepfather a note that he was going to train and was out the door by 5:30.

Before he left the driveway, he reviewed the situation like a pilot running a preflight checklist.

His phone was powered down and in his car's cup holder, not to be touched again until safely back at the house to obviate any chance of his movements later being tracked. He'd avoided coffee to minimize the chances of urinating at the park, and thus leaving behind anything biological. Plus, he was wide awake and energized, caffeine unnecessary. The forecast was for clouds but no rain, and the hour was early enough that other park visitors should be at a minimum. Reassured, he buckled his seatbelt and set off.

An hour later, the sun hadn't quite broken the horizon as he pulled into the park's lot. Birds chirped in the predawn light, and a damp thick mist clung to the ground giving the park an eerie lunar quality.

He casually examined the trailhead while stretching. No other cars were present, and the air was still. He'd long since confirmed there were no video cameras of the lot, but it having been weeks since his last excursion he double-checked the area. The only thing he saw on the light poles were swarms of bugs bouncing off the still-lit halogen lamps. He pulled up his sweatshirt hood, swung his fanny pack toward the small of his back, and started down the trail at his customary light trot.

After twenty minutes, the trail eased into a downhill and cut through a dense stand of cedar trees. This morning, back in the thickest of the trees and perhaps thirty yards off the trail, he noticed a small sky-blue tarp suspended a few feet off the ground. He stopped short, never having seen it there before. From this distance, he saw no movement in the area.

Looking around to make sure he was not being observed, he stood with his hands on his hips for five minutes, timing it by his watch to temper his impatience. He shifted his weight from one foot to the other as the time ticked down, with no signs of activity from the blue sheet of plastic, nor from the trail.

He broke from the jogging path and began quietly walking in the direction of the tarp. Halfway there, he heard something that made his chest tighten in anticipation—deep, resonant snoring.

Pausing again to look around, he confirmed no one else was in the vicinity. As Henry neared the tent, he began rolling his feet, an old Boy Scout trick for stealth.

The tarp sat in a small clearing, perhaps twelve feet by ten. The plastic sheet was suspended over a rope tied between two trees, forming a crude tent. Fist-sized rocks pinned down the tarp's edges. The camp's detritus made the vicinity look post-apocalyptic, a sea of drained pint bottles, empty sardine tins and bean cans, and cigarette butts. Sniffing, Henry smelled the pungent odor of fresh scat in the area and told himself to watch his footfalls, so he didn't step in any fecal land mines.

At the tent's opening, his eyes narrowed as he studied the shelter's occupant. The skinny vagrant wore a filthy red flannel shirt and black ski cap crammed atop long, unkempt gray hair. A bushy beard spilled over the man's chest, and his cheeks puffed out when he exhaled, like a feral Dizzy Gillespie. He lay curled in the fetal position, his hands tucked in his armpits for warmth, a near-empty pint bottle of tequila and a tattered Louis L'Amour paperback by his elbow.

Henry squatted, forearms on his thighs, fingers interlaced as he studied the man and debated. The early morning sun had burned off the mist and was now dappling through the trees. A sliver of light broke through the cedars and cast Henry's long shadow across the vagrant's recumbent form, literally the shadow of death. Taking that as a sign, he made his decision.

Reaching into the fanny pack, he removed the light gloves he wore when he went dove hunting with Sully. He then pulled out a pair of handcuffs he'd bought months before at a San Antonio sex shop.

Waddling forward, he ducked under the flap of the tarp. The plastic crinkled loudly as he did so, making him wince and freeze in place. The cadence of the vagrant's snores continued unchanged, and Henry crept forward, carefully positioning himself behind the man's back.

He collected himself, took a slow, deep breath in through his nose, and out through his mouth, focusing. Then with lightning quickness, he grabbed the vagrant's left arm and pulled it backwards hard, slapping one cuff on the man's wrist. The man snorted awake as Henry pushed him onto his stomach and kneeled in the small of his back before yanking his right arm behind him roughly and cuffing that wrist.

Shifting to a straddle, Henry flipped him onto his back as the man continued to cut through the cobwebs of sleep. Wadding up a handkerchief, he stuffed it into the vagrant's mouth and sat on the man's chest. The back of Henry's head rubbed against the tarp, and he could feel moisture from the dirt grinding and soaking the knees of his cotton sweatpants, but those things couldn't be helped. In control of the situation, as he waited patiently to give the man a few more moments to come fully awake and realize his predicament, Henry realized he had an erection.

The man wriggled, trying to free his wrists in vain. Fully cognizant, the vagrant became bug-eyed with fear, and he began to emit muffled screams against the gag, his shrieks of terror building then receding for over a minute until they gradually subsided, and his nasal breathing became a pant.

Suddenly the man began to thrash, flailing his head from side to side, trying to scream through the gag once again. He tried to buck Henry off his chest, but Henry's weight and leverage were too great. His legs kicked at the air, then he dug his heels into the dirt, trying to piston his torso upwards unsuccessfully as Henry rode him like a bull at a rodeo.

Finally, exhausted, the man lay still. His eyes, which had been squeezed shut during his exertions, now opened and stared directly into Henry's who whispered, "There. There it is. That's what I want."

Henry began to stroke the front of the man's throat with his gloved thumb. As he did so, the vagrant's eyebrows lifted in a plaintive expression. Henry's thumb stopped when it was over the man's windpipe, then he slowly pushed. As he did so, he leaned in close, his face within six inches of the doomed man's. Henry wanted to see what the man's eyes looked like when the light behind them dimmed.

He found out.

Afterwards, Henry opened the vagrant's mouth. Gnarled, rotten teeth sagged from the gumline like crooked tombstones. Henry pulled a utility knife from the fanny pack and opened the small set of pliers. He pinched one of his victim's incisors with the metal jaws and wiggled. No movement. He moved to the adjacent tooth, wiggling again. This time the cavity-ridden brown nubbin wiggled out of the socket easily, coming free with almost no pressure.

Methodically, he went tooth to tooth, ultimately finding five such souvenirs. He noted their roots were so necrotic the sockets didn't even seem to bleed. He put them in a metal mint tin he'd brought just for this purpose and cleaned up the scene, before turning the vagrant back into the sleeping position in which he'd found him.

His back, stiff from bending forward for so long, screamed at him as he emerged from under the tent, the suspensory rope rubbing his hood off his head for a moment as he emerged. Henry quickly flipped it back up, then looked around furtively once again. Still no one around. He retraced his steps to the main trail and set off back to the parking lot at a trot.

A few hours later, Henry spied some hardscrabble in a bar ditch a few miles from the park and pulled over. Pieces of busted concrete from some long-completed highway work littered the gravel-lined trench. Selecting a chunk that weighed several pounds, he slipped it into a small duffle that contained the handcuffs, gloves, and handkerchief.

When he got to the bridge that crossed over the San Antonio River several miles further down the road, he pulled his car onto the shoulder in the middle of the span and turned on his hazard blinkers. He waited until no traffic was visible in either direction, then exited the car and tossed the bag into the middle of the brown river where it made a muted splash and left a brief trail of foam and bubbles as it disappeared into the murky depths. Starting the drive back to Three Rivers, he reviewed the morning and searched for any details he may have missed that could be problematic.

He knew for a fact that cell phones were untraceable when powered down. Check.

No cameras and no witnesses. Check.

He was never going back to the park again, so no stupid blunders possible there. Check.

He wore gloves through the whole event. Check.

Footprints? Those were a possibility, but he wore a common brand of running shoe that he'd bought at a large retail sporting goods store months ago, paying cash. The earth between the trail and the vagrant's camp had been overgrown and unlikely to yield a quality print, and the camp itself was tamped down to a point that he thought would be similarly improbable to be helpful. He was confident of that. Besides, there was fuck all he could do about that at this point. Just something to keep in the back of his mind.

DNA evidence? He'd researched this thoroughly in preparation for the day's events, and he knew leaving some DNA behind was inevitable simply because he couldn't very well go wandering down the park's trails in head-to-toe plastic wrap. Early on, he'd come to grips with the fact that there was going to be some risk in this regard.

But he knew enough about how the world worked to suspect that a vagrant turning up dead in a park in south San Antonio wasn't going to be high on the city's list of concerns. If he was lucky, sloppy and/or overworked authorities would chalk the dead body up to natural causes and no one would even know a crime had occurred. If the authorities suspected anything, they'd likely attribute it to a squabble with one of the other vagrants in the park.

He also knew the camp was going to be exposed to the elements for however long it took for the vagrant to be discovered, degrading any biological clues he might have left behind. Finally, assuming the highly unlikely worst case came to pass, that they did bother to collect any DNA and were successful in doing so, what would happen then? The police would still have to connect it to him somehow. He obviously wasn't in any criminal databases, so they would be stuck with a DNA fingerprint with no match.

Finally, his souvenirs. He shook the metal tin once again, excited at the rattle it generated. This was his only connection to the scene he controlled. A part of his mind screamed at him, telling him to wipe the can down of his fingerprints and toss the teeth in the next river he came across, that knowingly keeping a link to the scene among his possessions was beyond stupid, it was the closest thing to a death wish.

But he knew he could no more throw away his souvenirs right now than he could keep his eyes open when he sneezed.

His souvenirs were an acceptable risk, he told himself. They would stay with him until, well, until they weren't an acceptable risk.

Henry recognized he'd crossed a dangerous line with the day's activities, and it was one with which he had to continue to be very careful. Texas was still Texas after all, and the consequence for what he did today was getting the needle up in Huntsville.

As he thought about this, he wondered what he would do if capture looked inevitable. Henry supposed that was the kind of thing you didn't really know until you were there.

CHAPTER EIGHTEEN

6:15 a.m.—Sunday, October 20ᵗʰ

On the morning of the dove hunt, Alex barreled down a county road away from Three Rivers, blowing on a cup of coffee, high beams on. Rain from the day before had cleared, and the east horizon glowed a dull red, shooing away the night. A good day in the making. He stretched behind the wheel, causing the LeSabre to drift, and when he jerked it back the coffee sloshed and stung his thigh. The parallel lines of barbed wire converged to a common dot on the horizon as he headed southwest of town to meet Stu, tapping his finger on the steering wheel in time to the radio.

He passed through fields of harvested cotton, the skeletonized rows giving the illusion of a stiff-legged giant sprinting to keep pace with his car, and pastures with cattle still in their bedded clusters from overnight. The second cut of hay lay in round bundles, scattered across green meadows waiting to be hauled away.

Nine miles outside of town he saw his turnoff, a break in the fence on his right with a dirt road that led past a large, low prefab barn painted with a Lone Star. Passing the barn, he followed the weed-choked ruts as they skirted the edge of a sorghum field for half a mile before coming on a line of four vehicles in a pasture. Recognizing Stu's truck, he pulled up next to it where six people in head-to-toe camo stood by the tailgate, chatting and drinking coffee.

Stu hailed him, "Morning, Alex. Glad you could make it."

"Thanks for having me," he said and nodded to the others.

One of the group, a stocky Hispanic man whose baldness made his age difficult to guess, waved to him then said to the group, "Me and *mijo* came out here over Labor Day to hunt hogs."

A burly redheaded man with a peeling sunburn asked, "Y'all put a hole in anything?"

"Yes, we got six. Enough for a batch of tamales."

"See any birds while you were here?"

"*Si como no*. They were thick, especially close to the stock pond."

Stu made introductions. In the group were a Minnie Pearl look-alike named Alicia Mansell and her husband Jon, both older and married as well as owners of a local hardware store. The red-headed man was Doug Idriess, and he was joined by his brother Randy, both insurance agents in town. Stu introduced the hog hunter as Ernesto Arias. "Ernie's the best goddamn county judge we've had around here in the last thirty years," Stu added.

Ernie laughed and said, "Only thirty?" He smiled warmly as he shook Alex's hand, "*Mucho gusto mi amigo.* Stu speaks very highly of you."

"Beautiful morning," Alex said. "What'm I gonna be shooting with today?"

"Come take a look," Stu said as he opened the cab of his truck and pulled a large gun case from behind his seat.

He laid it on the tailgate and popped the briefcase-style latches before lifting the lid.

Alex gave a low whistle.

From the hundred-year-old walnut stock to the engraved silver inlay, the two guns crisscrossed in their foam-crate resting place looked magnificent. Stu said proudly, "Belgian-made Brownings. Twelve-gauge, double barrel, improved cylinder chokes on both. Mine's an over-under, hope you're okay with a side-by-side?" He gingerly retrieved one shotgun and handed it to Alex like a mother passing her newborn.

"Stu, thank you, but I can't—"

"Bullshit, I wouldn't offer it to you if I didn't want you to use it today. Go on. My hunt, my rules," he said, extending it once again.

"Stu, the barrel alone on this thing costs three grand," Alex said as he pushed it away.

"So be careful with it," he said and pushed it back.

Amused, Alex carefully took the weapon and cradled it, then broke the gun's action, admiring the box lock. He snapped it shut again and said, "Well, if I come in empty-handed, there's no blaming it on the gun."

The sun was close to emerging over the horizon, so Stu handed Alex a pair of amber-tinted shooting glasses and explained the plan while the other hunters tended to their gear.

"Place belongs to Ignacio Negrete, friend of ours, farmer here in town. Normally, he'd be out with us today but poor bastard's in San Antonio getting over a knee replacement. We'll be working this milo field here, heading up in the direction of the water source Ernie was talkin' about," he said as he pointed west. "Sound good?"

"Yup. It's been a while since I've dove hunted. Not that it'll probably matter much for me, but what's the limit?"

Stu smiled wryly and said, "Fifteen a day. And if you really haven't been bird hunting in as long as you say, if you limit out today, I'll run a lap around City Hall bare-ass nekkid come Monday morning."

Overhearing this, Alicia laughed and called out as she retrieved her own gun case, "Now Stu, would that be punishment for you or for us?"

Stu handed Alex a shooting vest similar to his own and each of them stuffed three boxes of shells into the back flap. The group clearly had experience hunting together as they wordlessly paired off and spaced themselves far apart in a manner smooth and long-practiced.

"Why don't you stick with me since it's your first time with this bunch?" Stu said to Alex.

Stu inspected their line one last time, then, satisfied, put his fingers to his mouth and cut the still morning air with a shrill whistle. As one, they set off in a westerly direction across the grain field.

For ten minutes, Stu and Alex crunched across the rows of milo, not spooking any birds but enjoying the predawn tranquility. The air was heavy with the earthy smell of fresh-turned soil and the musty scent of sorghum stalks, ground down and scattered in the harvest, now just so much brittle debris underfoot. Alex studied the inert rolling irrigation systems sitting at the pasture's edge, looking like stretched out bedsprings. Interspersed along their paths, dove decoys spun their plastic wings gently in the breeze, a parody of flight. The sun had now cleared the horizon, and for the first time they cast long shadows.

Looking fifty yards off to his right, Alex watched the brothers where they'd stopped and knelt, appearing to inspect something in the dirt. Randy scooped a handful of soil and peered at it intently before sniffing it and letting it drop, dusting his hand on his pants and saying something to his brother.

An explosion of sound ripped the air behind Alex, making him yip in surprise. Chagrined, he turned and looked back just in time to see the parabolic arc of a wounded bird. Smiling, Stu broke the action on his gun and extracted the spent shell before sticking it in his vest pocket while walking in the direction of the downed bird.

Abruptly he said to Alex, "Single, left."

Alex simultaneously swung the gun up and shouldered it, trying to lead the bird, then pulled the first trigger. The gun erupted, kicking hard against his shoulder. The bird's path continued to dart frantically to and fro. Gun still up, Alex tried to quickly re-center the sights and pulled the second trigger. The gun sang again, but the bird flitted out of range then out of sight.

The smell of burnt gunpowder was thick, and his ears rang with a high metallic note. It was like trying to hit a goddamn zig-zagging light bulb, Alex thought as he reloaded.

Stu walked up with the dead bird in hand and stuffed it in the large pouch sewn into the vest's backside. "Hmm. Never seen that before," he said to Alex.

"What's that?"

"That bird actually bent the middle feather on its wingtip when you missed. Be damned if I don't think it was flipping you off," he said with a droll smile.

Alex said, "Best watch what you say while I've got a loaded shotgun in my hands."

Stu feigned indignation. "Lookit the sack on you. Well, I tell you as long as you were aiming at me, I think I'd be pretty safe." Grinning, Stu began the slow march west once again.

That marked the beginning of an increase in the action for the morning. Alex began to consistently hear the hollow pop of shotguns and, judging by the frequency with which he saw the other hunters stooping to retrieve dead birds, they appeared to be a remarkable bunch of marksmen.

At the end of the hunt, the other hunters drifted to Stu's truck and compared notes.

Stu, Alicia, and Randy had limited out, so Stu reached into his glove compartment and retrieved three cheroots.

Keeping one, he handed the others to Randy and Alicia who proceeded to proudly unwrap theirs.

"Sort of a tradition we started a while back. Limiting out gets you a cigar and bragging rights," he explained to Alex as the three of them lit up.

No one else had gotten fewer than twelve birds. When asked how he'd done, Alex shrugged and rubbed the back of his neck. He had three shells remaining from the seventy-five with which he'd started the day, and to show for his efforts he had a sore shoulder and two birds bagged with more luck than skill when a covey took wing directly in front of him. He almost hadn't had to aim as both he and Stu had just discharged two rapid succession shots into the flutter of feathers alighting in their path.

"Don't worry about it, Alex. Smoking's bad for you anyway," Alicia said as she puffed and smiled, the cherry glowing.

"Shooting like that, you definitely won't have to worry about lung cancer," Randy said as he tried to blow a smoke ring, only to see it whipped away by the light breeze.

Stu chuckled as Alex returned the gun, and clenching the cigar between his teeth said, "You've got to have some thick skin to hang with this bunch. Two birds won't make a meal. If you want, I'll clean yours for you and freeze 'em with mine. Then I promise to have you over whenever we cook 'em up. Sound okay?"

Gratefully accepting Stu's offer, Alex shook a round of hands once again and bade them goodbye. As the LeSabre bounced away on the rutted road, Alex gave a quick glance back and watched as they turned their attention to dressing and plucking their birds before putting them on ice, the wisps of smoke whipped around their heads as they worked.

Once back at the apartment, Alex took a package of peas out of the freezer and held them to his sore shoulder. Of all the things he'd come to appreciate about Stu, the biggest was his restraint in asking any questions about Alex's past. He had to have known something about the story—Alex was realistic about that—but despite having spent two full days around the man now, he'd never made a peep about the circumstances that had led to Alex's arrival in Three Rivers. Thinking about this, he texted:

> Alex: *Thx again. Good 2 have a friend here*
> Stu: *My pleasure & word of advice: if burglars break in, try negotiation. U will prob miss if u try 2 shoot them*

CHAPTER NINETEEN

12:05 p.m.—Monday, October 21ˢᵗ

Alex tapped on Principal Cunningham's open door but found her on the phone. He pantomimed coming back, but she waved him in and motioned for him to sit down, then pointed to the phone and rolled her eyes.

Checking email while he waited, the first message was from Gabriella stating she'd just finished filing the paperwork to try to get his student loans included in the bankruptcy declaration and that she'd keep him posted.

He could just hear the voice on the other end of Jen's phone, the words indistinct but the tone animated. Jen looked pained as it went on at length until she broke in. "Well, goddammit, Henrietta, this can't come as a surprise. You and I both know that son of a bitch is so crooked if he swallowed a nail, he'd spit up a corkscrew."

Henrietta had some more thoughts about this as she

started up again, but Jen cut her off. "Look here, Henrietta, I got somebody in the office. I got to go...okay...okay... Love you too. Bye."

She hung up the phone in exasperation, saying, "Lord, that woman taxes me so. Family is family but goddamn.

"Anyway, I didn't call you in here to hear my tales of woe. I just wanted to touch base. Been getting good report cards on you. Control your class well, students seem to be learning, interactions all professional. Helping out some students on your own time. Bottom line, so far so good."

Without realizing he'd been holding his breath he exhaled in relief. Truth to tell, he didn't really have a sense of how he'd been doing, and it was good to get positive feedback.

"Thank you, ma'am. I'm glad to hear that."

"So tell me, how do you feel like things are going?"

"I'm kind of feeling my way along, but I think I have the kids' respect."

"That's good to hear. No problems from any of the parents?"

"Not so far. I'm realistic that by now they all know my story and how I wound up here. If they're talking about that, they're not saying it to me. In fact, if they are, I suspect you'd know about that before I would."

"Oh, I got a few emails from a couple of assholes in the first few days after some folks did some googling, but nothing too bad. Community this size you're always going to have some folks who're like that. Okay, any questions for me?"

"An easy one. I'm supposed to work the football game this Friday night, but nobody's told me what to do."

"Just touch base with Grady, the vice-principal. Can't miss him. Had his larynx removed from a pretty bad cancer a while back, now he's got one of them magic wands he holds up to his neck, makes him sound like Stephen Hawking. He'll give you the plan."

"Sounds good. Anything else?" Alex said, preparing to

leave.

"You having a chance to get out and see the community at all?"

Alex stopped. "Yup. The father of one of my students has been good about trying to introduce me around. Stu Perry, daughter's Janine. He invited me over to a barbecue he had at his place on Labor Day, and then took me dove hunting with some other folks this last weekend. My shoulder's still sore."

Holly looked at him. "Stu Perry. The lawyer?"

Alex nodded.

"Well good, I'm glad he's helping you out."

"Yep. Seems like a really great guy."

"Well, you take care and remember what I told you first day. Door's always open."

Heading back to the teachers' lounge, Alex couldn't shake the feeling Jen had looked worried after he mentioned he was getting to know Stu.

CHAPTER TWENTY

2:20 p.m.—Thursday, October 24ᵗʰ

A lightning strike illuminated the interior of Detective Rodrigo Lozano's unmarked car in Juan Seguin's parking lot, followed immediately by the boom of thunder. The body found by a park employee prior to the start of this downpour looked to have been there a while, he'd been told, so he figured a few more minutes' delay while waiting to see if the worst of this blew over wouldn't hurt anything. To pass the time, he unwrapped the audio CD boxset of the first Harry Potter book given him by his daughter.

Not having his bifocals on, he held the boxset at arm's length, eyebrows arched and the corners of his mouth downturned as he scanned the blurb. Muggles and magic? Not his usual thing, but speaking the language would be a good way to bond with his nine-year-old grandson who was obsessed with that universe.

The Cuts that Cure

Fifty-nine years old, Lozano wore the swollen, bumpy nose that bespoke his years as an alcoholic. He'd been sober for the last twelve after suffering a Damascene moment, one for which he still thanked God daily. In the decades leading up to that day, he'd hid his alcohol intake from his wife, Anette, by drinking in a machine shop he'd built onto the side of his garage. She was uncomfortable in the workshop and rarely visited, as though the miter saw and metal lathe might spring to life autonomously. He drank out there most nights undisturbed, and the dead soldiers accumulated quickly. In his drunken laziness, he often procrastinated on their disposal.

One Monday night he took his empties to the curb for a Tuesday morning pickup, and the numerous bags filled the garbage can beyond capacity. Tired and drunk, bleary and languid, he overstuffed the can, heaping bags so high the lid sat at a forty-five-degree angle. He considered the problem for a moment, then shrugged and went to bed.

Overnight, however, a dog or raccoon whom he'd later consider to be sent by God tipped the can over, shredding the bags and scattering the evidence of his habit.

Lozano came out in the morning to get the newspaper with his usual hangover, clad in bathrobe and slippers, only to find piles of empty beer cans and whiskey bottles scattered along the gutter, his yard, and his driveway. Cans that had landed in the street lay squashed flat by passing cars, and two empty Jack Daniels bottles by the base of his mailbox had been politely set upright by the mailman.

The quantity of empty containers of alcohol would have embarrassed a fraternity cleaning up after a toga party. Checking his watch, he realized this tableau had been in plain sight of his neighbors and the passing world for several hours.

Shoveling the bottles and cans into new bags as heads turned in cars driving to work and school, a light had gone off in his head telling him that this wasn't normal.

That was close enough to bottom for him. He'd called

in sick that morning and attended his first Alcoholics Anonymous meeting. He still attended faithfully, going to at least one meeting a week and acting as a sponsor for two other cops.

Both his glasses and his girth were heavyset, and after thirty-three years on the force his retirement plans were starting to seem less abstract. While he didn't say it around the precinct, he secretly felt it couldn't come quickly enough. He just didn't have the energy that he used to have five, hell, even three years ago. Anette was convinced after listening to one too many commercials that he was "Low-T" and kept insisting that he get checked. As far as he was concerned, Low-T was just code for getting old.

After fifteen minutes in the car, the pounding rain didn't show any signs of letting up. Lozano sighed and hit pause. He found his glasses, zipped up the yellow rain slicker with SAPD stenciled on the back in large black letters and flipped up the hood. Swapping his loafers for rubber boots, he steeled himself before popping the car door enough to quickly open an umbrella and walked out into the pelting rain.

He legged it around an ambulance parked in the spot closest to the trailhead, and as the backs of his thighs became damp he broke into a trot, headed in the direction of a small pavilion covering a single picnic table. Once under the pavilion, Lozano had just collapsed his umbrella when a Parks Department vehicle drove by too fast, throwing a wall of spray on him.

A gangly young man with shaggy blonde hair that stuck to his cheeks like a Centurion's helmet sat before him on the picnic table. His soul patch wicked water down his chin, and his gray Parks Department uniform—open to his navel and framing a puka necklace—now clung to his torso like he'd stepped out of the shower. He was shivering despite the warmth of the rain.

The downpour thrummed on the pavilion's tin roof, amplified so that Lozano had to raise his voice. "Morning, sir. I'm Detective Lozano. You the man who called this in?"

A forlorn, "Yeah."

"Your name?"

"Mitchell. Mitchell Gansereit."

"Mr. Gansereit, can you tell me what happened? Start from the beginning."

"Me and Colin McPherson was detailed to pick up some trash out of the crick that runs through the back side of the park. We knew it was 'posed to rain today so we wanted to hurry up and get to it so's we didn't get soaked.

"We was at it for couple'a hours and was getting close to done when a man come up to us while we was working back there. He said he was jogging on the other side of the park over where all them cedars is and that he come up on a smell that was somethin' awful, like somethin' died."

"Did you get that man's name?" Lozano asked, interrupting the man's story.

"No, he just took off jogging again. Me and Colin didn't think much of it, lotta deer back in here, we figured one had died.

"Anyway, I told Colin I'd go check it out, mostly just so's I wouldn't have to carry the bags of trash back out to the truck.

"I went back up in them cedars and right off I could smell what the fella was talking 'bout. Smelled like Bigfoot took a shit on a pile of rotten eggs. I followed to where it was getting stronger, kept thinking I'd come up on a carcass, you know?"

Lozano nodded.

"Smell took me up to a blue tent about a hunnert feet off the trail. Once I figured out the smell's comin' from there, that's when I started getting a bad feeling. Little sick to my stomach, not just from the smell. There's 'bout a dozen homeless guys more or less live up in here full time. Generally, they don't do no harm to nobody so's we mostly don't bother 'em. Figger live an' let live.

"So I come sidling up to that tent, calling out, like.

'Hello? Anybody home? Knock, knock', like that. But I didn't get no answer. Man, I didn't wanna go look up under that tarp for nothing."

His speech had been rapid to that point, but it slowed, and he looked down between his feet where they rested on the table's wooden bench, as though trying to read the graffiti carved there.

He cleared his throat then continued, "Finally, though I decided it was time to nut up. I come 'round the back of the tent and looked inside.

"Sir, if I close my eyes right now, I can see it perfect, just like I'm sittin' here looking at you. I seen this fella, laying on his side, knees pulled up, hands folded under his head like this"—Mitchell demonstrated, pantomiming sleep—"like he was sleeping or something. I called out loud to him, 'Hey! Wakey wakey!' You know? But he didn't move a muscle. Smell by then was so bad I had to pinch my nose and try just to breathe through my mouth, but that smell was so goddam strong I could taste it. It was like burning up in my eyes, my nose, all sick-sweet."

Here he gave another shiver, closed his eyes and shook his head.

"I went to give him a shake, but when I took aholt of his leg, it was reeeeal cold. Then when I tried to turn him over onto his back, at first he wouldn't budge, not an inch. Just stiff as a board. Finally, I just pulled hard on his leg and his whole body come up, but still without bending his arms an' legs. They was frozen in place, just sticking out in the air like they was one a' them dummies you see in a store window.

"That's when I seen his face and hands was all purple and green and puffed up, like somebody'd blowed him up all full of air or something.

"But sir, it's the last part that'll haunt me for the rest of my days. God as my witness, it was somethin' I'll take with me t' my grave.

"When he come up off the ground, his mouth was open

just a little bit, and dear sweet baby Jesus I heard him make this long moan sound, like he was in pain, and for a half a second I thought he was gonna open his eyes wide and reach out to grab me, gonna grab me and hug me to him.

"Lord help me, I went ass over tea kettle backwards. I just remember gettin' tangled up on that rope and that plastic and then runnin' like the devil hisself was after me. Ran all the way back to the truck."

Now his voice cracked. He reached into his shirt pocket and took out a pack of cigarettes, hands trembling. He tapped one out and put it to his lips, but his fingers shook so badly he had difficulty lighting it.

He took a long drag and restlessly bounced his leg. "Colin wasn't no help. I asked him, hell, begged him to call it in. Chickenshit asshole kept saying that going to check out dead bodies ain't in his job description. The son of a bitch."

Lozano squished down the trail hunched under his umbrella. The wind picked up, whipping the bottom hem of his raincoat around his legs. The dirt path had transformed into one long puddle of inch-deep mud. In the trees off to his left, yellow-slickered bodies milled about, so he bushwhacked in that direction.

At the scene, the officer who'd first responded stood under his own umbrella talking on his phone just outside the police tape. Inside the camp, a technician from the medical examiner's office, a short Asian man with Clark Kent glasses, took pictures as quickly as he could, the rain so intense it sounded like bacon frying.

Since the cop was occupied, Lozano started with the tech. With the rain, both men got to business without the usual pleasantries. "Lozano. What have you got so far?"

The tech huddled under the umbrella to get a temporary respite. Lozano glanced at his lanyard, catching the name Vincent Chang. Rubber-gloved, Chang pushed his glasses back up the bridge of his nose with his bent wrist.

"Male, no ID, stage of decomposition makes age and race difficult to determine right now. Gun to my head, dead four to six days, but we should be able to give you a more accurate guess once we get him back to the office and take a better look.

"No blood anywhere, no obvious external trauma jumping out at me so far, but again it was a pretty quick look. Looks to have been a vagrant living out here. Mud everywhere rules out any chance of getting meaningful information from footprints.

"Found these in one of his pockets," the technician said as he handed Lozano an evidence bag containing a small cellophane baggy with three small dull-yellow pills, each with "OP" stamped on one side and "40" on the other.

"What are they?" Lorenzo asked as he leaned forward, squinting to see them better through the two layers of clear plastic.

"Oxycontin. Must have been saving them for a special occasion?"

"Hmph. Anything else on him?"

"Pint flask next to him, and then there was this tucked in his belt." From a second evidence bag he pulled a large hunting knife with a worn leather scabbard, the belt loop broken and flopping. He pulled the knife from its sheath. "Tip's bent as you can see here, probably from trying to pry something open. Blade's clean, though, no blood." He re-sheathed it and replaced it in the evidence receptacle.

Lorenzo sucked his teeth then asked, "So what do you think?"

"Given the position he was found in, looks most likely to have died in his sleep. Means that statistically speaking, pills and empty alcohol bottle, plus this living situation"— he gestured, waving his hands around them in the air for a moment— "you'd bet on an overdose. No way of knowing accidental or intentional.

"Other big possibility is a catastrophic medical event while he was asleep. Big myocardial infarction, stroke, something like that. The fact that he was on his side when he died makes it less likely that he vomited and aspirated, so probably didn't pull a Jimmy Hendrix. Weather's been mild, so unlikely that ambient temperature played a role."

"Chances of foul play?"

"Well, again if you're talking statistically, that would mean your most likely suspect would be one or more of the other homeless guys in the park here. But a fatal assault by one of his neighbors would be highly probable to spill one whole hell of a lot of blood or have left him with a caved-in skull. It doesn't look like the guy ever took this pig-sticker out"—he indicated the vagrant's knife— "so if it was an assault, he didn't see it coming.

"Bottom line, common things are common. I think you got a homeless guy who just turned up dead from one of a half dozen possible natural causes. John Doe here'll get an autopsy, and that may or may not give us better information, but for now I don't think there's going to be anything here for law enforcement."

Lozano nodded, then stepped past the tech to look under the makeshift tent. The rope which had been the support for the canopy had come untied from one of the trees, with that end lying coiled serpentine in the mud. As a result, the shelter, losing half its support, now sat looking like a pyramid open on one side. And like those Egyptian tombs, this one also held the dead.

The dead vagrant's upper torso lay covered by the shelter, but his legs jutted out below the knees from the rumpled edge of the collapsed plastic. Lozano suspected it was Gansereit's panicked retreat that had knocked the shelter down.

The technician came around and started taking pictures of the vagrant's legs sticking out below the border of the tarp. Squinting into the viewfinder, he said, "Reminds you of the Wicked Witch of the East, doesn't it?"

Lozano didn't smile. He went to the other end of the tent that still stood erect and open. Peering inside, he found the stench much stronger, as this was sheltered from the rain. The corpse lay there on its side. He fished a pair of rubber gloves from his pocket and put them on before pulling the man's hair out of his half-open eyes. Lifting the closer of the two lids, he saw the eye was dull and milky, like those of fish on ice at the market.

He was about to leave when he saw something curious. Pulling a penlight from his pocket, he flashed it on the white of the vagrant's upward-facing eye.

Scattered across the milky surface of the eye were several small, red dots, like rosy freckles. Frowning, he turned the vagrant's head to face him and inspected the other eye. Again, he found the same punctate red spots spread across the white sclera, each no bigger than a period at the end of a sentence in a magazine article.

He'd seen those red dots on a case years before, long enough ago that he was still drinking at the time. Lozano had been called to the Hilton when an out-of-town businessman—an accountant, Lozano vaguely remembered, in town for some kind of conference—missed his check out.

When the maid came to clean his room, the situation was already bad enough when she found the accountant hanging by his neck from a belt he'd looped around the bar in his closet. It was made worse by the lace bra and nylons he was wearing when she found him, as well as the array of pornography he'd arranged in a semi-circle in front of him. When the E.M.T.s arrived there was nothing they could do for a case of autoerotic asphyxiation gone wrong, Lozano recalled, but they had to sedate the poor housekeeper.

Poor bastard, Lozano had thought as he watched the investigative team chat animatedly and sift through the man's belongings while his corpse dangled a few feet behind them. All these years later, he could still remember the man's name: Brett Harnolde. It was funny, the things that stuck.

When he'd examined the accountant's face, with its bulging, purple tongue and the eyes set in a glare of concentration that was now permanent, he'd noticed these same subtle, red spots on the eyes. He couldn't remember the medical name for them but what he did remember vividly was what the medical examiner had told him later after the autopsy.

They were indicative of choking. As he squatted over the vagrant's corpse that gave him pause.

Seeing nothing else of interest, he peeled his gloves off, pocketing them as he said to the technician, "Thanks, hope you get outta here soon." He turned to slog his way back. The cop was still on his phone, so Lozano waved his goodbye before pushing through the sodden overgrown grass to get back to the main trail.

Making his way back to the car huddled under his umbrella, he found himself eager to get back to the car and hear about the Dursley's efforts to flee their house on Privet drive and go into hiding.

CHAPTER TWENTY-ONE

2:20 p.m.— Friday, October 25ᵗʰ

The long, black hearse crept backwards toward the knobless double doors set into the concrete wall. From his vantage point on the steps leading to the coroner's office, Lozano could see through the gaps in the white ruffled curtains that the rear was empty. The driver, a skinny middle-aged black man in an ill-fitting jacket and crooked tie opened the rear door and left it ajar, then leaned against the rear quarter panel and lit a cigarette while he sent someone a text. Tapping ash on the asphalt, he glanced up and noticed Lozano watching him from a short distance away. The driver gave Lozano a curt nod then went back to looking at his phone while he waited to pick up his cargo.

Lozano pressed the red button on the intercom next to the locked entrance and waited. The building's structure matched the nature of the work that took place in its bowels:

126

grim, unattractive, but functionally necessary. Not for the first time, he thought the entire edifice resembled a large hollowed-out cinder block.

A minute went by with no answer. He could see through the pane in the door the receptionist desk was unoccupied, so he leaned on the button a second time, generating a long, uninterrupted buzz. As he watched, a heavyset white woman wearing a chambray dress emerged from a door behind the desk, and without sitting down leaned over to key the intercom.

"State your business," the curt woman said.

"Detective Lozano, SAPD I was called down here by Dr. Reinhard. Said she had something she wanted to show me." Per protocol, he took a step back and looked up directly at the video camera set under the eave of the small porch that covered the entrance's three low concrete steps. There followed a loud buzz and he entered the spartan lobby.

"Sign in," the receptionist said as she handed him a clipboard with a pen chained to the metal clasp. Through the doorway behind her, Lozano saw three people with a half-eaten birthday cake and plates of melting ice cream, chatting and laughing.

She handed Lozano an adhesive name badge with VISITOR written in block letters. It immediately began to curl at the edges when he stuck it on his lapel.

"You know where you're going?"

Lozano nodded and, taking him at his word, the receptionist returned to the back room. The left exit led him down a windowless, unadorned concrete hallway, thick with the smell of fresh paint and lit by a single row of sickly fluorescent lights, some with missing covers and naked bulbs. The only sounds were the hum of the lights and the clopping of his footfalls. Wandering these halls made him feel like he was in a bunker, not an office building.

At a small, nondescript elevator door, he summoned the lift. When the elevator door slid open, the smell of formaldehyde billowed out as though the car exhaled a breath it had taken deep in the building's guts. Wrinkling his nose, he pressed the button for the basement, arriving a few moments later in the Bexar County Morgue.

The air was a pungent combination of tissue preservatives and disinfectants overlying decay. Most of the basement was one large working space with room for as many as eight autopsy tables, although only three were out and occupied at the moment. Doctor Sabine Reinhard was working on the body closest to Lozano as he approached. The other two corpses lay patiently under their white sheets.

Dr. Reinhard split her time between working with pathology residents at the local medical school and doing autopsies for the county. Lozano had gotten to know her reasonably well through that time, and he'd found her to be a born teacher. The county's other two pathologists would have just emailed him the findings. Dr. Reinhard summoned him to discuss face-to-face. He didn't mind making the trip, as he usually learned something on these visits.

Slender in her physique and subtle in her make-up, Dr. Reinhard looked younger than her forty years. She liked to work to classical music, and Lozano could hear her humming along as she concentrated. She wore her longish blonde hair up in a low, looped bun and the front of her green rubber smock was smeared with fatty grease and blood, a startling contrast with the serenity of the symphony.

"That's nice. Relaxing."

"Mozart," she replied, looking up and smiling. "Serenade number thirteen for strings in G major. Thanks for coming by, Detective Lozano."

"My pleasure. This about that kid we sent you couple days ago, six-year-old? Supposedly fell into the river when stepdad wasn't paying attention?"

"No, although I should have those results for you later this afternoon. The tech is doing the child's x-rays now." She pointed toward the far end of the morgue where a white-coated technician wearing noise-cancelling headphones wrestled x-ray equipment around a pitifully small shroud.

Lozano said, "The vagrant from the park, then?"

"Yep." She threw the sheet over the corpse in front of her and peeled off her rubber gloves in a wadded elastic bunch, then hooked a thumb in the elastic wrist and pulled the rubber fingers back before snapping the wad like a slingshot into a red biohazard bag eight feet away. Pulling on a clean pair, she led Lozano to one of the other tables and gently pulled the drape back just enough to uncover the homeless man's upper torso down to the umbilicus before snapping on the harshly bright overhead surgical light and centering its glare on the cadaver's head.

His skin was waxy-appearing, a decomposing pastiche of greens, purples, and yellows. His neck rested on a small wooden block. The vagrant's face was bloated, eyes swollen shut, lips slightly parted. There was the usual large Y-shaped incision over the chest and abdomen that Lozano had come to know over the years, but this one had a long extension going up along the neck, like an upside-down peace sign. Another large incision buried in the hairline went across the scalp from ear to ear.

Reinhard asked, "I hear the tech at the scene was thinking this was death from natural causes, correct?"

"Yeah, that's why I called you afterwards."

"Before we get to that, just a little house-keeping first. Here's his tox report." She handed Lozano a clipboard. "Blood alcohol three times the legal limit, and a mix of opiates and drugs that come from a family of sedatives, called benzodiazepines. Valium, Xanax, that sort of thing."

While Lozano flipped through the report's pages, Reinhard retrieved two small V-shaped retractors with what looked like a cat's claws from a nearby surgical tray. She hunched over the corpse's face and placed the retractors between the swollen eyelids. Once they were in place, she then opened the retractors as widely as the hinge at the crotch of the V would permit. The eyelids were pulled in opposite directions, completely exposing the white surface of each eyeball and giving the vagrant a look of wide-eyed surprise.

Handing him a magnifying glass, she said, "You were right to call. Take a look."

Lozano leaned in close, to within a matter of inches of the vagrant's bloated face. The stench was overpowering, even with mouth breathing. With good lighting, the magnifying glass, and the retractors in place, the red spots on the vagrant's eyeballs were now clear, almost obvious.

"What do you call these spots again?" Lozano asked.

"Petechiae. Tiny little spots where someone bleeds into their tissues, and they definitely shouldn't be there if this was natural causes. They're associated with asphyxiation. That's what causes the pinpoint bleeding, when the victim is pulling so hard for a breath that the negative pressure actually causes tiny little blood vessels to rupture. You get them all over, but they're easiest to see in the eyes because the whites make the red color of the dots stand out."

Reinhard continued, "If he O.D.'ed from the sedatives in his system, you wouldn't see petechiae because an overdose slows down your drive to breathe. Petechiae arise when you're trying to breathe but can't. But we have a saying around here that goes 'Believe what you see, don't see what you believe'. So, the next question you ask yourself as a coroner is, 'Why would someone whose drive to breathe is intact still asphyxiate?"

Clearly enjoying herself, Reinhard said, "And that list is as short as it is sinister—strangulation."

Lozano said, "Okay, now you have my undivided attention."

"Usually, that's done with some kind of a ligature, like a belt or a piece of rope or something. Alternatively, you can try to strangle someone with your bare hands. But both of those methods generally leave marks on the neck, either finger-shaped bruises or a straight line, and as you can see there's nothing like that here. When I dissected the tissues under the skin I didn't see anything out here on the sides of the throat that was consistent with a ligature. I did see this, right here in the middle of the neck, right over the windpipe."

She lifted the skin edge by the neck incision she'd made. "You can see that the tissues right here in the middle of the throat directly over the windpipe have a small amount of what may be discoloration, but if it's real, it's subtle.

She then pulled the skin flaps on the wound back further and lifted the entire voice box out of the neck and held it in her hands.

"Moving on from the idea of bruising, I took a look and there's no broken cartilage in the proximal windpipe or larynx. Again, things you'd expect if someone used a looped ligature of some kind.

"There were other things that didn't go with the idea of strangulation during a struggle. For instance, if somebody's trying to choke you out, what are you going to do? You're going to punch, scratch, claw, right? But I didn't find any bruises on his knuckles, skin under his fingernails, anything like that."

Lozano kept listening, but he was beginning to play out different scenarios in his imagination.

Reinhard continued. "Then something occurred to me. What if our guy was awake but unable to fight back? That would take something like wrist restraints."

She lifted the cadaver's wrists up where Lozano could see them easily. "Take a look here. Externally, there was subtle discoloration, hard to really get a sense of whether that's real bruising or not. But" –she lifted back the flaps of skin to see the tissues beneath—"underneath you can see it easily. Two completely circumferential, neatly circumscribed lines of bruising. That's definitely real."

"What caused them?" Lozano asked.

"Maybe zip ties, maybe handcuffs. Less likely to be rope just because of the time it would have taken. But frankly, the cause of the bruises is less important than the fact of the bruises themselves. While the bruises are present, the ligature causing them is gone, which means that they were removed, probably immediately post-mortem. And by definition that means…?" she asked leadingly.

131

"Proof of another person," Lozano finished.

"Last thing. Look here," she said.

Reinhard opened the vagrant's mouth and shone the overhead light inside.

"Guy's got horrible dentition, right? No surprise. I counted a total of eleven missing teeth. But look here." She pointed at one empty socket toward the back which she picked at with a small dental hook. When she extracted the hook, a small glob of what looked like grape jelly the size of a pencil lead sat on the tip.

"That's a small blood clot. Not much of one, in fact not even big enough to see with the naked eye, I needed the magnifying glass at first. While six of the sockets were obviously old missing teeth, I found that five of the spots where teeth were missing had similar clots at the base of the root. I checked his stomach, and he didn't swallow them, and no teeth were listed among the evidence found at the scene."

Lozano finished her thought. "I think somebody took some souvenirs."

When Lozano arrived back at his office, he found a maintenance man working in the drop ceiling above his desk. Four mineral fiber tiles had been removed, and the man was shoulder-deep in a hole noisily replacing a mass of tin ductwork in the darkness. Years in that decrepit building had taught him how to block out such distractions, and he settled in to review the vagrant's file again.

With the advanced state of decomposition, Reinhard had only been able to place the time of death as sometime between the 19th and the 22nd. Physical evidence from the scene was nonexistent. With multiple days' worth of exposure to the elements ending with that rainstorm, he had nothing to go on.

There were no cameras anywhere near that part of town, so the likelihood of getting a plate or a picture was zero. None of the other homeless people who lived in the park had seen anything suspicious, and Lozano made a note to go back and have them interviewed again.

He clasped his hands behind his head and leaned back in his chair, staring at the work going on in his ceiling. He sat deep in thought for the better part of a minute, and then started doodling on the yellow legal pad in front of him.

The previous summer, he'd attended a talk given by his Captain on the Supreme Court's ruling in the case of *Carpenter v United States* and what it meant for law enforcement in regard to the information gleaned from cell phone histories.

As the Captain explained, the case arose when the FBI demanded that a cell carrier in Detroit turn over cell phone records as part of an investigation of one of their customers. The court decided that a demand wasn't enough, that a search warrant should be required, in a manner no different than if they wanted to enter the suspect's house.

Not being tech-oriented, Lozano focused on the background given by the Cap about how cell carriers work. As he explained it, there were cell phone towers all over the city run by private companies. Whenever a cell phone turned on, it communicated with all towers in its vicinity. Each company's network constantly looked at the phone's location, and if that phone made an attempt to call or text, the network would decide which tower was closest and least busy, and then routed the call to that tower.

According to the Captain, if a single tower out in the middle of nowhere showed that a given cell phone was in proximity to it, all you could tell was that the phone was somewhere within a circular area of coverage with that tower at its center.

If two towers picked up a given phone simultaneously, though, you could tell that the phone was physically present within the roughly diamond-shaped overlap of the two towers' circular coverage areas. The companies tracked the data about every cell phone's location tower-by-tower and stored it, usually for ninety days.

This opened up all kinds of possibilities as Lozano and his partners saw it. Everybody had cell phones. Hell, even he used a smart phone, and he was a Luddite. All that information was accessible so long as you got a warrant.

Returning to the moment, Lozano realized that if the perpetrator had a cell phone on his or her person and it had been turned on during the commission of the crime, there would be a record of that with the cell phone companies' towers.

He went to the SAPD website and navigated to a map of the different cell phone towers in the city. Collapsing the map down, he saw four towers encircled the park. That meant that anyone in the park with their phone on at any given time would have their number show up on the records of all four of those towers simultaneously.

So now he would be able to get the numbers of every phone that was turned on in the park during the window of time that the crime had occurred.

It was as good an avenue as anything else he had at the moment, he said to himself. He pulled out the paperwork to get started on the affidavit.

Of course, if whoever did this turned off their phone before coming to the park, this would all be moot.

CHAPTER TWENTY-TWO

6:40 p.m.—Friday, October 25ᵗʰ

Henry and Tracy held hands as the line of students shuffled forward to get into the Friday night football game. It was still short-sleeve weather on this October evening, but despite the warm and humid air, Tracy chose to wear Henry's letterman jacket. She pressed against his side, leaning into him so hard at one point she knocked him off balance.

"Jesus, watch it," he said as he caught himself.

"Sorry," she said and kissed his shoulder, leaving a smear of lip balm streaking the fabric. His annoyance flared, eyes rolling while he wiped at the smudge with his thumb.

Ahead, Henry saw Mr. Brantley manning the ticket office, a plywood booth so small the door couldn't open all the way without bumping against the stool. The low sun kissed the horizon, shining directly into Mr. Brantley's eyes in his seat at the cutout window.

At the counter, Henry pushed a twenty across and said, "Evening, Mr. Brantley. Two please."

While Mr. Brantley made change, he smiled at Tracy then said, "Say, Henry, at practice Saturday, you were saying something about an all-girl band I should check out who sounded a lot like the Whiskey Sisters. What was their name again?"

Henry said, "The Trishas. In fact, they're having a reunion show in a few months at Gruene Hall if you want to see them live."

Alex tore two perforated raffle tickets off a roll, passed them to Henry along with his change and said, "Cool, thanks. Y'all enjoy the game," before turning his attention to the next couple in line.

They passed through the gate and up a concrete ramp to the stadium's rows of aluminum benches. Tracy asked, "You and Mr. Brantley seem like y'all are gettin' pretty close, huh?"

"I guess," he said as they scaled the rows. Each step generated a clomping metallic reverb. "Where you wanna sit?"

She ignored the question for the moment. "My momma says she heard Mr. Brantley's some kind of pervert or something."

"Naw, he's alright," making a command decision and taking a seat.

"No, let's go further over here," Tracy said tugging at his arm. She led him to a spot in front of where the cheerleaders would be, where most eyes would be focused.

Their long shadows reached the racetrack as the sun sank lower behind them. The metal bench was surprisingly cool despite the warm air and the facing sky gave the first hints of dusk.

After a minute of sitting in silence, she asked again, "Seriously, Henry. You're spending all this time training with him, spending time after school with just you and him in his office gettin' tutored. I'm gettin' to be worried about this whole situation. I was reading the internet about it, the way child molesters go pickin' their kids. They even got a word for it, they call it 'grooming'."

Exasperated, he snapped, "Look, I told you it's nothing. Why are you making such a big deal out of this?"

Looking hurt and angry, she answered, "Well, if you can't see why I might be wondering why my boyfriend won't talk to me about hangin' out with a man who's a known pervert then I don't know what."

He knew his silence would egg on her aggravation. Maybe if she got upset enough, he wouldn't have to navigate a sexual encounter later that evening.

She stewed beside him, forearms on her thighs, hands clasped between her drawn up knees. "Fine, then. You can just feel free to run all over God's creation getting molested by who knows how many dirty old men all day long for all I care. Just don't come crying to me after. I'm not going to ask about this no more." She turned her head in a snit.

"Works for me," he said, distracted as he scrolled his phone.

CHAPTER TWENTY-THREE

8:30 p.m.—Friday, October 25th

At halftime, Alex closed the ticket window and reported to a generator-powered shack wedged under the stadium's slope of seats where a line snaked thirty feet out. In the concession stand, a frazzled computer sciences teacher, Wendy Cobb, looked like she was a few minutes from just throwing all her food supplies across the countertop and letting the crowd have them in a free for all.

Wendy was raven-haired with pale skin and freckles, a quirky smile and a Roman nose. With no makeup, Alex judged her to be early thirties. A smear of chili tattooed her cheek, and her hands were sticky-stained with snow cone juice in all the primary colors. All the bills in the small cash box sported multi-colored fingerprints.

"Need some help?" Alex asked.

She sagged with relief, "Yes, please."

Under a pair of naked 60-watt bulbs, they spent the rest of the game pouring can after can of thick, fluorescent orange goo over paper baskets of chips. They spooned gallons of hot chili into innumerable corn chip bags, and troubleshot the cotton candy machine when it abruptly quit spinning its pink, sugary cobwebs. With two sets of hands, the work was pleasant, the customers were generally cheerful, and no one threatened to call the Health Department when he and Wendy licked spills off their fingers.

While they worked, Alex noticed how little the sounds of high school football had changed since his day. It was all familiar: the band gamely struggling through the *Hawaii Five O* theme song; the cheerleaders with their staccato claps and chants; the crowd's machine gun stomps in unison on the aluminum risers, building in volume and speed to a crescendo, then releasing with a roar. It felt timeless.

In the middle of the fourth quarter, Stu ambled up to the counter. "Well, looky here. New folks drew the short straws I'm guessing?"

Alex laughed. "Yeah, it's not a mystery why we're down here. Y'all know each other? Wendy, Stu. Stu, Wendy. She's the new computer sciences teacher."

Things had slowed for the moment, so Wendy wiped her hands and threw the towel over her shoulder before shaking. "Pleasure." With a jut of her lower lip, she blew a puff of air straight up at her forehead to clear the dangling hair from her eyes then leaned on the dented, sheet metal countertop.

"What you in the mood for?" Alex asked.

"Two popcorns, two diet drinks, whatever kind you got."

"Coming right up."

While Alex tended to the order, Stu asked, "So Wendy, where do you come to us from?"

"My people are from El Paso, most of them're still there. I went to Texas State, and got a job working at Dell in

Austin after I got out of school. Did that for about ten years before I figured out I was ready for a break from the corporate world. After I listened to my better angels, I decided to give working with kids a try."

"Whatever happened to ol' what's-his-name? The fella who used to teach computers at the school? Anthony something?"

She dabbed her sweaty neck with a napkin. "They told me he caught a bad case of rehab," tipping her thumb and pinky fingers toward her mouth.

"Shame. My daughter liked him. Well, glad we got you out of the deal, though."

"Thanks. I've enjoyed my time here so far. Job's been fun and the people seem nice."

"Glad to hear it." Turning his attention back to Alex, Stu said, "Say, while I got you here, let me ask you something. How's your Spanish?

Alex said, "I know just enough to get myself in trouble. You want butter?"

"Nope. Second question. What do you know about *Día de los Muertos*?"

Alex handed the bags across and worked on scooping ice for Stu's drinks. He pointed at Wendy's mostly empty paper cup and, when she nodded, topped her off with fresh ice and a full soft drink. "*Día de los Muertos*? Big festival in Mexico, sort of like their Mardi Gras I think. Past that, not much. How come?"

"You're right, it's a big party all over the whole goddamn country. Lasts a couple of days, always the tail end of October or early November. I do a lot of business down on the border, and I've got some clients in Nuevo Laredo that do it up right every year, first class all the way. These guys are the real deal. They've had me down a handful of times over the years as their guest, and we usually howl at the moon. This year they're not only bringing me but also two fellas from Europe that we've all been working on some projects together. There's a good time to be had. I was wondering if you'd want to come along? Leave on a Friday after school, back Sunday night?"

Alex paused while he let the soft drink bubbles foam down before dispensing more. "Man, Stu, I don't know. The border? We used to go down there some back in the day, but nowadays it seems like a good way to wind up zip-tied in a car trunk with a hood over your head, don't you think?"

"I'll grant that if you're a drunk tourist crossing over for a night of liquored-up assholery there's no telling what kind of mess you're liable to find yourself getting into. But we won't have to worry about that with these *muchachos*. They're upper crust Laredo, all the way. Trust me, nobody's going to mess with 'em. They're putting us up in style, and I know my way around the city. Plus, I'm bringin' these two Croatian fellas who're doing a project for me. They're great guys, lots of fun. It'll be a couple of days of good music, and even better food. I don't need an answer right now, just be thinking about it and let me know."

"Will do. That'll be nine even."

Stu paid him and balanced the food and drinks. He smiled at Wendy, "Nice meeting you, ma'am." Then to Alex, "Later gator," and wandered off whistling along with the band as they struggled through an off-tune cover of "Eye of the Tiger."

Wendy shook the ice in her cup and said, "Nice guy. Y'all known each other long?"

Making himself a chili pie, Alex said, "Just since school started. Yeah, he seems like good people."

Wendy cocked her head. "I feel the urge to ask: you know him well enough to think about going down across the border with him at night? I mean, in El Paso, we've quit crossing the river into Juarez because it's like a goddamn war zone down there right now."

"I don't know. He made it sound like it would be alright as long as I'm with him and his people."

Wendy scooped a handful of ice from her cup and held the cubes against the back of her neck. "All that to say, *Día*

Arthur Herbert

de los Muertos is a lot of fun. We used to go every year when I was a kid. My parents took us over and we would stay with friends on the outside of Juarez."

"You went when you were a little kid?" Alex asked in surprise.

"Yeah. You hear festival and you think party-time. While there's that for sure if you want to find it, the spirit of the holiday is family-oriented."

"Is that right?" Alex asked.

"I can't tell if you're being sarcastic," she said and smiled.

"No, go on. This is interesting."

She bumped her shoulder against his in an avuncular fashion, and pulled her hair behind her ear with one finger. "It's all about remembering family who died, sort of supporting them as they go through the spirit world. Mexicans view death as a part of life, so during the festival they're being reunited with their dead family members, that the dead walk among us. That's why you'll see so many people paint themselves with the death mask."

"The what?"

Wendy pulled her t-shirt off her shoulder. There, under her bra strap and over her scapula, was a tattoo of a skull, the sunken eyes blackened, white cheek bones offset by a crown of blood-red roses.

"When we were teenagers my sister and I got matching versions of this. I have some great memories of the festival from back in the day."

Impressed, Alex said, "Clearly."

It was just after midnight by the time Alex made it back to his apartment. Standing on the landing while he searched his key ring, he could hear Brutus snoring inside. The dog still didn't wake up even after he entered the apartment and dropped his bag, only lurching awake when Alex nudged his hip. The bleary bulldog followed Alex outside and down the steps, sniffing the monkey grass that lined the driveway before urinating on it. While he waited for the dog to finish, Alex thought about Wendy. Good-hearted and tomboyish, confident and competent. She'd seen something of life, and he found that as attractive as her plain Jane features and slim physique. It had been so long since he'd flirted with anyone he'd forgotten how, but she'd taken the lead, asking him for his number as they stowed equipment and supplies at the end of the night. The look she'd given him when she asked had been expectant, as though she knew he'd say yes. He sensed his life leveling out, establishing a sense of normalcy.

His thoughts turned from her to what she had to say about *Dia de los Muertos*. The nature of the festival started to appeal to him, celebrating death as a part of life rather than fearing it, belief that the dead walk among us, that there's something after this, and it's joyous.

The thought of spending a weekend immersed in that culture sounded pretty good. It would do him good to get out of town for a few days and spend time in an atmosphere like the one she described. In a moment of spontaneity, he reached for his phone and texted:

Alex: *Im in 4 DDLM. Let me know the deets.*

Three grey dots shimmered for a moment, then:

Stu: *Roger that u will b glad u said yes*

CHAPTER TWENTY-FOUR

11:10 a.m.—Saturday, October 26ᵗʰ

After receiving the warrant, Lozano drove to the wireless carrier's regional office and served the on-site manager, explaining the situation and the SAPD's request.

"I'll just have to let legal look at this," the woman said in a tone cordial if not enthusiastic. "Assuming everything's legit, we should be able to turn the information over later today, tomorrow at the latest."

Surprised, Lozano asked, "That quick?" He was embarrassed that a part of him had pictured people wading through boxes of documents.

"Yep. Piece of cake."

He was just putting papers away in preparation to go home when he received an email from the manager with the attachment. The cell phone carrier's output had been translated into a two-page document containing a table with five columns. Expanding the list with a finger-spread, he squinted at the headers. It looked like the first column was a list of phone numbers, the second a column for the date each phone came into the area of triangulation. There was a column for the time each phone entered the area and one for its time exiting. The last column had the name of each phone's owner. A quick count showed there were fifty-eight phones in the query. *Now that's what I'm talking about.*

Fifty-eight phones over four days. He thought about that. *Gives me a rate of a little more than one phone entering the park per hour each day during normal operating hours. You got a park that's out of the way, and some people maybe scared off by the place's rep for housing vagrants. Yeah, okay, I can believe that. About one phone per hour.*

He scanned the list of names, not really expecting anything to catch his attention. They all seemed innocuous.

A knock at the door to his office interrupted his thoughts. Doug McBride, another homicide detective leaned in his office at a forty-five-degree angle, one hand on the doorknob while the other held the door frame, supporting his weight. "I'm so behind on my reports I've got a late night coming. Making a coffee run before I dive in. You want me to grab you anything?"

"Yeah, medium roast, black. I got a bunch of calls to make, gonna be here a while, thanks." McBride gave him a wink-and-a-gun and disappeared.

Lozano started at the top of the list, crooking the phone in his shoulder and dialing the first cell number on the carrier's list. Witnesses, suspects, information: at this point he would take whatever he could get.

The name typed next to the phone number on line forty-three was "Wallis, Henry."

CHAPTER TWENTY-FIVE

11:45 a.m.—Monday, October 28ᵗʰ

The air smelled of rain.

Henry sat on a low brick wall that surrounded the field house on three sides and watched a dark line of thunderheads drift in his direction. On the football field, a handful of crows busily pecked at bugs around the thirty-yard line until a landscaper on a riding mower spooked them into flight, cawing as they scattered. Finishing his lunch, Henry wiped his mouth with his forearm and shot the wadded up brown paper bag like a jumper, wrist bent and fingers curled, at a trash can fifteen feet away. The bag arced toward the can, and then missed wide left where it landed on the grass. Henry never considered picking it up.

The U.I.L. cross country regionals were coming up and his training was going well. After seeing his times from the last week, Coach Volkner made it sound like a scholarship was a real possibility. "Division I schools might be a stretch," he'd told Henry the previous week after reviewing the boy's times, "but for a Division II school you would def—"

His ring tone interrupted the thought. Fishing his cell from his pocket, he let the unknown caller go to voice mail.

A moment later, he toggled over to retrieve the message. His stomach immediately went cold.

"Hi Mr. Wallis. My name is Detective Lozano of the San Antonio Police Department. I'd like to speak to you, as I'm hopeful you may have information that can help an investigation I'm conducting. Please call me back at this number when you get a chance. I look forward to speaking with you. Take care."

His face and fingers tingled, and his saliva instantly tasted of copper, like sucking a penny. It was as though a bucket of water had been thrown at him, a splash-shock that took a minute to pass.

He replayed the message, impossibly hoping he'd heard it wrong. The visceral reaction to hearing the detective's voice was not as severe on the second listening, and he could already feel the adrenaline surge receding, his thoughts coming under control.

Opening a search engine, he typed in "detective lozano san antonio police." The first link was a bio page on the department's personnel tab. In the picture, Lozano had tired eyes and a grim scowl. Henry expanded the picture on the phone's screen and studied it closely, thinking he was looking at a serious man who was not to be fucked with.

Of more concern to him was the information in the short blurb of a bio. Homicide Division.

How was this fucking possible?

A steady breeze kicked up, and a grey wall of rain came from the thunder heads, looking static from this distance. The temperature had dropped, and he pulled up his sweatshirt's hood. Okay, work the problem.

There had been a loose end. It remained to be seen was

how serious it was. At least the content and tone of the detective's message didn't make it sound like there were going to be squad cars waiting for him in his driveway when he got home.

He briefly considered deleting Lozano's message and ignoring it. What was the worst that could happen?

Gaming it out, it was hard to believe that were he to delete the message and act like he never heard it, the situation would just fizzle out and disappear. No, more likely he would wind up coming home one day soon to find the serious man in the picture sitting on the couch in his living room wanting to talk while his mother looked on in horror.

Plus, the denial plan was just plain ridiculous anyway. There was no way he could walk around with this kind of uncertainty hanging over his head. He'd be constantly jumping at shadows, worrying every time he heard a siren go by. He couldn't ignore the Detective Lozano problem.

He needed more information, which meant calling Lozano back.

As the initial shock passed, an icy resolve took its place.

Henry stared at the clock through his afternoon classes, his thoughts far away. When the final bell rang, he snatched his backpack off the floor and trotted to his car through a drizzle as light as a wet dog shaking. Slamming the door, the only sound was the gentle patter of scattered raindrops on the roof. He took a deep breath and exhaled. Then he hit the call back button.

The phone only rang once before a gruff, "Lozano."

"Hi Detective Lozano, my name's Henry Wallis. You called?"

A pause during which Henry could hear pages flipping. "Yes, Mr. Wallis. Thanks for returning my call. I'm in charge of the investigation of a murder that took place in Juan Seguin City Park about a week ago. It appears that you were in the park around the time of the crime, and I was hoping you could answer some questions for me."

"Am I in trouble?" Henry asked.

"I'm hoping you have information that could be helpful to the investigation." The detective sounded noncommittal. "Understand, you have the right to refuse to talk to me, but it's my hope that you'll answer my questions."

To Henry's ear, Lozano hit "refuse" menacingly, like only guilty people would choose that option.

Henry watched the rings made by rain droplets on the surface of a puddle outside the driver's window. "No, I understand. Ask away," he said, trying to sound nonchalant.

"You were in the park early on the morning of October twentieth, is that correct?"

"I really don't remember."

"You don't remember being at the park on that day, or you don't remember going to the park at all?" Lozano asked.

"Both. I run cross country at my high school, and so I run at a lot of different places to break up the routine."

"I see. You go to these parks as a part of a training regimen."

"Correct."

"How long of a run do you usually go for?"

"Five kilometers, usually. Takes me a little over forty-five minutes, all total with stretching and a cool down."

"So you said you go to lots of parks in the area to train?"

"Yeah, I like to mix it up."

"Mmm-hmm. What are some of your favorites?"

"Oh, I don't know, they all kind of blur together after a while."

"Okay. This particular park is on the southwest side of town, has a small pavilion to the left of the main trail entering the park, and a creek that makes up its north border. Lot of winos live in the park too, probably hard to spend much time there without bumping into some of them. Any of that sounding familiar?"

"Vaguely. Can I ask what makes you think I might have been at this park on the day you're talking about? Might help jog my memory."

"Your cell phone was in the park early on that morning."

Confused, Henry said, "That can't be right." Immediately he regretted it, squinching his eyes shut in fury. *Fucking idiot.*

Quickly he tried to do damage control. "I usually leave my phone at my house when I go for a run. I don't need the weight or the distraction. You know, trying to focus."

"Yuh-huh." Lozano said. Henry heard the papers ruffle again on Lozano's end before he asked, "You live in Three Rivers, is that right?"

"Yes sir."

"That's an hour away. Why don't you bring the phone with you and just leave it in the car while you run? That way you've got it around if something happens."

Henry's mind scrambled for an answer, but all he could come up with was, "Well, you know, I'm not one of these people who needs to constantly be on my phone. It feels good to get away from it sometimes."

"Alright. Well, Mr. Wallis, I'll get to the reason for all this. It appears that a murder was committed in the park during a period of time that we know—" Lozano hit that word hard "—you were in the vicinity. If you're telling me that you don't remember going to the park on the day that we know you were there, could I ask that you meet me at the park? We could walk around together, and once you re-acquaint yourself with the place, we can see if anything comes back from your visit."

"Like what?"

"Anything. Something or someone that you saw mostly."

"When would you want to do this?"

"As soon as possible. After all, this is an active investigation."

"Alright, how about Thursday after I get out of school?"

"Sounds good. I look forward to meeting you."

When Lozano hung up, he put his pen down on the yellow legal pad of notes and leaned back to stare at his newly repaired ceiling. He'd been making good progress contacting the list of phone owners who'd been in the park around the time of the murder, yet none had proffered any helpful information so far. But the phone call with this kid Wallis felt different.

Lozano used a well-practiced tone with his cold calls, one purposely designed to sound uninviting, almost threatening. No matter the crime he was investigating, the vast majority of people he interviewed weren't involved. As a result, he figured it didn't hurt to let the average citizen sweat a little. After all, he reasoned, everybody has something they're feeling guilty about. Maybe a spook would help them be better people in the future. And for those rare occasions when he was unknowingly establishing first contact with a perpetrator, a menacing tone would hopefully start the anxiety train rolling.

Lozano looked at his printout. Henry's phone had been at the park for an even sixty minutes on the morning in question. He'd said that his runs took about forty-five minutes. Lozano could spot him that.

But who doesn't remember whether they've visited a park an hour away within the last few weeks? And he says he left his phone behind when going to run that far from home? Lozano had no more insight into the mind of most Texas teenagers than he would have a Martian that landed on his front yard and walked into his living room, but one thing he knew with absolute certainty was the average kid these days would rather leave an appendage at home than their phone, especially for that long a period of time.

Lozano's ears began to feel warm. Yes, this phone call definitely felt different.

Ten minutes after finishing the phone call with Lozano, Henry was back in the school library's computer lab. The rain was now a downpour, throwing wavy reflections on the walls from the windows. The third computer terminal he checked was still logged on from a previous user, so he set his backpack on the floor next to the carrel and poked his head outside the doorway. An elderly librarian's assistant slowly pushed a cart overflowing with books between the stacks while re-shelving, the only person in sight. He returned to the unattended computer.

At the computer, he opened a search engine and thought hard. He was certain he'd powered down his phone on the day in question, he'd bet his life on that. Actually, he had bet his life on that. Until fifteen minutes ago, he also thought he'd been certain that no one could track a phone that was turned off. Now he needed to learn more about that.

His first search was simple. He typed in, "Can police trace a cell phone that is turned off?"

The first three links seemed to confirm his belief. As he skimmed over the source material on three tech websites, they all confirmed what he thought he knew. If you completely powered down your phone, its physical location could not be traced. Period. It was basically as if the battery had run out on the phone. It just wouldn't work.

This made him worry all the more. So why did Lozano contact him? What else could he have on Henry?

Curious, he clicked a link to a Reddit sub-thread. The first part of the thread described various users' frustrations with Android phones then got technical with complaints about coding problems. He wondered why this thread showed up on his search when he suddenly came across the relevant portion.

A user with the screen name "gearhead82" posted:

> "All Android users should be aware of a new trojan making the rounds that's been named "PowerOffHijack." When you press

the power button on your device, the virus will make a visual appear that fakes the dialogue box and shutdown animation sequence displayed on your phone's screen when actually shutting down. It leaves the screen looking black as though a proper shutdown occurred, and then proceeds to spy on you in the background. Apps purchased through Google Play Store appear to be okay but beware when buying from any of the third-party app stores that have looser restrictions. The code for the malware appears to contact Chinese servers, so be aware!"

Henry felt uneasy. He used an Android.

He searched the term "PowerOffHijack" and a long list of links appeared. Clicking on several at random, they confirmed the Reddit poster's warning. It wasn't a conspiracy theory or over-hyped internet bullshit. A virus was making the rounds of Android phones which mimicked a power down, but secretly stayed active and prowling your phone, as well as continuing to interact with cell phone towers.

This was bad. If the virus had infected his phone, he'd left an electronic fingerprint behind every time he'd gone to the park. And now he was getting phone calls from a homicide detective.

He took out his smart phone, toggled over to Norton mobile security and ran an anti-malware scan that took about ninety seconds to complete. Sure enough, a results screen notified him that one virus had been detected, associated with a third-party zombie-killing game he'd downloaded for free about a year before. A helpful button at the bottom of the display asked if he wanted to uninstall the app.

"Not just yet," he said out loud. Uninstalling the app now would clear the virus but wouldn't tell him the malware's identity. Instead, he set the Android aside for the moment and pulled his laptop from his backpack. After it powered up, he went onto a tech site and pulled sample code to help with diagnostics for thousands of viruses world-wide. Within ten minutes, Henry found the code for PowerOffHijack. Copying it, he then went onto a website he'd encountered during his explorations of the dark web. This site was a community for hackers, with a chat board whose participants protected their identities with layers of security that would make the CIA jealous.

Checking his watch, he saw that he was running late to get home and he made a mental note to text his mother with an excuse when he finished. Then he posted:

"Need to backdoor my way into my android to check for PowerOffHijack code. Suggestions?"

He crossed his arms and watched the rainwater cascade down the panes of glass, periodically hitting refresh. Six minutes later, he'd received his answer. Plugging his Android into the laptop, he followed the instructions of the anonymous user and was rewarded by a display box on his laptop that displayed reams and reams of code, the equivalent of his phone's genetics, rolling on and on. Henry opened the search function, then pasted the virus' code into the query box and hit "search."

The hit was immediate. The virus' code was buried somewhere in his phone's guts.

The phone had been running the entire time Henry was at the park, and that was how Lozano had found him.

He stared at the screen for a few moments, then took a long, deep breath and exhaled slowly before deleting the virus as an afterthought, electronically closing the barn door after the horse escaped. This hadn't been the news he'd wanted, but at least it was better to know. Now he could make plans.

He gathered up his gear and left the computer lab, texting his mother a lie in a manner long-practiced.

CHAPTER TWENTY-SIX

5:40 p.m.—Thursday, October 31st

Two does grazed on clover at the base of the Juan Seguin Park sign as Lozano pulled into the parking lot. He had the lot to himself except for a lanky teenager leaning against the quarter panel of a tan Buick sedan, legs crossed, palms on the hood. That's not the pose of a kid who's nervous, he thought.

"Henry Wallis?" The kid nodded, unsmiling. "I'm Detective Lozano." As he extended his hand, he assessed the kid, giving him a long look.

Lean, verging on scrawny, definitely a runner's physique. Close-cropped black hair, strong grip. His expression was vacant, his eyes narrow and, in this light, yellow.

Lozano got to the point. "Any of this looking familiar?"

"Yeah, I remember this place now that I see it again."

"Do you remember where you went for your run?" Lozano led Henry over to a lacquered map of the park's trails painted on a large piece of plywood at the trailhead.

"Mm-hmm. I try to run north-south so I don't have the sun in my eyes when it's coming up." He traced his finger along the trails' dotted lines, drawing a loop that Lozano saw would have taken him past the vagrant's camp.

"You see anything suspicious while you were on your run?"

"Suspicious? No."

"Did you leave the trail at any point?"

"Mm-mm. Nope. Just concentrating on my pace."

"Okay. Let's go take a look at the area that's of particular interest."

Lozano led the way down the trail. Wallis followed far enough behind that Lozano had to raise his voice slightly to ask questions as they walked.

"On the day of your run, did you encounter any of the homeless people who live in the park? Maybe any other park visitors?"

"Not to my recollection," Wallis said. "In fact, I came out here late yesterday right before the park closed to walk around by myself and see if anything jogged my memory. Nothing did."

Reaching the spot on the trail closest to the murder scene, Lozano saw boot prints and thick mud created a new path to the encampment, a vestige from the law enforcement personnel trudging back and forth during the storm. The partially collapsed blue tent was visible in the clump of trees, the police tape still squaring it off.

Stopping and turning, Lozano said, "By the path you took, you would've come down this trail. How about this spot? Any of this look familiar?"

"Nope," Wallis said as he caught up, looking around blankly. Then, pointing, he said, "Wait a minute. I just had some flashback with that blue tarp over there." The kid closed his eyes, as though thinking hard, trying to dredge something up from the depths. "Shit, what was it?" He pinched the bridge of his nose in an effort of concentration. "Can we go take a look over there? Maybe it'll jar something loose."

Lozano let Henry walk first, staying close behind. The kid walked slowly, swiveling his head, scanning the area. The kid looked nonchalant, the furthest thing from anxious. So why couldn't he shake his feeling about this kid?

The kid ducked under the yellow tape then stood in silence at the base of a large tree at the back of the hobo's camp. Wallis spun in a slow circle, studying the scene closely, arms crossed, brow furrowed until he faced Lozano once again and said, "No, I'm sorry, Detective, I was wrong. I had thought this looked familiar but—" He snapped his fingers suddenly and pointed at Lozano as a look of realization crossed his face. "You know what? I know what it was. This tarp reminded me of a tent I saw on a Netflix show I was watching, a murder mystery. 'The Shantytown Killings,' or something like that. You seen it?"

"No," Lozano said without inflection.

Nodding, Wallis said, "It was pretty good, you should check it out. Anyway, that's what I was thinking of. I've definitely never been here before."

Lozano couldn't shake the feeling things were not as they seemed. If this was his guy, was the kid getting some kind of ego trip out of standing at the crime scene with his pursuer? Contrary to what one saw on TV and in the movies, most of the murders he'd worked in his career weren't dramatic. People usually killed each other without forethought in arguments about the three great motivators in life: money, power, and/or sex. Momentary rages combined with judgments impaired by alcohol or drugs, that was Lozano's wheelhouse. In over three decades on the job, he could count on one hand the number of times he'd dealt with a cold-blooded son of a bitch who enjoyed cat-and-mouse games with the cops, and this kid's expression was so blunted, he didn't appear to be getting a thrill from this.

"Okay. Well, I appreciate your coming out this early to meet me," Lozano said, heading back through the mud toward the trail.

"No problem. I'm sorry I couldn't be more help to—" the kid paused, his speech cut off in mid-thought.

Lozano stopped and turned. Wallis was staring hard at the base of the tree next to him, the one to which the tarp's rope was tied. As Lozano watched, Wallis squatted and said, "What's this?" then reached toward the tree's gnarled roots.

Realization hit Lozano like a lightning bolt.

He leaped at the teen, shouting, "Don't move, goddammit!" The two men were separated by ten yards and Lozano closed the distance in a few seconds. Wallis' fingers had just touched the moist soil when Lozano ran into him hard, throwing his weight behind a forearm to Wallis' shoulder. The impact bowled the boy over, his feet momentarily pointing toward the leafy canopy before he came to rest on his side amid the undergrowth.

In a flash, Lozano was on him, pinning Wallis down with one knee on his chest. The kid held a clump of moist earth in a right fist closed so tight his fingers blanched. Lozano grabbed the wrist in an immobilizing grip, the two men tussling in silence broken only by their grunts of effort, both aware of the consequences for the winner and the loser of this struggle.

Lozano slowly overpowered the younger man, peeling his fingers back to expose the contents of Wallis' closed fist.

There on Wallis' palm, sitting among the dirt and a few leaves and stray grass roots, lay the vagrant's five rotten teeth.

Wallis wheezed from his position under Lozano's knee, "I saw these sitting at the base of the tree over there. Do you think this is something that might be important?"

Lozano sank back then stood, his knees popping as he breathed heavily from the sudden exertion. It had all come to him in an abrupt flash. The kid's off-hand mentioning that he came to the park the previous day alone. His voluntary disclosure of the path he'd taken which ran by the campsite. His conjuring an excuse to get to the campsite accompanied by Lozano. It all made sudden sense, but just a fraction late.

The kid had wanted to dispose of the teeth in a way that assured they could never be used against him as evidence. Now the teeth were out of his possession, with a good explanation for why his DNA would be found all over them. Wallis had come last night and planted them at the base of this tree, and he'd told Lozano that he'd come to the park the previous evening to explain his presence if any efforts were made to place him in the vicinity again.

The fact that Wallis discovered the teeth by himself despite the area already having been searched by investigators would be blamed on sloppy police work and the rainstorm. Any defense lawyer worth their salt would be able to make the argument that their well-meaning client, there only to assist the police in their investigation, had actually helped the investigators, doing their job for them in finding this important evidence, and in return for his trouble, he was made the target of harassment. The only question would be whether the judge tossed the case as a summary judgment or not.

Wallis stood and brushed the dirt off his t-shirt and shorts. Then he said, "I assume you'll be wanting these?" He poured the teeth, dirt and all, into Lozano's palm, then said, "I'm guessing we're done here?"

For the first time, Wallis' gaunt features broke into a crazy grin. His yellow eyes locked on Lozano with a stare so intense the entirety of both pupils were visible, and Lozano knew he was seeing on the kid's face an expression that he'd only shown to two people in the world, with the other finishing his days on a slab at the Bexar county morgue.

Lozano said, "This isn't finished. Not by a long shot, you cocky little fuck."

That look of insanity was still plastered on the kid's face as he said, "Maybe so, maybe no." He left Lozano standing in place, heading down a path he clearly knew well back toward the parking lot. The last thing Lozano heard was the kid whistling to himself, a tune that sounded familiar. It came to him in a flash of recognition. His grandkids loved the song, playing it all the time. It was "Bring It On."

CHAPTER TWENTY-SEVEN

6:20 p.m.—Thursday, October 31st

On the drive back to Three Rivers, Henry allowed himself ten minutes to fantasize about feeding a bound and gagged Lozano into a wood chipper feet-first before getting to the business of replaying the events in his mind.

He went over his conversation with the detective analytically, probing for details that he may have missed in real time which could become problematic. He'd taken a huge risk with this plan, planting the teeth, knowingly exposing himself as the killer to Lozano. In the end it had been close, the old cop had caught on at the last second and almost ruined everything. But Henry had pulled it off. He'd permanently gotten rid of the only physical connection that existed tying him to the murder and now no matter what Lozano knew he couldn't prove anything, and Henry knew enough about the law to be certain that was the only thing that mattered.

He cursed his broken brain that it had come to this. Not so much its drive to commit the murder in the first place. That was what it was. But he'd discovered something else about himself in the last few days, something that was unsettling for his future prospects.

He'd recognized immediately after the phone call with Lozano that he had to get rid of the teeth. They were his only physical connection to the crime, the only evidence that could prove anything. It killed him to have to part ways with his souvenirs given what he'd gone through to acquire them, but there was just no other option. They had to go.

That night, he'd told his parents after supper that he was going out for a quick run. Taking the teeth with him, he'd trotted along a path he took where town ended and the desert started. At a point where the trail made a hard-right turn by a bend in a creek, Henry paused and checked for any other joggers or hikers. Seeing none, he splashed across the shallow stream and scrabbled five feet up the far bank, the cascading muddy mixture making it difficult to get footholds. Once up on the other side, he jogged in the moonlight for a quarter mile away from the trail, bushwhacking his own path through the creosote bushes along the flat escarpment. Standing among a cluster of nondescript sotol bushes several minutes later, he stopped and checked his surroundings again. Confident that he was alone, he hit his knees and used his hands to quickly scoop a ten-inch-deep hole in the sand and clay. He took one last, lingering look at the teeth sitting in the cup of his palm, then poured them into their resting place before filling the hole back in.

The disposal complete, he paused at the creek on his way back to the trail to wash his hands. Inspecting them in the moonlight, he would have to work on the clay under his nails later at home, but for now, he'd fixed a huge problem. An existential one even. So, he wondered as he trotted back down the trail toward his car, why didn't he feel any sense of relief after throwing them away?

It only grew worse on the drive back to the house. Something gnawed at him, and it grew with every mile he put between himself and the hole he'd dug. He tried to be logical about it. There was no human way that anyone could stumble across the teeth accidentally. He was fine, in the clear. This was done. Relax, meet with Lozano, keep answering all of his questions with I don't know and I can't recall, and he would be home free. This anxiety about the teeth was something he needed to get over, right now. Tonight.

By the time he walked through the front door and hung his keys on the small butterfly key holder though, it felt like his brain itched. His mind created a scenario for the teeth's discovery that Henry recognized as being irrational. Lozano had secretly been following him with night vision goggles, and even now was digging at the hole with a team of investigators as a DNA analysis machine waited on standby. Try as he might, he couldn't make this image disappear. The doubts kept popping up, like a perverse game of Whack-a-mole. A war raged within him, the higher self versus the primitive lizard brain.

Lying in bed, arm thrown over his eyes, his rational side admitted defeat. The uncertainty that accompanied his imagination was unsustainable. It would not be enough to simply hope the teeth would never be discovered. A different solution would be required.

Two hours later, he trudged with a flashlight across the stream. His footprints made it easy to identify the spot of his crossing, but the sotol bushes had been harder to find. Everything looked alike. *Yeah, no shit* his higher self screamed at him. Twice he had to go back to the point of his entrance onto the escarpment to reorient himself, cursing. Finally, he found the familiar orientation of the sotol bushes and the fresh-turned earth. Scooping at the hole, he was grateful that on his first visit he'd over-ridden his reflex to just fling the teeth into the escarpment's darkness. Had he done so, they'd have been impossible to find and he would lose whatever traces of sanity he still possessed.

When he returned the teeth safely to his pocket, the itch instantly disappeared, the sense of relief like taking off a pair of shoes that were too tight.

Henry checked his watch. The green glow read 04:14. Exhaustion came over him suddenly, like a child jumping on his back. He shuffled back to the trail and didn't bother washing off. He would make up whatever lies he needed for his mother and Sully if they asked questions later. This had been an inconvenient time for him to develop obsessive compulsions, but now that it was a reality it would have to be handled.

On the walk back to the car, he'd tried to think of ways to destroy the teeth, but as those dysfunctional pieces of his brain saw it, sledgehammers and the like amounted to breaking the teeth into smaller pieces, not destroying them. Then the plan for this morning's subterfuge came to him all at once, fully formed. It came with risk but what in life didn't? As he rotated the plan in his mind, probing it for chinks and weaknesses, he liked it better and better. By the time he pushed the button on his key fob and his car blinked back, he'd decided. He would have to expose his guilt to the detective, but do so in the course of an act that made him untouchable.

Collapsing on his bed in his clothes, the last conscious thought that went through his mind before sleep consumed him was that he had this situation under control.

CHAPTER TWENTY-EIGHT

4:45 p.m.—Friday, November 1st

The two young Croats jabbered enthusiastically in the backseat of the LeSabre as the miles of south Texas desert sped by, animated and pointing out the windows at the landscape in childlike excitement. Watching them in the rearview mirror, Alex couldn't help but smile.

When he'd taken Stu's call the day before, he first thought he hadn't heard right. "You want me to do what?"

"Just drive 'em down," Stu had repeated. "I'm already here in Laredo, and they're both in San Antonio right now. They've been working on a special project there for me for the last couple weeks. Neither one of those swingin' dicks speaks a lick of Spanish. Hell, only one speaks English, and he'd have trouble driving a two-button elevator. If you bring 'em down you can save me the trouble of driving a hundred and fifty miles just to turn around and drive back."

And so he found himself chauffeuring two Croatians whose names he kept having to re-ask. The young men seemed good-natured and effete, almost prissy. Both late twenties, Roko was short and pudgy, well-moussed with wire-rimmed glasses and a goatee. Simun was tall, beak-nosed, and long-necked with a mop of stylishly unruly blonde hair. Roko's English was fair, Simun's nonexistent. Their fashion choices tended toward European tighter fits, and their black leather boots were ankle high with zippers on the sides, pictures of hipster refinement.

The two chatted and argued nonstop, with Roko intermittently pausing the conversation to translate for Alex. When asked what they did for Stu, Roko said they handled cyber security for his firm. While they could generally do their work for him from Croatia, this project required face-to-face meetings. This would be their first time in Mexico and, after reading about *Día de los Muertos*, they were excited to be getting out of the hotel room for a weekend, especially at the prospect of first-class accommodations.

As the time and miles passed, Alex found he liked them. Young, interesting, and energetic, they made good road companions.

The traffic waiting to cross into Mexico backed up to the middle of the river bridge. Inching forward in stops and starts, Alex said, "Now listen up. When we get our turn up here, no screwing around. We clear on that? The *federales* do not have a sense of humor."

Roko translated for Simun in a clipped tone as Alex pulled up to the booth, stopping when the large overhead light snapped from green to red. The Mexican Customs Authority official gave Alex's passport a perfunctory glance but spent a long time staring at the two Croatian passports, frequently glancing into the backseat while he inquired about their business in Mexico. Then, snapping the passports shut, he waved Alex out of the main traffic flow toward a single lane angling in the direction of a low concrete building where more officials crawled through a pair of parked cars like ants.

Alex grimaced and muttered, "Son of a bitch."

"What is it?" Roko asked.

"They're gonna toss the car."

"What does this mean, 'toss the car'?"

"You'll see."

Alex piloted the car through a serpentine path of concrete security barriers and into a spot by the inspection station. A different Customs official approached the car accompanied by a soldier in camouflage fatigues carrying an assault rifle at port arms.

"*Apaga tu motor*," the unsmiling official said.

Alex obeyed, killing the motor.

"*Sal del auto.*"

Alex gestured to his companions, opening the doors and slowly exiting the vehicle. Simun raised his arms for a moment, then lowered them again, confusion flitting across his face.

"*Siéntate aquí*," the official said, and pointed at the curb at the head of unoccupied stall nine.

Alex sat where the agent indicated, and signaled the Croats to join him, patting the concrete.

The official waved over a subordinate with a pole attached to a small mirror mounted on four wheels. Together, they rolled the mirror beneath the car, inspecting the reflection of the underside of the chassis for contraband. Finding none, he told Alex to open the trunk then pulled the men's bags out and unceremoniously went through them right there on the hot asphalt. Still finding nothing, the official next waved over a man restraining a German Shepherd tugging hard at its leash.

While Alex and his companions watched the dog, the official watched them, searching their faces for signs of apprehension. The dog snuffled excitedly through all of their belongings with long-practiced movements, registering nothing. The dog's handler then moved on to the car's interior, giving the animal enough slack to jump onto the seats front and back.

Again, finding nothing, the official dismissed the dog and its handler before waving toward the exit and scowling at the three gringos, "*Yaváyanse a la chingada.*"

Alex began stuffing his clothes back into his suitcase and Simun followed his lead. Roko, however, stood looking expectantly at the official and at his own clothes piled in a heap.

"Something to say, *pendejo?*" the Mexican said in lightly accented English.

"*No, todo bien,*" Alex said, giving Roko a look and pulling him down to a squat.

As the young Croatian began repacking his bag, Alex hissed, "How do you say 'dumbass' in Croatian?"

After crossing into Mexico over the river bridge at *Puente Internacional Número II*, the first difference Alex noticed between this Nuevo Laredo and that of his youth was the visibility of the military presence around the city. Amid the throng of raucous festivalgoers—faces painted in death masks and sporting garlands of roses—grim-faced soldiers with automatic weapons slung at odd angles were stationed at random street corners as they closely watched the passing revelers.

Sitting at a light, Alex and the Croats saw a large *mercado* ringing a park. The shoppers and vendors haggled and carried on, unperturbed by the armored personnel carrier stationed yards away in the middle of the grassy square. A soldier in the turret, his helmet crooked, leaned on a mounted fifty caliber machine gun and smoked a cigarette.

The atmosphere felt gritty and real, exhilarating with just the right amount of danger. The smell of roasting meat would waft into the car from time to time, alternating with the odor of mud or cleaning products. Many of the side roads were cobblestone, and the foot traffic on the main thoroughfares bustled with rowdy crowds, the street economy alive and well. With the windows down, the interior of the car filled with music from passing radios, shouts from small *tiendas*, sirens, and horns. It felt good to be back, he said to himself. He'd missed this.

Stu had arranged a villa for the four of them near the top of the *Palacio Imperial*. Blooming agave lined the luxury hotel's long, looping driveway. A clean-cut bellman appeared from nowhere and greeted them enthusiastically, saying he would see to getting their bags to their room.

The marbled lobby amplified the indistinct chatter of the well-heeled crowd. A domed glass atrium threw natural light on an ornate fountain in the center of the entrance hall. Atop the plinth stood a woman in long, flowing robes holding a bouquet of flowers and looking to the sky in a pose of supplication while jets of water shot in long, low arcs from her pedestal. Three small children groped in the water to retrieve coins while their mother reprimanded them, an escaped tendril of hair dangling in her face.

Minutes later, Roko and Simun chattered excitedly as the elevator attendant closed the antique brass scissor gate and the lift groaned upwards.

They found Stu pacing the living room of their suite with a drink in his hand, chatting on his phone in easy conversational Spanish, the Nuevo Laredo skyline behind him through floor-to-ceiling windows that made up the entire wall.

Holding the phone to his chest, he said, "Bar's over there, grab a drink and pick a room, I'll be with y'all in a minute." As he resumed his conversation, the Croats disappeared to explore the opulent space. Alex grabbed a beer from the refrigerator and stood, taking in the view in silence. The Rio Grande snaked its way between the two cities like a glinting silver ribbon.

After hanging up the phone, Stu said, "Glad you boys made it in okay. No problems?"

"Meh," Alex said. "Car got stopped at the crossing. Gave Frick and Frack here a taste of what can happen if you fuck around, though, so there's that." Then, looking around, "This place is incredible."

"Courtesy of a buddy of mine named Luis Espinoza. He's a big boy over here. Luis's got lots of different interests, one of them real estate. We've been doing deals together coming up on twenty years now. Great guy. You'll probably get to meet him at some point this weekend."

"That him on the phone?"

Stu shook his head, exasperated. "No, that's going to be our other companion for the evening, Luis's brother-in-law, guy named Marco Corrales. Man doesn't have the sense to piss downwind. Even Luis doesn't like him, but hell he's family, so what's he gonna do?

"Luis said he's got some kind of high-society obligation tonight for the first night of the festival, a no-gringos-allowed type thing, so it'll be just us and Marco for the evening. Luis's wife has been pushing him to start giving Marco more responsibility in his business, so over the last couple months I've noticed that he's been around more. This trip's supposed to be about me getting to know Marco better, but frankly, over the last couple months I've already seen enough of that asshole to form an opinion."

By this time, it was dusk. Roko asked, "Is there any particular place you are planning to go, or shall we just see where the evening takes us?"

"Marco wants to head down to Boys' Town."

Roko looked confused. "Explain, please?"

Stu said, "Texans have been coming to border towns to howl at the moon since forever. So, a long time ago, Nuevo Laredo decided it would be a good idea to concentrate the seedier side of things in one place to kind of insulate it from the rest of the city. Here they called it '*La Zona de Tolerancia*', but on the Texas side it was mostly just called 'Boys' Town.' That's where most of the prostitution was focused, nightclubs, hot sheet joints, that kind of thing. They built big concrete walls around the place so there's only one way in or out, and it has a police checkpoint. Even got its own little police station.

"Since they first built it, though, the city got a lot bigger and those businesses outgrew *La Zona* so now you can find whatever you're looking for in pretty much any part of the city. It was before my time, but I'm told *La Zona* itself hasn't changed much since the '70s. It isn't nearly as nice as all this"—he gestured at their luxurious surroundings—"but Marco loves it down in that sleazy shit-hole. For fellas who've never been here before, though, it'll make a fun place to start the night."

Roko smiled as he translated all of this for Simun, who grinned widely and gave Alex and Stu a thumbs up.

Stu said, "Okay fellas, it's time for 'Stu's Rules for the Road' down here. First thing, put a hundred dollars in your wallet and the rest in your shoe. Then if you run low, you go to the bathroom and take more out from your shoe, a little at a time. Keeps you from flashing too much money around," he explained. "People around here notice a big wad of cash. For *gringos*, you start looking like a target. The exchange rate right now is about nineteen *pesos* to the dollar, so you're gonna see that your money goes a real long way. Trust me, you won't need your wit and charm to impress any of the girls you'll be meeting tonight.

"Second thing, keep your wallets and passports in the front pockets of your pants. Nothing you care about goes in your rear pockets. Pick-pockets are all over the place down here, especially when you get in a crowd and people start jostling."

Next, he turned to Roko and said, "Lift your shirt."

He looked confused. "I'm sorry, I do not understand."

Stu tugged upward at Roko's shirt. "Come on, lift it up."

Still looking puzzled, Roko did as Stu ordered, untucking his pressed black shirt and lifting it to his nipples.

Stu pulled a Sharpie from his shirt pocket and began writing in thick block letters on Roko's plump belly. When he finished he stepped back to admire his handiwork. Roko couldn't read the writing upside down, but the others could see Stu had written the name and address of the hotel in clear block letters and numerals.

"Sharpie won't run when you get sweaty. We should be together all night, but worst case and we get separated, all you got to do is lift your shirt and tell your ride 'Take me here.' Don't ask me why I know to do that." Roko translated for his countryman while Stu did the same for Alex and Simun.

Stu continued, "Last thing. All the *federales* down here are corrupt as hell. There's two kinds of interactions you can have with the cops in Nuevo Laredo. The first kind is just the hassle. You'll be minding your own business, when some *federale* who thinks you look like you can afford it'll come up with a bullshit reason to stop and frisk you. Meantime, he'll plant a knife in your back pocket, then take you to jail on a weapons charge. You post bail, which he sticks in his pocket, and you walk. It's expensive but at least there's no real consequences other than you're out a little bit of money.

Stu's expression became grim. "The other kind is when you actually do break the law in a serious way, and if that's the case, God help you. Anything is on the table, up to and including winding up in a hole in the desert. You boys understand?" Once again Roko translated all of this for Simun.

Alex pointedly said to Simun, "So if a cop starts to fuck with you like happened back at the border crossing, instead of getting an attitude, what are we going to do this time?"

"Suck it up, buttercup," Simun said with an eye roll, practicing the phrase Alex taught him after the incident at the inspection station.

Stu smiled and finished his drink. "Alright then ramblers, let's get ramblin'."

CHAPTER TWENTY-NINE

7:45 p.m.—Friday, November 1ˢᵗ

They were to meet Marco at a *cantina* called *El Coyote Borracho*. The rendezvous was a short three blocks from the hotel, and they strolled, taking their time as they pushed through clusters of small children who swarmed them on the sidewalk. Like moths to a flame, the children circled and collided with the four *gringos*, jostling each other and jumping in the air to attract the men's attention to buy their trinkets. The children followed them for half a block until, sensing futility, they dispersed before reconvening by the hotel entrance to await another prospect.

They heard the sounds of the festival in the near distance. The crowd flowed at a right angle to their path, heading eastward in a sea of decorative costumes toward the sound of Tejano music.

"Big kickoff to things tonight out on the *Plaza Ignacio*

Zaragoza—that's where all these folks are going," Stu said.

El Coyote Borracho felt old in a way that contrasted with the youth of the crowd. Narrow-walled, the stamped tin ceiling was easily fifteen feet high, with fans that barely moved the smoky air. A weathered oak bar ran the length of one wall, backed by a mirror that reflected the light of a string of gas lamps. Hundreds of pictures of coyotes covered the walls to the ceiling. Old photographs and new paintings, charcoal sketches and black velvet; the medium didn't seem to matter to the owner. It was kitschy bordering on obsession.

Stu blazed a trail through the crowd and into the depths of the bar, the others following him like a conga line. An unpretentious wooden door opened onto a small courtyard where a dozen people milled about. The brick patio was framed on all four sides by high brick walls, and when they craned their necks skyward, the four men could see a square of stars.

Stu headed to a short bar on their left, but Alex was drawn to a grotto of stacked stones. In its center was a large bronze sculpture of the Capitoline Wolf with its two suckling babes. Several fresh red roses lay at the base of the statue.

Stu tapped the shoulder of an overweight Mexican sporting a pompadour and a Pancho Villa mustache. Turning, the man threw his hands in the air in excitement at seeing Stu, then bear-hugged him with a shouted greeting, spilling some of his cocktail down Stu's back. He wore an expensive-looking suit with a dress shirt open to the third button, and high-end Italian shoes while the gas lamps glinted off a flashy watch. His pinky ring and a necklace looked to have multiple diamonds, Alex estimated the man's ostentatious ensemble ran well into five figures head-to-toe.

The man swayed slightly as he gesticulated, engrossed in telling a story. Stu's expression suggested his captivity in the conversation was causing him physical pain, but the man seemed oblivious. It dragged on for several more seconds before the man abruptly bellowed in laughter and slapped

Stu on the back so hard he momentarily lost balance.

Catching Alex's eye, Stu motioned him over.

"Alex, got somebody for you to meet. This is Marco Corrales. Marco, this is Alex, a friend of mine from Three Rivers."

Alex extended his hand, but Marco swatted it away before pulling him in close and drunkenly hugging him. In close, the smells of alcohol, cigarettes, and cologne fought for dominance.

"This is how we greet new friends here *mi amigo*. A friend of Stu's is a friend of mine," he said with a touch of an accent.

As Marco resumed his previous conversation with Stu, Alex tuned him out and surveyed the crowd. Roko had struck up a conversation with two women nearby. Simun looked on, mute but smiling. Practicing his slang, he told the taller of the two, "If loving you is wrong, I do not want to be right."

Looking at Alex, Stu made a twirling motion in the air with one finger, then pointed at Marco, the signal to round everyone up because Marco had decided they were leaving.

Outside, Alex got out his phone to hail a ride, but Marco said, "No, no *amigo*. It is a beautiful night, and a walk is a reminder that it is good to be alive, no? *Venga, venga*." He set off down the sidewalk.

It was now fully dark, and Marco and Stu led the way, Marco carrying on a monologue in Spanish. Roko and Simun brought up the rear, speaking in Croatian and seeming to enjoy themselves. As the blocks rolled by, the neighborhoods transitioned, with fewer festivalgoers. Street lamps changed from high-end halogen suns to those that cast a dull, pallid glow. After twenty minutes of walking, they found themselves heading down a street with dark buildings where young men in shabby clothes loitered in unlit doorways. Some watched the quiet of the dimly lit street out of boredom, some for opportunity.

By these sallow arcs, Alex surveyed the beggars lining their path, squatting or sitting with their backs against the cinderblock walls: all old, mostly male, many infirm. Their filthy clothes hung from their frames, revealing sunken rib cages and scaphoid abdomens. Shoeless, they shook clay bowls and solicited alms. None of his companions seemed to notice as they carried on their spirited conversations in other languages around him, but Alex continued to study the street dwellers as they drifted by.

Alex pulled up short. While other beggars were trying to get the attention of the night's pedestrians, calling out and rattling their change receptacles, here was one who simply appeared to be staring straight ahead, indifferent to the world on the sidewalk in front of him.

Staring would be the wrong word, Alex realized, as the milky corneas covering both of his eyes suggested that *sus ojos* had been unseeing for some time. The beggar's right leg was angulated below the knee, a fracture that healed without setting of the bone, and a pair of crutches lay across a plastic trash bag to his left. The man sat hunched, back against the cool concrete of the wall and chin tilted upward, mouth agape. His knees were bent, and his bare left heel was pulled up under his right thigh. His hands were beside him on the sidewalk, empty palms up, Christ-like.

Alex squatted in front of the beggar. Through his thick mat of beard, he appeared edentulous. His forehead, nose, and cheeks were scarred, suggestive of the caustic injury that cost him his sight. He found himself wondering how old the man had been when he suffered the injury, whether it had been an accident or had someone done this to him. He wondered whether it had been the injury that set him on this path.

The man's unbuttoned shirt revealed a few dozen telltale circular scars scattered across his chest and abdomen, the marks of a heroin habit caused by cigarettes falling from stoned lips during the drug's initial kick.

But what caused Alex to break his stride was his instinctive recognition, even at a glance from several feet, the man did not appear to be breathing. Alex squatted there, watching the man's chest for several seconds. No movement. Steadying himself with one hand, he leaned forward and placed two fingers on the man's neck. No pulse, and the beggar's skin felt cold. Dead. And for no more than a few hours.

Roko and Simun stopped and witnessed all this, but Stu and Marco hadn't noticed until they were well down the block.

Turning, Marco called out, "*Oigan, pendejos,* what are you waiting for? *Venga.*" He waved them to continue walking, but when they ignored him, he and Stu backtracked.

Looking around, Alex did not see any signs of violence, nor did he see any paraphernalia that suggested an overdose. With his arms at his side and palms skyward, the Mexican's corpse seemed to be gesturing in surprise or confusion, asking whomever was in front of him what had happened.

Roko asked. "What is happening?"

"Poor bastard's dead," Alex said, continuing to look down at the man's remains with pity.

"Should we not be doing something?"

"Like what?"

"I do not know. Call for an ambulance?"

"No, he's been dead for a couple of hours. Nothing for an ambulance to do."

At this point, Marco and Stu arrived.

"*¿Qué pasa?*" Marco asked, gesturing at the scene.

Alex answered solemnly, "I noticed this guy wasn't breathing when we were walking by. Looks like he died within the last couple hours."

Marco was unfazed, "He may be dead, but we are not. Come, come." When no one moved, Marco said, "He is past the point of caring, *amigos*, I promise you. Watch." He bent down and slapped the corpse twice in the face, hard, his open palm making a sound like the crack of a bullwhip. He shouted in the man's face, "*¡Oye, hombre! ¡Hola! ¡Hola!*"

The other four men watched in appalled silence.

"¿Estás ahí, viejo? ¿Eh? ¿Te gusta eso?" Marco shouted, and began to laugh. He slapped the old man again, then grabbed him by the shoulder and shook him violently. The old man's head whipped to and fro, as though vigorously nodding yes. *"¿Eh, te gusta eso? ¡Hola, hola!"* Then Marco shoved the old man's corpse back toward the concrete wall. It hit with a dull thud before coming to rest slumped to the right, his head lolling like a chicken's after its neck has been broken.

Marco stood and looked at the four other men, satisfied he'd made his point. He began to walk down the sidewalk once again, gesturing for the others to follow.

"Are we just going to leave him here?" Roko asked.

Alex nodded glumly, and he and Stu began to head in Marco's direction.

Simun and Roko spoke in Croatian, then followed. As they caught up to Alex and Stu, Roko said, "I have never seen a dead body before. That seemed disrespectful."

Alex checked that Marco was still out of earshot and answered, "Yeah, I hear you. Stu, man, what the hell? Jesus, what was that show that Marco put on back there?"

Stu shook his head and mumbled, "Look, fellas, I'm sorry but babysitting this shit heel for tonight is the price of admission for the weekend."

They turned onto *Calle Monterrey* and shortly the imposing, gray walls of *La Zona* came into view. If not for the graffiti, the scene would look medieval. The Croatians were getting re-engaged with the prospect of fun, walking more quickly, urging on their companions. Stu and Marco were deep in conversation and had slowed their pace, causing them to lag behind.

At *La Zona's* checkpoint entrance on *Circunvalación Casanova,* two policemen manned the swinging arm of the gate. One, a raconteur, was telling an elaborate story about two *gringas* he'd suspected of smuggling drugs, only to find after detaining them that not only were the two women clean, but one was the daughter of the mayor of Laredo. Without interrupting his own story, he waved Alex and the Croatians over and patted them down perfunctorily. His engrossed colleague listened in rapt attention, raising the arm on the gate as an afterthought.

When Stu and Marco caught up, they received an entirely different reception. The *federales* greeted them with familiar waves and smiles, and raised the gate's arm with a manner that seemed almost apologetic. Marco and Stu barely broke stride, nodding to the two policemen as they entered Boys' Town, obviously knowing where they were going.

The unpaved roads in *La Zona* appeared soupy. Marco and his expensive shoes stayed out of the street. There was a good deal of foot traffic about for this early in the evening.

As they walked down *Lucrecia Borgia Avenue*, Alex saw little had changed since his last visit years ago. Most of the establishments were still dirty, low-lying buildings with primitive hand-painted signs leaning next to unpainted wooden doors or strings of glass beads that rattled like a diamondback's tail. Other businesses just had door-shaped holes in the stucco walls, or a limp sheet hanging across the entrance in the breezeless air. From the street, all the interiors appeared as dark as the sins inside.

They occasionally passed abandoned structures claimed by weeds, untended and forgotten. Two buildings had been gutted by fire on one block, their roofs gone leaving only charred joists and studs jutting toward the sky like black ribs.

Tired-looking women in easy-access attire leaned against the walls, smoking and watching. They bobbed their heads in time to muffled music thumping from the larger, finished buildings and propositioned passerby who made eye contact with "*¿Quieres fiesta?*" Some women smiled while doing their hectoring; others were more blasé.

On one muddy side street, the men came upon an argument between a diminutive woman wearing a merry-widow with a pleather skirt and a milquetoast man in a worn denim jacket. The five of them stopped and watched as she screamed at him nose-to-nose in such rapid cadence that Alex had trouble following her Spanish, but the gist was she questioned his manhood for not defending her honor in an argument with some *vaqueros,* punctuating her points with slaps to his head and torso. These were delivered with such vigor that her too-large top drooped, allowing her saggy left breast to slip out of its lacy confines. It swung to and fro, like a violent wrecking ball.

The man cowed and tried to shield himself in an effort as futile as keeping the ground dry by catching raindrops. In a moment of respite as she caught her breath, he mumbled something the five men couldn't hear. His inaudible comment made her shriek with fury and she flew into an even more virulent rage, launching herself upwards at him and clawing at his eyes.

He stumbled backward in panic and threw his hands over his face to keep from being blinded. Losing his balance, he fell into the mud.

In a flash she was on him, straddling him and continuing to scratch at him in an out-of-control fury as he begged for help from bystanders and God.

The Croatians ran over and, each taking an arm, lifted her off him. She continued to try to get at the man, screaming obscenities and kicking at the air, her skirt now bunched around her waist. While they restrained her, Roko yelled at the man in English to escape. With her temporarily incapacitated, the man slowly stood and wiped his cut and bleeding face with a stained handkerchief before returning it to the rear pocket of his mud-stained blue jeans. He spit on the ground and unleashed a stream of invective that started as a rumble but quickly built to a roar as he jabbed his index finger in her direction. She wrenched free from Roko and Simun and leapt at him once again. As they tumbled into the mud once more, the two young men looked at each other and shrugged.

"Fuck them, they deserve each other," Roko said as he and Simun returned to their amused colleagues.

"If you are through playing *los santos de la Zona*, we leave now?" Marco said, grinning.

"Yes, that was our good deed for the day. By the way, where are we going?" Roko asked.

"You will see."

They followed Marco down *Casanova*as, which looped to follow the concrete wall's perimeter. Presently, the road made a right turn to parallel the southern wall for a distance of several city blocks. It was in the middle of this stretch that they saw a windowless two-story structure, the sign on its façade reading "Dallas Cowboys", outlined in navy blue, silver, and white. A crowd of backlit figures were visible in silhouette behind the roof's parapet.

In contrast to the gaudiness of the frontage and sign, the entrance was a simple stainless steel door offset from the middle of the building. Two large Mexican men stood at each side of the door and Marco greeted them effusively, hugging each and giving back slaps. Putting his hand on Stu's shoulder, he said something to them in Spanish, then gestured to Alex and the Croatians. The men nodded, and one of them rapped hard on the heavy metal door. It opened from the inside, and disco music spilled out at them.

Marco led the way inside, and the door clanged shut behind them.

CHAPTER THIRTY

9:45 p.m.—Friday, November 1ˢᵗ

In a dark anteroom, a mountain of a man appraised them while disco music pulsed so loud Alex felt the bass line rumble in his chest. Well over six feet tall, his stomach hung over his belt buckle, and tufts of back hair escaped over the collar of his plain blue t-shirt. Pulling back the left half of a dark green velvet curtain, he said without a smile, "*Diviértanse.*"

The interior of the club was brightly lit, large and open, the size of a small warehouse. Mirrored walls reflected a rotating spray of lights over the clientele while multiple disco balls and water spots dotted the ceiling.

A long runway dominated the room. Multicolored concert lights illuminated the stage, alternately bathing dancers in red, blue, or white while long-legged women clung to poles mounted on the stage, spinning and grinding.

Clothed dancers circulated the floor, working the crowd of about twenty patrons for private performances. The sound system played "It's Raining Men."

A short, round man in an ill-fitting suit with a greasy ponytail approached, squeezing his girth through the maze of tables and chairs on the concourse.

"*¡Bienvenidos, caballeros! ¡Marco, qué felicidad verte de nuevo! ¿Cómo estás?*"

Marco replied, "*Muy bien, mi amigo, muy bien. Es la primera vez que mis amigos vienen aquíi.*"

"*Entiendo. Por favor, siganme.*"

The grubby carpet stuck to their shoes with an adhesive crunch could feel as they walked. At a candle-lit table on the main floor, he pulled up five upholstered, armless chairs and gestured that they sit. Waving over a waitress, she brought three bottles of champagne in ice buckets. The manager told Marco it was compliments of the house, then bowed and wandered off toward the bar. Marco told the waitress to keep the champagne flowing.

An Amazonian dancer, dark-complexioned and muscular, approached Simun smiling. Simun looked to be a shade over six feet tall, and barefooted she might have been taller. Now in six-inch heels, she towered over all of the men in her red corset and blonde wig. "*Te gustaría un baile?*"

Alex asked, "*¿Cuánto cuesta?*"

"*Nueve dólares.*"

"Tell Simun she's asking if he wants a dance, it's nine bucks American," Alex said to Roko.

"I will do no such thing," Roko said, looking up at her with lust. "Tell her instead that I would very much like a dance from her."

Smirking, Alex said, "Roger that. *A mi otro amigo le gustaría un baile.*" She nodded and the other men dutifully moved their chairs to make room. As she signaled the transaction to the manager, Roko said, "This is the price that Simun pays for not knowing the language."

Facing Roko, she straddled him. The chair groaned like

an old man, as though it may break under their bulk. The dancer's towering frame swallowed him. One-handed, she reached behind her back and released the hook-and-eye closures on her corset before tossing it at Simun where it landed in his lap. She laughed, clearly enjoying Roko's reaction, then closed her eyes and began to sway, head back, feeling the music. She leaned toward Roko, brushing her breasts side to side across his face. She began to rock in his lap, seductively, grinding her G-string clad pelvis against Roko's.

Roko was lust incarnate, grasping her buttocks, urging her onward. He tried once to let his hands drift toward the fabric covering her crotch, but she gave him a playful slap and wiggled a finger, no. He faux-pouted, causing her to wink, then lick her lips while reaching down to caress his crotch through his denim.

Finally, the song ended. She stopped her gyrations and smiled again, the mood dispelled. She did not get up, however—instead, raising one eyebrow at Roko.

"What is Spanish for 'again'?" Roko asked, without breaking eye contact.

"*Otra vez*," Alex answered.

"*Otra vez*," Roko said, looking deep into her eyes. She made a quick gesture toward the manager to keep the meter running, and he responded with a curt nod.

Like meerkats, the other dancers working the floor drifted over to the other four men. Simun selected a short and chubby girl, and his hand rubbed circles in the small of her back as she settled onto his lap. Alex looked at the juxtaposition of the two Croats and their partners.

Stu leaned forward and said, "Notice anything funny?"

Alex smirked and said, "Yeah, each of them basically chose a version of the other one."

"So it's not just me?"

"The heart wants what the heart wants," Alex said. Stu laughed, and clapped him on the shoulder.

For the next few hours, Marco went through champagne

and lap dances, distracted and ignoring his companions. Stu selected a girl of his own for a dance, while Alex was content to just keep pouring champagne.

As he got drunker, Roko became increasingly infatuated. The stripper pulled up a chair of her own, and when not dancing for him sat with one massive leg draped over Roko's thigh. Holding his hand in both of hers, she occasionally traced a finger along his jawline or massaged his erection through his pants. Her upper arm was the size of his thigh, and even draped over his leg, her foot sat flush on the floor.

She leaned down to whisper to him, playfully darting a tongue in his ear, closer than needed to be heard over the music. Alex eavesdropped as they taught each other simple words in their languages, Roko occasionally leaning over and asking Alex how to say things like "beautiful" and "stunning."

Alex asked, "Don't you think you're laying it on a little thick? I mean, if you want to take this further than a dance, it's not a seduction, it's a negotiation."

Roko looked hurt. "It is not like that. Yolanda and I have made a connection."

"A what?"

"A connection."

"Without being able to talk to each other?"

Roko slurred, "We speak with our eyes."

Stifling a yawn, Alex checked his watch. Almost two in the morning. He'd lost count of the bottles of champagne that had cycled across the table. The woman perched on Stu's thigh at the moment had a sun-shaped tattoo around her navel and lipstick on her teeth. She sat with her thick legs crossed; her silver stiletto had slipped off her heel and she bounced it off the bottom of her foot to the music. She, Stu, and Alex all sat mute, a sideshow in a decadent circus.

The Croats showed no signs of slowing down, both

happy drunks and sweating profusely. Simun had acquired a feather boa at some point, and Roko had taken to doing tequila shots out of Yolanda's navel.

Marco, on the other hand, became quieter and withdrawn as he continued to drink. As his mood darkened, he would snap at the waitress or dancers, cursing them in slurred Spanish before lapsing back into silence. Marco's eyes swept the room, and locked on Alex's, giving off an air of menace.

Marco stood abruptly, spilling the two girls on his lap to the grimy floor before grabbing one by the elbow and pulling her up. Short and painfully thin, her ribs stood out and accentuated the thick, poorly healed C-section scar on her lower abdomen. Her heavy eyeliner accentuated the fear in her eyes as Marco whispered in her ear, then she tentatively nodded. Pulling her roughly, he led her toward the back of the club as she struggled to keep up in her high heels and they disappeared through a thick green curtain next to the runway.

Alex asked Stu, "The guest of honor appears to have taken his leave. How much longer you wanting to keep this party going?"

"Yeah, you can stick a fork in me, I'm done. That asshole can make his own way home." Stu caught the waitress's eye and made a check mark in the air.

Five minutes later, she brought him the tab. He was running through the charges when a sound like a heavy door slamming shut echoed through the club. The dancers on stage stopped and stood, frozen, watching as two bouncers sprinted through the green curtain, followed by the waddling manager.

The music stopped and the sounds of men shouting and a scuffle could be heard from behind the curtain, followed by an eerie silence. After a few moments, the manager appeared at the curtain, and, finding Stu's eye, gestured for him.

"Aww, hell's bells, what now?" Stu groaned.

He and Alex rose and made their way toward the commotion. Roko and Simun tried to follow, but Roko staggered sideways and ran into a small table, knocking over the beers of two cowboys and soaking their laps. One of them shoved Roko who knocked over an empty table and hit his head on the main stage as he fell. He lay stunned, all thoughts of heroics gone.

Alex turned back and played peacemaker, shouting, "Hey, hey, hey! Easy fellas, easy, sorry about that, just some drunk assholery. Let me get my buddy out of here. He's had enough fun for one night." Two more bouncers rushed over, carrying slapjacks and knocking over empty chairs in their haste to restore order.

"Best be getting that asshole outta here," shouted one cowboy, pointing at Roko and wiping his soaking crotch.

"Working on that, trust me." Alex threw a twenty-dollar bill on the table and said to the waitress, "*Dos más para mis amigos nuevos.*" He motioned for Simun to render aid to Roko, then headed to the green curtain to join Stu.

Behind the drape, Alex found a horror show in progress. On a short hallway lit by bare red bulbs, everyone congregated around the last of three doors where Marco was wild and agitated, enraged at everyone and everything. The front of his suit was bloodstained. In one hand, he held a Glock, jabbing the pistol at the floor in emphasis of his words. Muffled crying and screamed obscenities came from inside the third room. The smell of gunpowder hung thick in the air.

The manager and Stu were talking to Marco in gentle, hushed Spanish while a bouncer looked on. Alex had trouble hearing them over the sound of tears and cursing, but he picked out assurances that everyone there respected him, they all knew he was the man, and he just needed to holster his weapon so no one else got hurt.

Alex peaked in the room and saw Marco's girl sitting on the edge of a loveseat, sobbing and retching while holding a blood-soaked white towel to her face. Blood ran down her

Arthur Herbert

bare chest and puddled between her feet. Across from her, a bouncer sat on the floor with his eyes squeezed shut and cursing loudly while he banged the back of his head against the plywood wall. He writhed in pain while clutching his bicep, and blood trickled steadily down his arm, dripping off his fingertips. Red footprints tracked all over the room and hallway, reminding Alex of an old *Family Circus* cartoon if Billy had lost his mind and ax-murdered the family.

Stu's voice was hypnotic, soothing as he tried to de-escalate Marco. It had its effect as the pistol gradually dipped then dangled by Marco's side. His breathing slowed, and he spoke at a normal volume, but without moving to holster the Glock.

Stu asked Marco if it would be okay for Alex to look at the wounds in the room. Marco nodded, so Stu jerked his chin toward Alex before returning to Marco with that same mesmerizing lilt.

Examining the girl first, Alex said, "*Relaje, señora. Deme la toalla.*" She allowed him to hold the towel, then gently roll it away from her face. "*Necesito examinar su herida.*"

He grimaced at what he found. Her nose was broken, as was her right cheekbone. A ragged four-inch laceration ran across the bridge of her nose to the corner of her mouth. *Shit, that's going to leave a hell of a scar.* At least most of it had stopped bleeding.

As her sobs slowed to sniffles, she asked, "*¿Se ye muy mal?*" To keep the situation controlled, he lied and told her no, he didn't think it was bad. She started crying again, but with an element of relief.

He said, "*Sujeta la toalla.*" She held the towel once again, and he turned his attention to the wounded bouncer, saying, "*Mueve su mano.*" The man's breath slowed to ragged huffs and his hand shook as he removed it from his upper arm. A single nickel-sized wound with tattered edges sat over the muscle belly, and the arm wobbled as though he had a new joint between his shoulder and elbow. The bleeding that arose from the wound had a slight pulsatile arc to it. Alex told the man to hold pressure on the wound, then reached over and removed the man's belt. Retrieving the bouncer's slapjack from where it lay on the floor, Alex used the two to make a crude windlass tourniquet. The Mexican yelped in pain as Alex tightened it, but the pulsatile flow of blood from the wound slowed then ceased.

"I got the bleeding stopped but this guy needs to get to a hospital A.S.A.F.P. That bullet broke his arm and cut an artery. He needs an operation. She needs to go get checked out too and get that cut irrigated out and fixed," he said to Stu.

"Understood," Stu said, still not taking his eyes off Marco. "Marco, is it okay if these folks go to the hospital?"

Again, Marco nodded. Stu motioned with his head and the manager backed into the room. Without taking his eyes off Marco, he removed his suit jacket and placed it over the woman's shoulders. It hung on her like a dress, and she clutched the lapels together with one hand while she held the towel to her midface with the other. Still closely watching Marco through the doorway, the manager helped the bouncer to his feet. The man's arm flopped by his side at an odd angle while he held the tourniquet in place. The manager muttered, "*Venga,*" and the three of them slowly made egress to the green curtain and disappeared.

Once they were out of sight, Stu said, "Marco, *mi amigo, mi compadre*, I need you to put the gun away now, okay?"

Almost in a daze, Marco replaced the gun in his shoulder holster. It was testimony to his tailor that Alex had not noticed the weapon's bulge through the night. It also caused Alex to ask himself why Stu was hanging out with guys who needed to have their suits tailored in such a fashion. That was a question for later.

Stu walked Marco back through the club and toward the exit, continuing to speak to him in the same soft cadence. The music remained off and everyone watched Stu lead him like a Sherpa. Marco shuffled more than walked, throwing one foot in front of the other, bumping haphazardly into chairs and tables as customers and dancers cleared their path as though Marco was contagious.

Meanwhile, Simun was smiling now that the situation was defused, and he squatted next to his friend. Roko rubbed the back of his head, and when he brought his fingers away, saw they were bloody. He said something in Croatian to Simun, who smirked before nodding and helping him to his feet. Roko swayed and reached for a chair to steady himself. He gratefully accepted a stack of cocktail napkins from Simun and held them to the back of his head.

Yolanda stood nearby, smiling sardonically with her arms crossed under her bare breasts. For the first time, Alex noticed the discrete scars just above her ribcage through which some plastic surgeon had placed her implants. She plucked the last of the champagne from Marco's ice bucket and took several long pulls straight from the bottle, her Adams apple bobbing as she swallowed. Holding the bottle by its neck, she picked up her corset with her free hand, winked at Alex, and ambled away through the curtains at the back of the bar.

When Stu reappeared Alex asked, "What's the tale, nightingale?"

Stu said, "I stuck Marco in a taxi."

"Okay. So...what the fuck?"

"What the fuck, indeed." Stu saw the shape Roko was in and said, "I'll tell you the story in a minute but first, now that we got Larry taken care of, get Curly and Moe out of here while I finish settling up. I want to get the hell out of here before something else happens."

Roko wobbled like a baby giraffe. Once outside, he mumbled something and sat down hard on the slicked mud at the edge of the thoroughfare. Alex removed the bloody clump of napkins from the back of his scalp and pronounced,

"Just a small laceration, maybe an inch. I think you'll live." Alex replaced the napkins and gave Simun a thumbs up. Simun nodded, then turned back to surveying their surroundings.

When Stu emerged from the club moments later, he took a long deep breath and exhaled, decompressing. Seeing Roko's head bob with sleep, he smiled and said to Alex with a heavy sigh, "He's strong out of the gate, but not much for stamina."

Stu spat in the mud and began the story. "First thing you've got to know is the owners of the place are in tight with Luis, and as a result they know Marco real well. They don't like the asshole either, but they tolerate him to stay in good with Luis.

"Marco's a regular here, coming in all the time and acting like a big shot. Name-dropping, demanding respect he hasn't earned, bullying the staff and customers, you know, that kind of shit. He knows what being related to Luis means, that anybody who fucks with him had best come heavy.

"Most of the time its girls and booze he's after. They wind up comping him for everything, having to stand there and smile while they watch him run up a tab. It pisses them off, but there's fuck all they can do about it.

"Not for nothin', but usually Marco behaves himself pretty well. A few times he's been known to pick an argument, occasionally there's some pushing and shoving but nothing like tonight. Up 'til tonight, they've just looked at dealing with him as the price of doing business.

"The manager's a friend of mine, guy named Jorge. According to him, Marco demanded a blowjob from that poor girl he took in back. The girls—and sometimes the boys—here know the deal same as everybody else. They look at the job as tiresome, maybe expensive because they can't be out front working paying customers, but that's it. It also incentivizes them to finish Marco off quick so they can get back out front. Jorge told me that tonight word got around quick among the dancers that I was out front too and spending money, so they figured they could still wind up doing okay for the evening.

"Once Marco got that girl in back, though, he had a bad case of brewer's droop. She'd worked on him a while but Marco got pissed, started blaming her, saying something about if she couldn't do the job he'd go back out and find someone who could.

"Jorge said that then Marco accused her of giving him a look, and he just lost his shit. He starts yelling at her, pulls out the Glock and holds it to her head, tells her if she didn't get after it, he was going to spray her brains all over the shitty little walls. She started to cry, so the motherfucker pistol-whipped her."

Stu grimaced and shook his head. "So Jorge said the first bouncer comes charging in but held up after seeing the gun and the man behind it. They'd all been told a bunch of times that the rules don't apply to Marco.

"Marco's bloodlust was up by then. He points the gun at the bouncer and then just out of the blue pops him, right in the arm. Didn't even look to be aiming, could just as easily have hit him between the eyes. Looking back on it, that girl and the bouncer were both lucky to get out alive. Hell, we all were. A mean drunk waving a pistol? That's a headline waiting to happen. Anyway, you know the rest from then on."

Roko's hand began to slide from the back of his head, obeying gravity as the bloody clutch of napkins slipped from his grasp and littered his lap. Head slowly nodding, he dozed where he sat. "Tell you what," Stu said to Alex. "Why don't you get the kids here back to the hotel and tuck 'em in? I got some things to take care of still tonight and Roko here looks like he's had his fill of life's rich pageant for one night."

CHAPTER THIRTY-ONE

10:10 a.m.—Saturday, November 2nd

The next morning, the four men went to the heart of the city for the festival and were quickly swallowed up in a sea of revelers, music, costumes, and drink. They passed graveyards strung with streamers as families busied themselves cleaning the gravesites of loved ones. Passing through smaller neighborhoods, marigolds—thought to be the pathways that guide spirits—lined the sidewalks. Altars covered with brightly colored oil cloths bore photos and other mementos of the dead, with *ofrendas* of food and flowers arranged below. Everywhere were *calaveras*, the skulls made of candy or clay.

They found themselves on an out of the way plaza where six adolescent girls in white dresses with red rose embroideries performed a ritualized, choreographed dance for the crowd. Bellies full and drinks in their hands, Roko and Simun stood twenty feet away talking to a Mexican couple they had met moments before.

Stu and Alex hadn't talked further about the previous night's ending, other than Stu's assurance they were done spending time with Marco for this trip.

"Unfortunately, I still have to do business with that jackass moving forward," Stu said as he watched the smiling Roko try to mimic the dance the girls were doing, much to the crowd's amusement.

"We meeting up with Luis at some point today?" Alex asked.

"Don't think so," Stu said as he finished his beer and turned back to the bar to order another. "He said he had something come up with one of his businesses that he was going to have to tend to today, and he thought it would be a while."

"Too bad. I was looking forward to meeting him."

Stu didn't say anything to that.

CHAPTER THIRTY-TWO

1:18 p.m.—Sunday, November 3rd

A slight breeze rippled the lake's surface, rich with the smell of fresh cut grass. It ruffled the tail feathers of a brown hawk perched in the branches of a gnarled tree on the shoreline, scanning the sawgrass and cattails, silhouetted against a bright blue sky. The squawk of walkie talkies marred the idyllic setting, and the dull chug of the outboard motor on the SAPD Zodiac spoiled the peacefulness as it circled a patch of water forty yards from the shoreline. From this distance, Lozano could just see the bubbles of the recovery divers breaking the surface.

He'd already taken a statement from the recreational diver who'd first found the body at the bottom of the lake a few hours before. The poor lady had been so shaken she'd been unable to drive home. Stumbling upon a dead body when enjoying a weekend dive was bad enough. Finding that body wrapped in hundred grade chain and tied to a Danforth anchor would be fodder for nightmares.

With nothing more to watch at the moment than the boat making its slow loops, he stewed over the Henry Wallis case. Since meeting Wallis at the park, it was all he could think about, like a rock in his shoe. The balls on that kid, he kept thinking.

Lozano's phone rang. It was Beatrix Dominguez, one of his partners. "Hey Bea, what you got for me?"

"I just finished with those phone numbers from Juan Seguin that you gave me while you're out there at that new scene," Bea said. "How's it going by the way?"

"Divers still working on bringing the body up."

"How'd you get stuck with a new case so fast? I thought your plate was full right now."

"Miranda's maternity leave started yesterday, so we're gonna be a little short-handed for a while."

"Say no more. Anyway, I wish I were calling with good news. I saw what you meant when you said those last three names on your list were tough to get ahold of. I actually had to drive out to their home addresses since they weren't returning my calls either. But I just finished interviewing the last of them ten minutes ago. Sad to say, none of the three had anything to offer that was helpful."

"Did you—"

"Yes, I gave them Wallis's description too, still nothing. Sorry."

"Goddamit," Lozano muttered. He'd held out hope that the last three names on his list might have seen something, anything that could connect Wallis to the scene. Now having struck out with all the other phone owners who had been in the park and with no chance of finding any physical evidence to implicate the Wallis kid either, it was getting harder and harder to see how this worked out well.

"Fuck me, Bea. Kills me to say it, but I think there's a good chance this *pendejo* walks away."

"*Lo siento, mi amigo*," she said grimly. "We all been

there."

A yell from the boat and a flurry of activity on the water grabbed his attention. A bright yellow lift bag the size of a yoga ball breached the surface and bobbed up and down on the police boat's wake. Tethered by the divers to an underwater, heavy-duty body bag, it reminded Lozano of one of Quint's barrels in "Jaws".

"Looks like the body's up. Gotta go. Thanks anyway, Bea."

"Let me know if there's anything else you need," she said and hung up.

What I really need is to catch a break. He pocketed his phone.

CHAPTER THIRTY-THREE

6:45 p.m.—Monday, November 4th

Chris Melville sat slumped in a chair in the darkened homicide offices with his collar unbuttoned, tie loose, feet propped on the corner of Lozano's desk. The reading lamp threw a small island of light on the two men as one of the custodians went desk-to-desk emptying wastepaper baskets.

Once the custodian left, Melville double-checked to make sure they had the after-hours office space to themselves, and said to Lozano, "So the Department of Justice decided to give an award to the best law enforcement community in the country, and the finalists were the FBI, the CIA, and the SAPD

"They couldn't decide who to give the award to, so they decided to have a contest. First, they took the FBI out to some desert island. Then they brought out a rabbit, and let it run off into the jungle. They gave the rabbit a ten-minute head start, then they told the FBI, 'Go find the rabbit.' The FBI agents waded off into the jungle and come back three days later, all scratched up and tired, holding the rabbit.

"Next the guys from Justice take the CIA agents out to the island, same thing, release a rabbit into the jungle, and tell them, 'Go find the rabbit.' The spooks tear off into the jungle, and they come back two days later, same thing all cut and scratched up, looking gassed, holding the rabbit.

"Finally, the guys from Justice bring some cops from SAPD out to the island, and release the rabbit. They tell the cops, 'You gotta beat two days.' The SAPD said, 'Easy,' and wade off into the jungle. The cops came back twenty minutes later dragging a badly beaten coyote that was saying, "Okay, I'm a rabbit! I'm a rabbit!"

Melville laughed uproariously, slapping the armrest, but Lozano only smirked before saying, "You're such an asshole."

Melville wiped a tear from one eye and said, "Lookit, that's funny and you know it."

Lozano said, "Swear to God, before it's through H.R. is just going to set up a standing weekly meeting with you."

Melville, still chuckling, stood and smoothed out his tie. "You kidding? They love me over there. I bring a box of donuts every time we meet." Then, "I've had all the fun I can stand for one day. You coming? I'll walk out with you."

"Nah, I'm gonna hang back and work on my press release disavowing any relationship with you for when the inevitable press conference happens."

After Melville left, Lozano sifted through the stack of manila folders on his desk and selected the one for the vagrant's murder. It was mockingly thin. Since Bea called him at the lake the day before to say she'd finished contacting the list of names for him with no luck, Lozano had put this on the back burner only because there was nowhere else to go. There was no physical evidence beyond the teeth and for all practical purposes those were worthless. They'd previously circled back to reinterview as many of the vagrants in the park as they could find and that had led nowhere. And no one on the list of cell phones had anything to offer.

Lozano tried to distract himself in the interim by working on other cases, hoping illogically that something external would happen in the vagrant's investigation, some divine intervention that would illuminate a path forward. None had.

The lack of options frustrated him, and in the old days would have led to a bender. Now, sober and grayer, he took frustration in stride. He'd come to believe in karma, and as Lozano saw it just because the kid might not face a judge in this life didn't mean he wouldn't ever be judged. But thinking about it now in the dark homicide offices after hours, man, did he want to be there to see the kid get his.

He flipped open the folder. After his initial report, he found a PDF. of the ME's exam. He reread it closely and did so again, hoping some detail would jar a memory loose, some pebble that would start an avalanche. After ten minutes, he said, "Bupkes."

Next was the list of vagrant interviews from the park. On the first round, they'd found four. Going back a second time, with no rain and more motivation, eleven. He'd accompanied the officers for that set of sit-downs, which impressed upon them his seriousness. One thing occurred to him, they hadn't known at that time to show Wallis's picture around. Now he made a note to himself to go back to the park and reinterview the other vagrants and show them Wallis's picture to see if that jogged anyone's memories. A long shot, granted, but he felt desperate.

Next came the DNA report from the teeth. Three sets of male DNA had been isolated, presumably the teeth's dead owner, plus Lozano and Wallis. Since Wallis had a reason to explain that away, it was worthless. Lozano sat and stared at the report. If only he'd been a split second faster in knocking Wallis down as the teen reached for the dirt. Everything would be finished had that been the case. "Goddamit," he said and turned the page face down, moving on.

The last document in the folder was the printout from the cell phone carrier and, paper-clipped to it, the pages from the yellow legal pad where he'd scribbled his notes from the conversations. He flipped through them, looking at his scrawled notations of people's responses. Mostly joggers, a few dog walkers, one teenager dirt-biking. Nobody on a picnic, but that probably wasn't too surprising given the itinerant homeless population. Not that their reasons for being in the park mattered in the end. No one besides Wallis had been evasive, and in fact most had expressed regret they had nothing to offer. But in the end, no help.

He looked at line forty-three, "Wallis, Henry." He stared at the name, squinting, as though he could conjure justice telepathically. Doodling, he drew stars out to the side of the name, then underlined it, then drew several circles around it. He stood the pen on end, running his fingers down to the base, before flipping it around, over and over, each slow revolution leaving a small blue ink spot on the printout around the name as he stared at the letters trying to will an insight into being.

Irritated, he tossed the pen down and stared out the window at the parking garage across the street, before heaving a sigh and rubbing his eyes with the heels of his palms until he saw light bursts.

Looking at the page once again, his eyes wandered to the circles he'd haphazardly drawn around Wallis's name. The loops of royal blue ran across the names above and below several times, but the names were still legible: "Meyer, Deborah," "Santana, Fernando," and "Bodline, Jamarcus."

The list had been created in order of the time of entry into the network's coverage area, meaning that these three individuals had entered the park immediately before or after Wallis. Looking at the times on the network carrier's printout, in fact, all three were in the park at the same time as Wallis: Meyer's time in the park overlapped with Wallis by forty-four minutes, Santana and Bodline by fifty-two. The problem was, the park was so large it was possible, in fact probable, they hadn't been in a position to see anything.

Turning to his yellow pages of notes, Lozano found his interview with Meyer. At that time, she'd told Lozano that, yes, she'd driven to the park with her dog on October 20th and taken him for a walk on the east side trails, that this was a routine she did most weekends. She always kept him on a leash and the trip stood out in her mind because at one point on the walk she'd spooked a deer. When her dog saw the animal it tried to bolt, knocking her off balance, scraping her knees and hurting her shoulder from the sudden jerk on the leash. Lozano had memorized the park's layout by now and knew that her path took her well away from the murder scene. Lacking anything else to do, he dialed her number again. She picked up on the second ring.

After they exchanged greetings, Lozano said, "Miss Meyer, I'm just circling back to you because I've gotten some new information. It now looks the crime I'm investigating may have occurred during the time that you were actually in the park."

"Really? Jesus. Kind of gives me the heebie-jeebies to think that. You close to catching somebody?"

"We're certainly trying our hardest. Meantime, I was wanting to know if you've remembered anything new since the last time we spoke? Anything at all, no matter how insignificant you think it may be. Think hard."

"Gee, like I told you before, Detective, I got nothing. Plus, I've been taking lots of pain killers. Turns out that getting yanked like it did by that leash plus falling on it funny messed up my rotator cuff pretty bad. They're talking like it might need surgery."

"Mmm, sorry to hear that. Nothing more miserable than a bum shoulder. One last question before I let you go. Have you been back to the park since that day?"

"No, I don't think I'll be going back, even once my shoulder's healed. I'm going to stick to my neighborhood for my dog walking."

"Okay. Well, if anything at all comes up, you've got my number. Hope you feel better."

Hanging up, he looked at the name below Wallis's, Fernando Santana. Reviewing his notes, he remembered that Santana was a thirteen-year-old who'd ridden his bike to the park to meet up with the Bodline kid, his running mate. According to his scribblings, both boys said they'd hung out for about an hour, never venturing too far into the park, until they got bored and went home. When pressed for what hanging out meant, Fernando had replied, "Just talking and stuff." He, too, had said he'd seen nothing that was of interest or unusual.

Lozano called Fernando's number once again, but the voice that answered was feminine and mature. "Hello?"

"Good evening, may I speak to Fernando?"

"This is his mother. Who am I speaking to?"

"Hi, ma'am. My name's Detective Lozano with the SAPD Homicide Division. I need to speak with Fernando regarding an investigation I'm conducting. Is he there?"

"I'm sorry, did you say you're a police officer? Is he in trouble?"

"No ma'am, Fernando didn't do anything, but I'm hoping he may have information that may be helpful to an active investigation. We know from his cell phone records that he was in Juan Seguin City Park at the time that a crime was committed there. In fact, I've already spoken with him once about this matter last week and he couldn't remember anything that was helpful. I'm hoping to check in with him again to see if he's remembered anything new since then."

"Yes, he's up in his room, hold on one moment." The phone scritched as she covered its face, then a muffled shout, "Fernando, telephone! Get down here right now!" Returning, she said, "Sorry about that. He's grounded, that includes no electronics. That's why I'm answering his phone."

Making conversation while he waited, Lozano said,

"When I was that age it seemed like I spent half my time getting in trouble, and the other half being grounded for it."

"That one is the reason my hair is turning gray already and I'm only thirty-six."

"If you don't mind my asking, what'd he do?"

Lozano was doodling on the legal pad through this conversation, politely killing time. He expected to hear her offer some tale of adolescent hijinks, caught with cigarettes, or chucking rocks at an abandoned house's windows. But as Mrs. Santana answered in a good-natured, boys-will-be-boys manner, a comment she made caused Lozano to pause. Putting his pen down, he leaned forward as she continued, suddenly listening intently. When she finished speaking, he no longer cared about speaking to Fernando.

Barely able to contain his excitement, he said, "Mrs. Santana, listen to me very carefully..."

CHAPTER THIRTY-FOUR

8:04 am—Tuesday, November 5th

Lozano paced the scuffed linoleum in front of the police station's front desk, wide awake despite not sleeping well. The bemused cop working the desk watched Lozano make slow laps around the lobby, hands in his pockets, stooped so his dangling shield bounced rhythmically off his chest in time with his footsteps.

Lozano looked up eagerly each time the sliding glass doors whooshed open, like a man waiting on a blind date, only to be disappointed at the sight of a fresh-scrubbed administrator starting their day or a bedraggled family member summoned to post bail.

"As long as you're down here anyway, Detective, you want to take my shift at the desk?" the cop asked, smiling.

Lozano grunted. "I'd rather have a jalapeno enema."

"Ouch." The cop grimaced.

"I did my time sitting there back in the day, you can too," as he resumed his slow loops.

He stopped short when a balding, baby-faced man with rimless glasses entered with a slouching boy by his side. The man approached cautiously before asking, "Detective Lozano?"

Lozano could read the skepticism on the man's face, and got the feeling his visitor was one menacing comment away from turning around and walking out. Conjuring a smile that was courteous but stiff, Lozano extended his hand. "Yes, and you must be Mr. Santana. And I guess that makes you Fernando," he said with a grin that felt too big as they shook. "I really appreciate your meeting me this morning." He tried to make his tone as welcoming as possible so as not to spook the man. He knew he could legally compel Santana for all of this if it came to it, but that would be messy and labor-intensive. Lozano badly wanted to keep this from becoming adversarial and if that meant being a little obsequiousness, fine.

"No problem," Santana said brusquely. "Shall we get started? We're both busy guys."

"Absolutely. Follow me."

Lozano led the way down two flights of stairs into the bowels of the police department's basement. Coming upon a heavy white door, he card-swiped them through with a loud metallic clack and into a hallway that looked primitive, with exposed ductwork and zip-tied cables running overhead.

They passed a break room where a woman with spiky hair and an eyebrow ring worked a French press. Slight, almost mousy, she swam in her oversized Army surplus jacket and purple corduroys that bunched at her ankles. From the doorway Lozano said, "Morning, Aubra."

Aubra pushed her glasses up her nose and answered without looking up as she concentrated on pressing the plunger through the brown, steaming liquid. "Morning, Detective. Want some coffee? Awesome Guatemalan dark roast I picked up just yesterday."

"None for me, thanks. Mr. Santana?"

"I'm good."

"Don't know what y'all are missing," she said, pouring herself a cup before brushing past to lead them down the hallway to a nondescript door. Inside, she pulled on a dangling beaded cord, and a fluorescent tube light flickered on.

The room was claustrophobic. Electronics were crammed on top of each other amid spaghetti strands of coaxial cables and cords. Every inch of counter space on three of the walls held high-resolution monitors or hard drives, and when Aubra took her seat in the room's only chair it left Lozano and the Santanas with barely enough space to stand without touching. Apropos to this spider-hole in the basement, her screen saver was a picture of Milton from "Office Space" with the quote, "I believe you have my stapler."

Aubra logged on, then blew on her coffee and asked, "Okay. May I see it?"

Still looking dubious, Santana reached into his pocket and fished around for a moment. He pulled out a small Ziploc bag containing the memory card from a high-end drone.

Passing it to Aubra, Santana said to Lozano, "Like I told you last night, Detective. I'm reserving the right to stop this process the moment I see anything that could go against my son's legal interests."

"Again, Mr. Santana, I can assure you that we don't have any concerns that your son might be involved in the crime we're investigating."

Santana shook his head. "It was stupid enough for him to sneak my new drone out to that goddamn park with his friend without my permission, but I feel like I should have my head examined for letting y'all review that memory card without having my lawyer here."

Trying to change the subject, Lozano asked, "How did you discover he'd taken your drone without your knowledge?"

"It didn't take Sherlock friggin' Holmes to figure it out. He put it back on the charging pad facing backwards."

Lozano mused, "Now it makes sense why all he told me the first time I talked to him was that him and his buddy were just hanging out at the park." To Fernando he asked, "How much longer after we talked was it that your dad noticed you'd snuck his drone out of the house and used it?"

Fernando mumbled, "Two days."

Mr. Santana said, "I'm getting pissed off all over again just talking about it. I'd taken him to that park a couple of times before to fly it. You always want to fly over public property if you can so that if it goes down there're no arguments with a land owner."

"And you know for sure there's video from October twentieth on that memory card?"

"Yeah, it's time stamped. After my wife and I spoke with you on the phone, I watched it myself late last night to make sure there's nothing on it that's obviously going to be a problem for my boy. I wouldn't have agreed to this otherwise. I don't know what I was looking for, but nothing jumped out at me that looked like it might get him in trouble." He threw a sideways glare at his son. "More trouble, I mean."

Aubra interrupted to say, "Okay, its downloaded. Looks like there's nineteen minutes, forty-seven seconds of video. Here we go."

The resolution was high quality. The group watched as the image began with a close up view of green grass, the individual blades looking like a dense jungle. As the drone lifted off, it caught a glimpse of the two boys looking excited as Fernando concentrated on the hand controls. Slowly, the drone ascended, higher and higher. As it panned, it caught a better view of the two boys again, now showing their bicycles lying on the ground behind them.

Lozano instantly recognized the boys' location. A water tower sat atop the park's tallest hill, and the boys were in its shadow.

"You want to be able to keep the drone in sight," Mr. Santana said. "Higher you get, the further you can let it go."

"What're the drone's specs?" Lozano asked.

"It's rated for a range of three miles, but I'd never think of letting it go that far, too easy to lose it."

"How about elevation?"

"What they can do is different from what they're allowed to do. The record altitude for this model's eleven thousand feet, but that was illegal as hell. Regs are you need to keep it under four hundred feet, so you don't run the risk of interacting with manned aircraft." He pointed at a rapidly increasing number at the bottom left of the screen. "That's the altimeter there. In a minute, you'll see Chuck Yeager over here decides that rule doesn't apply to him. The highest that he let it get for this flight was seven hundred and three feet."

The video bounced as the drone ascended. "Wind gusts while he's climbing," Mr. Santana said. The image smoothed out momentarily as the drone leveled itself, revealing a beautiful, elevated view, the park's patchwork landscape looking like a quilt.

The vista crawled forward. As the drone banked, a jerky view of the parking lot crawled across the top of the screen from left to right.

"Freeze it right there," Lozano said. Aubra obeyed, pausing the feed. The view of the parking lot in the top right corner of the screen was smeared, like a painter sneezed in mid-brush stroke.

"Can you advance frame by frame?"

"Hang on," Aubra said. A brief burst of keystrokes, then she methodically hit the down arrow on her keyboard, moving the image forward incrementally. The picture came in and out of focus, alternately pristine and blurry.

"Find me the clearest view of the parking lot you can," Lozano said.

She reversed the image until she found a freeze frame

with the lot clearly visible in high-resolution, the size of a fifty-cent piece at the top edge of the screen.

"Okay, can you enhance this car?" Lozano asked, pointing. More keystrokes, then Aubra moved the cursor over the car in question and clicked the mouse several times. The image serially magnified, zooming in until the car occupied the whole screen. The resolution remained sharp through the magnification, and when she finished the screen was filled with a clear picture of a tan Buick sedan, driver's side.

"There's no view of the plates from this angle," she said.

Lozano said, "That's okay." He recognized the car as the one Wallis had been driving on the morning they'd met at the park. It was exciting to have new information, but seeing the car in the lot didn't advance his case since Wallis admitted to being in the park around the time the murder had been committed. "Can you capture that as a still image for me?" Aubra grabbed a screen shot and saved it.

"Okay, can you resume the footage, but play it at, say, half speed?" Lozano asked.

Aubra said, "Tell me what you're looking for. More sets of eyes, the better."

"Looking for a bright blue tarp sitting in a clearing, surrounded by a stand of trees."

"How big's the tarp?" Aubra asked.

"Small. Pup tent-sized."

"Roger that."

The image on the screen crawled forward, the horizon waggling intermittently as Fernando's inexperience showed. From the drone's elevation, small splashes of color were what stood out from the verdant landscape's muted greens and browns. Lozano's eyes locked on a bright white object for a moment before recognizing it as a large propane tank behind an equipment shed. A bright yellow pinprick stood out, a flash flood warning sign at the edge of the creek that ran through the park. A red blotch that became the t-shirt a different vagrant wore as he reclined next to a shopping cart full of supplies. Movement across the barren top of a hill caught his eye, recognizing it as two deer casually crossing the clearing, heading in the direction of the park's creek.

The view shook for a few seconds, and the altimeter rapidly dropped about forty feet.

Mr. Santana gave a smug, "Hmph. Lost radio control there." Turning to his son, "Bet that made you shit your pants for a few seconds, huh?"

Fernando remained silent, and the image steadied itself before continuing on its path. With every passing minute, Lozano could feel himself growing more anxious as the timer on the bottom of the screen ticked away. He found himself concentrating on the screen with such intensity that he irrationally felt himself getting angry at the kid whenever the screen bounced, wasting a few more seconds of footage. The beginnings of despair crept into the back of his thoughts.

Suddenly he heard Aubra say, "There."

His stomach tightened with excitement when she hit pause at the eight minute, sixteen second mark and pointed to the bottom left of the screen.

There it sat, nestled among the grey-brown packed earth at the edge of a small clearing. A splash of blue like a mirror reflecting a piece of sky. Lozano felt his stomach leap at the sight. Aubra enhanced the edge of the screen, bringing the tarp up, larger and larger. What Lozano saw made him hold his breath.

A figure wearing a gray hoodie could be seen facing the tarp, perhaps ten yards away and heading in its direction through the knee-high grass.

Fighting to keep his voice under control, Lozano said, "Zoom in on that person."

The aerial point of view came from a slight forward angle. Only the nose and chin were visible, protruding from under the hoodie's edge. The person's hands could be seen clearly, with a skin color that appeared to be Caucasian but with no identifying features. The figure had Wallis's height and habitus.

Without meaning to, Lozano had leaned in tight over Aubra's shoulder, his hands resting on the back of her chair, close enough that he could smell her coffee breath. "Okay, now advance the feed slowly. Let me see the next few seconds."

The tarp crawled across the bottom of the screen, from left to right as the camera panned, visible for exactly six seconds before it passed from view. In that six seconds, the figure that Lozano knew to be Wallis took three slow steps in the direction of the tent.

As Wallis and the tarp's images disappeared from the bottom of the screen, Lozano couldn't help but feel the clutch of hopelessness. That goddam hoodie. This had been his shot to get something usable on the kid, and to get this agonizingly close and come up short stung in a way he hadn't felt in a long time.

Aubra rewound the six seconds and they watched it a second time, then a third, looking for anything identifiable on the person's clothing or skin that they missed. Each time, the subject's face never came into sight. A Nike swoosh was visible on the front of the sweatshirt, a popular enough piece of apparel that Lozano knew even if he seized the sweatshirt from the kid, it would never stand up in court. Finally, in resignation he sighed, "Okay, enough of this. Go back and get me the best screen shot you can of Wallis."

"You mean the hoodie guy?" Aubra asked.

"Yeah, sorry. The hoodie guy."

"Done. Proceeding with the review."

As the drone continued its course, Lozano tried to push down his fatalism and focus. But as the drone continued on a path that took it further and further away from the scene of the murder, his concentration waned. His thoughts kept drifting back to his options. Could a circumstantial case be made against the kid? He immediately dismissed the possibility. What he had in hand was wet-tissue paper flimsy. Lozano knew the District Attorney personally as they'd started in the system around the same time. The man possessed the risk-averse philosophy of all career bureaucrats, and rumor had it he had aspirations to higher office. This caused him to be conservative about bringing charges, and he typically only proceeded on slam-dunk cases. Charging a kid for capital murder with no physical evidence except Lozano's story about the teeth, and a video that only showed a suspect matching his skin tone and body shape? The DA would give himself a hernia laughing before suggesting Lozano needed to get tested for dementia or neurosyphilis.

For the next several minutes, the drone took an aimless path. It made a slow figure-eight, then banked, the water tower visible a few times far away at the edge of the horizon. As the drone made progress in a loop along the park in stops and starts, it hovered in place for several seconds and then for the first time began to travel in a straight line at the eighteen-minute mark. The charge icon blinked to red and showed "10%."

Santana said, "He waited too long to bring it back. You'll see it ran out of power about a quarter mile short of the launch point, but he was able to land it in a clearing before the battery died completely, so it didn't crash."

Fernando said meekly, "We ran and picked it up. I was a'scared somebody would try to steal it while it was just sitting there on the ground."

Lozano nodded, half-listening. The foliage below moved now with purpose, the meandering finished. From this height, it still did not seem to move with real velocity, its land speed disguised by the altitude, the way an airplane seems to crawl across the sky.

In a tone that made clear he'd rather be anywhere else on the planet, Fernando asked, "Can we go home now?"

"In just a minute, buddy," Santana answered as he leaned back to crick his spine, then put his hand reassuringly on Fernando's shoulder and gave it a squeeze. The gesture of kindness seemed to say he was done beating the boy up over this, the lesson had been taught and he was moving on. "You want to stop at Denny's after this and grab some breakfast?" he asked graciously.

"Yes, sir."

Eighteen-fifteen. Eighteen-thirty. Eighteen-forty-five. The charge icon, already red, was now blinking at the bottom of the screen as it counted down the draining power. Nineteen minutes. Even Lozano found himself thinking, yeah, some breakfast does sound good.

Then, at nineteen minutes and seven seconds, a familiar bright blue spot appeared at the top-right of the screen and inched along parallel to the drone's flight route.

"Hang on. We got lucky, the tent was in the return path," Aubra said. Watching her repeat the routine of freezing the image and enhancing the tent, Lozano refocused.

At first no one was visible in the campsite. Then the middle of the tarp bulged outward, lifted by something underneath, and the rope suspending the tarp briefly swayed between the two trees to which it was tied. In a moment, the reason for the movement became clear as the hooded figure emerged from under the edge of the tarp wearing gloves.

Aubra froze the image as the hooded figure came into view. Lozano could not believe his eyes. He had to bite back a primal scream of rage when he saw the angle of the drone's camera—behind and to the figure's right—gave him no view of the kid's face. From this angle, he couldn't even see the figure's nose and chin anymore. His chin dropped to his chest in defeat. "Not looking good for the home team, Detective," Aubra said as she hit play once again.

Abruptly, she said, "Check that."

Lozano's head snapped up as she hit rewind. Frame by frame, the figure emerged once again from under the tarp's edge. As the footage advanced, the top of the murderer's head momentarily scraped against the rope suspending the tarp. The rope pushed the hood back, bunching the cloth around the figure's neck, revealing a full head of closely cropped black hair. The face still pointed away at an angle, only giving Lozano a view of the murderer's right ear and some of his smoothly shaved cheek. But what made Lozano's heart race had nothing to do with the subject's face: clearly visible in the assailant's neatly clipped hair was a sickle-shaped scar curving widely around the right ear. Lozano's eyes went wide as he remembered that scar clearly from his day at the park with Wallis, having been tempted to ask about its origin before deciding to hold off. Seeing it now, he knew that scar was damn near as good as a fingerprint.

Tingling warmth started in Lozano's chest and spread outward. Three minutes earlier, he'd convinced himself the only retribution Henry Wallis would ever suffer for his crime was of the divine type. Now, he was thinking the young man might get a taste of the earthly variety after all.

CHAPTER THIRTY-FIVE

4:30 p.m.—Wednesday, November 6ᵗʰ

Lozano circled the parking lot of Lorenzo De Zavala looking for the Wallis kid's car. He found it parked near the far exit and pulled up in front of the bumper, blocking it, before putting his own car in park.

Lozano loved this time of year. College football was in full swing, and the autumnal air signaled deer season lay ahead. This November felt sweeter than most, though. The drone footage had been like an early Christmas present.

He left the heater running and checked email while he waited, a toothpick in his mouth. Inside the building he heard the muffled clatter of a school bell, followed by a horde of students leaving the building and scattering among the parked cars. Within a few minutes, the Wallis kid appeared, heading in his direction and looking unfazed. He walked up to Lozano's driver's-side window and leaned in. His face bore a smile that didn't make it to his eyes.

"Afternoon, sir. I'm gonna need you to move this thing so I can head to cross-country practice. You're welcome to come if you want, might do you some good. Right about now, you look like if you sneezed, you'd pop this door clean off your car."

Without looking up from his phone, Lozano said, "You know Henry, I've been sitting here working on my cell while I waited, and it got me to thinking. If I wanted to, I could call my sister in Germany, or text a picture of that baseball field over there to a friend of in Korea, or look up Reggie Jackson's batting average in nineteen seventy-eight. I know your generation takes shit like that for granted—trust me, I don't hold it against you—but for folks my age a lot of those things seem like magic. Know what I mean?"

Wallis stood silent.

"Yeah, when you get to be my age, technology just never ceases to be amazing. Whether it's the internet, digital TV, smart cars, what have you, it can seem like science fiction stuff."

Lozano retrieved a manila folder from the passenger seat and handed it through the window to the kid. Wallis opened it and studied the eight by ten glossy photo inside, a still frame blown up of his scar as he ducked out from under the vagrant's tarp.

Lozano took the toothpick from his mouth and gestured with it to the folder. "Recreational drones. That's another little piece of technology that I never would have guessed would be a thing when I was a younger man. What a time to be alive, huh?"

The kid's expression didn't change as he handed the picture back.

Waving the picture, Lozano said, "This changes things, kid. Tomorrow morning, you're going to need to come into my precinct for formal questioning. Let's say, eight o'clock?"

A smile crept into the corner of Henry's mouth and he

was silent for a long moment before he said in a voice that had dropped an octave, "Think you got me, don't you?"

As he put the car in drive, Lozano said in a threatening tone, "I don't think. I know. Tomorrow morning. Don't be late."

Heading toward the highway, Lozano reflected on the encounter. If the kid showed up with a lawyer in the morning, it would force his hand to charge the kid or let him go. He hoped it wouldn't come to that. The end game was in sight, but he didn't want to rush too quickly to an arrest, a mistake he'd made a few times early in his career. The evidence he had in hand, both concrete and circumstantial, would ultimately get a conviction. Now that he'd caught the kid in his lies, he needed to question him on the record. If the interview went well, he would charge the kid at its completion. He just needed to make sure there didn't exist some problematic piece of information, some last-minute hocus-pocus of which he was unaware, something that would embarrass him or the DA. Assuming there wasn't, this time tomorrow the kid would be in jail.

He hadn't liked that last smile Wallis had given him, though. It made him worry the kid knew something he didn't.

CHAPTER THIRTY-SIX

5:45 p.m.—Wednesday, November 6th

Eyes burning from chopping onions, Rebecca blinked through tears to see Henry's car pull into the driveway. She heard him enter the house, and shout-asked without turning around, "Hi, honey, how was your day?"

"Okay, I guess," Henry shouted back.

"Sully's working the eleven to seven, so we'll eat when he gets home. I'm making taco salad." She wiped her eyes with the back of her wrist.

"I'm going to go play *Call of Duty* for a while."

"Just don't snack on anything in your room, mmkay?"

She heard his bedroom door close and continued to putter. As the meat browned, the smell of cumin and chili powder drifted through the house. Sully would be home around seven fifteen, and he would be hungry. Not for the first time, she thought how nice it was to have a husband about whom she didn't have to worry. She had a memory of sitting in the car as a young girl while her mother dispatched her brother to go into a beer joint to find their father and tell him mommy wanted to know when he'd be home. Looking back, she was mortified for her mother.

At 7:18, she heard Sully's car pull in while she shredded cheese. A moment later, he hollered from the entryway, "Man, somethin' smells good." He untucked his uniform shirt as he came into the kitchen and flipped through a stack of mail. Next, he, sidled behind her and kissed the nape of her neck. "How long before dinner's ready?"

"Almost done." She frowned as she looked at the back of her fingers. "I saw a man on TV who said he didn't know why they call this a cheese grater, said they should call it what it is, a knuckle scraper."

Sully got a beer out of the refrigerator, then sat while she added the pile of cheese and tossed the salad before setting the large wooden bowl on the Formica tabletop. She shouted in the direction of the bedrooms, "Henry. Supper's ready." Turning back to her husband, she asked, "How was your day?"

"Long. But I found out they may give us a chance at some overtime next week."

"Yeah?"

"Yeah, Riley Storkey's wife got sick, he's going to have to take FMLA for a while. Came up sudden."

"That's awful. Is it serious?"

"Serious enough that he's takin' FMLA. Don't know anything past that."

She hollered again, "Henry. Dinner." She paused, looking toward the hallway that led to the three bedrooms. When he didn't emerge, she muttered, "Probably got his darn headphones on." Going to the door, she rapped loudly while saying again, "Henry! Dinner!" When there was still no answer, she cracked the door an inch and peeked in.

His backpack lay on the still-made bed and his computer was closed, with Henry nowhere to be seen.

She crossed the room and knocked tentatively on his bathroom door, "Henry?" No answer. She tried the doorknob and found it locked. It could only be locked from the inside, so he had to be in there.

Now worried, she knocked harder and louder. "Henry, are you in there? Are you okay?" Still no answer.

She returned to the bedroom door and called in a voice that quivered slightly, "Sully, can you come back here please?" Then back to the bathroom door, she knocked louder. "Henry, please open the door!"

Sully appeared, asking, "What's all the commotion?"

As panic began to creep into her voice, she said, "Henry has locked himself in the bathroom, and he's not answering the door."

Innocently, Sully asked, "Why would he do that?"

"*Do you think I fucking know?*" she shrieked, hands clutched into fists and shaking.

Caught off guard, he tried to soothe her. "Hon, he's probably takin' a dump with his earbuds in. Give him a couple minutes."

"No, something's wrong!" She threw her shoulder against the door, then again.

"Okay, okay, okay," Sully said. "If that's how we're gonna do this, then just stand back."

She stepped to the side, and Sully drew himself up. He muttered so low she barely heard him say, "Jesus, please don't let that boy be jerkin' off in there."

Still wearing his steel-toed boots from work, he dealt the cheap particleboard door one vicious kick right next to the knob. The door exploded inward, pulling the lock and a fist-sized piece of the doorframe with it before slamming against the doorstop.

Rebecca had gone with a monochromatic ivory white when she'd decorated the bathroom. Shower curtain, walls, ceiling, linoleum, every inch of every surface the same bleached shade. Sully had joked at the time that standing in the bathroom made him know what a chick felt like inside the egg right before it hatched.

Henry's face was chalk-white, matching the tiles against which the back of his head lay, but their eyes were drawn to the bathtub full to the brim with blood-red water. He lay chin deep, eyes closed, head tilted. The scene almost looked serene, the only movement coming from small ripples in the bathwater made by a few floating plywood splinters. The water was so thick with blood they couldn't see his submerged body, only his bent knees where they broke the surface. Henry's pocketknife sat on the edge of the bathtub, a thin line of blood on the blade's edge.

Rebecca would later say she only remembered fragments from that point on, like stills in a photo album. She had a distinct memory of Sully shouting, "Oh, Christ!" but in her mind the voice was muffled, like it came from an underwater speaker. She hazily remembered watching while Sully's training kicked in as he pulled Henry from the tub, and the red water as it sloshed over the porcelain and soaked the white bathmat before running across the linoleum. She vaguely recalled the wet smacking thud Henry's body made as it hit the floor, like a fish landing on a pier. She remembered the feel of being jerked at the waist, hard, three or four times as Sully frantically tugged at her belt, then used it to tourniquet the long gash above Henry's right wrist. She could dimly recall snippets of Sully checking for a pulse and finding none, starting chest compressions, yelling at her to call 911, then, frustrated at her paralysis, doing it himself. Through it all, she felt like a detached observer, like Jane Goodall watching a particularly interesting silverback.

Posted to Henry Wallis's Facebook account at 6:22 p.m., eighty-seven minutes before the paramedics pronounced him dead:

> *For as long as I can remember, I've had a*
> *lot of problems. I think this will be for the*

best. Mr. Brantley always says every problem has an answer. I think he's right.

P.S. Sorry about the mess.

CHAPTER THIRTY-SEVEN

8:15 a.m.—Thursday, November 7th

Lozano gave Wallis a quarter hour before deciding he'd had enough. Yesterday as he left the high school, he'd put it at even money as to whether the kid actually showed for the interview, so it didn't come as a surprise.

His first guess was that the kid had made a panic move and bolted. In a way, Lozano actually hoped that would be the case. It would strengthen the case against him, and he didn't care how cool a customer the kid seemed to be, he wouldn't be able to just disappear. Between phones and debit cards, Lozano knew the modern middle-class teenager couldn't go to ground for long. The kid was smart enough not to use any plastic, but the problem of a renewable cash stream would quickly lead him to a choice between petty larceny or sucking off long-haul drivers at truck stops. They'd probably find him breaking into a car in Shreveport or El Paso, and then it would be a quick transport back to San Antonio. As he accessed the kid's home address on his desktop, he started mentally composing the speech he would give Wallis's parents if he found them at home when he got there to arrest the kid.

A little over an hour later, he parked across the street from a modest one-story, seventies-style ranch home with earth tones and a mansard roof. Bay windows gave views of two large, well-tended crepe myrtles that swayed in the brisk wind. He looked up and down the street. Quiet, shade-strewn, with lots of box hedges and garbage cans on the curbs. All in all, he thought, you'd be hard-pressed to tell you weren't looking at a replica of Mayberry.

There were no cars under the aluminum carport. A gray mailbox mounted on a stacked stone column in front bore the name Sullivan. With his tie whipping around his face in the breeze, he rang the doorbell, and when no answer came, knocked loudly. He repeated this twice more while he looked around. Stepping carefully in a mulch bed at the bottom of the street-facing walls, he leaned over a short shrub line and rapped gently on the bay windows, holding his shield up and calling out as he did so.

Peering in the plate glass through cupped hands, he surveyed the interior. He could see a darkened living room with cozy furniture, the only illumination sunbeams falling through twin skylights, lighting up dust particles floating in the air. Gingham curtains ruffled in the breeze, and Peekaboo cherub figurines sat at each end of a mantel. An inexpensive family portrait hung over the fireplace showing a trail winding through pine trees where stood a youngish, wholesome-looking couple. Each rested a hand on the shoulder of a gangly adolescent boy, all toothy smiles. Lozano recognized a younger version of Wallis. He favored the woman in the picture around the eyes, the man not so much.

Okay, looks like I'm headed back to the high school. Checking his watch, the administration should be able to tell him by now whether Wallis had shown up for school today.

On the way, he stopped at a Valero to get gas and a cup of coffee. He found himself in line behind two women making small talk, but in tones that sounded morose. One wore mirrored Raybans, the other had her hair pulled back by an off-center scrunchy.

Raybans was saying, "After I heard, it just made me want to go in and hug my little Sherry-Anne to me."

Scrunchy nodded her agreement. "What's so scary is how you just never know what's really going on with them. Jason's with his dad this week. I tried to call him this morning after I heard and tell him he needed to sit Jason down this evening and have a serious talk with the boy to make sure he's not thinking of doing any of that copy-cat business you hear about."

"Copy-cat? What do you mean?"

"Girl, you ain't heard about this? That when one child commits suicide, sometimes you see other kids at the school do it too in the next few days. Almost like it's catchin' or something."

Raybans shook her head. "Oh, Lord, please don't tell me that. You just give me one more thing to worry about."

"It's true. I saw it on 'Ellen' a while back. She had some psychiatrist on their talkin' about it."

"So did he say he was gonna talk to Jason like you asked him to?"

"What do you think? That shit heel told me"—she dropped her voice a few octaves in husky imitation— "'Oh, the boy's fine, I know my son, you worry too much, blah, blah, blah.'"

"Unbelievable," Raybans said with a disapproving tsk.

"Don't worry, he drops Jason back off tomorrow and I'll make sure he's alright then."

"Well, I'm sure he is. You're so involved with his life, I can't imagine that you wouldn't know if he was havin' the kind of trouble that makes him think about killin' himself. He should be grateful to have you as a mother."

"I try." Scrunchy was silent for a moment, then followed with, "I mean, in one sense I get his point"—here she leaned in conspiratorially and whispered low enough that Lozano could barely overhear— "You do have to wonder just what kind of mother wouldn't know, you know?"

"I know," Raybans dropped her voice in turn and put her hand on her companion's forearm in a gesture of agreement. "I had just that same thought. A good mother always knows when something's wrong with her child…"

"I admit, I had my suspicions about what kind of mom she was ever since that PTA meeting when she wouldn't vote for that 'stranger danger' proposal." To the clerk as they made it to the register, "Pack of Salems."

As the bar scanner beeped her friend's purchases, Raybans muttered, "Did you hear how she didn't even help try to revive him after they found him?" Shaking her head, she said, "How could anyone just stand there?"

Handing over her debit card, Scrunchy said, "I shouldn't say this, but I'm not totally surprised. Do you remember how we had to twist her arm to get her to help with that bake sale with the Auxiliary couple years ago?"

As Lozano eavesdropped, his disinterest morphed into disquiet. He interrupted. "Excuse me, ladies. I'm sorry, I couldn't help but overhear. Are y'all talking about a kid committing suicide around here recently?"

The pair flashed a split second of annoyance at him, but it didn't last long compared to the opportunity to dish on a scandal, even to a stranger.

Scrunchy said, "Yessir. One of the students at the high school killed himself last night. Stabbed himself in the stomach."

"I thought I heard he cut his own throat?" Raybans asked her.

"No. Lloyd McHenry was the paramedic who was there, and supposedly he told Joselyn's husband that when they got there, they found the knife sticking out of his stomach."

"If you don't mind my asking, do you know the kid's name?" Lozano asked.

"I should, he was one of my son's friends. Henry Wallis," Raybans said.

"Such a shame," Scrunchy said as she shook her head one last time.

CHAPTER THIRTY-EIGHT

1:45 p.m.—Thursday, November 7th

The McMullen County Medical Examiner's office was small in size and aspirations. As the sheriff explained to Lozano when the detective called to inquire about where he could find Wallis's corpse, Live Oak county partnered with nearby McMullen county to split the cost of a coroner's office since neither had the volume of deaths to support the service by themselves.

Located where town ended and desert started, the squat single-story building wasn't much to look at, and Lozano's footsteps kicked up brown clouds of dust as he approached the front door. Serving a population, a fraction the size of San Antonio, the diminished scope showed through in its informality. Pushing a button by the door handle, he heard a doorbell chime inside. Moments later a young man holding a sandwich and wearing a smudged smock opened the door a crack and asked around a mouthful of food, "Can I help you?"

Lozano flashed his shield. "Hi, I'm Detective Lozano, SAPD. I'm out here on an investigation and I'm hearing from Sheriff Leighton you've got a body of a kid named Wallis, suicide from Three Rivers yesterday?"

The man took another bite as he stepped aside. "Yessir. Let's get in here out the cold."

"I'd like to take a look at the corpse if I could, confirm it's him?"

"That's easy enough, I guess. I'm the tech, name's Ernie. You need to talk to Dr. Johnson? He's at lunch if so, be back in 'bout forty-five minutes."

"Not if you're comfortable showing me the body."

"Naw, should be alright. C'mon" He popped the last bite of sandwich in his mouth as he headed through a door and into the building's only other room.

The cramped morgue contained a wall refrigerator with two doors for body storage. There was room for just one exam table. It sat empty, tolerant of the delay. A stainless steel sink crowded the autopsy table, forcing Ernie to turn sideways to pass.

"We don't get a lot of young folks comin' through here, but this kid makes the second this week. First fella was some scabby tweaker they found dead next to the dumpster behind a burger joint couple days ago. OD'ed on Oxycontin, looks like. Unusual for around here. Course, there weren't no mystery about what happened to this kid." He pulled a linchpin out of the handle on the left drawer and popped the handle. Reaching into the darkness, he pulled the sliding table out and threw back the white sheet covering the head, like an unmasking.

Wallis lay in repose, eyes closed with a hint of stubble on his cheeks and chin. His ivory skin was discolored as lividity followed gravity's pull, his expression peaceful. *Far more peaceful than he had a right to be.*

Ernie flipped the sheet off the right wrist and lifted it to display two gashes, each four inches long and running parallel to the axis of the forearm. Lozano's nose wrinkled at Ernie's not wearing gloves.

"If you're gonna do it, that's how," Ernie said, almost approvingly. "Folks cut straight across, the edges of the arteries contract down, sometimes enough to stop the bleeding. Cuttin' along the lines of the arteries like you see here keeps that from happenin'. Arteries cut like this'll keep bleedin' 'til you shuffle off to your eternal reward."

Lozano said, "You gonna give me a hard time if I ask for a few moments alone with him? I'd like a little closure."

To the idea of denying a policeman's request, Ernie said, "My momma might'a raised an ugly child, but not a stupid one. Take your time. I'll be out front grabbin' a smoke."

Once Ernie left, Lozano stood staring at Wallis's face, as though if he concentrated hard enough some truth would reveal itself. Why would a kid like this undertake premeditated murder? It was unknowable, like explaining the color blue to a blind person.

But it was enough that he'd gotten his man, a victory for cosmic justice. As he found his career winding down, he found more pleasure in these wins, savoring them in the moment because he didn't know how many more he would have coming to him.

Waving goodbye to Ernie who stood near the doorway smoking, Lozano was at peace as he climbed in his car and cranked the engine. Speeding up the two-lane Highway 37 towards home, his final thought on the matter was that the kid had gotten his.

CHAPTER THIRTY-NINE

6:45 a.m.—Monday, November 11ᵗʰ

Rebecca watched Sully's truck back out of the driveway for his first day back at work since the funeral. He'd been as supportive of her as he could muster, but there'd been no mistaking his eagerness to get out of this house and back to a normal work routine where life was simpler.

Returning to the couch, she felt the layers of emotions might suffocate her like so many heavy blankets. While she felt a natural sense of maternal loss, there was also an element of relief that the monster she'd borne was gone. Since finding out what Henry was that day in the woods with the rabbit, she'd often wondered: if her future-self had appeared early in her pregnancy and told her how evil—and there was no other word for it—her unborn child would turn out to be, would she have continued with the pregnancy? She could honestly say she didn't know.

That was why above all of the guilt, shame, and relief, the supreme emotion she experienced was anger. Anger that Henry had put her in this position. Anger that he'd publicly violated the uneasy and unspoken truce they'd declared that day in the woods with the campfire and the rabbit cage.

Her worst fears had come to fruition. Not only had all of her nagging insecurities and doubts about her fitness as a mother been ratified, but in a manner that put them on display for the world to pick through, like leaving her journal in the town square with a blinking sign inviting the curious to leaf through it.

She had no desire to talk to these people. After their pro forma condolences, she was certain when they gathered later there would be whispers.

And at the moment she saw no option other than taking it. As she saw it, the town viewed this as her failure. It was her fault. From now on, she would walk among them marked with her own version of a scarlet letter. Pugnacious by nature, Rebecca wanted to fight back, tell them this wasn't her doing, it could have happened to any of them. But coming from her, they wouldn't believe it. They'd all seen Henry's final Facebook post in which he wrote of having problems.

If not her fault, she felt sure they would ask, then whose?

It was in these doldrums that she had her idea. It revealed itself, a vision, a solution, an escape. It so surprised her that she sat up suddenly, leaning forward off the couch, holding her terry cloth robe clutched at her neck, staring ahead without seeing.

Could it work?

As she thought it through, she nodded, slowly leaning back to resume her position. So the town would want some kind of proof that she wasn't at fault? She would just have to give it to them.

For Alex, the past week at the high school had been a blur of grievance counselors, expressions of shock and grief, reduced assignments and expectations. On a parents' night, counselors imparted lessons on how to recognize signs of risk in one's own children as well as how to talk to them about the events. Teachers were told to be on the lookout for other students who may be at-risk, and Principal Cunningham held an assembly so the school could meet as a community. One of the students started a website on which students and faculty could post their feelings, and Jen assigned Alex the responsibility of monitoring it.

The sense of shock Alex felt at receiving the news of Henry's suicide was echoed by all the faculty. He'd liked Henry, and never in all of their training sessions nor their tutoring-meet ups had he gotten any sense that the kid had been in crisis. At his own worst, he'd so clearly been a mess that it would have been obvious to anyone. The same could not be said here. It just goes to show, he told himself, one never really know what's going on in somebody else's head.

CHAPTER FORTY

12:10 p.m.—Thursday, November 21ˢᵗ

Since he only had the noon break to meet with his lawyer Gabriella, Alex dismissed his last class five minutes early to avoid the crush of traffic when seniors left for off-campus lunch. He'd already spent ten minutes of it trying to find a parking spot around the town square, and as he circled, he made a mental note to avoid making appointments during Dinah's lunch rush from now on.

After parking on the far side of the square, he cut across the courthouse's neat lawn. Approaching the diner, he saw the sandwich board man again, bundled against the unseasonably cool south Texas autumn, extracting bottles and aluminum cans from the city can on the corner. Pedestrians gave him a wide berth, but he didn't appear agitated, the sign propped on itself like an A-frame nearby. He'd changed the verse so it now read, "Psalm 58:10. The righteous shall rejoice when he SEETH the vengeance: he shall wash his feet in the BLOOD of the WICKED."

Inside the diner, Gabriella waved to get his attention. She'd upgraded her wardrobe since their last visit, dressed in a woolen gabardine suit with a pair of stylish designer cats-eye frames. The look suited her. *Hope that's a sign her practice is picking up.* Alex slid into the booth across from her.

After they ordered coffee, he gestured at the plate glass window. "Meant to ask you before. Who's the bundle of joy out there?"

She poured a splash of milk and craned her neck to see what he was talking about, then explained, "Around here they call him Crazy Milton. Poor guy has been at it for years. Lots of different stories about Milton. When I was younger, my father told me he fried his brain with drugs. The DA told me he'd heard it was from exposure to Agent Orange. I don't think anybody knows.

"He just wanders around with those signs, talking to himself and not bothering anybody. He mostly stays around the town square here because when the weather gets bad, the sheriff lets him spend the night in an empty cell at the jail if they've got one. Plus, sometimes the staff here lets him have food before they throw it away. His people are outside town, and they keep an eye out for him too."

Gabriella got down to business. "I filed the Chapter 7 bankruptcy, and that went routinely. I also formally petitioned your student loan holders to bundle your student debt into your bankruptcy filing and, as we expected, they laughed at me.

"Again, according to plan, I then filed the adversary proceeding in which we asked the judge to determine whether your student loan debt is dischargeable based on your new financial circumstances.

"We got assigned to Judge Lucinda Stansfield. I spent my first two years out of law school clerking for one of her good friends and got to know her somewhat. She's a good lady.

"I'm sorry to say, though, Alex, it didn't matter. She denied our request yesterday afternoon, and when she turned us down, she used the exact argument I was worried about. She was nice about it, but she said that the most logical plan as she saw it was for you to do what was administratively necessary to return to practicing medicine. Now we can appeal that, but it means that the process is likely to keep getting dragged out with no guarantees of a different outcome. In her ruling, she even threw in some language about the moral obligation everyone has to repay borrowed money. That's something that a lot of judges are going to be sympathetic to."

Alex tilted his head back, then closed his eyes and cricked his neck side to side, making it pop.

"Okay. Hypothetically, what if I just refused. What would the consequences be? I mean, they can't put me in jail, right? As much as the sons of bitches may want to, debtors' prison isn't a thing anymore. And all you see in the news is about students who're unable to pay their debt."

"Well, no, that is true, you don't have to worry about jail. But your circumstances are different from, say, a college student with a classics degree who can't find work. The important difference is that, as opposed to a younger graduate who wants a job but can't find one, in the eyes of the system, you have the opportunity to service the debt and would be refusing to do so. The consequences for you would be much more severe.

"You could expect them to garnish your wages and trash your credit history. Because your salary would never be able to relieve a debt that massive, these would be permanent conditions.

"Further, for cases deemed egregious—and that is how they would consider your refusal to return to medicine now that you've been psychiatrically cleared to do so—they have the ability to petition the court to suspend your teaching license in order to pressure you toward the more lucrative path. You would become unemployable."

"Unemployable?"

"For this amount of money, they would use every weapon at hand. Frankly, the only other option that I can see for you would be to say that your mental illness has returned, making you unfit for any type of work. Obviously, you would have to resign your position at the school, and for the sake of appearances, you would have to apply for disability. They could not fight this, but what I can promise you is that they would watch you very closely. The moment that you stated your psychiatric issues had resolved well enough to seek meaningful employment, even years from now, they would turn the dogs loose on you again. You would in effect be forced to live off social security disability funds for the rest of your days."

He scowled, but Gabriella held his gaze. "As your lawyer, I have to say at this point I don't just think going back to medicine is your smartest option, I think it's your only option."

CHAPTER FORTY-ONE

2:07 a.m.—Monday, November 25ᵗʰ

For the next week, Alex felt like a prisoner who'd made parole and gone home only to find a deputy waiting on his doorstep, saying there'd been a mistake, and they were taking him back to jail.

With Brutus's chin resting on his bare foot, Alex sat in boxers and a white cotton t-shirt, pondering his meeting with Gabriella.

There had to be a better option than returning to medicine. He turned the conundrum over and over in his mind, probing it for weak spots. Try as he might, though, he didn't see an alternative.

A feeling of disquiet grew with each passing minute. He felt like he stood at the top of a staircase that led down into an unlit basement, the darkness inky, familiar. Bad things happened down there. That place scared him.

He felt his chest tighten, like some ghostly hand reached through him and squeezed his heart. His breath wouldn't catch, and his hands trembled so badly he locked them and pressed them between his knees.

Through a conscious effort of will, he worked to calm himself. Long, slow, deep breaths in through his nose, and out through his mouth—just like the doctor had taught him. Focusing on that and nothing else, over and over. Gradually, he regained control of his thoughts, de-escalating his emotions. The mental door going to the basement closed with difficulty, like fighting rusty hinges.

Finally, he felt under control, but it left him with the realization of how perilously close to the edge he was living at the moment. That left him vulnerable to a slip, a nudge. Then the only thing left would be the abyss.

Sleep didn't come easily these days. Tossing and turning, he listened to leaves scrape across the concrete driveway below his window while the chimes of an ormolu clock Mrs. Wright had gifted him marked the passing hours Eventually, he gave up and showered and dressed. Getting to the school at first light, despite the near-empty lot he still parked in his usual space on the far side, a creature of habit.

Sleep-deprived, he plodded through his day, class after class. Despite drinking enough coffee to give him a fine tremor, a fog hung in his head. During his sophomore chemistry class, in the middle of a discussion of Heisenberg's Uncertainty Principle, he broke into a massive yawn, eliciting a titter from the class. *Not my best day*.

When the last bell rang, he felt like he'd finished a marathon. Stuffing his briefcase with the day's quizzes and lesson plans he headed to the LeSabre. Right now he needed sleep. After a catnap he'd have a clear head, and maybe could return to troubleshooting his legal problems.

He'd just unlocked the car door when he heard, "Alex? Is that you?"

Two men in jeans and sports coats approached him from the next row of cars over. The man in front had a broad smile as he took off his sunglasses to get a better look while his trailing partner looked on nonplussed. "That is you, isn't it, you old son of a bitch! How are you?"

Alex tried to place him but couldn't. He felt awkward, given the man's familiarity. "Hey, how's it going?" he said noncommittally while searching his memory.

The man helped him out. "Remember me? Connor Barbosa? We went to high school together." Turning to his friend, politely smiling with his hands in his pockets, the man said, "Me and Alex go way back, ran in some of the same circles in the day. Man, it's good to see you. This is my friend Scott. Scott, this is Alex…" He snapped his fingers twice and looked away briefly. "Shit, I'm sorry Alex. Was it Branson, Bradley, something like that?"

"Brantley."

The man's demeanor changed. His smile disappeared, replaced by a serious frown as he reached into his jacket pocket, pulled out a thick envelope and thrust it at Alex.

"Consider yourself served." He jerked his thumb at his partner, "Witnessed." Still unsmiling, both men turned and wordlessly walked back toward their car.

It took him a moment to comprehend what had just happened. The realization came in time for him to yell, "Assholes!" after the two men.

Ignoring him, they climbed into a white Oldsmobile and headed toward the lot's exit.

"Assholes," he said again, muttering as he looked at the envelope. The return address was a legal firm in San Antonio he'd never heard of. Goddamnit, Gabriella hadn't told him getting counter-sued by his student loan company was a possibility. God only knew what this would cost him in legal fees, or how this would impact their strategy. If he couldn't repay his loans through the normal payment schedule, how could they expect him to pony it up all at once by suing him for the money? He'd been prepared to deal with collection agencies, not this.

He scanned the first page, and felt strength drain from

his legs, his knees weakened then caught. He whispered, "No, it can't be."

The subpoena didn't have anything to do with his student loans. His eyes flew across the text, picking up key words, words like, "negligence," "wrongful death," "practice outside the scope."

The moment felt otherworldly, as though he was dreaming. He felt shocked. Shocked and angry.

The Sullivans were blaming him for Henry's death.

CHAPTER FORTY-TWO

3:30 p.m.—Wednesday, November 27th

The smallish room felt crowded. Two lawyers and their paralegals pored through documents across from Alex and Principal Cunningham, while another partner chimed in on speakerphone. In the middle of introductions, Alex's phone pinged with a request from Gabriella that they sit for a brief meeting that afternoon. After agreeing, he realized the lead counsel, a Mr. Friedlander, had asked him a question.

"Sorry, sir, can you repeat that?"

"I asked if you understood the nature of these proceedings?"

"Well, yes and no. Yes, I understand that y'all are here because the school district was named in the suit, and that you'll be representing me in this matter. I also know I've been placed on administrative leave because of all this." Frustration crept into his voice as he said, "What I don't understand is what it is exactly that they're accusing me of doing?" He squeezed the pen in his hand so hard his palm hurt.

Friedlander said, "I can see how this would be unsettling, Dr. Brantley. The heart of the matter is this. In their suit, the Sullivans are alleging that Henry had a psychiatric disorder of major depression of which you, and only you, were aware. They go on to allege that upon discovering this disorder, rather than referring him to a qualified mental health professional, you decided instead to treat his psychiatric condition yourself, therefore practicing medicine as a psychiatrist and in a legal sense taking him on as a patient. They further allege that you elected not to share your discovery of your patient's psychiatric diagnosis with them, despite the fact that he was a minor and in the state of Texas you're required to get parental consent for treatment. They claim that you chose to practice as a psychiatrist, despite lacking board certification in psychiatry or having an active medical license, and that you therefore did so poorly, with a quality that didn't rise to the standard of care.

"They argue that but for this negligence, Mr. Wallis would be alive today. Finally, since you were a member in good standing of the Three Rivers School District faculty throughout this time, they contend the school district also bears culpability in his death."

"And why would I have supposedly done all this?"

Friedlander looked at the rest of the table, then back at Alex. "Your situation is a matter of public record, Dr. Brantley, so we expect them to argue you were motivated by recklessness, that the same poor judgment that in the past led to the suspension of your medical license now led you to believe you were capable of competently delivering psychiatric care to Mr. Wallis."

Holly looked down at her folded hands, studying her thumbs as she rubbed them together.

Alex rubbed his eyes. "You know this is nuts, right?"

Friedlander nodded his head in sympathetic

exasperation. "I know. Stupid, isn't it? But what you've got to understand is that's just the excuse we expect them to use, their cover story for what they're really after in this suit."

"And what's that?"

"This looks like a shake down, a money grab. Their real target is the district and its deep pockets. You're just collateral damage to them. The problem for you is that, as an agent of the school, you're the linchpin to their argument. They'll go after the district vicariously by going after you directly." Friedlander leaned forward. "That being said, we also suspect there may be an emotional element to this as well."

"What do you mean?"

"Well, if they can get a settlement saying this young man's suicide was the school's fault, you know whose fault it wouldn't be in the eyes of many of the folks in town?"

"Let me guess. His parents?"

"His parents." Friedlander echoed as he scribbled a note. "Obviously, that's conjecture on our part, but it would make sense. You know, small town perceptions and all that."

"Okay, well, please tell me then that they don't have a fucking case. I mean, I knew Henry and I liked him, but this? Suggesting that I had anything to do with his death? It's obscene." He spat the words.

"That's a little harder to say. I can tell you what they've got right now. In their filing, they provide depositions from Mrs. Sullivan and a Ms. Tracy Garcia who both testified that in their opinions you had a relationship with Mr. Wallis which went beyond the normal student-faculty relationship and which concerned them for having crossed a line to being inappropriate.

"Further, as evidence that you had in fact taken on the role of a medical professional with Mr. Wallis and were dispensing psychiatric care, the Sullivans cite a text message that their son sent them which read" —he put on his half-rim glasses— "*I lost track of time. Having a good talk with Mr. Brantley, he has some great ways to think about things. On my way home now.*"

"That's bullshit," Alex raged, his lips flattening against his teeth. "He was talking about how I taught him—"

Friedlander held up a hand, cutting him off. "They also cite as evidence of your alleged therapeutic relationship Mr. Wallis's Facebook post which functioned as a suicide note in which he wrote, '*For as long as I can remember, I've had a lot of problems. I think this will be for the best. Mr. Brantley always says every problem has an answer. I think he's right*'.

Alex rolled his eyes and threw his head back. "Are you serious? That's what all this is based on? Some text messages, and his mother and girlfriend having a problem with me?"

"At the moment, yes," Friedlander explained. "But you've got to understand that those texts and depositions were just what they needed to get the ball rolling. The next part of this process will be going through what's known as discovery. That's when we'll have to turn over your phone and email accounts. They'll subpoena your disciplinary file with the state medical board and go through your file at Three Rivers. They'll do a deep dive on your internet presence and social media history. All that will be a fishing expedition, but they'll be looking for something that can embarrass you and the district in a way that will pressure us to settle. We all get the feeling they don't want this lawsuit to ever get anywhere near a courtroom."

They met at the diner in their usual booth.

"How are you hanging in?" Gabriella asked him.

"Not so great. Actually, pretty bad. It's been a rough week."

"So I heard."

"You heard?"

"Yes, I was at the courthouse today working for another client and overheard a couple of lawyers talking about the filing. Made me think I'd better check in with you."

"Jesus Christ."

"Part of small-town life," she said, stirring cream into her coffee.

"I knew there was no way that this bullshit lawsuit would stay quiet, but still."

"Listen, Alex, I know you've got a million things on your mind, and so I won't keep you long. But this is advice now from a lawyer friend and not your counsel, Okay?

"If they haven't already, the lawyers from the school district are going to want to meet with you soon."

"Yeah, I was actually in a meeting with them when you texted."

"Okay. They said they're representing you, correct?"

"Yeah."

"While technically that's true, they're actually paid by the school district to represent you as a member of the faculty."

"Right."

"What that means is they have the school district's interests first, and yours second. If the two overlap as they sound like they do right now, great—they can function as effective advocates for you. But make no mistake, if the two start to diverge, they will cut you loose in a heartbeat."

Alex looked confused. "Cut me loose like quit representing me?"

Gabriella shook her head. "Like acting in ways that may be in the school district's interests but not in yours. Maybe they pressure you to take a bad deal to limit the district's costs, maybe they recommend the district fire you as a way to buy good will with a judge or limit the district's liability. There's all kinds of ways that you could become expendable."

"Great, so what do you suggest I do?"

"If all things were equal, I would recommend that you get your own lawyer, someone who's only loyalty is to you. And I'm not saying this to get myself the business. Frankly, you're moving into areas now that are outside my sphere of expertise. I wouldn't feel comfortable taking this on even if you asked me to."

"I appreciate the advice, Gabriella, I really do. But I gotta be honest, at the moment it's gonna be tight for me to get you paid just for the work you've done for me on my loan issues. Taking on somebody else now, I just don't have the money."

"I understand. At least you now know where you stand with these guys, that when they say they're your lawyers that there's a big, unspoken asterisk there."

Alex looked out the plate glass window at the courthouse with its rough-faced limestone trim, the inscription above its entry just visible: *To No One Will Justice Be Sold, Denied, or Delayed.*

For a minute, Alex forgot to censor himself. "Gabriella, I have no fucking idea what I'm going to do."

"Rebecca, I just don't know about this," Sully said again.

She sighed. He'd said that earlier in a fast-food drive through on their way to this meeting with Mr. Childes and his legal team, then again when checking in with the receptionist. Rebecca had already apprised their lawyers that Sully had misgivings about suing Dr. Brantley and the school, and so far during today's update Sully had sat quietly in his chair with his crooked tie and baggy suit.

"I know, sugar." She laid a hand on his thigh, but he didn't return the intimate gesture. A chill lay between them, thin but there, like a skim of ice on a puddle.

The idea for the lawsuit had come to her suddenly, fully realized. The impossibility of making the case that she and Sully weren't at fault with Henry's suicide. As she saw it, no one in the community would believe that she and Sully didn't bear some responsibility for their son's death, seeing any excuses as self-serving. But if the courts were to say so, well, that brought credibility. And, if it happened to have the benefit of bringing a financial windfall, all the better, no? After all, who would walk away from life-changing money?

If she'd had any remnants of qualms, Mr. Childes had quickly dispelled them during their first meeting. After hearing her version of events, he made it sound like the school district's negligence in harboring a werewolf like Dr. Brantley was so clear, so pronounced, she had a moral duty to proceed with a lawsuit. After all, how else would they learn? This was the only way to make them see the error of their ways, to have a reckoning with the fact that their administrative sloppiness and corner-cutting had cost a young man his life.

She and Mr. Childes had seen eye-to-eye from the jump. But Sully had been a harder sell.

Sully was grounded. While his formal education may have ended with a high school diploma, he knew people. Rebecca suspected that made him a good prison guard. He could relate to the inmates, see things from their side, and most importantly he knew right from wrong. It was one of the things that had initially attracted her to him.

Rebecca had attended the first meeting with Mr. Childes by herself. On this, their second meeting, she'd brought Sully so the lawyer could walk him through the plan. He laid out their argument for Dr. Brantley's culpability, why his actions had led to Henry's death, why the school system should be held responsible too. Throughout the lawyer's explanation, Sully sat with his arms crossed, lips pursed in thought, as though listening to a fast-talking used car salesman. When the lawyer finished, Sully flipped through a copy of the lawsuit while Mr. Childes plucked lint off his expensive suit, ready to answer questions.

"I need to think about this. You got something I could drink?"

"Of course. Janine, will you take Mr. Sullivan to the break room for a cold drink?"

Mr. Childes waited for the door to close before turning back to Rebecca. He was silent for a moment, twirling his

Mont Blanc pen before saying, "Mrs. Sullivan, I understand that this can be an incredibly difficult time for a couple. Losing your only son through the negligence of others, feelings of despair and sadness that I can't even comprehend, much less relate to. It's not uncommon for couples in that situation to be in such a state of grief that they have difficulty in dealing with matters like the ones we're discussing. I hear it all the time. 'This won't bring my son back.' If y'all aren't on the same page with this, there's nothing stopping you from proceeding alone. But I will tell you it makes it harder to prove our case if the parents aren't in it together."

"Thank you for your understanding, Mr. Childes, but you don't need to worry. Sully'll get there," she said.

Sully didn't say a word on the ride home. Walking into the quiet house, Rebecca said, "Hon, why don't you take a shower while I order us a pizza?"

He nodded and walked off pulling his tie over his head, knot intact. Hearing the shower start, she dug through the coupon drawer in the kitchen. Sifting through the ratty-edged discounts on bleach and toilet paper and two-for-one mac and cheese, the specials on Chinese food and sandwich shops and oil changes promising to pass the savings on to her, she began to get angry. The hundreds of Sundays she'd spent over the years combing through the paper, clipping and tearing these God-forsaken coupons to save a few cents here and there. In her eyes, that drawer symbolized their lower middle-class status.

But not for long.

CHAPTER FORTY-THREE

6:40 p.m.—Sunday, December 1ˢᵗ

The apartment had taken on the feel of a sanctuary. Through the Thanksgiving break, Alex had only gone outside long enough to let Brutus out, and he let all of Wendy's calls go to voice mail. His sweatpants and flannel shirt were on their third day, and he'd walked the soles of his white cotton socks to a dingy gray. The room's only window marked the passage of time, and as the light faded on the day, he thought was Sunday, a dark blue band on the horizon presaged the first blue norther of the season.

The problems over the student loans had been bad enough, but now with the added stress of the Sullivans' lawsuit, he felt overwhelmed. There were no outs he could see, and according to Gabriella, he couldn't trust the district's lawyers to be his advocates. He felt trapped.

Sitting on the floor, leaning against the wall with his

forehead on his knees and arms wrapped around his legs, he wanted this to be through: the fatigue, the anxiety, the self-loathing.

Brutus stretched out next to him, spine pressed against Alex's thigh and fast asleep. The bulldog broke the room's stillness when he pricked his ears, then snapped his head up. He muttered a low woof, then a loud bark before running to the door, continuing to yap. A moment later, a knock came followed by a familiar voice.

"Alex? Open up. It's me, Stu. Come on, open up."

Alex ignored it for the moment, hoping the man would leave.

"C'mon, I know you're in there, your car's in the driveway. I can wait you out if you make me."

Alex sighed and called out, "It's open."

Stu entered bundled in an Anorak coat and carrying a fast-food bag and drink. Brutus snuffled his boots, then heaved himself up to stand on Stu's thigh. Stu scratched his head and gave him a couple of French fries from the bag before nudging him off. He wrinkled his nose, "Christ, it smells like shit in here." The trashcan in the kitchenette overflowed and the apartment reeked of spoiling food and sweat. The temperature outside was in the forties, and Alex had turned the heat up on his window unit, making the odors simmer and cloy.

"In law school, I never had to go to the state prison in Huntsville for anything, but I think this is what the place must be like on the day a man gets the needle," he said looking around. "I was gonna eat this, but you look like you could use it more."

Wordlessly, Alex took the bag and inspected its contents. Stu went into the small bathroom and left the door open while he urinated.

"Tell me why you're here," Alex said to Stu's back.

Over his shoulder, Stu said, "I heard about your problems. Figured we should talk."

Alex swallowed a bite of cheeseburger, then said,

"What do you mean?"

"What do you mean, what do I mean? Everybody in town is talking about it."

"Oh, fuck."

"Oh, fuck indeed," Stu said as he came out of the bathroom, zipping his fly.

Stu squatted to play tug of war with Brutus while he let Alex finish eating. Once Alex had wadded the brown bag and tossed it in the direction of the over-stuffed trash can, Stu stood and with his hands on his hips said, "Come on, get up and get showered."

"Where're we going?"

"To the goin' place. Come on, get your ass moving."

"Pass."

"I'm not asking. Now come on."

"Stu, seriously—"

"Goddammit, you're so lazy you'd shit in your own bed and kick it to the bottom with your feet. Now c'mon. Move."

Alex rose and shuffled toward the bathroom. Stu took a place on the love seat and monitored Alex's progress while scrolling his own cell phone.

A short time later, Alex, scrubbed pink and wearing his cleanest dirty shirt, presented himself for inspection. Stu said, "Good enough. Grab your coat."

Alex obeyed passively. Heading down the sheet-metal stairs toward Stu's truck, he said, "You still haven't told me where we're going."

"My place. Time's come for us to have a talk."

The temperature was dropping as the leading edge of the cold front made its presence known. The hinges of the old truck's doors squealed as they climbed in the cab. Stu cranked the engine and drove them off as the last of the light faded from the dark blue, winter sky.

CHAPTER FORTY-FOUR

7:50 p.m.—Sunday, December 1ˢᵗ

They drove in contemplative silence, neither in the mood for small talk. In front of Stu's house, Alex saw a black Escalade parked on the gravel road's pull out next to the closest oak tree. Stu parked and led the way around back to a tongue of flagstones that extended in the general direction of the far-off river. Down two short steps, a bonfire blazed in a six-foot fire ring.

A Hispanic man sat on a cut stump stool, staring into the fire. Seeing them, he stood and smiled. The taper of his Carhartt coat suggested a lean and wiry physique and with his close haircut gave him the impression of being sleek, like a bullet. He looked comfortable in his worn jeans and scuffed boots, and Alex had a sense that if the man wore a suit much of the time, it was a costume for doing business.

The man extended a hand. "You must be Alex. I am

Luis Espinoza. It is wonderful to meet you after having heard so much about you." His English was accented, his manner refined. He had a tight smile that appeared genuine and his handshake firm without pumping.

Alex replied, "Nice to meet you."

"If I may?" He turned to their host, "Stu, may we open my present now? It is a thirty-year-old Balvenie and it is magnificent." He put his pinched fingers to his lips in a mwah gesture. "A perfect accompaniment to a campfire." He turned back to Alex and gave a sly wink. "I know that tequila is the drink of my country, but I have to confess to a love affair with single malt Scotch from the first time it touched my lips."

"Sounds good, I'll be right back," Stu said. The screen door screeched as he cut through the porch. Through the kitchen windows, Alex saw him grab glasses and rip open a gift-wrapped box. Two stocky Mexican men sat at the kitchen table looking on, positioned for easy lines of site to the fire pit and the long slope of lawn as it disappeared into darkness towards the river.

While they waited, Luis sat again and asked, "Alex, I trust you enjoyed *Dia de los Muertos*?"

Alex rolled a similar cut stump over and tipped it on end to take his own seat. "Yeah, very much. And I'm glad to have this chance to say thank you for hooking us up like you did. That was very generous."

"It was my pleasure. Stu is a valuable partner as well as a very good friend. He is—how do you say?—a lovable scoundrel." That tight smile again. "Any friends of his are friends of mine."

Stu returned with glasses in one hand, a straight-back chair in the other, and the bottle under his arm. Handing out the etched glass tumblers, he examined the Scotch's label before breaking the seal. He poured each of them two fingers before collapsing in his chair, the bottle clinking when he set it on a flagstone. Exhaling toward the sky, his breath made a white plume, so he scooched closer to the fire, the chair legs scraping like nails on a chalkboard. He rolled the first sip around his mouth, experiencing it as he held the amber glass before him, examining it by the fire light before swallowing. He said an approving, "Oh, my."

"I do not lie, do I, my friend?"

"Least not about this," Stu said and they both laughed.

The three men savored the expensive Scotch, in no rush, watching sparks corkscrew toward the sky, the silence interrupted only by the pop of steam pockets in the mesquite logs.

Finishing his, Luis held the empty glass out towards Stu. While Stu poured another splash, Luis asked, "Alex, did you grow up in Three Rivers? Is this home for you?"

"No, we moved around a lot when I was younger. My dad had an oil-field job that kept us moving from town to town."

"When did you move to Three Rivers?"

"August."

"Have you always wanted to be a teacher?"

"No, I came to it later in life."

"That is interesting. I myself changed paths onto the one that I am on now. Was your decision to change a hard one?"

"Not really."

"Mine was agonizing. I grew up in *Parras*, west of *Saltillo*. My father and my grandfather were both farmers who worked the fields for *Casa Madero*, a famous vineyard in Mexico. Neither man could read nor write, but they were smart and loyal and could work other men their ages into the ground. The owners of the land, the Garcías, were good people, and they recognized that tending to the fields was backbreaking work. I am happy to say that they treated my family well. When my grandfather became too old to work, they continued to support him and my grandmother until the day they passed on. When my mother had to have surgery in Monterrey and suffered complications, the Garcías continued to pay my father while he stayed with her for almost two months. Yes, the Garcías were good people.

"I had seven brothers and two sisters, and as the oldest son, it was expected that I would follow the same path. We would do some schoolwork in a small classroom on the owner's land, but as a child my passion was being in the fields with my father and grandfather. At their knee I learned how to tend the vines, how to fertilize the soil—not too much, not too little, like Goldilocks—and when to mix in clay or sand to the rows. I learned how to properly prune the vines and the correct way to manage the canopies. I gave that soil my sweat, and when I was young, I could imagine no better life for myself.

"Once I was in my twenties, however, I began to see that while the life my family led tilling the soil was a good one, I wanted more. I was thinking of changing the last name of a pretty girl whom I met, and I was attracted to the idea of a life where my opportunities for advancement would only be limited by my talents. I let this idea nurture for a while, tending to it like I did the grapes. I did not want to seem impertinent.

"As part of my responsibilities at the vineyard, I had to drive a truck to Laredo once a week to make deliveries and pick up supplies. On one of these trips, I met a man who introduced me to some other men, who then introduced me to others. They were entrepreneurs, and I thought, this is a world that has possibilities for me.

"So I began to make excuses to be able to spend the night in Laredo when I went on these trips. I would spend those nights around these men, listening and learning, helping them build their trust in me and what I could do. This went on for many months.

"Then on one of my trips, they came to me and said, 'Luis, we have a job for you.' It was simple, really. I was only to make a delivery of a package to one of their business partners in Piedras Negras. They stressed to me that it was very important that the package arrive without problems. They said that the business relationship that they had built with the man was a new one, and they needed to make sure that he saw them as professionals. The package was about, oh"—he squared his hands off in an area a little larger than a shoebox— "this big."

"As you can imagine, I was excited to have this opportunity to show them my worth. 'Of course', I told them. 'I will take care of this'. So, I called my father and told him a small lie, that the truck had broken down and would not be ready until the following day, and I set out to Piedras Negras for the two hour drive to make the delivery for these men.

"I was just a little more than halfway there when I came upon a roadblock in the highway manned by *federales*. They stopped me and without asking me questions made me pull over. I had hidden the package well, or so I thought: under the chassis and behind the gasoline tank where it could not be seen by mirrors under the truck. But that is directly where they went, and my heart sank as I watched them pull the package down. It was clear to me then that someone had betrayed me.

"They opened the package and it held money, most of it in small bills. I watched as they counted out eleven thousand dollars."

Luis smiled and got a wistful look in his eyes. "A rounding error to me now, but at that time that was all the money in the world."

"Having taken the money, they let me go, and I returned to Nuevo Laredo with my tail between my legs.

"I went back to the men who had given me the assignment and I told them everything. I explained how the *federales* had allowed other cars to go through and had pulled me out of the line, how they had gone directly to my hiding place, how they had acted content with the money in hand to let me go with no talk of jail. How I was sure that someone had tipped them off about my assignment.

"They listened to me without interrupting. When I had finished, they thanked me for bringing the fact that there may be an informant to their attention. Then they asked whether I planned to return to Piedras Negras that day or the next.

"I was confused. Was this another assignment?

"They told me that, no, as they saw it, I had been given the responsibility of getting eleven thousand dollars to their colleague in Piedras Negras. Nothing had changed in their eyes. It was only a matter of when I planned on making the delivery so that they could let him know when to expect me.

"I looked at these men, these hard men. I could have stammered and made excuses, whined about how this was not my fault, that it was unreasonable to expect me to procure an amount of money that I had never before seen in my life until that package was opened on the side of the road. But I could see from their faces and knew from their reputations that it would do no good. Like it or not, I was accountable. So, I asked them if I could have a few days. They said I had twenty-four hours.

"As I drove away, I was panicked. I thought of taking flight, trying to start over in another part of the country, maybe even fleeing to the US. But I knew to do so meant my family would pay a price. Not so much over the amount of money, but over the principle. They would be unlikely to kill someone over that pittance, but it was probable that my father or my brothers would be trying to work the soil with seven or eight fingers instead of God's ten after these men finished with their pruning shears.

"Now you must understand, Alex, I have always considered myself to be a good man. I believe in our Heavenly Father and life everlasting, I have always remained faithful to my wife, I keep my word, and I help the less fortunate with no expectation of praise. But this was the first time in my life that I ever really considered going against the church's teachings. I was desperate. I could see no other way out of my situation. Everything seemed to be at stake. A life, career, marriage, children, everything, and the thing standing between me and the life I wanted was that money.

"Frequently, it is only with the benefit of hindsight that you realize that you truly came to a crossroads of a decision, one that could change your life drastically. Here, I knew it in real time."

Luis fell silent. A knot exploded in the fire, causing the logs to collapse a few inches and sending a shower of embers up toward the starless sky.

Unable to take the suspense, Alex asked, "So what'd you do?"

Luis took another sip before answering. His voice was mild but when he looked up from the fire to meet Alex's gaze, he was now shark-eyed. He said, "There was a middle-level drug dealer in Nuevo Laredo who was known to have gotten sloppy, flaunting his money, staying high all the time. He had hired a bodyguard who worked *cheap*." He spat the last word.

"That night I crawled through his bedroom window and cut his throat from ear to ear while he slept. His bodyguard was nowhere to be found, but the girl who was with him awoke in the struggle and saw my face. She did not leave the bedroom. To this day, I do not know who she was."

"The money was exactly where I had been told it would be, in a compartment beneath a rug in the bedroom. I snatched a pillowcase from the bed and threw it in, then ran. A few hours later I would find that it totaled nineteen thousand, six hundred forty-five dollars, a number I will remember for the rest of my days.

"So, the next day I made the delivery without incident, with two hours to spare. The client actually acted frustrated that the money was late from the original deadline, but there was nothing I could do about that. And my new employers— that was what I was calling them by that point—never acted impressed, just very matter of fact, like I had done what was expected. No more, no less.

"They told me that they would have another assignment for me in a few days. I used that time to buy my own car with the extra eight thousand-some-odd dollars, a used pickup truck that looked like something a pimp would be too embarrassed to drive." A weary smile crossed his face. "At twenty-one years old, it was what success looked like to me.

"I drove my family's truck back home. A friend followed me in the truck that I had purchased. In my panic, I had forgotten to tell my family that I was going to be an extra day, and their relief that I was okay quickly turned to anger over my lack of consideration in making them worry. But that anger was nothing compared to the fury I encountered when I told them that I was quitting the farming business to move to Laredo to make it in the business world. Then, amid all their questions and indignation, I just walked out to my truck and drove back to Nuevo Laredo.

"I have thought many times over the years about the compromises I have had to make to get to where I am now, sitting at this campfire with you tonight, Alex. They were concessions that were made out of necessity, because usually it was an acknowledgment that there really wasn't a choice to be made about the actions that were needed. Rather, it was a choice about whether I had the will to go down the only road that was being offered."

Along with his earlier sense of grace, Luis now gave off a feeling of menace, like a coiled snake. Stu sat next to him, staring into the fire, legs crossed, the flames reflected in his pupils. Alex wondered how much of this story Stu had heard before.

Alex asked, "You ever have any regrets?"

"Of course," Luis replied. "You would have to be a monster not to, and call me what you will, I am not a monster. But just because I have regrets does not mean I would have done anything different." He paused for a moment, then said, "Stu tells me that you know something about hard choices and desperation."

Yeah, I know something about hard choices. How do you say I've got my dick caught in a wringer in Spanish?

"It's been a rough stretch, that's true."

"Would you mind telling me about them? After all, I've

told you my secrets. I think fair is fair, no, *mi amigo*?"

Alex recapped his problems with his debt and the Henry Wallis lawsuit, then touched on his license revocation. He talked about what he hoped for his future, the kind of life he wanted. The trickle of words became a flood, as if someone turned a tap in his brain. He felt powerless to stop. No, not exactly powerless, just that he didn't want to stop—saw no need to. This night was like a prism that broke the beam of his conundrum into its constituent parts, making them easier to see in their relationship to the whole.

As he purged, Luis and Stu sat intently, not interrupting while they listened, unmoving except to pour another finger. When he finally finished, he felt like he'd run a sprint. He breathed a little heavy and found that he'd been clutching the tumbler of Scotch so hard his forearms and wrists were fatigued.

Luis said. "My heart goes out to you, Alex. These problems sound overwhelming. Being blamed for the death of a student whom you considered a friend, employers who may or may not have your interests at heart, a judicial system pushing you toward a career that you cannot stomach, and a debt of over three hundred seventy thousand dollars hanging over your head. Faced with these same problems, Job himself would have felt besieged."

Alex nodded in appreciation, then paused.

Wait a minute. He replayed his diatribe in his head. Had he mentioned the exact number?

Luis had been sitting ramrod straight, but he now leaned forward and looked intently at Alex. "May I suggest an option for dealing with these hardships that God has seen fit to visit upon you?"

"Okay."

"Let me begin by asking you this: what was your impression of Marco?"

Surprised by the question, and not knowing how much Stu had told him about his brother-in-law's actions on their first night at the festival, Alex was deferential. "I dunno.

Seemed like a guy who liked to have a good time."

Luis said, "My brother-in-law is not a good man. He enjoys suffering for its own sake. No control over his impulses, he is pure appetite. Drink, drugs, food, women. I have tolerated this for a long time because, as I say, he is *mi cuñado*. I have spoken to him many times over the years about the fact that his actions reflect on me. With him it is always the same. Promises to do better, promises to think before acting. Always, promises, promises." His voice trailed off.

"We have a complicated relationship, he and I. My wife and I met in *Parras* when we were teenagers. She came from a family of unskilled laborers, working very hard during the harvests of grapes or cotton, and scraping by in between with whatever work they could find. As I began my courtship of her, I came to know Marco as well.

"One story in particular will make you understand. He and I were teenagers at this time, working in a barn, cleaning equipment for my father. In the course of our work, I lifted the heavy metal lid of a feed bin that I had been told was nearly empty. As I looked, I found two rats inside running around frantically, trapped. They had crawled into the bin to finish the last stray kernels of corn and found themselves unable to climb the sheer metal walls to escape.

"As the rats scratched about, panicked, I fetched a shovel to kill them quickly. Marco stopped me, however, telling me to close the lid and let them be. The look on his face was what I can only describe as glee at the thought of prolonging their fear and suffering, leaving them to die of thirst. I was disgusted. I can remember thinking what kind of person is this, who takes such pleasure in the pain of others?

"Not wanting to argue, I did as Marco told me, only to return a short while later alone where I dispatched them quickly. But that day foreshadowed the problems I would face with Marco in the years to come.

"While it was no secret within our community that

Marco was hot-headed, untrustworthy, in his parents' eyes he could do no wrong. He was their only son, you see. I sat and listened to them make excuses for him for many years, how it was always the other person who had started the fight, how his supervisor was foolish for firing him. And all the while I knew that if my plans for my life and career went as I hoped, he would one day be trouble for me.

"When I left to go to Nuevo Laredo, I promised my Magdalena that once I became successful, I would return to claim her hand and give her the life she deserved. For twenty-two months we wrote every day—there was no email at that time for children of those who worked the fields— and I worked hard, establishing myself, making my name, working my way up the ladder. I will confess, every time I received one of her letters, I hoped it would bring news that something had happened to Marco. Killed in a car wreck while drinking and driving, stabbed after picking a fight with the wrong man, shot by a jealous husband. You get the idea. But no, that man lived a charmed life. I guess it is true. God looks after babies, drunks, and fools.

"Finally, when I did return to take my Magdalena back to Nuevo Laredo so we could begin our life together as man and wife, there was no question Marco would be going with us.

"At first Marco seemed grateful for the opportunities I created for him. I introduced him to people, vouched for him, taught him the ways to work his way upward in the organization. It did not surprise me to see, though, that he was the same old Marco. Unreliable, quick-tempered, poor judgment, insincere, always looking for the easy way out.

"While Marco was squandering opportunities, I was continuing to rise. Then I began to receive word that he was trading on my name. Once again, his behavior was being excused, but instead of his parents, this time by the world with the phrase, 'Leave him be, his brother-in-law is Luis Espinoza.'

"And yet for all of the power his relation to me gave

him, rather than gratitude I sensed resentment rising within him. As he saw his career plateau and mine continue to rise, through many small things—a sideways look, a missed opportunity to express gratitude, a hug given with a chill rather than warmth—I noticed a growing bitterness. He would never dare speak such a thing out loud, of course, but it was there. If we get to know each other better, Alex, you may find your way into a poker game I hold once a month at my villa. But if you should decide to sit with us and play cards, be aware I am skilled at reading a man's face."

A trace of weariness crept into Luis' voice. "And so I think it was out of this sense of resentment that it came to pass several months ago, it was brought to my attention that Marco was stealing from me. He had probably started with amounts that were too small to be detected but had grown increasingly bolder.

"My close circle suspected something was going on with his receipts, so before coming to me they confirmed it beyond a shadow of a doubt: he was skimming two to three percent of his collections before turning them in. Regrettably, he had also enlisted two junior associates in his scheme. They were either too naive or too stupid to know not to throw their lot in with him.

"These two flunkies were dealt with easily enough, but unfortunately I cannot use the same remedy for Marco. My wife knows who and what Marco is, and she shares my contempt for him. But at the same time, he is her family. Many years ago, she made me promise that no matter what happened, I would never have him killed, no matter what he did. I promised, and I am a man of my word. But I cannot let this activity, this theft, go unanswered. And so, I have come up with a solution that will solve my Marco problem for me once and for all, while allowing me to keep my word to my wife. The fact of his theft is not widely known, so neither she nor the world will know the reason why the fate I have planned will befall him. He has made enough enemies in Nuevo Laredo that the list of people who could be responsible for what is to come will be long. I suspect that even he will not know. So much the better."

Alex interrupted, "I'm still not clear why you're telling me all this."

"Because, Alex, I could use your assistance."

"I'm not following you."

As Luis began to explain what he had planned for Marco, Alex listened first in disbelief, then with nausea. When Luis finished, Alex sat in shock as Luis stared at him, his steely eyes unblinking.

"I can't believe this," Alex said.

Luis acted like he hadn't heard. "And in return, I can make the problems that plague you disappear. I will pay off your debts. It is also within my power to make the lawsuit brought against you by the Sullivans vanish.

"Alex, I have put a great deal of thought into this. Stu has been aware of my conundrum with Marco for months. When you arrived in Three Rivers in August, Stu read about your background on the internet, and the problem with your debt and the legal battle you have undertaken to rid yourself of it has been the subject of gossip at the courthouse. He told me all of this, and the seed of my plan was planted at that time. He told me he thought it was likely that the legal maneuvers that you and your lawyer were undertaking would not work. He also got to know you better to try to predict what your reaction would be to my offer. I did not want to be going through all of this only to see you talk of going to the authorities and leaving me no choice but to dig a third hole in the desert next to those two *pendejos* who aligned themselves with Marco." Luis cocked an eyebrow at him and let the threat hang in the air for a moment before continuing.

"It was at my suggestion that you came to the festival along with Roko and Simun, and it was at my suggestion that Marco accompanied you on your first night so you could see him and who he is. When we found out about the most recent ruling against you and your debt, we decided it was time to approach you. While we were making arrangements for this meeting tonight, the lawsuit from the Sullivans was an unforeseen development. While admittedly unexpected, we are confident it can be dealt with easily enough.

"So now you know everything. The only thing remaining is your answer."

While Luis talked, Alex held his glass up to eye level again, rolling it gently, watching the way the flames danced off the surface of the liquid. Luis was in his line of vision above the Scotch, and as he spoke Alex thought it looked like the devil's face hovering over a lake of fire.

CHAPTER FORTY-FIVE

11:15 p.m.—Sunday, December 1ˢᵗ

The cold front's gusts swayed the electric icicles under the house's gutters and ruffled the shriveled rubber of an inflatable snowman's puddled remains on the lawn. Red and green lights outlined an ornate nativity scene where a plastic Baby Jesus emanated a dull yellow glow that reflected off Mary and the Wise Men. The home's owners had aimed for Biblical accuracy in their lawn decorations, but nowhere in the New Testament could Alex remember reading about the long orange extension cord snaking out from the back of the manger.

He'd been walking his neighborhood for the twenty minutes since Stu dropped him home. The biting cold wind made his eyes water. The temperature continued to drop as the front moved through, and the chilly air made his chest hurt with each deep breath. During the ride home, he'd felt surreal, like he was moving through a dream. For the moment, the cold helped clear his head so he could think about Luis's proposal.

While he watched, a wise man tipped over, bouncing off the manger and landing face down. Alex crossed the yard's gentle upslope and stood the hollow plastic figure back up, but it blew over again as he walked away. He left it this time and kept walking down the sidewalk. As he licked his chapped lips and hunched his back against the wind, his mind returned to the bonfire. He realized he was thinking the unthinkable. What he'd been asked to do was premeditated evil, and premeditated evil was a foreign thought to him. Foreign and fearful.

What Luis proposed went against every fiber of his being. Willfully visiting the type of harm that Luis proposed on another human being was an affront to the moral order, and while he no longer thought of himself as a doctor, he had taken an oath once upon a time to first, do no harm.

But that was a long time ago, another part of his brain spoke up. And Lord knows, if ever a human being deserved the type of consequences that Luis planned, it was Marco.

Luis had left him with this. "Think hard about my offer, Alex. You are on the losing side of thirty, with insurmountable problems that have caused you to unravel. I am offering you a chance at a new life. A chance to start over."

Alex gamed this out.

What if Marco ever found out somehow that Alex was the one who had carried out Luis's plan? Would that be a possibility? He didn't want to spend the rest of his life looking over his shoulder.

As Alex thought about this, he realized if he did his job right, that would not be a problem.

What about the Sullivans? When Alex had asked, Luis had only promised no harm would come to them, but he wouldn't elaborate.

He had a momentary, ugly flash of a thought: *fuck the*

Sullivans. He suppressed that and tried to answer his own question. In the end, he didn't have anything to go on other than Luis's assurances. And yet, he had a sense that would be enough. When Luis told Alex he was a man of his word, he believed him. Truthfully, were he not a man of his word, he would already have just had Marco killed and told his wife that someone else must have done it. Now that Alex thought about it, they were going through this whole exercise because Luis had given his word to his wife that he would not have Marco killed and he said he planned to keep it.

Alex could not believe he was considering doing this. But now that the prospect of a life reset had been offered, it became impossible to unthink, like being told not to picture a purple elephant.

But at what cost? Was this who he was now?

An unoccupied bus stop granted shelter from the wind. Cold from the metal sign on the bench seat leeched through his jacket. His ears burned and the tip of his nose was numb. Stamping his feet to get some feeling back in them, he watched the traffic light cycle green to yellow to red a few times.

He got out his phone and called Stu. It rang twice, then a quick, "Hello?"

"I'm in," Alex said.

"Alright, we'll be in touch." Stu hung up.

As he walked back to his apartment, his teeth started chattering. He told himself it was from the cold and not fear at the events he'd set in motion.

CHAPTER FORTY-SIX

1:20 p.m.—Tuesday, December 3rd

"Say again?" Alex asked in confusion.

"I said go get yourself a fishing license. Then be outside your apartment tonight at straight-up midnight. Plan to be gone about a week and a half, two weeks tops," Stu answered.

"Why the fishing license?"

"Don't worry about it right now, just do not forget it. We don't move ahead if you don't pick up a freshwater license. Understood?"

"Yeah, I hear you."

In the days since he'd agreed to Luis's plans, his imagination had run wild with the demands that would be placed on him. The banality of this requirement caught him off guard.

That afternoon, Brutus gave Alex a pitiful look when he

dropped the dog off to board for two weeks. Wendy had offered to keep him for the weekend when he'd gone to *Dia de los Muertos*, and the dog had looked excited when Alex dropped him off at her place. This time, he whined in a way Alex had never heard, apparently sensing that something was amiss as Alex did paperwork at the kennel's reception desk. When he saw Alex walk back toward the exit without him he barked until the sound was blocked out by the closing of the door.

The call to Wendy had been trickier. More than a friend, less than a girlfriend, he wasn't sure what he owed her but he knew he didn't want to lie to her. He decided as he hit her contact to keep it vague.

She picked up on the first ring. "Hey stranger, I'm glad you called. You forget how a phone works?"

"Yeah, contrary to any rumors you may've heard, I'm not actually part of a sleeper cell that's been activated."

"I've been worried about you."

He paused. "I appreciate that. Don't let it weigh on your mind, though. I'm getting to a better place. In fact, that's why I'm calling. I'm going to be out of town for a couple weeks, just getting my head screwed back on straight."

"I'm glad to hear that. The way you dropped off the edge of the world there for a while I passed the time coming up with odd jobs you may have taken up if you'd decided to blow town. My two best guesses were that you were either working a boom mike on low budget porn movies in Romania or harvesting black-market kidneys for transplant in India."

Alex laughed. "Nothing so sexy I'm afraid. I'm just getting off the grid for a while. The lawyers told me to go get away from all this, that there'd be time to mess with the depositions and such after the holidays, so I'm going to take their advice and head out to the desert, see if I can find some answers out there. Call it a walkabout, I guess." That explanation had the benefit of being true.

"Okay. Go mend your wounds."

After hanging up, he felt relief that she hadn't pressed him. If Luis's plan worked out, if he was successful at getting a do-over in life, well, he was coming to realize he wanted Wendy to be a part of it.

The hours until his pickup crawled by. With Brutus gone, the apartment felt empty and abandoned. He tried to sleep but found it pointless. He thought about going for a run but nixed that, not wanting to chance a last-minute injury throwing a wrench in things. In the end, he settled for watching a whole evening of *Seinfeld* re-runs.

At 11:52, a white extended cab GMC pulled up to the curb by his driveway and sat idling, chuffing exhaust into the night air. Carrying his canvas kit bag, he went to meet them. The passenger was young and Caucasian, the driver older and Latino, both holding cups of coffee.

Alex said, "Good, you're early."

The passenger replied, "If you're early, you're on time. If you're on time, you're late. Got your fishing license?"

Alex patted his hip pocket. "Right here."

"That all your gear?"

"Yup."

"Okay, let's roll."

They headed southwest in the inky darkness, keeping to the speed limit. Shy of two hours later, they motored through the small town of Zapata, Texas where at one of the town's two stoplights, the driver turned due south. Before long Alex could see the two-lane road came to parallel the shoreline of a massive body of water, the far shoreline not visible in the darkness. After several miles, the driver slowed and he and the passenger closely watched the right-hand side of the road, illuminated by the high beams. It was the driver who first spotted a break in the wall of sawgrass, tapping the back of his hand against his partner's chest and pointing. A rutted gravel path appeared, headed in the direction of the water and guarded by two crooked iron posts and a padlocked, heavy-duty chain. The passenger nodded in agreement.

The three of them swayed in unison as the truck dropped off the highway's gravel apron and bounced across a large pothole in the short distance to the chain.

"You don't mind getting it, I suppose?" he asked of Alex, unbuttoning the cuff of his flannel shirt and rolling up his sleeve. The man held his bare forearm up to the dashboard lights. "Padlock combination's—" he squinted to read the scrawl on his arm— "three-seven-seven-eight. You can hold off on lockin' it back up since we ain't gonna be here long once we drop you. I'll get it on the way back out."

Alex exited the truck and stretched before dutifully opening the lock and letting the truck pass through. The crimson brake lights turned Alex, the creosote scrub brush, and the surrounding bulrushes a harsh blood-red. He thought the hellish appearance appropriate considering the job he'd come to do.

After a short drive, the end of the gravel road widened just enough for vehicles to maneuver. A Tundra pickup hitched to an empty boat trailer crowded the primitive cul de sac. Nearby, two men stood smoking on a short dock where a nineteen-foot Ranger bass boat bobbed gently in the dark water, tied up by the bow and stern cleats.

"Okay, they'll take care of you from here," the passenger said with a tired smile to Alex, but when he turned to look at the two men on the dock, a lip-curling sneer replaced it. Some unknown bad blood caused him to yell, "*¡Oigan! ¡Cabrones!*" When the men on the dock looked over, he flipped them off as the truck pulled away in a spray of gravel.

The noise of the truck's engine disappeared, leaving Alex and the two men with only the gentle sound of waves lapping on the shore and the soft bumps of the boat against the dock as the moonlight reflected off the water like luminous cobblestones.

One of the men retrieved a Coleman lantern from the flat bow of the boat. Lifting the glass housing, he flicked a lighter at the two mantles, resulting in a flash and a muffled whoomph. He hung the hissing lantern on a nail and for the first time all three men could see each other clearly in the bright bubble of light. The men's faces shared the same sad eyes and heavy monobrows, the same dimpled chins and flared nostrils. While identical twins, though, they gave off different vibes. One man had sculpted his wavy hair with mousse, with a leather jacket unzipped at the wrists and a gold hoop in one ear. The other twin's shaved head glistened in the moonlight, with a pearl snap western shirt and faded jeans. The only trait the two men shared beside their genetics was a solid teardrop tattoo at the corner of each right eye.

Alex didn't bother with introductions. "You speak English or *prefieres Español*?"

With a heavy accent, Hairdo said, "English is okay."

"Alright then, what's the plan?"

Hairdo once again. "This is Lake Falcon. She was made when the *gringos* make a dam on *Rio Bravo*" —the man used the Mexican term for the Rio Grande— "so the lake, she sit on the border between *México* and *los Estados Unidos*. When you on east side, you in the US. When you on west side, you in *México*. When you on water, you no need *un pasaporte* anywhere. *Pero,* when you on land you can be check by that country *policía*."

Hairdo said something to his brother in Spanish, too low and fast for Alex to follow, then continued. "*La policía*, they have many boats on the water, *pero* they check people most on land. In the morning, we take you across to *México*. If *la policía* make stop, we say we fishing. *Entiendes*?"

Alex nodded and stepped aboard the boat. Six rods strung with tackle lay under bungie tie downs on the carpeted bow, while further aft, he found boxes of fishing lures and even an ice chest with sandwiches and drinks. An Evinrude three hundred fifty horse-power outboard engine supplied the speed. He had to give it to them, they were thorough.

A few hours later, the boat bounced along in the chop, the cold spray thrown by the bow glinting in the first rosy fingers of sunrise. The chill December wind stung Alex's face and pulled his hair back from his skull. They sped down Lake Falcon's main channel, the water wide enough that they could barely see a strip of land to each side. The engine didn't break a sweat as they clipped along through the deep water at medium speed while light crept into the eastern sky. They only passed one other boat this time of the morning, a worn jon boat, paint-chipped and dented, bobbing at anchor in the two-foot swells. Its solitary occupant ignored them as they motored by. Minding one's own business was second nature for most people out here on the border.

They motored north for twenty minutes before Hairdo turned toward the Mexican shoreline. He cut the throttle as they passed out of the main channel and as the RPMs dropped, the boat settled lower in the water, the sound of the bow cutting through the water now audible alongside the chugging of the engine. With an experienced hand, Hairdo piloted the boat through a maze of tree stumps poking clear of the surface like stubbled whiskers as they crept toward the muddy shore. The brothers had a brief unintelligible exchange, after which Baldy tapped Alex on the shoulder and pointed farther north along the shoreline. Following the direction of his finger, Alex saw what appeared to be a steeple beyond an intervening low ridge.

"*¿Esta una iglesia?*" Alex asked. Baldy nodded.

Rounding the spit of land, a small, abandoned church came into view on the Mexican bank. Hairdo cut the engine, and all three men craned their necks around the main lake, looking for company. Seeing none, Hairdo held out his hand and said, "*Necesito su teléfono.*"

Alex obediently handed over his smart phone. Hairdo waved it at him and continued, slipping back and forth between languages in the way common among those who made *la frontera* home, "This stay in *Estados Unidos*. If *la policía* look *más tarde*, they think you in *Estados Unidos* whole time. We give you back when finish."

Baldy handed Alex a prepaid mobile phone. Hairdo continued, "Is for you. You no make phone call. *Solamente* answer.*¿Entiendes? Nunca, nunca, nunca* make call youself. Very important."

Pocketing the burner, Alex thought he couldn't call out even if he wanted to as he knew no one's phone numbers. Hairdo nudged the boat against the shoreline, and said, "You wait inside church. *¿Preguntas*?"

Alex shook his head, and holding his kit bag jumped off the bow, sinking ankle-deep into the muddy shoreline. When he tried to take a step, the mud made a sucking sound and pulled off his left shoe. Dropping his canvas bag, his arms pinwheeled as he tried to keep his balance, and he planted his left socked foot. He pulled on his right leg, causing his left foot to sink deeper while his right shoe came off. A shrill whistle cut the air, and he turned to see Hairdo jerk his chin at the bow. Tossing his kit bag forward into the sawgrass, he toddled back through the mud in his socked feet and waded into the cold lake water up to his shins. Locking his knees, he lowered his center of gravity and pushed the bow off the shoreline while Hairdo revved the reversed engine. The boat's resistance pushed his feet further into the mud, but the beached boat cleared the gooey bottom and idled backwards until Hairdo spun it around and began distancing them from the shoreline. Alex returned to his shoes, knelt, and dug them out of the fetid-smelling muck before making his way up through the brown, withered bulrush toward the sawgrass and the church beyond.

Caked with cold, wet mud from the knees down, his teeth chattered as he held his shoes in one hand and his bag in the other, looking at the crumbling church before him. A chill passed over him and his stomach tightened as he realized this was the first moment in which he was actually committing a crime. Having crossed the Rubicon, he wondered how long it would be before he had a feeling of safety again.

He pulled his shoes on over his stained, squishy socks and went to the church at a trot, his untied laces dangling and flopping. The heavy front door hung on one intact hinge, leaving a narrow opening that he could just squeeze through. His first instinct was to notice the muddy tracks he left behind, his second to wonder whether he was being paranoid. He thought about it for a moment, and decided, no, for the duration paranoia was probably going to be a healthy attitude. As far as his footprints, though, for the moment that couldn't be helped.

He'd expected to meet his next escort inside the dilapidated building, but found himself alone except for a pair of pigeons cooing in the rafters. The church was a single, simple room, built with space for only five or six pews. Now only three pews remained, scattered across the middle of the room forming a lazy "N" with their wood screws rusted through and sheared off the waterlogged timber.

Behind the humble wooden altar hung shattered blue-green-white stained glass, the only recognizable depictions remaining those of a pair of clasped hands holding a rosary and a serpent coiled around the globe.

The room smelled musty and sour, and a soft buzzing noise caressed the air, like a gently-pulled zipper. Both the noise and a smell of decay grew stronger as he crossed the warped planks of the floor to approach the altar. He found where rubble had been pulled into a rough circle and, judging by the scorch marks and ashes, used as a fire ring. The buzzing came from a cloud of blowflies working over the nearby carcass of a javelina, the disarticulated skeleton evidence of someone's supper at some point in the last week.

The clay walls in this part of the church were pockmarked with bullet holes too numerous to count, clustered together and making the wall look like the surface of a golf ball. He traced the outline of one bullet hole with his index finger, feeling the change in texture from the smooth outer wall to the sharp edge and craggy base. He pulled at the edge with his finger, pulling off a small piece of the dried clay.

The rotting javelina corpse seemed to be proof others had been forced to spend the night here. Is that what they expected of him, he wondered? Squatting in the church's dark, gloomy interior he cursed himself for not having asked Hairdo questions when he'd had the chance. He began to feel nervous, like something had gone wrong. He wondered if they were going to call him, then panicked, thinking that the burner phone wasn't turned on. What if they had been trying to call him, and, not having answered, they'd called everything off? Frantically, he dug at his pocket, scrambling for the phone, scared that his stupidity had gotten him stranded in Mexico with no way home. A wave of relief washed over him when he saw the phone was on. He'd received no calls. Scrolling to the contacts, he saw none listed.

He went to the crooked door to breathe fresh air and see the early morning sunlight, thinking both would help him relax. He pressed his face to the crack and inhaled deeply, savoring the smell of the nearby water. Over the sound of water lapping against the shore, he heard the sound of an engine. He strained to listen. It got louder, clearly heading in his direction. He withdrew to the interior of the church and peered through the slats of a broken shutter toward the direction of the vehicle. As it grew closer, Alex wondered what he would do if the red and blue lights of a *federale* hove into view.

A brittle sound like an alarm clock cut the tension, causing him to flinch in surprise. It took a moment to realize he still held the burner phone in his hand and it was ringing.

He hit accept. "Hello?"

The voice on the other end was husky and deep. "Who am I speaking to?"

"This is Alex."

"Very good. Are you still at the place where you were dropped off?"

"Yes."

"I will see you in two minutes."

CHAPTER FORTY-SEVEN

7:20 a.m.—Wednesday, December 4th

To call the overgrown, rutted path from the church back to the highway a road was too generous. It appeared to be a game trail, a worn path winding between chaparral and creosote bushes, over hollows and limestone shelves. The ancient F-150 had no shocks, so Alex and its driver bucked and bounced, pitched and swayed, like riding a bull with seatbelts on. Sometimes the trail disappeared altogether, forcing them to bushwhack their way along as the wiry scrub brush slapped up against the grill with hollow tinks before being whipped scratching under the chassis.

The driver, Guillermo, smiled at Alex and tried to carry a conversation, but Alex couldn't hear him over the squealing of the metal cab, the thudding of the truck's frame with each impact on the desert pan, and the roar of the engine. Smooth-faced and mid-twenties, chubby and serious, Guillermo wore new black denim jeans and the pointy, curly-toed boots favored by hard-core *vatos*. His truck showed its years. The nylon bench seat extruded foam ticking through long lacerations, and Alex's floorboard had a baseball-sized rusty-edged hole through which he could see the desert floor flying by. While most drivers would have prioritized replacing the spider-webbed windshield, Guillermo instead had apparently spent the money on an ornate knob for the gearshift where a gold cobra looked up at Alex with ruby-red eyes, wings flared, coiled and hissing. The appearance of his vehicle aside, Guillermo himself gave off a cool and professional air.

Alex said a silent prayer of thanks when they found paved road, and Guillermo turned north. The ride became smooth and in the silence of the cab the stress of the long night caught up with Alex, and he dozed off.

He was awakened sometime later by Guillermo's gentle "*Despierta, dormilón.* We are here."

"Where's here?" Alex asked as he cut through the cobwebs.

They were parked in front of a flat-roofed, adobe structure surrounded by a thigh-high retaining wall. A scrawny cottonwood tree threw skeletal shade across a pen where five goats watched them indifferently. A two-story windmill stood next to the pen, its spinning blades a blur in the desert wind, the pump rod shaft gliding in and out of the draw pipe to suck water from the ground into two troughs, one for goats, the other for humans. Looking around, Alex could see no other signs of humanity from horizon to horizon, just miles of rolling Chihuahua desert.

Guillermo smiled. "We are about fifteen miles outside of Nuevo Laredo. This is where both you and I will stay while final arrangements are made. I stayed here last night because I was to find you so early *esta mañana*. It is a simple house, but that clears the mind, no?" He said the last part while tapping his index finger against his temple and squinching that eye shut.

"How long will it take while final arrangements are made?"

"*No sé, pero* it is likely to be at least a few days, perhaps longer. During the day, I will come and go, but it will be best if you stay here. You should not be seen during this time. That is for your safety, *comprende*?"

Entering the austere house, Guillermo set a grocery bag on a rough-hewn table surrounded by four mismatched chairs, and went to an old potbelly stove where steam drifted from the spigot of a blue percolator coffee pot on its hot plate. He poured himself a cup before gesturing toward Alex, lifting both the cup and pot. Alex shook his head no, and Guillermo replaced the pot before tossing a few pieces of wood from a small stack by the stove into its belly.

Two folding cots with pillows and bedding were pulled up tight to the stove, one with a bag of clothes beneath it and looking slept in. Guillermo smoothed the thick blanket out, then sat hard, making an *oomph* sound before he took a small pistol out of his right boot and set it on the floor. Kicking his boots off instep-to-heel, he drank his coffee.

A counter in the rear of the room held cutlery and pots and pans. "*Tiene hambre?* There are eggs and bacon on ice over there, and the stove is hot." Guillermo gestured toward two Yeti coolers on the floor by the front door. Next to the coolers sat a smaller table with a deck of cards and a short stack of tattered pulp paperbacks, all in Spanish. Alex flipped through the book atop the pile, *Morir en el Ocaso*. Its illustrated cover showed a determined-looking *vaquero*, pistol in one hand and a bundle of dynamite in the other, standing spread-legged in front of a swooning *señorita*. The book had clearly passed through many hands.

Guillermo lay propped on one elbow, legs crossed, one socked foot bobbing. "I will need a list of the supplies and equipment that you must have for your job. Please be specific when you write them down. I will spend tomorrow getting things together for you." He drained the last of his coffee at one gulp and set the cup on the floor by his boots and the pistol. "We get our water from the trough, basins for washing are outside. I will care for the goats, and if you desire *cabrito* for supper one night, simply ask. It gets cold at night here, so I will pick up more firewood when I am about tomorrow." That said, he lay back and closed his eyes.

Alex went outside and sat in the tree's shade, alternating between watching the goats and staring out into the empty desert. In a few minutes he heard Guillermo's snores. Since arriving at the house, things had felt surreal, like any minute he was going to wake up from a dream. Over and over he asked himself, what the hell am I doing here?

The days crawled by. Guillermo turned out to be good company as well as an excellent cook, and he took pride in the meals he prepared. They quickly fell into a routine in which they would have a large breakfast, sometimes *huevos rancheros*, sometimes *chorizo* hash. Then Alex would clean up dishes while Guillermo made a run into town, always whistling *"Rancho Grande"* as he made his way to the truck. He would shop for food, pick up newspapers, and buy bundles of firewood. Alex spent his time going for long walks, and reading an English copy of *All the Pretty Horses* that Guillermo found for him at a bookstore.

Since both men had packed light, they ran out of clean clothes on their fourth day at the house, so after breakfast Alex washed them by hand while Guillermo headed to town. When he returned that afternoon, he found Alex standing at the clothesline naked in his cowboy boots, clothespins held between his lips while he hung their wet clothes out to dry. Guillermo paused with one foot in the cab, one on the truck's running board, then doubled over laughing at the sight.

"Hruckyu," Alex tried to curse at him around the mouthful of clothespins.

"Will you marry me?" Guillermo asked and came at him with his arms out and his lips puckered before Alex whipped a clothespin at him. He went back into the house giggling and wiping away tears.

Alex helped feed the goats and burn their trash. Guillermo spent a lot of time playing solitaire, hunched over a worn deck of cards. Other times he would look through classified ads for an apartment, as he said he was thinking about moving in with his girlfriend, and hand-rolling his cigarettes. When Alex asked about the latter, Guillermo explained that it reminded him of good times with his *abuelo* who had the same practice.

In the evening, Guillermo would make a feast. Skillet steak, *arroz con pollo*, *tortas*, and *huaraches* with pinto beans and chicken, like a Mexican pizza. He took obvious pleasure in Alex's enjoyment of the food, and it seemed the only thing that was off limits was alcohol, as the young gangster said simply that the time for drinking would come after the job was through, not before.

After they ate, Guillermo would light a stick of incense—he said he believed it brought good luck— and they would chat as tendrils of the exotic smoke curled toward the ceiling unmolested in the dead air. They spoke of the job, of course, going over details and logistics. But they also shared stories of their lives, and the trials that had brought the two of them to be temporary roommates. Guillermo had been a star *futbol* player in school, with dreams of playing professionally and using the money to lift his family out of poverty. A knee injury had ended those hopes, and he rubbed his pudge and smiled as he said it was clear his days of being an athlete were long gone.

He listened with interest as Alex told him his story, asking questions and nodding in appreciation of his conundrum as he flicked ash onto his empty dinner plate.

Despite his pleasant companion, the anticipation of the job was killing Alex. Sleep was only coming with difficulty, and on the first night when it did, he dreamt of Marco. Marco was in his suit with the prostitute's blood staining the front, sitting by Stu's campfire in Luis' stead, making small talk before mentioning that clouds were coming in, and pointing.

Alex turned to see a fire red sky, lit like the brake lights he'd seen cast on the desert scrub.

Alex awoke with a start, in a cold sweat despite the chilly temperature. In the dark on the other side of the stove, Guillermo's back was to him, blankets pulled up to the crown of his head, his barrel chest rising in time with his deep snores. Far off in the darkness, he heard a coyote howl at the moon.

Rolling off the cot, he wrapped the blanket around his head and shoulders like a Bedouin before walking outside, grabbing one of the hand-rolled cigarettes off the table as he passed. Meandering over to the windmill, he watched its blades spinning, visible in the dark profiled against the backdrop of the starry sky.

On the afternoon of their eighth day, Alex walked off his lunch by following a dry *arroyo* that ran behind the house. The creek bed cut a path ten feet wide through the underbrush, and its liner of oval rocks worn smooth by long-distant waters made for an easy trek. He'd taken to walking that route in the afternoons when the sun dipped behind a *mesa* to the west. On his return to the house, Guillermo's F-150 was in the driveway, having completed his chores in town. Rather than finding him inside preparing supper, though, his companion was out front, leaning backward against the retaining wall and smoking.

Guillermo said, "Tonight, we go. Supper will be light. We will need to leave here at one o'clock in the morning. Bring all of your belongings with you because you will not come back here when we are through."

CHAPTER FORTY-EIGHT

1:35 a.m.—Friday, December 13th

Ten hours later, Guillermo navigated them through the back streets of Nuevo Laredo. Alex tried to stay oriented, keeping track of the twists and turns but soon gave up and resigned himself to being lost for the duration of the night's activities.

In the warehouse district, Guillermo pulled up to a parking lot surrounded by a fence topped with barbed wire, and pressed a button on a garage door opener clipped to his visor. As the gate's rack wheels obediently trundled open, the chain link jingled like a runty tambourine. Guillermo circled the lot and parked with a good view of a large warehouse across the street on the next block. A sign on the building's facing wall had the name and logo of a large discount clothing store. Three stage lights provided illumination for the sign, but their meager glow didn't reach to the sidewalk, leaving it in shadow where Alex could see only the glow of a cigarette.

"That is where it will be," Guillermo said. They could see their breaths, so he kept the engine running to let the heat from the engine compartment bleed into the cab.

Alex said, "That warehouse looks like it's in use during the day. I'm worried about that."

Guillermo cocked his head and answered, "If the Big Man says we do it here, we do it here. *No te preoccupes*, he will have worked it out. You just worry about taking care of your part of the job."

With no response to that, Alex went back to watching the façade of the massive storeroom. Checking his watch, he realized it was Friday the thirteenth.

Shortly after 3:00 a.m., a crimson-colored Crown Vic pulled up in front of the warehouse. A passenger got out and furtively looked around before the cigarette smoker joined him from the shadows. After a brief exchange, the cigarette smoker pulled the warehouse's large sliding door for truck deliveries open a few feet while the passenger popped the trunk. Together, they hauled out a hooded man with bound hands. When they tried to stand him, whether from fatigue or fear his legs collapsed. They half-dragged, half-walked him into the warehouse, then slid the door closed behind them.

Once the Crown Vic disappeared down the dark street, Guillermo looked at Alex and nodded. Hunched against the chill, they walked the short distance to the warehouse where he put out a hand to stop Alex short of the door before rapping twice. A moment later, the door opened on its own and a short man with thick glasses stepped out. He wore rubber gloves; Alex didn't offer to shake.

The man said, "We are securing him now. It will only be a few moments." He closed the door once again.

Alex nodded and looked around, nervous about standing out in the open even though it was in shadow.

Guillermo asked, "How will you be able to do this with only that man to help you? Will Marco not fight you?"

Alex shook his head no. "I'm going to be giving him a medication called Ketamine. You go out of your head for about fifteen minutes, during which you feel no pain. At the doses I'm going to be using, it won't affect his breathing so all I'll have to do is work fast. I'll probably have to re-dose him one or two times to get everything done, but it means that I can do this without him bucking and fighting me, so I won't need an anesthesiologist."

"So, you simply give him a shot of this, how do you say? *Ketamina*? And begin to work?"

Alex said, "*Más o menos.*"

Guillermo nodded his head and took one of his hand-rolleds from behind his ear. He'd only taken a few drags when the door slid open once again, and the short man came over to them. Already looking tired, he said with grim seriousness, "From this point on, do not talk. He is blindfolded but can still hear for the moment, so we do not want him able to recognize any of our voices later. Point, gesture. If need be, write something down. But do not talk until he is unconscious. Do you both understand?"

Alex and Guillermo nodded.

Now he said just to Alex, "He thinks that very soon he will die a dog's death, and he is terrified. Desperate people are dangerous people. Be careful until the medication is given. Do you understand?"

Again Alex nodded, then followed him back into the warehouse and slid the door closed.

CHAPTER FORTY-NINE

3:10 a.m.—Friday, December 13th

They pushed through the translucent plastic straps of a vinyl strip door and entered the warehouse's cavernous interior, their footsteps echoing on the polished cement floor. Circular racks of clothing wrapped in clear plastic were scattered about, interspersed with stacked bins of neatly folded children's clothes. A few dozen brown-skinned mannequins were haphazardly scattered about, and pallets of broken-down cardboard lined most wall space. Deep in the recesses of the building, two forklifts stood mutely in the shadows. All of it looked to have been laid aside by people who would be returning in the morning, and Alex found himself not for the first time having to trust that Luis knew what he was doing by setting this up here.

In the middle of the warehouse, a rough circle several yards in diameter had been cleared amid the floor's clutter.

A half dozen mannequins had been hurriedly pushed out of the way and now stood at the edge of the circle in a tangled knot. Thinking they looked like a jury, Alex struggled to push the thought from his mind and focus.

Klieg lights lit a primitive stretcher at the center of the circle. On that stretcher lay Marco, still in his suit and blindfolded with duct tape over his mouth. Both wrists and ankles had been shackled to the stretcher, and he was shouting against the tape. In response to hearing the door slide open, he lurched side-to-side, causing the stretcher to rock. Two burly men, one of them with the hood stuffed in his back pocket, stood at its sides to keep it from tipping.

As Alex pulled on rubber gloves and approached the stretcher, Marco calmed, straining to assess the situation with his remaining senses, listening for clues as to what was happening. His nasal breathing sounded harsh and labored. A snot bubble sucked in and out.

Alex used a large pair of shears to slit the right sleeve of Marco's jacket and dress shirt. Placing a rubber tourniquet on his bicep, Alex slapped his forearm and hand looking for a suitable vein. With the contact, Marco began to thrash again, like a snake caught in a handler's snare before Alex gestured for one of the men to hold his arm still. When he felt the prick of Alex's needle, wetness spread at Marco's groin, and the ammonia smell of urine filled the air as Marco pissed himself.

The IV in, Alex moved to a small stainless steel table covered by blue surgical towels and the instruments he'd requested: a small braided wire with a steel loop on each end, several silk and nylon sutures, a large Velcro surgical tourniquet, four small clamps, and a needle driver to manipulate the sutures. The bottle of ketamine, a small bottle of antibiotics, and a hypodermic syringe sat next to a stack of sterile gloves. Seeing everything that had been on his list, he turned and nodded to the other men before turning back and drawing up the ketamine into the hypodermic while the short nameless man set to work cutting off the rest of

Marco's clothes with the shears.

Naked under the harsh lights, Marco sobbed, drawing long breaths in through his nose, head rising off the stainless steel of the stretcher and bobbing rapidly in time with his blubbering. His penis and testicles had fully retracted in the chill and fear. They saw Marco shaved his pubis, and with his retracted genitals he resembled a two-hundred-pound infant.

Alex stuck the loaded syringe into Marco's IV and pushed the drug, watching the medication creep through the curled tubing like a pigtail and toward his unwilling and last ever patient. Marco's sobs continued a few moments longer, then grew weaker, his head drifting backward until it gently contacted the stainless steel and lay still. Alex waited to make sure the Ketamine had safely sent him into the purgatory between life and death for the next fifteen minutes. Then, assured it had, he pulled the duct tape from over his victim's mouth. Marco's jaw was slack, and his mouth hung open in silence. His breathing appeared regular and unlabored.

Alex pulled the table of instruments over and set to work.

CHAPTER FIFTY

4:50 a.m.—Friday, December 13th

Two paramedics pulled their rig into the parking lot of a large grocery store on the east side of Nuevo Laredo to eat a late meal. Working the eleven-to-seven shift meant developing a working knowledge of all-night eateries. The taqueria they just left had great food and no line—not that crowds were often a problem at that time of the night.

The older and more experienced of the two, Josefina, had worked nights most of her twelve-year career and loved it. She slept during the day while her kids were at school, and it gave her the late afternoon and early evening to spend time with them and her husband. Plus, there were fewer of the nonemergent phone calls that were the bane of the day shift. Had anyone told her when she applied to the paramedic vocational program that she would spend as much time responding to calls for rashes, heartburn, and twisted ankles as she did on the day shift, she wasn't sure she would still have gone into it. Say what you would about working nights, she told people, nobody calls for an ambulance at two in the morning because their mole looks funny.

Her partner Carlos had only been a paramedic for five months and seemed to hate night work, complaining often to her that while his body had gotten used to it, his mind hadn't. She knew the difficulties of that adjustment. At first, the reverse rhythms of life had made her feel like a vampire, immersed in the city yet isolated from it. Spending most of her waking hours driving down dark streets and seeing closed storefronts and empty sidewalks had made her feel like she was living in the aftermath of the apocalypse.

Josefina had adapted, though, and she encouraged Carlos to give it time. But he'd recently confessed that his live-in girlfriend, Consuelo, was showing signs of having had enough of this life. It had started when he hung blackout drapes in their bedroom. Those only lasted a week, and he said he came home one morning to find them stuffed in the trash can outside the back door. He told Josefina his girlfriend rolled her eyes when he turned down social events to sleep, and he was starting to pick up little things that made him suspicious she may be seeing another man. Rather than confront her, he'd decided to request a transfer to working days.

He'd told Josefina he'd miss working with her, and the feeling was mutual. She'd taught him to be cool under pressure—although she hadn't been able to break him of his habit of chewing his fingernails when he got nervous—and she didn't mind being patient with his inexperience. At times, he jokingly called her Mama, but that was almost how she felt towards him.

They'd just dug into their *tortas* while discussing the quality of the new defibrillators the department issued when the crackly voice of their dispatcher broke into the cab.

"Dispatch to thirty-six, dispatch to thirty-six."

Carlos keyed the mike, "Go ahead for thirty-six."

"Thirty-six we have a request for medical from law enforcement, six-one-two-one *Arroyo*." A half-mile from their location.

"Roger that, thirty-six on the move." Sighing, they stowed their food and hit the lights and sirens.

Pulling up to a warehouse a few minutes later, they saw three cars belonging to the municipal police force, *Dirección de Seguridad Ciudadana*, parked at odd angles to the sliding door and yellow tape bearing the DSC initials squaring off the area where a lone policeman stood guard. A light drizzle moved through, and the harsh blue strobe lights of the DSC cars illuminated the scattered raindrops, freeze-framing them like snapshots.

White light tumbled out of the back of their rig as they retrieved their gurney. Through a two-foot-wide gap in the warehouse's sliding bay door, they could hear a man's throaty screams echoing around the interior.

Josefina looked at Carlos and arched an eyebrow, then took the handle at the front of the gurney and ducked under the police tape as she led the way.

The screams became louder as they entered, reverberating off the walls of the vast space. Josefina pulled up short, unsure for a moment exactly what she was seeing. The only light sources at the moment were the flashlights of two policemen and the sliver of light that eked through the cracked doorway behind her. She could barely make out a path leading through a maze of plastic humps and cardboard toward the middle of the building where the two flashlights danced.

To Josefina's ear, those weren't screams of pain, but anguish. She crept forward slowly, the stretcher nudging her buttocks like a coffin bumping the hips of pallbearers.

Josefina held her breath. The source of the screams appeared to be a naked man on some kind of table or stretcher in the middle of the room. The man was screaming curses in Spanish at whomever had done this to him, but it was not clear what this was.

The pair of flashlights' beams swept around the area rapidly, like searchlights scanning a prison's grounds, allowing only momentary glimpses in which the mind could register but not contextualize the images. There were snippets: the naked man with his back arched; the policemen's faces; a surface that flashed of steel or chrome; bright reflections off the dull plastic shrouding the clothes, the mannequins standing their posts, some whole, some in pieces; a few scattered small spatters of dark liquid on the floor. As she moved forward in the low lighting, Carlos bounced his end of the stretcher off a cardboard box, and she felt one of her front wheels snag. She couldn't see the cause of the blockage in the darkness, and when she kicked at it, it did not come free. She tried to back up the stretcher, but met resistance in Carlos' momentum forward.

Frustrated, she shouted at the policeman nearest to her, "*¡Oye! Necesitamos luz aquí!*"

He responded, "*¡En eso estamos!*"

Great. You're working on it. Meanwhile, we're groping our way along.

She continued to pull the stretcher, then kicked again at the wheels, still unable to free them. Just as she braced herself to tug hard on the stretcher's handle, they heard a loud *thunk* from the far wall as some cop threw a breaker, and the warehouse was awash in light.

She reflexively threw a forearm up to shield her eyes and squinted. As her eyes adjusted, she first saw a cluster of half-assembled mannequins at the edge of a clearing at the center of the maze. Looking down, a piece of one of those mannequins, a plastic leg, had been carelessly tossed aside and now lay wedged under the stretcher's front wheels. She reached down to toss it aside so it wouldn't bother Carlos, but as soon as she picked it up, she knew something was wrong.

The texture was soft, and it had more heft, more weight than the hollow plastic she was expecting. Her brain was still piecing this together when she looked up at the man who lay screaming on the table. For the first time, she saw him clearly.

The man's arms and legs had been cleanly amputated. She could see what appeared to be neat, professional suture lines closing the incisions on his elbows and knees. The man waved the stumps of his arms and legs like a deranged conductor, writhing on the table since he could not leverage himself. Josefina's gaze drifted down to the burden in her hands. Sickly, she realized it was not, in fact, a piece of a mannequin but the man's right leg. She screamed and dropped it where it hit the ground with a moist smack. Scanning the floor, she saw his other leg, as well as the man's arms scattered around the concrete.

Josefina told herself to get it together. Leaving the stretcher where it was, she advanced and tried to talk to the man. He was incoherent, shouting a disjointed stream of profanity amid guttural noises. Over her shoulder, she heard Carlos retch and the sound of his stomach contents spattering on the floor. She inspected the table's surface and, seeing the equipment and medication vials, tried to piece together what happened.

One of the policemen came forward and said, "Detectives are on their way. Any idea what all this was for?"

Josefina first turned to Carlos where he stood bent over with his hands on his knees, spitting. The stethoscope he wore dangling around his neck had vomit on the earpieces. Pointing at it, she said, "*Carlito,* clean that and when you are ready start your assessment."

Carlos spat and used his collar to wipe his mouth and nose before standing erect and saying, "*Sí, mamá.*"

As Carlos began to check Marco's vital signs, Josefina turned back to the policeman and pointed at a long strip of black Velcro that was on the floor next to the man. "This is a tourniquet like the kind used in surgeries. Whoever did this put the tourniquet on above each arm or leg so there would be little loss of blood while they carried out this mutilation."

She continued to inspect the scene, then said, "Do you see this?" She pointed at the braided wire with loops at each end. "This is called a Gigli saw. The coarse nature of the wire allows it to cut through skin and bone with only a few pulls on the rings at the end, like lumberjacks sawing a tree trunk." Next she pointed at the clamps and cut pieces of sutures on the back table. "These were used to tie off the blood vessels once the amputations were done so that there would be no further bleeding, and to suture the incisions closed." Finally, she walked back over to the amputated arm that she had dropped. She saw a long incision running from the cut end at the elbow to the wrist. Seeing this, the policeman asked, "Why did they continue to mutilate the arms and legs once they were removed?"

Josefina said, "Not for further mutilation, no. Look." She splayed open the cut ends of flesh and pointed.

The policeman asked, "What am I seeing?"

Josefina said, "Whomever did this destroyed the pieces of the blood vessels and nerves that go to the hands and feet."

"I do not understand, why would someone do that?"

"That removed any possibility of trying to reattach his arms or legs after we found him and took him to the hospital."

The policeman was silent for a moment then said, "I recognize this man. His name is Marco Corales. He is a mid-level soldier in the Sinaloa cartel. He has a reputation for being needlessly cruel."

Josefina said, "You make it sound like there are times people need to be cruel."

The policeman thought about that. "*Pues, está mal.* I am reminded of a saying of my father's. 'When you give a lesson in meanness to a dog or a child, do not be surprised if they learn the lesson.'"

Josefina asked, "Meaning?"

"I suspect whoever did this to him tonight learned a lesson in meanness at Marco Corales' hand sometime in the past."

She returned to help Carlos move the screaming man onto their stretcher. As they began to maneuver their way back down the path to their waiting ambulance, Josefina said partly to Carlos and partly to herself, "Tonight I will pray for this man."

Carlos asked, "And what about the men who did this to him?"

She was silent then said, "May God have mercy on their souls."

CHAPTER FIFTY-ONE

7:15 a.m.—Saturday, December 20ᵗʰ

According to the booklet Roko picked up in the rear of Sacred Heart's nave, the church had been established in Three Rivers at the end of World War I. He read its history with interest as he ate dawn toast and marmalade at Dinah's before starting his day's work. The original parishioners had worshipped in the barn of the town's founder, a cattleman named Woodrow O'Keefe. From those humble beginnings, the church had survived the great American Depression and grown into the quaint cathedral he'd visited yesterday afternoon. Much like the town itself, he'd found the church had an unassuming tranquility.

The booklet told of how the church took its mission of Christian charity seriously, and as part of that service conducted a year-round clothing drive. To help with collections, the parish placed a telephone booth-sized receptacle at the southwest corner of the church's parking lot where parishioners deposited sartorial items that had been outlived or outgrown.

None of the booklet's information about the clothing drive had been new to Roko, of course. In his prep work prior to actually visiting Three Rivers, he'd learned that every Saturday morning a volunteer would collect the items, trundle them into the elementary school's gymnasium, sort them, discard anything that was too threadbare. Then they'd wash them using the school's equipment before folding and stacking them in the vestibule of the Ladies' Auxiliary building next to the priest's residence. He'd even committed the schedule of volunteers to memory. After all, he was a professional.

Even his visit to see the inside of the church had been done more in the interest of thoroughness than necessity. But he was used to the formal grandeur of European cathedrals, and since he'd had time to kill, seeing the simplicity of the small-town church made for a nice distraction.

It was in doing this preparation that he'd learned Rebecca Sullivan always signed up to work the clothing drive for the first Saturday of every month, and that since her son's death she'd taken to volunteering for most of them. He'd also discovered that this had been noticed by the other ladies of the auxiliary, who tacitly approved as this seemed a constructive outlet for a woman who'd suffered such an unimaginable loss.

After finishing the booklet, he dusted his hands of the crumbs, finished his strong, black coffee and left his waitress a twenty-five-percent tip before driving to the gymnasium.

He wrestled a large cardboard box out of the backseat and set it down with a thump on the asphalt. Licking his thumb, he grimaced and rubbed it along a scratch on the rear bumper where he'd backed into a post in the motel parking lot the night before. Shaking his head, he hoisted the box and staggered a serpentine path to the main gymnasium door.

In the gym, Roko could see through the glass walls of

the laundry room that Rebecca was alone with her earbuds and her thoughts, folding and stacking clothes amid the rhythmic churning of the washer and drier. He slammed the gym door loud enough to get her attention, and lifted the box once again before waddling under his burden in the direction of the laundry room He saw her look up and notice him, pulling the ear buds out and pocketing them.

"You can just set it down right there, I'll be there in a second," she hollered through the door as she finished folding the blue jeans in her hands. Roko stopped and managed to set the box down without splitting it, smiling toothily at her.

Walking over, she saw the box was full of good quality clothes and jackets. "Wow, that's quite a haul," she said. Giving them a quick sniff, she said, "Clean too."

They should be clean since I just plucked them off the shelf at the Salvation Army last night. He said, "As I was telling myself, this is the season for doing good, no?"

"Here, help me get it over to the sorting table."

Together, they dragged the box toward two side-by-side card tables and shook the contents out, spilling them across the vinyl surfaces, sleeves and pant legs sticking out at odd angles like a denim octopus.

"You need the box?" she asked.

"No, you can have it. I will need a receipt, however, for the deduction."

"Actually, I'm not set up to do that. Normally, folks just deposit the clothes anonymously in that bin by the parking lot. Today's really just the day we handle the donations."

"I see. That is disappointing. I will tell you what, could you just hand-write something, showing what you accepted and the date? It would be better than nothing."

"I don't know if it'll do you any good, but yeah I can do that. Follow me."

Roko bent and retrieved an accordion folder that had spilled out of the box along with the clothes, then followed her to the Phys Ed teacher's office connected to the laundry room. Rebecca pulled a blank piece of paper from the printer and scribbled an informal receipt-of-goods for the fake name Roko gave her.

As she held it out to him, Roko made a show of digging through the accordion folder. "I have a special folder for receipts. I'm sorry, please bear with me. I really must organize this one of these days." He continued digging, pulling sheets of paper out and scanning them before returning them to the folder, all while she patiently held out the receipt.

"Here, would you mind holding these for just a moment?" He handed her two xeroxed pages and went back to rummaging. As she took them, he noticed out of the corner of his eye that she couldn't help flicking her eyes toward the contents of the top sheet. In that split second, she picked up a suggestion of an image, a reflexive recognition like ocular muscle memory, of the word Wallis at the top of one of the pieces of paper. She angled the paper to see it better as Roko continued to fumble. There it was, Wallis, Henry.

Seeing her reaction, Roko stopped rooting in his accordion folder and watched her. She gave up any pretense of not appearing to snoop and began reading the first piece of paper.

The first page was a xeroxed copy of the medical record generated by Henry's visit to the Austin psychiatrist following the rabbit episode. The psychiatrist had been meticulous in her notetaking, detailing with excruciating accuracy the events of that awful day and the impressions she'd gleaned. While Roko suspected that the doctor had couched her conversation with Mrs. Sullivan diplomatically at the time, her written assessment had been unflinching, almost cruel in its frankness that Henry showed sociopathic traits with a high risk for escalation of his cruelty even with intensive therapy.

The second page was a copy of a progress report written by Detective Lozano to his superiors detailing his progress on the vagrant's murder. He described the cellphone and drone evidence that led him to Henry, and the conversations he'd had with the boy. Noting the temporal relationship between his last conversation with Henry and the teen's subsequent suicide, Lozano concluded the report by writing that Henry should be posthumously considered a person of interest in the investigation, and in Lozano's opinion the case would now go unsolved as the totality of the evidence led him to conclude he'd been the perpetrator.

Rebecca leaned backward against the folding table before mumbling, "Where did you get these?"

Roko guided her over to a chair. "Please, have a seat and put your head between your knees. We will talk after you are feeling better." He didn't need her to faint and hit her head. He'd been doing Stu's dirty work for years, with hacking being a large part of his responsibilities, but he'd always worked with the understanding that he would not perpetrate physical violence. Frankly, Roko didn't think he could even if it was needed. But if she hit her head, he could not leave her, nor could he call for help and get entangled in that mess. Better that it should all be avoided.

She did as he said, and a short time later, she sat back up. He pulled a pointed paper cup of water from the dispenser in the coach's office and held it out. "Here, take a sip of this."

Robotically, she took the cup, but her hand shook so badly the water slopped over the edges. She steadied it with her other hand and took a sip, then another.

She tilted her head back and repeated, "Where did you get these?"

"May I assume that you are well enough to talk?"

She nodded.

Roko shook out a cigarette and offered her one. She shook her head. He lit up, and took a drag before exhaling a cloud of smoke. He got down to business.

"Have your lawyers talked to you yet about what discovery is?"

Still pale and shaking, she nodded yes.

"Ah, good. So that will save me some time." He took another drag. "Mrs. Sullivan—may I call you Rebecca?"

Another nod.

"Rebecca, I know you. I know you better than Mr. Sullivan. I know you better than Henry did. I know you well enough that I was able to find out about the information on those pieces of paper in your hand. Depending on how self-aware you are, I may even know you better than you know yourself. Here, watch this." Putting the cigarette in his mouth, he took another piece of paper from the desk and scribbled on it, shielding it from her view. He then folded the paper into quarters and handed it to her where it hung limply in her hand. Roko said, "I want you to think of a color. Can you do that for me?" She nodded. "Okay, do you have the color in your mind?"

"Yes."

"What is the color?"

"Green."

Roko jerked his chin at the piece of paper. She unfolded it and saw written in his rough scrawl the word, Green.

Taking back the piece of paper and putting it in his pocket, he saw that he hadn't needed to pull this parlor trick out, she was already on board. Still, it was one of his favorites. The average person would be amazed at how easy it was to figure out a stranger's favorite color when you searched their online clothing purchases.

"Rebecca, if you proceed with your lawsuit, I will anonymously send these documents to the lawyers for the school. I will anonymously send copies to the Three Rivers newspaper. I will create false profiles and saturate Facebook with these documents. They will be seen by Mr. Sullivan, by your neighbors, by the world. Do you understand what I am telling you?"

"Yes."

Now the shock was wearing off and he could see she was beginning to feel the first stirrings of anger.

"And if you do not wish for that to happen, if you wish

for the secrets that you have kept for so long to stay secrets for a while longer, all you must do is walk into your lawyer's office Monday morning and tell him that you have thought it over, and you wish to drop your meritless lawsuit against Alex Brantley. If you do that, you have my word that you will never see me again for the rest of your life. So, what is your decision?"

As the color ran back into her face, he saw that her edge suited her. He liked her better like this, it made him feel less like he was kicking a puppy.

"You can go to hell," she said, her bright bird eyes flashing with indignation.

Roko stared at her unblinking, giving her an appraising look. The quiet stretched for a full minute.

The way he studied her face finally made her ask, "Well?"

"I am trying to decide if you think I am someone you can fuck with," he said nonchalantly. In response, her lower lip betrayed her by quivering, and he saw tears well up.

Roko laughed, but there was no humor in the sound. "Very good." Standing up, he pointed at the copies she held in her hand. "Think it over. You may keep those."

He headed toward the gym's exit. Opening the door, he heard a roar of effort and fury behind him as she began flipping over the tables.

From his driver's seat in the rental car, he called Stu's burner from his own.

"Yeah?"

"All done."

"And?"

"We will see. I am confident this will have a happy ending."

"Okay. Safe flight home."

He started the hour-long drive to the San Antonio airport. Homesickness had been tugging at him of late, and the thought of going back to Croatia for a while, getting back among the familiar, comforted him. These trips never seemed to bother Simun. Roko's own family was in a small town outside Dubrovnik that was not unlike Three Rivers, and he missed much about small-town life. After all, isn't that what everyone wanted in the end, to go back home?

CHAPTER FIFTY-TWO

8:45 a.m.—Monday, December 22nd

A black wreath hung on the Sullivan's front door since Henry's funeral, an incongruity in a neighborhood full of Christmas decorations. Sully had asked her the week before how long she planned on keeping it up, and she didn't have an answer for him, other than, "A little longer." When she'd returned home on Saturday after meeting the awful, accented man and his accordion folder, she lifted the wreath off its hook and carried it inside with her, setting it in the bottom of the coat closet.

Now on Monday morning, after getting Sully off to work, Rebecca's gaze drifted around the house—she couldn't bring herself to call it a home. A home was where memories made you smile doorways with hatched lines marking children's growth into young women and men, cabinets with collections of souvenir shot glasses acquired over lifetimes of family road trips, scratches on wooden furniture from children's make-believe sword fights.

No, this house was only the mundane trappings of three—sorry, make that two—peoples' existences gathered under a seven-year-old asphalt shingle roof. It most definitely was not a home. It reminded her of the pictures she'd seen of Hollywood back lots—hollow buildings and store front facades propped up by sun-bleached braces of two-by-fours, structures built to trick audiences.

And what of the secret himself, her malfunctioning monster? Call him what you want, but Henry hadn't been stupid, and apparently he'd learned a thing or two about keeping secrets since that day in the woods.

It didn't occur to her for a moment to question Henry's guilt. She also felt a pang of guilt over the fact that she had culpability. After all, her years of passive inaction had led to this, a man's murder.

Rebecca pulled out the report the accented man had given her and googled the detective's name, then called his contact number on the SAPD website.

The man picked up, "Lozano."

She tried to speak and couldn't. Her mouth opened and closed a few times, like a gasping fish.

"Hello?"

She coughed and cleared her throat, then, "I'm sorry. Yes. Hello, Detective. My name's Rebecca Sullivan. I'm Henry Wallis's mother."

Now the pause belonged to Lozano. When he answered, his tone was guarded. "Yes ma'am. What can I do for you?"

"I understand you recently had the opportunity to interact with my son. I'm hoping you could tell me more about that." Her voice cracked slightly at the request.

"I'd be happy to," Lozano said in a clipped, professional voice.

The detective gave her a brief overview of the case against Henry: the dead vagrant, the dental souvenirs, the digital evidence against her son, his behavior when contacted about it.

Wincing, with her breath hitching, Rebecca said. "Thank you for giving me the gist, but if you don't mind, I'd like you to give me as many details about the murder as possible. Facts as well as your conjecture."

He obliged. She closed her eyes and put her hand to her forehead, trying to picture the scene as he spoke, imagining the poor victim, his canopy, the murderer she knew to be Henry stalking him, approaching him in his sleep, binding his wrists, torturing him with the fear of impending death and his helplessness to prevent it. The detective spared her nothing.

It was all too easy to envision. Her fear of Henry fueled her imagination's ability to fill in missing details to a level that made it seem as if she watched the act on a movie screen. Waves of revulsion, shame, queasiness, and remorse alternately washed over her as the detective methodically sketched out the known facts, first in a monotone, but morphing into judgment.

She hadn't asked for this detailed narrative out of morbid curiosity, but rather out of guilt that she shared in the responsibility. In her eyes, to be forgiven by her God she had to experience the act, experience the murdered man's fear and his final moments. The guilt and shame that Rebecca felt would scar her, a souvenir to show at her time of final judgment, and through that possibly gain forgiveness.

When the detective finished his narrative, her silence stretched long enough that he asked, "Mrs. Sullivan? You still there?"

"Yes, I'm here. Thank you for sharing that."

"Is there anything else I can help you with?"

"Yes." She took a deep breath before asking, "Is this through? Is it finished?"

"Yes ma'am, we're confident that Mr. Wallis was the perpetrator and with his death, this inquiry is closed."

"Thank you for your time, Detective," she said and hung up.

The phone lay in her lap, the silence of the living room broken only by the ticking of a grandfather clock. She sniffled, wiping her snotty nose with her sleeve. But no tears came. She realized she was all cried out.

Still sniffling, she called her lawyer's office, asking to be put through.

When Childes picked up, he said, "Morning, Rebecca. You saved me a phone call. I was going to check in with you today to see how you're hanging in and give you an update on things. We've made some good—"

"I want to drop the lawsuit."

"What? Hon, if this is about Mr. Sullivan, I'm sure we can—"

"No, it's not about him. This is about me. I want to drop the lawsuit."

Childes sounded flustered, like a man who's just realized he misplaced his winning Lotto ticket.

"Now, Rebecca, I can hear in your voice that you're upset right now. Please don't go making an emotional decision. Why don't you come in, I can take you to lunch, and we can talk this over?"

She said through gritted teeth, "That's the end of this conversation as far as I'm concerned." Then she hung up the phone, and let loose a scream, primal, equal parts sadness and fury, before hurling the phone at the cushions on the other end of the couch.

CHAPTER FIFTY-THREE

8:15 p.m.—Wednesday, December 24ᵗʰ

"What do you mean your favorite station's The Weather Channel?" Wendy asked, holding her empty wine glass out.

"What part of that don't you understand?" Refilling her, Alex rinsed the last of the soapy bubbles from the dinner plates and placed them next to the skillet in the dish rack. The basil-heavy scent of the evening's pomodoro was still in the air.

"Like, if your satellite package only allowed subscription to one channel, it would be—?"

"The Weather Channel, correct." Throwing the dishtowel over his shoulder, he grabbed his wine glass and padded over to the settee in socked feet, Brutus trailing him by a step. "It's just so relaxing. When they start talking about, I don't know, a low-pressure system on the Eastern Seaboard, it's like I can just feel my blood pressure go down."

Wendy laughed as she followed, plopping down beside him, and draping her legs over his lap. "I see why you waited 'til now to say anything about that. The only other person who talks that way about the goddamn Weather Channel is my grandfather. If you'd told me that when we were in the concession stand, there's no way I would have agreed to go out with you."

Alex began massaging her feet. In the background Lyle Lovett sang about the lights of L.A. County. Wendy closed her eyes, whispering the lyrics. "I love this song."

"It's the most romantic song about a mass murder I think I've ever heard," he said, and she playfully slapped his shoulder.

Alex had been nervous about cooking for her for the first time, wanting to impress her. A few hours before her arrival, he'd committed the recipe to memory, saying it over and over as though it were an assignment for a poetry class. He then measured out quantities into his palm and on the cutting board and stared at them, memorizing their sizes. Later, as she sat in the kitchen with a glass of wine watching him cook, in mid-story he'd nonchalantly thrown the tablespoon of marjoram or half cup of green chiles the recipe called for into the food, making it appear he'd done this impulsively because his refinement knew just what the dish called for.

On her third glass of wine, she asked, "You sure you can't get out of whatever it was you said you have to do tonight? Stick around here and play your cards right, you might get lucky." Her mouth curved into a smile as she ran her index finger around the rim of the wine glass.

"Next time. You got my word on that," he smiled in return.

An hour later, he sat in Stu's back yard, again in front of a roaring fire. The screen door slapped shut as Stu came outside, holding the same three etched glass tumblers and the mostly-full Balvenie, giving Alex déjà vu.

Instead of Luis, they were joined this time by a long-limbed Mexican man with a self-assured carriage, and stubble that looked maintained.

Pouring everyone two fingers, Stu said, "Alex, this is Miguel. He's part of Luis's legal team."

Miguel gave Alex a tight smile as he took a seat next to him. "I am sure we all have places we wish to be on Christmas Eve so I will get right to business. Alex, how are you doing since the events of eleven days ago?"

Alex took a sip, feeling the warmth coat his stomach. "I'm not gonna lie. It's been as hard as I thought it'd be. Mostly just been real jumpy. Every time I hear a siren go by, if somebody knocks at the door unexpectedly, when I hear my name called, even when the phone rings.

"I've packed a go-bag that I keep with me all the time, on the floor next to my desk in the classroom, in the child seat of the grocery cart when I shop. For the first week I even took it with me into the bathroom."

"These feelings of anxiety are normal and will abate with time," Miguel said. After a pause, "You have not had any thoughts of turning yourself in to the police?"

"No, no. Nothing like that."

"And since the Sullivans have dropped their lawsuit, has the school system made arrangements to reinstate you?"

"Yeah, when school resumes in January, I'm cleared to go back in the classroom."

Stu spoke up, "I heard they're relocating. Probably for the best." He spat in the fire.

Miguel said, "Very good. Then to the matter at hand." He reached to an attaché beside his chair and pulled out a sheaf of papers marked with several yellow arrows.

As he handed Alex a pen, he said, "Mr. Espinoza has made you a consultant for a medical device company in which he owns a majority share. It will require you to make a trip to San Antonio a few times a year for appearance's sake, and to log on to a monthly teleconference at which your attendance will be documented. This appointment will establish a paper trail for your new revenue stream, and since there will be no patient care you will not need a medical license. While we have no practical expectations that you will be contributing in any meaningful way to this venture, the business is a real undertaking, and it would behoove you to keep abreast of their work if only so that you can explain it in the unlikely event someone were to ask questions. You will be well compensated for this work, and if you manage your money well and live frugally, I calculate that you can expect to retire your debt in three and a half to four years. This revenue stream passes the sniff test."

As Alex signed the lawyer's papers, Stu said, "You'll see. You're on the downhill side of all this now."

CHAPTER FIFTY-FOUR

4:15 a.m.—Thursday, December 25th

That night, Alex awoke restless and sweaty. He'd dreamt he was strapped to a gurney, and Marco stood naked over him, spittles of fury at his lips as he tried to figure out how the Gigli saw worked. Alex shouted at Marco that he needed to apply the tourniquets first or he'd bleed to death, but Marco ignored him. Alex thrashed, screaming he didn't want to die, that this was not the agreement. He woke just as Marco began sawing through his right knee.

Breathing hard in the dark, he collapsed back onto the sheets. The adrenaline dump had made it pointless to try to go back to sleep, so he dressed and went for a drive.

With nothing better to do, he drove downtown to get an early breakfast. As he parked in front of Dinah's, he saw Milton dutifully shuffling back and forth on the sidewalk around the courthouse, like a sentry standing a post. Alex pulled open the diner's door, hesitated, then allowed it to close. Milton stopped pacing when he saw Alex approach and turned to face him. Nonchalantly, Milton retrieved a cigarette from his breast pocket then struck a kitchen match with a thick yellow thumbnail. He lit up while he stared Alex down.

Alex saw that Milton's sign now read "Mark 8:36 For WHAT does it profit a man to gain the whole WORLD and forfeit his SOUL?"

The two men stood staring at each other for a few more moments, and then Alex turned and went into the diner, where he took a seat and opened a menu. Milton watched him through the front window until he'd finished his smoke, and then flicked the butt away in a glowing pinwheel before continuing his lonely vigil.

EPILOGUE

The alarm.

It's jangling caused the bump under the sheets that was Wendy to stir for a moment, then lay still. Naked, Alex went to the bathroom to dress, Brutus padding along behind him, then he checked on Erin, cracking their daughter's bedroom door on silent hinges. A thin beam of light fell on her sleeping face, her long dark locks splayed Medusa-like on the pillow. She favored Wendy in her face, and at three years old, still sucked her thumb when she slept. A backyard barbecue had worn her out the day before. She'd spent much of it dancing while standing on his feet, and he'd had to carry her inside after she fell asleep on the short ride home.

In the modest room that functioned as his and Wendy's office, he opened the fire safe and took out his passport, then fetched his keys and looped the steel chain that bore his wedding band around his neck. Last night he'd waited until she was cold-creaming her face, good and distracted, before he'd mentioned this morning's trip in a way he'd tried to make sound off-hand, purposely vague. He had a wife now he was supposed to tell what? She hadn't pressed him other than to ask that he take the garbage out before he left.

Ten minutes later, he was in his F-150 heading southwest through the dark, barren desert. Trading in the LeSabre hadn't brought much, but the car had served as a reminder of times—well, times he'd rather forget but couldn't, like a sour mouth after vomiting. He caught himself thinking that inability to move on, to just learn to live with it, was what led him to this trip.

A few hours later, he was in one of Nuevo Laredo's eastern barrios, looking for a parking space on the street outside a dingy two-story building. In cursive script, a sign reading *Residencia las Fuentes* hung on the structure's brick façade surrounded by satellites of graffiti, and bald patches of dirt dotted the brown grass on the front lawn. Two men burned trash in a barrel twenty feet from the entrance, the steel drum belching black, acrid smoke to the sky.

Before leaving his truck, Alex donned the old white lab coat he wore at school, the one with no name stenciled above the breast pocket. Then on the floorboard he found the reason for today's visit, still wrapped in oil cloth. He dropped it in the lab coat's front pocket where the heavy metal pulled at the material, making it sag and bulge. He placed his hand in that pocket as camouflage and headed toward the building, stopping just long enough to pull a newspaper from a vending machine at the entrance and tuck it under his arm.

Alex still had a visceral reaction to the layers of smells on the other side of the porte cochere's plexiglass double doors: urine, microwaved popcorn, mildew, spoiled food. The linoleum had sticky spots that pulled at his cowboy boots as he walked.

At the reception desk, a young man in a scrub top sat reading. Alex confidently walked past the desk projecting an air of someone who belonged. The man didn't look up from his magazine.

In the nursing home's common area, three unmoving seniors watched a game show with the volume turned up loud. On the space's walls hung cheap prints of incongruous images, the framed mats placed in clusters with no attention to spacing or theme: *vaqueros* roping cattle; a cityscape at dusk, the skyline in the gloaming unrecognizable to Alex; an ice skater doing a split in the air, and a *futbol* player in midstride. Had he bothered to check the wall space behind each, Alex suspected he'd find they'd been placed where they were to cover holes in the drywall.

He navigated the hallways trying not to look through the open doors of residents' rooms at the sad tableaus of half-naked, sagging skin. He heard demented Spanish calling weakly for missing family, for assistance, for God. Alex fingered the cold, heavy metal in his coat pocket and walked faster.

Finally, he reached his destination. He paused at the closed primer-gray door and listened. Hearing nothing, he softly rapped twice and entered.

The door, poorly hung with an arc of scratches on the floor, always resisted, making him push hard. There on the nursing home bed, with a vacant expression on his face and dark circles under his red-rimmed eyes, lay Marco.

For four years, Alex's struggles with the road he'd chosen had been constant, like bailing out a leaky lifeboat. Racked with guilt, his dreams were a playground for his demons. Random events caused him to replay the events, sometimes with near-disastrous consequences like the time in a department store with Wendy when he'd almost broken down at the sight of a cluster of nude mannequins waiting to be dressed.

Looking back on it, he thanked God daily for his Wendy during those early days. She was an anchor to the life he sought, something tangible he could hold, smell, taste. In her arms, he could let go of the rest, temporarily escaping the storm that buffeted his psyche. In those days he'd consumed her like a drug, this wonderful woman whose humor, patience, and spirit touched his soul, calming it. His devotion to her was absolute, and more than once he'd grimaced at the thought of how things might have gone had she not been in his life.

As weeks turned into months turned into years, his internal tension evolved into an uneasy stalemate, like trench warfare. With the turning of the calendar, Alex's anxiety that at any moment a knock on the door would bring his new life crashing down became more manageable, shrinking without disappearing. He weaned himself from his go-bag in baby steps, and began to notice when he'd gone a matter of hours without subconsciously looking over his shoulder.

Whenever he allowed himself to reflect on the unseen threats, though, his imagination ran wild with images of twenty-four hour a day nursing tending to Marco's medical needs at a luxurious private compound while beefy gangsters stood nearby on high alert, forming a protective ring around him while Marco and his lieutenants gathered intelligence and plotted revenge upon his mysterious assailant.

It was because of this scenario that the turning of the calendar brought a new and complimentary emotion, one which crept in and which he found himself unable to conquer: curiosity. He had to know.

He realized the danger of what he was considering doing, like poking a skunk. In the end, though, he was confident that he could satisfy his itch without making Marco and his imagined team aware.

Finding Marco had been easy enough. Before he approached Miguel the lawyer, Alex invented a complex story to explain why he wanted to know his victim's whereabouts all these years later. But the lawyer offered the information in an offhand manner that made it clear he wasn't concerned about Alex's motivations. In retrospect, Alex realized this apathetic response foreshadowed what he would find.

The first time Alex visited the nursing home, he had few concerns that Marco might recognize him. Alex's face had filled out as he'd put on weight in the intervening years, and he now wore a goatee and close-cropped hair. For that first visit, he'd also worn a pair of John Lennon glasses, gold rims with plain glass lenses, in a dime store novel attempt at a disguise.

On that first morning, as he wandered the halls looking for Marco's room, he'd felt as though he was walking to the electric chair. He felt powerless to stop, though, as if willed forward by some invisible hand.

When he'd found the door with Marco's name on the sign, the door sat ajar. Cautiously, he crept up to the two-inch gap, his heart hammering in his chest and all of his senses keyed up for flight.

Alex had been shocked at what he saw. Burly once, Marco now had hollow temples and skin that seemed to be stretched over his skull. He'd aged, with a lined face framed by thinning gray hair that was wiry and unkempt, like a Mexican Einstein. His once-chubby arm stumps were now atrophied, pathetic pipe cleaners with sagging folds of skin obeying gravity. It was summertime hot, and in the absence of central air, a sheen of sweat glistened on Marco's forehead and cheeks where a single drop hung suspended from the end of his nose. A heavy leather belt with three fastened grommets ran across the front of his stained hospital gown, under his armpits, and looped around the mattress, securing him in place. The staff had raised the head of the bed to a steep angle where Marco dozed, his chin on his chest. No one else was in the room. No body guards, no visitors, no lackeys.

The relief Alex felt at the absence of danger was quickly overwhelmed by guilt. Alex stopped a passing nurse in the hallway. To his inquiry, she simply said visitors were rare for the man with no arms or legs, before shuffling off once again, apparently undisturbed at the idea of a strange *gringo* wandering the halls asking questions about the residents. On the walk back to his truck that morning, it was clear to Alex that Marco had been forgotten. And behind that realization, resolution followed. He planned to return, and to talk to Marco.

On his next visit, Alex wore the lab coat to lend credibility to his subterfuge. In a voice that cracked, he'd introduced himself to Marco as a new doctor working at the nursing home who would be dropping in from time to time. Marco's slack expression showed acknowledgement, but when he spoke his voice was quieter than Alex remembered. Every ounce of defiance was gone from him, squeezed out over the intervening years like a water-heavy sponge.

The only kindnesses that Alex extended that first day were to obtain a cup of ice which he fed to Marco, watching him crunch the cubes slowly, savoring them. When Marco finished, Alex saw neither smoke detectors nor sprinklers in the ceiling so he lit a cigarette and held it to Marco's lips, occasionally tapping the ash into the screw top lid of an empty specimen container Alex found on the nightstand. The cripple's eyes showed no gratitude, whether because of the emotion's congenital absence or its having been beaten out of him by time.

It had all come together that morning in a rush of emotion that made Alex's chin quiver. Alex took a deep, pained breath and averted his eyes, pretending to look at his phone while Marco finished the cigarette Alex held to his lips. The urge to confess his culpability to Marco welled up, so strong that Alex had to abruptly excuse himself, saying over his shoulder he would be back another time as he rushed out on dizzy legs. In the hallway, he caught his hitching breath, swallowing repeatedly to get himself under control.

Over the coming months, Alex continued to visit every few weeks. He would feed Marco, shave him, or brush his teeth. He did wound care for Marco's bedsores, and wheeled him outside in a wheelchair so he could feel the sun on his mangled skin. Once, even, Alex escorted a woman with a faux-mink jacket and lycra leggings down the hallways, her open-toed heels clacking loudly on the cracked linoleum. He showed her in Marco's room, then stood vigil at the door and played music on his phone loud enough to mask the sounds of her masturbating Marco.

Through it all the crippled man's gaunt features never showed a glimmer of recognition, nor appreciation. He never questioned why this new doctor was more concerned with dispensing small comforts than practicing medicine. And whenever Alex asked him what he would like to have brought to him on Alex's next visit, his answer was always the same: "Bring me an end to this."

On this morning, Marco's pillow had fallen to the floor. Alex retrieved it and placed it behind Marco's head, then went to wash his hands. The tap hissed out water that emitted a sulfurous smell, like rotten eggs. Then he stood at the foot of Marco's bed and fingered the cold metal weighing down his lab coat's pocket, stroking it with his thumb. He heard wastewater whoosh through an exposed iron drainage pipe in the corner of the room.

The blinds were closed. He knew from past visits that when Marco cursed at a nurse, the staff had taken to a simple, medieval punishment. They would pull the heavy blinds down on his window and close the door to his room. The clock in Marco's room was mounted on the wall behind his head, and with the head of his bed raised and the leather strap in place, he was unable to turn far enough to see its facing. This left Marco with only the sliver of light under his door as a frame of reference for the passage of time.

Alex asked, "How are you today, Marco?"

The cripple was silent, then shrugged. "*Mismo.*" Same.

"I have something for you."

"I do not want it."

"You do not even know what it is yet."

"Unless it is a release from this life, I care for nothing

else."

Alex pulled the heavy object from his pocket for Marco to see.

It was a heavy clock with an inset date display and a bracket at the base. Alex took a moment to affix it to the foot of Marco's bed within easy sight. "Will this help?"

Marco grunted.

Alex elevated the head of Marco's bed further, so the man was almost sitting up straight, and opened the newspaper on Marco's lap. "Tell me when you want me to turn the pages," he said as he opened the blinds. The room flooded with natural light, breaking the spell, and Alex blinked back into the outdoors' brightness. Marco squinted near-sightedly at the newspaper, his lips moving as he read, and Alex took a seat by the bed, next to the telephone that never rang. He opened a paperback from his pocket and began reading while he waited for Marco's command.

As Alex saw it, this was penance with the possibility of absolution for both men, the two of them forever linked in an unholy marriage. In this room, he could slowly piece together his broken image of himself. And that was enough.

A Note from the Author

Thank you for reading *The Cuts that Cure*. If you enjoyed this book, would you please consider writing a review of it on your favorite book-seller's website so other readers might enjoy it too. Just a couple of sentences. That would mean a lot to me.

Thank you!
Arthur Herbert

Connect with Arthur:

https://arthurherbertwriter.com/
arthur@arthurherbertwriter.com
https://www.facebook.com/arthurherbertwriter
https://twitter.com/HerbertWriter